WICKED AS THEY COME

"As good as it gets!"

—*New York Times* bestselling author Nancy Holder

"In Criminy Stain, Dawson has created a delightful rogue with a dangerously sexy edge."

—*RT Book Reviews*

"Mesmerizing . . . holds the reader spellbound from its opening line until its last. . . . This reviewer recommends you make a trip to the fascinating Sang immediately."

—*Bitten by Books*

"I can't recommend this book enough. It's like every genre I love so perfectly blended together. If you want to fall in love with two great characters plus an entire new world, this is your book."

—*Badass Book Reviews*

"One of the most refreshing reads I have read in a while. . . . A wonderful start to a new series, that had me dying to find out more. It is a dark macabre tale that Tim Burton would only wish to dream of. . . . Many a midnight hour was burnt with me not wanting to put it down."

—*Book Chick City*

Also by Delilah S. Dawson

DELILAH S. DAWSON

WICKED
AS SHE
WANTS

POCKET BOOKS

New York   London   Toronto   Sydney   New Delhi

Pocket Books
A Division of Simon & Schuster, Inc.
1230 Avenue of the Americas
New York, NY 10020

First Pocket Books paperback edition May 2013

POCKET and colophon are registered trademarks of
Simon & Schuster, Inc.

For information about special discounts for bulk purchases,
please contact Simon & Schuster Special Sales at 1-866-506-1949 or
business@simonandschuster.com.

The Simon & Schuster Speakers Bureau can bring authors to your
live event. For more information or to book an event contact the
Simon & Schuster Speakers Bureau at 1-866-248-3049
or visit our website at www.simonspeakers.com.

Manufactured in the United States of America

10 9 8 7 6 5 4 3 2 1

ISBN 978-1-4516-5790-6
ISBN 978-1-4516-5792-0 (ebook)

For Jan Gibbons

In addition to being the first kick-butt heroine I ever met, you were a great mentor and a greater friend. I miss you every day, especially when I see pictures of Gerard Butler.

Acknowledgments

Oh, I owe a lot of cupcakes this time around. Big thanks, hugs, and baked goods to so many.

To my parents, grandparents, children, and especially my husband, Craig, who once likened me to a classic Jaguar. Nice lines, plenty of power, but persnickety as hell—and yet he lovingly keeps me running. Rebels!

To my agent, Kate McKean, who keeps kicking butt on my behalf—and kicking my butt into shape. I might cry when she sends an edit letter, but it's worth it.

To my editor, Abby Zidle, who makes me happier than a fox with a marshmallow. To Parisa, Stephanie, and everyone at Pocket Books for taking such good care of me. And to the incredible copy editors who make me look smart by keeping track of this "blood/blud" business.

To artist Tony Mauro for another fantastic cover.

To the seriously dedicated and generous readers who helped spread signed bookplates to their local bookstores: Jamie Degyansky, "Goddess" Shel Franz, Phyllis Marshall, Lise Donnelly, Melanie Finnegan, Danielle Duffield, Heather Jackson, and Lee, Tammy, and Drea Hines.

For my very first fan e-mail, ever, to Michele Rotert. I will never forget the rush I got when I opened it.

To Ellen, Jackie, and Karen at FoxTale Book Shoppe in Woodstock, GA, for the best first-book launch I could possibly imagine. And thank you to everyone who joined me there! Best. Party. Ever.

And big thanks, hugs, and cupcakes go to: Nancy Holder, Stephanie Constantin, Ericka Axelsson, Debbie Pascoe, Jeremy Jordan, James R. Tuck, Janice Hardy, Kalayna Price, Alex Hughes, Chuck Wendig, Janet Reid, Beth Ho, Kathy Epling, Lindze Merritt, Charis Collins, Brent Taylor, Jon Plsek, Vania Stoyanova of VLC Photo, Croft Photography, Brooke of Villainess Soaps, Meghan Schuler, Kristen and Liz and the Cool Mom Picks team, Cakes by Darcy, Books-a-Million #232 in Canton, GA, Barnes & Noble at The Forum, Joseph-Beth Booksellers, and the girls at PLAY Activity Center in Roswell, GA. And because they threatened me, thanks to John Scalzi and Deanna Raybourn—for laughs and inspiration.

For inviting me to super-fun cons: Stephen Zimmer at FandomFest, Chris and Heather at Crossroads Writers Conference, Carol and Regina at the Dahlonega Literary Festival, and the three fantastic track directors of Dragon*Con who invited me to speak on panels: Doc Q of the Artifice Club, Derek Tatum, and Nancy Knight.

Thank you so very much to the book bloggers and reviewers who reviewed the book and invited me to do interviews or guest posts. Thank you to everyone who added, rated, or reviewed *Wicked As They Come*. Your support is invaluable to authors, and you rock!

I know I'm forgetting people, so please consider this a blanket thank-you to everyone. Everyone who's reading this, who read my last book, who follows me on Twitter or Facebook or reads my blog or just occasionally thinks of me when "Hey There Delilah" comes on the radio.

I love all your faces.

♥, d.

1

I don't know which called to me more, his music or his blood. Trapped in darkness, weak to the point of death, I woke only to suck his soul dry until the notes and droplets merged in my veins. Whoever he was, he was my inferior, my prey, and his life was my due. What's the point of being a princess if you can't kill your subjects?

His blood was spiced with wine; I could tell that much. As I listened, stilling my breathing and willing my heart to pump again, I realized that I didn't know the song he was playing. It wasn't any of the Freesian lullabies from my childhood, nor was it anything that had been popular at court. I could even pick out the sound of his fingertips stroking the keys without the telltale muting of suede gloves. Peculiar. No wonder I could smell him, whoever he was—he wasn't protecting his delicious skin from the world. From me.

He stopped playing and sighed, and my instincts took over. I lunged toward that intoxicating scent. But the attempt to pounce was painfully foiled by . . . something. Leather. I was trapped, tucked into a ball, boxed and balanced on my bustled bum. When he started playing again, my hand stole sideways toward the musty leather. With one wicked claw, I began to carve a way out.

The tiniest sliver of light stole in, orange and murky. Fresh air hit my face, and with it, his scent. It took every ounce of well-bred patience for me to remain silent and still and not fumble and flounder out of whatever held me bound like a Kraken from the deep. My mother's voice rang in my mind, her queenly tone unmistakable.

Silence. Cunning. Quickness. That is how the enemy falls, princess. You are the predator's predator. The queen of the beasts. Now kill him. Slowly.

My fingernails had grown overlong and sharper than was fashionable in court, and the rest of the leather fell away in one long curve. I lifted the flap with one hand and dared to peek out.

The room was dim and mostly empty, with a high ceiling and wooden floors. Spindly chairs perched on round tables. Across the room, lit by one orange gas spotlight, was a stage, and on that stage was a harpsichord, and playing that harpsichord was my lunch.

Seeing him there, the princess receded, and the beast took over. Body crouched and fingers curled, I sidled out through the hole, my eyes glued to my prey. He hadn't noticed the creature hunting him from the shadows. His eyes were closed, and he was singing something plaintive, something about someone named Jude. I wasn't Jude, so it didn't matter.

The refined part of my brain barely registered that I was dressed in high-heeled boots and swishing taffeta. I knew well enough how to stalk in my best clothes and had been doing so since my days in a linen pinafore and ermine ruff. As I slipped into the shadows along the wall and glided toward the stage, hunger pounded in time with my heartbeat and his slow keystrokes. It felt like a lifetime had passed since I had last eaten. And maybe it had. Never had I felt so drained.

I made it across the room without detection. He continued moaning about Jude in a husky voice so sad that it moved even the animal in me. I stopped to consider him from behind deep-red velvet curtains that had definitely known better days. But I didn't see a man. Just food. And in that sense, he had all but arrayed himself on a platter, walking around with his shirt open, boots off, and gloves nowhere to be seen. Exposed and reeking of alcohol, he was an easy target.

He broke off from his strange song and reached for a green bottle, tipping it to lips flushed pink with blood and feeling. I watched his neck thrown back, Adam's apple bobbing, and a deafening roar overtook me. I couldn't hold back any longer. I was across the stage and on him in a heartbeat.

Tiny as I was, the momentum from my attack knocked him backward off the bench. The bottle skittered across the floor, and he made a pathetically clumsy grab for it. I had one hand tangled in his long hair, the other pinning down his chest, long talons prickling into his flesh and drawing pinpoints of delicious blood to pepper the air. I took a deep breath, savoring it. The kill was sure. I smiled, displaying fangs.

His red-rimmed eyes met mine in understanding, and he smiled back, a feral glint surprising me. Something smashed into my head, and he rolled me over and lurched to his feet with a wild laugh. Red liquid streamed through my hair and down my face, and I hissed and shook shards of green glass from my shoulders. The uppity bastard had hit me with his bottle. If I hadn't already planned to kill him, I now had just cause.

As I circled him, I wiped the stinging wine from my

eyes with the back of my hand. I was dizzy with hunger, almost woozy, and he took advantage of my delicate condition to leap forward and slice my forearm with the jagged ends of his blasted bottle. I hissed again and went for his throat, but at the last minute, something stopped me short. He didn't smell so good, not anymore.

The beast within receded, and my posture straightened. My arms swung, useless, at my sides. His finger was in his mouth, and when he pulled it out with a dramatic pop, his lips were stained red with my blud. Now he just smelled like me. And less like food.

"Not today, Josephine," he said with a cocky grin.

I struggled to stand tall and not wobble. Now that he had swallowed my blud, the beast wasn't controlling me, and there was nothing holding me up. I was as empty as a cloud, light as a snowflake, beyond hunger. My heart was barely beating. And I felt more than a little bewildered.

"Oh, my," I said, one hand to my dripping hair. "I do believe I might swoon. And you've ruined my dress as well. Your lord is simply going to draw and quarter you."

I did swoon then. As the world went black, I felt his hands catching me, his delicious—if no longer maddening—blood pumping millimeters away from my own.

"Easy, little girl," he said. I smelled wine and sadness on him and something else, something deep and musky and not quite right.

I was delirious as he gently helped me fall to the ground. I could barely mumble, "I'm not a little girl, and you're the most badly behaved servant I've ever met."

The world fell away, and his laughter and music followed me into my dreams.

2

Before my eyes were open, before I was actually awake, I was drinking. Four great gulps, and I gasped for more. I clawed at the empty glass tube held to my mouth and flung it to the ground.

"More," I rasped. "I demand more."

Another tube replaced it, and I sighed and swallowed again. Someone chuckled. The blood ran down my throat, cool and warm at the same time. It tasted exotic. Must have been the local flavor.

"How long have you been hiding in that old suitcase?"

I opened my eyes, suddenly aware of the unladylike nature of my predicament. I sprawled on the ground, legs splayed out over the dusty wooden boards. A man's arm was around my shoulders, his ungloved human hand holding a vial to my lips as I drank the blood as greedily as a child with holiday sweets. My hair had fallen to disarray, and some of the straggling locks around my face were tinted red with what smelled like old wine. I slapped the vial to the ground—after I'd finished the last drop, of course.

"You varlet," I growled in my most ladylike growl. "You blasphemous dog. How dare you touch me? I'll use your blood for ink."

I jerked out of his hands and tried to stand, but my legs couldn't hold me. Without his body behind me, I toppled right back over and flopped on my back like a fish. Whatever had been done to me, two vials of blood wasn't enough to get me back on my feet.

But what *had* been done to me? And by whom?

"You," I said. My eyes narrowed, focused on him.

He sat on his haunches a few feet away, elbows easy on his knees, watching me. I'd never seen so much exposed skin on a servant who wasn't being offered as a meal. His eyes were bright blue, regarding me with curiosity and a noticeable absence of fear and respect.

"What did you do to me, offal?"

He chuckled and grinned. He had dimples. "I'm pretty sure I saved your life, right after you attacked me. I don't hold it against you, though. Looks like you were drained."

"Drained?"

"You can't even stand, little girl."

I tried to lift a hand to crush his throat, but my arm weighed a ton. I was starting to get woozy again, as if there was a block of stone on my chest. It was a struggle to breathe. Movement caught my eyes, and I saw a fresh vial of blood glinting in his hand, flipping back and forth over his knuckles. I'd never seen anything so beautiful, and I had to swallow down an unbecoming drop of drool.

"Give me that," I said, voice husky and commanding.

"Tell me who you are first."

I was starting to pant, watching the blood twirl around his fingers. He may have ingested my own blud and calmed the beast within me, but he still smelled like food. If I could have ripped his throat out, I would have been sunk to my ears in his neck, drinking in ecstasy. But

I forced that image from my mind and met his steely blue glare, fighting for control over the beast beginning to surface again.

"Let us understand each other," I said, enunciating every word clearly. "I am not little, and I am not a girl. I am twenty-seven years old, and I am a princess. And you, whoever you are, are my subject. You owe me obeisance, fealty, and blood."

"Come and get it, then." His grin taunted me with unexpected good humor as he held up the vial, the amber light glinting off the glass.

"You know very well I cannot," I spat, struggling for control. I had never been so helpless, and he was mocking me, and it was untenable. Once I was strong again, he was going to pay.

"Then we'll have to strike a bargain, won't we?"

"I don't bargain."

"Then good luck, princess."

He stood and walked back to his harpsichord. Long, tangled chestnut hair rippled over his stained white shirt, and I pledged to make a mop out of it one day. Rage consumed me. Rage and hunger.

As if sensing my fury, he turned back and winked with one damnable blue eye, then threw the vial into the air. I swallowed hard, watching the precious glass tube flip over and over in a perfect arc. When it smashed against the floor, I let out an inhuman wail and tried to drag myself over the worn boards. I was a princess, but I would gladly have licked the glass-dusted blood from the dirty ground. I couldn't move, not even an inch. All the training and breeding and hunting in the world had never prepared me for such utter helplessness.

"Wait," I gasped, my black hands scrabbling against the floorboards. I winced at the sound of my long white talons scritching uselessly over the wood. He had to be right; only draining could reduce me to mewling like a kitten. To begging and desperation.

"Hmm?" He turned around to grin at me again with those hateful dimples.

"Let's make a bargain."

"I knew you'd see it my way." He walked back to me, pulling another vial from his shirt pocket. He sat down cross-legged, just out of reach, and began flipping it over his knuckles again. The way I felt reminded me of a wolfhound my father used to have, the way she would gulp under her jeweled collar when he forced her to balance a bone on her nose until he gave her the signal to eat it. I gulped, too.

"First of all, who are you *really*?"

I closed my eyes, fighting for control of my emotions. I had never begged before, never been in any position that didn't involve absolute power. I had definitely never been helpless at the bare feet of a Pinky, a servant, a paltry human. My hands made fists in the ice-blue taffeta of my gown, the talons piercing the ruffles and digging painfully into my palms.

"I am Princess Ahnastasia Feodor. My mother is the Blud Tsarina of Freesia, and we reside in the Ice Palace of Muscovy."

At the mention of my name, his face underwent a strange ripple of emotions, from recognition to understanding to what appeared to be pity.

"Bad news, princess. I follow the papers. You were declared dead four years ago. They said you were kidnapped and that your ashes were returned to the palace in your engraved vial case."

I would not have guessed it possible that I could feel weaker and dizzier than I already felt, but fear and anger roiled through my barely breathing body. Me, kidnapped and drained? I imagined my parents holding the gold case they had given me on my sixteenth birthday to carry the vials of blood collected from only the most highly valued, most pedigreed servants. I tried to imagine what my mother's regal face would look like at my funeral ceremony, whether her carefully studied mask would break as my supposed ashes blew away in the wind of a snowstorm. Would she cry? Did she even know how?

I swallowed hard, my throat gritty. "This is not possible."

He cocked his head at me, squinting as he looked me up and down. I was accustomed to seeing awe, fear, and polite admiration in a Bludman's eyes. I had never had a human look so brazenly into my face, seeming to reach down into my soul and question what was found there. But this man did just that. And the answering expression on his face showed an unwelcome sympathy. I flinched under his scrutiny.

"You do look like the broadsheets, although the drawings showed you a little younger. If you've been drained and hidden in that suitcase for years, I guess it could be you. If you really are the Princess Ahnastasia, your sister is also missing, and your brother is sickly." He looked down to fiddle with the vial of blood, and my eyes followed. "I don't know how to tell you this, but your parents are dead. They were executed a few months ago in a coup by a gypsy sorceress named Ravenna, and she's a heartbeat away from complete control of Freesia. Tell me, princess, what do you remember?"

"I don't . . . I can't . . ." I faltered and closed my eyes. They were too dry to produce tears. "I need more blood," I whispered. "Please."

With another look of pity, he uncorked the vial he held. I allowed him to lift me into a sitting position and gulped the blood as politely as possible, so stricken with grief that it was like swallowing past a stone. After I'd emptied the vial and licked the lip of the glass clean, I muttered, "More."

He obliged, producing yet another vial from his shirt pocket. I had enough strength by then to slap his hand away and hold the vial myself, but I let him keep his arm behind my back, supporting me. My talons were atrociously long, the pinkie fingers beginning to twist into unfashionable corkscrews. At least my mother would never see me this way. I grimaced as I set the vial on the floor. The blood loss, the heartbreak—it was too much to bear.

"That's all the blood I can find." He pocketed the empty vials and dusted off his hands as if he didn't like touching them. "The delivery isn't due until this afternoon, I'm afraid. No one comes to the Seven Scars before lunch except me and Tom Pain. Isn't that so, Tommy?"

And then I smelled the strangest thing. An animal. A fellow predator but an unfamiliar and somehow non-threatening one. A rumbling noise started up, and an odd creature padded out from the shadows. It was heavy and black and furry, with one great, green eye that regarded me philosophically. The other eye was scarred over, an ugly slash against the creature's face. I had never seen anything like it.

"What is that monster?"

"It's not a monster. It's a cat."

As he reached to stroke the rumbling creature, I realized that I was sitting up on my own. I finally had enough strength to support myself again. The man focused on the animal, and I scooted unobtrusively toward the broken vial of blood, dragging my fingers through the red puddle and licking them clean with a new desperation.

"What, they don't have cats in Freesia?" he asked. "I thought cats were everywhere. Old Tommy has lived at the Seven Scars pub for much longer than any cat has a right to live. They say cats have nine lives, and he's on his tenth."

The man scratched the cat-thing under the chin, and the cat closed his eye in bliss and rubbed his head all over the man in an entirely unrepentant way that still managed to exude superiority. I began to like the cat. The man, on the other hand . . .

"I've answered your question," I said, my haughtiness returning with my strength. "Now you will answer mine. Who are you? And what are you? You smell wrong."

"I'm Casper Sterling." It was unsettling, the way his eyes held mine. I refused to blink as I waited for the answers he owed me. "I'm the greatest musician in London, maybe in the entire world of Sang. And I'm mostly drunk."

"That's not what's wrong about you. I know the smell of drink. It's something more."

"I answered your question, princess," he snarled. "Now we bargain."

"I will admit I owe you a debt," I said calmly. "And you owe me one as well. We are even."

He laughed, a dark, empty, reckless sound.

"I owe you? We're even? Bullshit. You attacked me, and I saved your life anyway. You owe me. Period."

"You cut me. Where I come from, those who threaten the lives of nobles are lucky to be drawn, quartered, and left for the bludlemmings and snow wolves. If you were my servant and you purposefully drew my blud, as you have, your entire family would be staked on the frozen hills and nibbled to death at a party. The debt you owe me is far greater than the one I owe you because I am naturally superior to you in species and breeding."

I glared at him. He glared back. Then he stood and walked over to me, his bare feet brushing the ripped and faded taffeta of my skirt. Leaning down, his face inches from mine, he bared his teeth at me. At me! I could feel the malevolence and alcohol rolling off him in waves.

"Hurt me, then. Go on. Bite me. End me. I've lost everything I ever valued. I would welcome it, princess."

It came out as a growl through shining teeth, and I flinched in spite of myself. I raised one shaking, black-scaled hand. Our eyes were locked, his pupils pinpricks in twilight blue. With every ounce of strength I could muster, filled with anger at his base nature and fury at his pity, I curled my sharp talons around his throat. I could see the pulse hammering there, smell the anger pounding through him. I tightened my grip, seeking the wet burst of his skin and the hard ridges of his spine.

"Do it!" His lips curled back over canine teeth that were sharper than I had expected. "End it! Send me back to the grave where I belong, you goddamn monster!"

I hissed at him and squeezed.

I couldn't even pierce his skin.

I let go of his neck, my throat convulsing in a sob. I couldn't even take what was mine. He was right—I was a monster. A broken one.

"That's what I thought," he said softly.

I fell back onto the boards and curled on my side, sobbing. A single tear rolled down my cheek and fell to my wrist, leaving a pink trail. The little strength I'd gained was gone. I needed more blood if I was going to kill him. And I *was* going to kill him, because any human who saw royal tears had seen his own doom.

"I'm going to end you," I whispered. "I'm going to find blood, and I'm going to get strong, and I'm going to drain you dry. Nothing shall be more beautiful than your death."

He looked at me strangely. "You do that," he said in a voice as ragged as torn paper.

I was starting to lose consciousness again, but I felt his arms around me, lifting me from the ground and carrying me. The velvet curtains whispered past, brushing my boots.

The last thing I heard before I passed out was his whispered, "Death has to be better than this."

3

My first thought upon waking was that all this passing out was terribly uncouth. My second thought was that I wanted to kiss whoever had taken off my boots. My third thought, as I wiggled my toes, was that I would probably have to kill them after I'd kissed them, because people can't just go around undressing princesses without permission. My fourth thought was that I wasn't a princess anymore. If my mother truly was dead, I was the Tsarina.

Then I realized that Casper was watching me.

I took stock of my body with eyes still closed and feigning sleep. Although I remembered everything that had happened since waking in the awful valise, I still had no idea where I was, what day it was, what year it was, or what my captor/savior wanted from me. I needed to strategize, but my thoughts were as muddled as a snowstorm on a moonless night.

"I know you're awake, princess. I can see you wiggling your toes."

"You again, servant?" I tried to sit up and smacked my forehead on something hard.

"The eaves are rather low," he said bitterly as I floundered. "I can't afford better. This ain't the Ice Palace."

My eyes adjusted to the dimness as I managed to roll onto an elbow. He was across the small room—more of a closet, really—sitting on a stool as he pulled on a pair of shiny knee-high boots with silver toe caps. I wanted to say something snide, but he was too interesting. The scruffy, careless, drunken wastrel I'd encountered earlier had metamorphosed into a sleekly handsome creature just this side of a dandy. Tight suede breeches, a flouncy shirt with feathery layers of lace, and a gem-encrusted coat winked in the twilight. His hair shimmered over his shoulders in glossy waves. He reminded me of my mother's favorite pet Pinky dressed up for a parade, although there was something vaguely threatening about him. I couldn't put my finger on what it was, his posture or his scent or his wolfish grin, but something dangerous lurked under the surface of Casper Sterling.

"It's time for me to perform." He stood, checking his image in a hanging mirror. "You need to stay right where you are. I looked up some old broadsheets, and anyone less drunk would recognize you in a heartbeat. So start thinking about what you can do to change that, starting with your hair."

My bare hand went to the long white-blond curls rippling over the side of the bed. Ye gods, had he taken the pins out while I'd slept? I was scandalized, to think of those long fingers buried in my hair. And he actually expected me to change my favorite feature? I couldn't alter the ice-blue eyes of my Muscovy heritage, so my hair was the only logical choice. Then I realized the implications of what he had said.

"Why should I disguise myself?" I pulled my shoulders back and stuck out my chin despite an unladylike position. "I am the princess. I will soon be Tsarina. Once the authorities are made aware of my whereabouts, I will be returned to the Ice Palace. You may even be rewarded for your trouble."

Before we drain you and eat your heart on toast, I added silently.

"This isn't Freesia. And Freesia isn't what it was four years ago. There's civil unrest there, talk of revolt against the landed Bludmen's harsh rule. The price on your head is high, and if you actually made it back home alive, Ravenna would have you killed. If the people still want you, they don't know it. They're completely in her power. Mesmerized or bullied or fed only propaganda. Perhaps all of the above."

"You're lying." Each word dripped icicles.

"Why would I lie? This is London, and I'm a has-been playing tunes for coppers in a third-rate Blud bar. I'm a dancing monkey. If I wanted to hurt you, I would have turned you in to the Coppers while you were asleep and taken the reward." He tied his cravat and flashed his dimpled grin. "It's up to a thousand silvers, you know. They think you're dead. But someone's not willing to bet on it."

On the outside, my nostrils flared. On the inside, I was breaking apart, cracks invading me like a glacier about to plummet into the fathomless deep. If he wasn't lying, my parents were gone, and the beautiful palace where I'd led a charmed life was more than a thousand miles away and no longer safe. The sea, the mountains, the wilds of the tundra standing in my way were rendered insignificant only by the understanding that someone wanted me dead. And they had very nearly gotten their way.

"I've got to get back." I had to discover what Ravenna held over my country and my last remaining sibling. If it was as bad as he had described, it was my duty to them and my birthright.

"I'd worry about standing up first. Looks like you were drained to the cusp of death. What's the last thing you remember?"

He leaned forward into a golden ray of sunset shining through a window so small it resembled a porthole. The bloodshot whites of his eyes served only to enhance the blue. I inhaled deeply and found that his smell nagged at me. He wasn't a Bludman, that was for sure. But what was he?

And where had I been for the last four years?

"The last thing I remember clearly was sitting by the fountain in the back courtyard. There was a thin layer of ice on top, like the film on blood brûlée. I was tracing patterns in the ice, watching the koi swim underneath, trying to reach my fingers through the crust."

"And then?"

"And then I was in the dark, plotting your death."

"Nice."

"I'm not nice," I growled. With a bit of a struggle, I pulled myself to sitting on the other end of the bed, where the eaves weren't so low. "Nice is for nursemaids and stable boys. I'm royalty. And I'm a pragmatist. And I wake up cranky. Why do you smell different?"

"None of your damned business."

"I don't like your attitude."

"I'm not your servant."

I hissed. "If you were—"

"Look, it's very sweet, you threatening me all the time. But you're weak, you're wanted, and you're in my power. Deal with it. I've got to be onstage in five minutes, or I won't have the money to buy more blood for you. Can I trust you to stay here?"

Finally, something I could work with.

I smiled my most beguiling smile, showing kitten teeth and batting my eyelashes. "Of course. I'll just take a nap while I wait, and then we can arrange transportation."

He chuckled, and my cheeks grew hot.

"You know, two years ago, I would have fallen for that, hook, line, and sinker. But a lot's happened since then, and now I know a lying woman when I see one."

My hands made fists in the scratchy blanket on his bed. I was growing accustomed to the feeling of my overgrown nails digging into cloth. It didn't bother me so much now. But as I settled my feet on the floor and curled into an attack position, he calmly put a gloved hand against my shoulder and shoved me, hard, back onto the bed.

I spluttered in indignation and fought gravity, but I was still very weak. It had cost me everything I had just to sit up. Shame nearly killed me, taking over where the draining left off.

"I don't trust you, princess. I don't know what you think you're going to do, but I don't trust you." He mucked around in a crooked drawer and held up a handful of silk cravats.

"You wouldn't dare."

"You can't stop me." He grinned.

I struggled, but it was no good. He hummed under his breath as he tied my hands together at the wrists. When he reached for my stocking-clad ankles, deeply bred propriety propelled my weakly kicking feet.

"No one," I gasped, "has ever touched my ankles."

"No one has ever threatened to kill me ten times in

ten different ways in one day." He neatly snagged my feet and wound my ankles around with a wine-colored length of silk. "But I need this job. I've drunk my way through every theater and bar in the city, and it's Deep Darkside and Beggar's Row after this. I won't let myself fall that far."

He was talking to himself now. I was bound, hand and foot, trussed up like a fly in a spider's web—or, to be more honest, like a spider temporarily restrained by a very foolish fly. My mind turned from escape to cunning, and I held very still, letting him go on. The more I could learn about my prey-turned-captor, the better my chances of besting him.

"What happened to you?" I asked softly.

"I died. You don't know what that's like. Or maybe you do, now. But music is the only thing I have left. I was famous. Celebrated, in two different worlds. And both times, I lost it. A girl I thought I loved told me that loss was supposed to be my salvation. But you know what? I don't feel saved."

"No one is ever safe," I added, my voice soothing.

He pulled a coin from his pocket and began flipping it back and forth over his knuckles. His eyes closed, and a look of pain flickered over his features. Faster and faster the coin spun in the last rays of evening, glinting in the light and showing me the copper-cast face of a kindly old man with a mustache. I didn't move a muscle. I simply studied my prey, as I had been taught. He swallowed hard, and I focused on his lips, on the sensual curve of the lower one, waiting to see what he would reveal next.

"Oi, Maestro," someone called, the voice tinny and echoing somewhere beyond the closed door. "It's your last chance, mate. You'd better get down here and start playing, unless you want to end up in the gutter."

"More threats," he said under his breath. "It must be Monday."

He checked the knots again, and seeing that I'd managed to wiggle just the tiniest bit loose, he yanked them hard enough to make me yelp in a decidedly unladylike manner.

"How dare——"

"You know very well how I dare." His gaze traveled over me, and he took a deep breath as if scenting the air. "Just remember when you've regained your strength that I could have done a lot worse to you." He licked his lips as his eyes lingered on the low cut of my gown, giving me a dark look that heated me straight through. I showed him my teeth.

He patted my hair, and I shook him off with a hiss. The movement pushed me past the point of exhaustion, but I hated the thought of his filthy peasant hands touching me. In my head, I killed him for the thousandth time, laughing as his blood painted my teeth.

"I won't remember what you didn't do," I said under my breath as I curled onto my side and prepared to sleep or pass out or whatever kept taking me over. "I'll only remember this."

4

I drifted in and out of sleep, too empty to dream. When I woke, I could hear the strains of his harpsichord somewhere below me, sometimes dulcet and slow and seductive, sometimes loud and brash and accompanied by the stomping of boots and ribald shouts and singing. Still, there was a melancholy undertone to the music, a sadness rippling under the surface of even the happiest tunes. I felt like that inside—a yawning chasm of sorrow that couldn't be filled. But I was going to do something about it.

When the door finally opened, I was mostly awake, lying on my side and diligently sawing through the silk cravat around my wrists with my fangs. I didn't try to hide it from him. I just smiled around what was left of his tie and continued gnawing. With the black cat trotting at his heels, he ducked through the door and went about his business as if I wasn't there. He tossed his gloves onto the dresser and cracked his knuckles one at a time, watching me in bemusement.

"You're a feisty little monster, aren't you?" he finally asked, slurring a little.

"I'm not a monster." I spat out bits of cravat and rubbed my sore wrists. The silk tasted too closely of human and

soap and something else, a musky stink that I didn't like.
I tossed it onto the ground, and Tommy Pain batted it
around as if it was a toy. It was charming, this cat creature.
But Casper wasn't. "But I wouldn't expect you to understand who I am or what I mean. You're uncivilized."

"I'm quite civil."

"Civility depends upon not tying people up."

"If our roles were reversed, you wouldn't hesitate," he
muttered. "You'd take your time killing me. I can see it
in your eyes. It's a shame, too. They'd be pretty, if they
weren't so set on murder."

I chuckled, low and sweet. He didn't know the half of
it. But I'd been thinking. I had figured out a way to get
what I wanted all around. My strength back, my life back,
my revenge, and, in time, his head on a silver platter.

"I don't want to murder you anymore." I smiled
sweetly. "I think we can help each other."

"Do you, now?" He turned his back to me. My anger
flared, that he thought me so inconsequential and harmless.

He was undressing. I had to turn my eyes—or at least
appear to. Not only because I was scandalized but because
despite the strange stink, he was still full of blood barely
contained by warm skin. As my beloved old nursemaid
used to say, even a cracked teacup made a fine vessel for
the right drink. And this teacup was far from cracked.

He tossed his glittering jacket over the dresser and
wrenched off his cravat. Next came the frilly shirt,
shrugged overhead and flung into the corner. His skin
was golden, almost unheard of in my country, where
ice-white was in fashion. He was more broadly built than
the royals I had grown up with, and his muscular shoul-

ders didn't need any padding. Fine curly hair on his chest caught in the lamplight, trailing down and down.

I heard the button on his breeches and may have peeked out of idle curiosity, but he seemed to recall where he was at that moment and stopped, eyes meeting mine with a sneer. Instead, he kicked his boots across the room and slammed a fist into the faded white paint on the wall. Tommy Pain shot under the low bed with a hiss. The cracked mirror hanging from a wire fell to the ground and shattered to pieces, each shard reflecting the pathetic little room and us, its pathetic inhabitants.

Me, a lost princess and future queen, far from home and so weak I couldn't untie the cravat around my ankles. Him, an uncivilized and fallen . . . whatever he was. I could read rage in the tension of his back, in the white of his fists against the crumbling wall where the mirror had been. Even in stillness, he was a tempest.

"That's seven years of bad luck."

"I've already put in three." He lightly banged his forehead against the plaster. "What will be left of me in four more?"

"If you accept my bargain, a wealthy man." I sat up. "Now, have you any more vials?"

He pulled away from the wall and pinned me with a steely blue glare. I didn't blink.

"Please?" I added, as much as it pained me.

With a chuckle, he fished three glass tubes out of his jacket and uncorked the first one Pinky-style, with two hands. By the time I'd downed all of the vials, I had enough strength to untie my feet and stand, although the ceiling didn't allow even my child-sized frame a decent stretch. I hadn't stood since I'd attacked him downstairs, and my corset hung loosely around my waist and itched. I was well trained enough not to scratch.

He watched me the entire time, cautious but curious and unsmiling. Casper made me feel self-conscious, which I deeply resented, since a princess existed only to be admired and feared. Another mark against him. I looked down at the rumpled sack of a dress hanging from my wasted frame. It had once been my third-best gown, the height of fashion, hand-sewn with golden thread. What must he think of me, weak and girlish and left to rot in a suitcase? And yet there was something hungry lurking in his gaze.

I would teach him what to think of me. I reached down to hand him his cravat.

"Here is the bargain I offer you." I folded my hands together and mimicked my mother's precise intonation. "I must return to my people. I understand that I am being hunted and that I am recognizable, and I admit that I know little of the squalid life outside of the Ice Palace. You will disguise me and escort me to Muscovy, acting as guide and guard. You will help me discover what power Ravenna holds over my kingdom, and you will help me depose her. If we are successful, you will be court musician to the Tsarina of Freesia, composer to the Snow Court of Muscovy. You will never want again. Whatever you are, you will have whatever you need. Whatever you wish."

"Whatever I wish?" One eyebrow went up, and a strange recognition shuddered through me. I ignored it.

"Within reason."

The cold silence hung between us, the shards of the mirror on the floor brighter than snow.

"You're not used to bargaining, are you?" he finally said.

"Excuse me?"

"You've basically told me that if I can do the impossible, keep you alive for more than a thousand miles, and depose one of the most powerful despots in the entire world, then I can sit around and play the harpsichord in the snow whenever you crook your little claw. But I'll still be an inferior, won't I? Your pet slave." He chuckled and leaned back against the wall, crossing his bare feet. "It's what they call a fool's bargain."

"You strike me as a fool."

"What, because I'm here, crouched in the attic and playing piano for blue-collar bloodsuckers who can't tell Beethoven from Brahms? Because I spend most of my time drunk and wishing for something stronger than drink? Or because I took pity on what I thought was a starving child but was actually a murderous little ice bitch with plans of world domination?"

As he panted with anger and hunched over, stalking toward me in the scant space between us, I saw in him the echoes of a Bludman's inner beast and wondered, in truth, what he was. But I smiled at his little tirade.

"You're a fool because you underestimate me." I ran a thumb over the edge of the mirror shard hidden behind my skirt, swiped from the ground when his back was turned.

Then I pounced for his neck.

It didn't take much strength or weight to knock him over—he must have been drunker than he seemed. His arm jerked up just in time to stop my slash for his jugular, and I hissed and aimed for his bare shoulder. The mirror shard plunged into his skin, and as he shrieked and struggled, I yanked out the tip and pressed my mouth to the wound.

Finally. Real blood. Straight from the animal, as it should be. Vials could never equal this rush, this eye-rolling pleasure.

Except.

I pulled back and stared at the blood dribbling from the wound. It wasn't right.

In that second of curiosity, as Casper clutched at his shoulder and swore in words I'd never heard before, something heavy landed on my back with a screech. Claws dug into the tender flesh above my corset, and teeth nipped against my neck. I growled in response and scrabbled at the heavy, furry shape with my talons. With one last, insulted hiss, Tommy Pain leaped off me and shot back under the bed, where he growled menacingly from the shadows.

I decided that I had mixed feelings about cats.

Casper erupted under me, dumping me onto the dusty floorboards in a heap. He lurched away to where the mirror used to be, then swore some more as he tried to find another way to assess the damage I'd done. I licked my lips meditatively, still wondering what the bitter taste might be. My already ruined dress now resembled a garbage sack, and creamy straggles of dusty hair tangled over my shoulders, sticky with blood and old wine. And I was still raging with hunger. His blood wasn't perfect, but it would have served its purpose if I hadn't stopped to deliberate.

Had I been a lesser being, I would have felt very sorry for myself. I might have endeavored to cry again. As it was, I held out a hand toward Casper and said, "You may consider us equal. Your blood in exchange for having restrained me. Shall we be friends?"

I didn't mean it. Not the *equal* part, not the *friends* part. I'd seen a human singing to some pigeons once, luring one close enough to twist its neck. I could sing like that, too.

He looked at my hand as if it still held the scrap of mirror. Luckily, his blood had already clotted, so it wasn't hard to control myself. I'd gotten a couple of good mouthfuls, and it was enough. But I wanted him to help me up. I wanted him to start thinking of himself as my servant. So I smiled. And I waited.

Casper stood over me so long that my arm started to shake. I had thus far managed to ignore my body's constant groans and aches since my emergence from the valise. But even fresh blood couldn't fix four years of starvation, stillness, and atrophy, not even on a Bludwoman's body.

"Hmm?" I added hopefully.

He dug into his pocket and dropped another vial into my hand instead. My black-scaled fingers curled around the cool glass on instinct, and I was already thinking of how good it would taste going down. I'd never drunk more than two vials in a day, but I felt that I would never be full again.

"Drink it," he said, his voice dull and deadly. "I have errands to run. If you still want to strike this ridiculous bargain, you'll stay here, in this room, and sleep. You're going to need strength and stamina for this to work. I'll be here when you wake up, and I'll be ready to leave."

"So you'll help me, then? You'll take me back to Freesia?"

The naive hope rose in my voice. Maybe that was what finally tipped his scales.

"Anything is better than this." He nodded once and stormed out of the room.

I was swallowing the blood before his bare feet slapped down the stairs.

I had guessed right—he was a fool. And I knew exactly what to do with fools.

5

I couldn't sleep. There was too much to contemplate—
and I didn't want to give Casper the satisfaction of my obedience. The longer I lay there, staring at the low ceiling,
the more I thought of what I had lost. My parents had not
been warm and loving—how could they, predators and
royal to boot? And my sister, Olgha, had been even worse.
But they had been my family, my anchor, the structure
around which my life had been planned. And now that
plan was gone, and I was alone and distraught.

All that, and the stupid cat kept making an entirely
inappropriate rumbling noise from underneath the bed.
So I gave up on sleep and did something I had never done
before.

I snooped. I tossed drawers, rifled through pockets,
hunted for loose floorboards, and even turned over the
mattress, much to Tommy Pain's chagrin. And I wasn't
sneaky about it, either. If Casper wasn't going to play nice,
neither was I.

The infuriating man appeared to own very little. His
clothes, a hidden bottle of wine sealed with wax, and a
small notebook with bizarre poetry in nearly illegible
handwriting. Angry slashes marred almost every page.

The first page said "Leaves of Grass," which seemed beyond ridiculous. Blades of grass, maybe. But leaves? I flipped through the book, trying to understand what appeared to be a very angry and scattered mind.

One phrase stood stark on a page, each word written in block letters with a heavy pen.

> *I, now thirty-seven years old in perfect health begin,*
> *Hoping to cease not till death.*
> *Fuck you, Walt Whitman.*

What a singularly bizarre man. With his things arrayed before me, I was no closer to mastering the servant I would pretend to befriend for the sake of my country. And I was running out of time. Improper and awkward as it was, I flopped onto the dusty floor and stuck my arm as far under the unkempt bed as I could. My hand grazed something small tucked against the wall, and I withdrew from the shadows with the object in my hand and a scratch from Tommy Pain for my trouble.

It was a little box of polished wood with a simple hinge and clasp. I flicked it open. Inside I found a single copper coin and a deep red feather.

"Trying to kill the Maestro wasn't good enough. Now you're stealing from him, too?" someone said from the door.

I slammed the box shut and threw it back under the bed, where it hit the mad cat with a hearty *thwack*. He shot out of the darkness and curled up in the corner to lick his nethers in an extremely improper fashion. I coughed politely.

Even if my height was never going to make me imposing, I still stood before I faced my accuser. And for once, I was taller than someone. Through the successive layers of grimy and stained clothing and the leather aviator's hat and goggles, I couldn't tell what it was. A girl, a boy, a child, a youth. Only one thing I could tell from across the small room: it was human.

And I was going to drain it.

"I lost a hairpin under the bed," I said crisply. "It's not my fault if he chooses to keep his sundries among the dustlemmings."

I glided toward my prey, my fingers curling into claws. The figure smirked and showed me a knife.

"Lesson one. Don't kid a kidder, kid. You suck on me, and Casper will turn you in for a thousand well-earned silvers unless I can gut you first. I'm Keen, by the way."

I nodded to the mongrel child. "Greetings, Keen. I am Ahnastasia, princess of the Great Snow Court of Muscovy, crown capitol of the Tsarina of Freesia."

"Yeah, and I'm the bloody king of Franchia." Keen grinned with surprisingly white teeth for what I had to assume was a diseased foundling. Tommy Pain had completed his vile self-grooming and twined around Keen's feet. When the stained brown gloves began to scratch under his chin, he rumbled like a steam engine.

"What do you care about that maddening man?" I said.

"None of your goddamn business."

"I seem to get that a lot here."

"That's because poor people like us hate rich people who try to make us feel like crap," Keen answered with slitted eyes.

"Do I look rich to you?" I held my hands out to show my ruined, blood-spattered dress.

"Maestro told me you've been stored in a suitcase for four years, so of course your frock looks like a handkerchief somebody sneezed in. But I bet that thread's still made of enough gold to feed me for a year. I see you staring at me like I'm nothing, like I should be bowing and kissing your feet. That's never going to happen."

I sat down on the bed, glaring. Taking a sphere of tarnished brass from a jacket pocket, the little urchin tossed and rolled it from one gloved hand to another with a private smile. I watched for a few moments, noting the markings and indentations in the metal, wondering what the thing was. Raised eyebrows told me I was being purposefully tortured. I sighed in resignation, exhausted from the small act of standing.

"Enough of this ridiculous standoff. Where is your Maestro?"

"Getting ready for the trip. He asked me to fetch you to the costumer's for your disguise."

"Why didn't he come himself?"

"I told you. He's busy."

I patted my dress and hair, as if anything I could do with my own two hands would prepare me for being seen on the street. What if there were people out there—and not people like Casper and Keen but People. Real people, people who mattered, people who might know me. I cringed inwardly and tilted my head benevolently.

"I suppose I am ready, then. Lead on."

"I got to do something first." Keen burst into a wide, toothy grin. I finally understood, seeing that brilliant smile, that she was a girl, a young and pretty one, hiding for some reason under short hair and shapeless clothes and a silly hat. Something evil glinted in her eyes.

"Very well." I crossed my arms and nodded. "Get on with it."

She reached into her jacket, tucked the sphere away, and pulled out a pair of jagged, rusty scissors, the sort of thing our gardeners would have saved for lopping off weeds and the heads of pesky bludlemmings.

"First, we got to cut your hair off."

I drew back and hissed, clutching long white-blond locks to my chest.

"No," I whispered.

"Deal or no deal, princess?" She snicked the scissors open and closed. "They always got room for bludwhores in the next bar over, if you ain't willing."

My hair had never been cut. Not once in my entire twenty-seven years of life. No, make that thirty-one. I had lost four years, and I was well on my way to being whispered about at court as a spinster, if I lived long enough for some snide baroness to call me such. But Keen left me with little choice, and I knew well enough that my hair was my most recognizable feature.

The little monster didn't even let me brush it first. As soon as I'd pulled out the few silver pins that remained, she darted behind me and wrapped a grimy glove around the knee-length mass. I yelped and fought her, but that only pulled the hair taut and straight, and I was still weak. She took advantage of my mistake to hack into the mess with her clippers, and tears stung my eyes in pain and sadness. The tugging hurt, but the injured vanity hurt more.

"Ha!" She held up more than three feet of my pride and joy, a hunting trophy. It was shiny, beautiful, and the color of buttermilk, if slightly dusty and blood-streaked buttermilk. The color was unusual in Freesia and had been my trademark. I grabbed for it, but she danced back, winding it around her hand and stuffing it neatly into a bag. She pocketed the pins, too.

"It's mine," I said menacingly.

"It's going to buy your disguise. Which we can't get until we cut off even more."

"No." I felt for the cruelly snagged ends of my remaining locks. They fell just below my shoulders. It was a tragedy. My fingers played with the rough curls, and I glared at Keen, imagining her head next to Casper's on a platter.

"Look, lady. It's simple. Do you want to live, or do you want to die? Somebody wants you to lie down and stuff it, and you don't strike me as the sort of bitch that's going to oblige. So let's get on with it before the shops close and your type fills the streets, eh? Short hair ain't so bad. And you're less likely to get the nits."

I shuddered. Common folk and their filth had never been a consideration before. Did I see things moving in her dull, mud-brown hair, or was that just my imagination?

She took a step toward me, scissors held out. I slapped her arm away, and quick as a snake, she slapped my arm with her free hand. It fell to my side, limp. I had never been struck before. The little beast took advantage of my shock to shove me onto Casper's stool. I tried to stand, but her foot pinned my skirts.

"I don't mind stabbing you," she said in a businesslike manner, "but you'll look nicer if you just let me take care of it."

In the end, I sat there, stunned and already grieving my youth and beauty. Each snippet of ice-white hair that fluttered to the ground felt like a year of my life. Instead of feeling lighter, my head felt weighed down by all the sorrow in the world. I was weak. I was lost. And now I was ugly.

"There we go," Keen said at last. "And a lovely job it is, if I do say so myself."

I thought about scooping up another shard of mirror to see the damage she'd done, but I knew that I was too distraught to stop myself from stabbing her, and then Casper would never help me. What was done was done.

"Put this on."

Keen shoved something green and smelly into my hands. I dumped it onto the floor, where Tommy Pain batted it about.

"You're going to want that hat, you know," Keen said. "Your hair stands out. You've got to cover it, at least until we can get some dye."

At the end of my emotional rope and badly in need of blood and non-Keen company, I shoved the hat onto my head. It was large and floppy and made of the itchiest substance I'd ever touched, the sort of thing an old servant man would wear to keep the rain off.

"Couldn't you find anything smaller than this monstrosity?" I tried to arrange it so it wouldn't itch. "I could fit Tommy Pain in here and still have room for—"

I looked at her, eyes wide. She grinned her evil grin again, the one that transformed her face into something beatific. And something that I wanted to destroy. I threw the hat at her instead. She caught it neatly and twirled it around a finger. Anger bubbled up in my chest.

"I could have stuffed all my hair in here, you brat. We didn't have to cut it off yet, or so badly. It didn't have to hurt."

"Nope. We didn't. But I think it was more fun this way. Don't you?"

"I'm going to see your head—"

"On a platter. Yeah, the Maestro told me about that. Why would you even want someone's head on a platter? It would just wobble around and leak and make a mess, and they'd be all staring at you with their dead eyes. A pike would be so much more dramatic. Or a fishbowl full of whiskey."

"Seems like you've been giving it some thought," I snapped.

"You're not the only one with enemies."

While we bantered, my traitorous hands crept up to what was left of my curls. My talons caught on the tangled ends, and my breath hitched. People could see my *ears*. It was the worst disaster since the last blood famine.

She snickered and patted the bag. "Going to get a good price for it, you know. Bloody idiots will think it's a unicorn tail with magical properties, make it into good-luck watch fobs. You should be proud."

"Magical properties? You've obviously never met a unicorn."

"Haven't met a sea monster or hellbear, either."

Now it was my turn to grin and flash my pointed teeth. "Then you haven't been to Freesia."

"Save the fairy tales for the kiddies, princess." But I had seen her tough façade falter, just for a moment. I was guessing she'd never been out of London and was scared of travel. She had reason to be, if she thought she was coming with us to Freesia. And now I had a little something to hold over her. Excellent.

"They're not fairy tales, ragamuffin."

"Well, we're still in London, and we're running late. So let's go."

I took my time tightening my corset and lacing my old boots back on. Four years ago, they had been as soft as a baby's cheek, perfectly tanned bludelk leather dyed to a deep gold. Now they were cracked with age and disuse, the laces hard and bent. As for my dress, there was nothing I could do about it, and I didn't want her filthy little paws on my person anyway. I snatched the hat back and draped it over my head, hiding my face under the sagging brim.

"You look like a drunk grandmother," Keen said with a laugh. "Just stagger about a bit and burp every now and then. They'll just assume you're blitzed on bludwine."

"On what?"

"Nothing. Let's go. Don't speak to anyone. Try to hunch over a bit like there ain't a red-hot poker up your bum. Don't say anything about heads on platters." She yanked a faded plaid blanket from Casper's bed and tossed it over my shoulders. It smelled like him, good and bad at the same time. "And keep this around your shoulders and neck. Hide your hands. They ain't so nice to Bluddies where we're going."

I arranged the pathetic little scrap of fabric the way I'd seen our old Pinky cook wear her shawl while making bloodcakes or mixing the potion for my baths. I hunched over, letting my head slump forward and bending my knees. It went against everything in my blud, pretending to be something less than I was. But I'd heard wild rumors of the Pinkies of Sangland, who held sway over the Bludmen in a blasphemous sort of power struggle that went against nature itself. I wasn't ready to be drained again or hit in the face with a moldy bit of vegetable.

Without a word, she led me out the door and down the rickety stairs. I was pleased to discover that I could walk, but I was still exhausted. It was like the dreamy ache of falling asleep beside the fire after a daylong hunt, but without the pleasant floaty feeling of a belly full of fresh blood.

We passed several open doors, one showing the empty music hall where I'd first found Casper and woken in the darkness. A jumble of crates, valises, and flotsam sat in the corner, and I thought I spotted the flap of leather from my own suitcase.

"Wait," I whispered, and Keen grunted. Before she could stop me, I darted over to the suitcase and scrabbled inside, feeling for some remnant of my old life, some clue to the last four years. The lights were low, since there were no windows, and even with my excellent night vision, I couldn't see much. I had nearly given up when my talon caught in the fabric lining, tearing it. I felt around between the ragged silk and the leather until something cool scraped my fingertips.

I pulled out my prize and sighed. I wasn't sure whether it was contentment or sadness. In my hand was the necklace I'd been wearing that day by the fish pond, the day that, to the best of my memory, was the day of my abduction. White diamonds and blue sapphires winked in a collar that made me look like a glacier carved of ice. It had been a gift from my father for my fifteenth birthday in those beautiful, dancing days before Ravenna had begun to insinuate herself into our family and our state.

"You find anything?" Keen called from the doorway.

I slipped the necklace down the front of my corset and called back, "No, nothing here."

But for some reason, I wasn't ready to leave the suitcase yet. It had been an unwitting prison, but it was the only clue to my apparent kidnapping. I pushed it over to investigate. Scuffed tan leather, thick and cheaply stitched. On one side, the curved flap I'd carved with my claws. On the other side, a host of odd stickers with strange names I had to squint to read. Stockhelm. Constantinoble. Kyro. Places I'd seen in my books and on the ornate, gemstone-dappled globe in my father's study. I had apparently been to those faraway places, unconscious and on the verge of death. I had missed the mountains, the sunrises, those abominations called camels that spit blud when angry. So much time and so many opportunities, lost forever.

And on the top, another sticker had been torn just enough to obscure the recipient's name. Written in dark red ink, the remaining words read, "-seinist, -uby Lane, -ontown, land."

They had shipped me, whoever they were. Like luggage. Less than chattel. Dumped in a case and passed along, hand to hand, never to reach my final destination. And now I knew, at least partially, to whom. And I wasn't leaving London until I'd learned why.

6

I was so busy fighting my way through the streets of London that I barely had time to register the details in the chaos. Head down and shawl-sheltered, I mostly saw Keen's back, the bag full of my hair bouncing against her grungy jacket. Every time I tried to look up and soak in the shops, the filth in the streets, the mouthwatering children plucking my skirts with innocent grins and handfuls of violets, I would nearly lose my guide. So instead, I focused on the spot between her shoulder blades, thinking about how pleasant it would be to plant a knife there.

She ducked down an alley, and I followed. We tiptoed over piles of rotten Pinky fodder, past drunks and fallen women, and through the lairs of the biggest bludlemmings I'd ever seen, their maroon fur bristling as they hissed at me. At last, Keen held open a nondescript door, and I stepped into darkness.

"Gods of ice, I'm sick of squalor," I muttered under my breath. We were in an antechamber, a sad little closet barely big enough for the two of us and the giant black cat that had apparently chased us all the way from the Seven Scars, bludlemmings be damned. I began to see why they called him Tommy Pain, because he certainly was a pain.

Keen knocked on the inner door, and locks clicked within.

"It's about time," Casper said through the crack before Keen shoved me through.

The room beyond was nothing like what I had expected from the dismal antechamber and Casper's room under the eaves. Bright red walls, a salmon-pink ceiling, and a wooden floor painted with giant swirls made my eyes hurt after the grim dullness of everything else I'd seen in London so far. Perhaps these people weren't as depressing and deadened as I had assumed.

"So here's ze little princess," mused a cultured lady's voice with a Franchian accent.

The tall woman at Casper's side was mostly uncovered, her skin shimmering with color, red and deep orange and violet like a sunset. Her eyes were black all around, and I would have sworn that feathers were somehow glued to her eyelashes, making them seem as long as fingers. A daimon. I'd never seen one outside of books or paintings.

I knew I was staring, and I knew it was rude. I forced myself to look down.

"Forgive me, madam. I've been out of the world for a long time and have forgotten myself."

It was the most polite I'd been in London, mainly because I could sense some common feeling in the proud carriage of this odd lady. If she wasn't royalty where she came from, she was something close.

"I understand what it is like to be alone among ze barbarians," she answered with a coy smile. "And I offer my condolences on the loss of your hair. I remember from ze broadsheets that it was quite beautiful."

My hand went to the heinous hat. I removed it and

dropped it right on Tommy Pain's head. He shook it off and glared at me with his bright green eye. I almost smiled.

"I am Madamoiselle Beaureve, but here they call me Reve. If you will allow, I will help you to bathe and dress in a disguise, so that you may travel unimpeded. The price, as you know, is your hair. Do you accept this arrangement?"

Keen handed her the bag, and Reve opened it with a look of awe. Her skin shivered in feathery patterns of violet and indigo.

"It is very fine. It will be a joy to work with such beautiful hair."

"What will you do with it?" I asked.

"Truly, you don't want to know, princess."

"There's some sick bastards in this town," Keen muttered under her breath. Judging by her bitterness, maybe she was older than she looked.

"It seems I have no choice but to accept."

My eyes met Casper's. I couldn't read what I saw there, a stormy mixture of determination and surrender, like a man being sucked into darkness and welcoming the maelstrom. He closed his eyes as if in pain and slipped out the door without a word.

Reve pooled my golden curls reverently on a worktable with a farewell pat. I told myself that my hair would grow back, that it would one day regain and surpass its former beauty, but I wasn't sure if I believed it.

The daimon walked around me, her long tail waving as she plucked my sleeves and felt the stuff of my skirt and tilted my head up with a hot-skinned magenta finger under my chin.

"This will be fun," she murmured.

She bowed me through another door. I was soon alone, soaking in a copper tub, the water from the steam pipes nearly boiling my skin. Once I got over my inbred fear of water and accepted that there wasn't a grain of salt in the sweet-smelling bubbles, I was able to finally relax. I hadn't realized how dusty and tightly wound I had been. The bathtub, clearly selected for Reve, dwarfed my petite form, and I stretched in ecstasy. In the workshop, the daimon would be plucking out the gold thread and burning my old dress, or maybe cutting it into ragged skirts for the less-picky whores. So it was done, then. I was ready to begin the next chapter of my life.

The water was soon cloudy with the filth of years, and it was delicious to scrub my short hair and feel the water running down my scalp. By the time I exited the steam-filled bathroom wrapped in a skimpy cotton robe, I was almost looking forward to life on the road. I'd never undertaken a journey before, and even if my main companion was an unpleasant ruffian like Casper, at least I wasn't half-drained in a valise.

Reve was waiting for me in the workroom, surrounded by heaps of fabric and ribbons.

"Oh la, *chérie*. You are ready? Good. We begin." She led me to a tall chair, and I sat, mesmerized by my image in the mirror.

She fluffed my damp hair with her fingers, which were now green. It curled loosely around my head in a pretty cloud of lightest blond, and I sighed.

"I know, *I know*. Sangland is a bland place, and you are accustomed to standing out. Brown dye will seem cruel to you, but it's the only way to avoid detection."

"Artifice," I said. "I don't like it."

She laughed, her voice like water over rocks. "You are Freesian royalty. You drank artifice with your mother's milk and blud. This is just a little paint."

With quick fingers, she mixed a strange concoction from bottles and powders and coated my hair with dull brown. Without a word and with an ease that suggested prior dealings with Bludmen, she clipped and filed my talons to the exactly proper length. When she finally washed the muck from my hair, I looked like a drowned bludlemming.

I was accustomed to being primped and dressed, and honestly, I wouldn't have known how to do half of it. I was more than content to let myself be manipulated as I meditated on my various plans. Heads on platters. Or spikes. Travel by coach or elegant airship, velvet couches, a parasol at my side. Sinking my teeth into Ravenna's throat and being welcomed back into the embrace of my country. Raising monuments to my parents and moving into the royal chamber.

I patted the robe's pocket, feeling the weight of my jeweled necklace there. I still had riches. It would be a piece of bludcake.

Reve helped me step into the bulky undergarments favored in London, frilly petticoats that would make my skirt stand out round as a bell.

"Now for your dress," she said, and I inspected the rich fabrics and trims draped everywhere.

My smile crumbled when she held out the dullest thing in the room.

"A sack?" I asked, acid in my voice.

"Oh, la, little princess. What you see here are costumes for performers. The dancers, the acrobats, the whores. They all come to me for the brightest, the lowest-cut,

the most daring. But you must do your best not to stand
out. You must escape notice. Eyes must travel over you
and never remember that you existed. That scarlet satin
would drop wagging jaws, and then you would find yourself in another suitcase."

I poked the dull brown thing draped over her arms.
Then I wiped my fingers off on my robe.

"Tell yourself it is a costume. Call the color bronze or
palomino. And don't give up yet—there is more to do."

With daggers of distaste in my eyes, I let her dump me
into the dress. The rough, canvas-like fabric grated against
my wrists and neck. I'd never dressed as a Pinky, never had
my throat covered up to my chin, and I wanted to gag
with the intimacy of the garment.

"This next bit is special," Reve said, interrupting my
sulk. She held something heavy and leathery out to me,
and I sneered at it.

"A saddle?"

"There are no stirrups, *chérie*."

She winked and lifted my arms to buckle the thing
around me. It was a leather corset. And it had to weigh at
least twenty pounds.

"Are you trying to torture me?"

"I'm trying to keep you alive, silly goose. A leather corset reinforced with steel bones and extra-thick panels. It
works both ways—not only will it keep you from being
accidentally stabbed or arrow-shot, but it will make you
look like the most frightened Pinky that ever walked the
earth. No Bludwoman in her right mind would wear such
a thing, no?"

I could barely move in it, and when she had finished
tightening the straps, I could barely breathe. As I panted

and glared, Reve glanced at a cuckoo clock and sucked at her lip.

"We are running out of time. Quit pouting and act useful."

She helped me back into my ragged boots and laced them for me, since I couldn't bend over. I put on the gloves she gave me and clenched my hands, feeling muffled and dull. I had never put on used clothes before, never had any fabric touch my body that had been touched by uncovered human hands, much less worn by the filthy wretches. It was like wearing trash. Ugly trash. I imagined what my proud mother would think if she saw me like this. Probably retch into a painted ewer at the sight of her favorite daughter drained, dressed in rags, and nearly bald.

But no. The dead don't retch.

"Come and see, *chérie*." Reve tugged me toward a looking glass.

"I don't think I want to."

But she didn't give me a choice, and the Bludwoman in the mirror was a complete stranger. From her huge ice-blue eyes to her hollow cheeks and dirt-colored hair, she was a mystery. The tan dress and dark brown corset went together like a steamer trunk; the little brass hooks up the front heightened the resemblance. Everything was so plain, so worn. There were no frills, no lace, no jewels, no clever wink of golden thread to glitter as I walked. I was no longer a princess. Not even a person. A thing.

"I am a portmanteau."

"You are beautiful, princess."

"My eyes are the only thing left of me."

"Ah, yes." She *tsk*ed. "We can't have that."

She tossed a hat at me and perched a pair of dark glasses

over my nose. The hat was a smallish topper that buckled under the chin, rough canvas, more tan with gray plumes. I tried to fasten it on correctly, but with my fingers entombed in gloves, it was hopeless. She snatched it from me and arranged everything.

"You'll learn how to do all of this yourself." She canted the hat at a slight angle, nearly choking me. "Casper has worked in a caravan. He can help you."

"I told him that if he touched me again, I would see his head on a platter."

"I know a man who once devised a platter for just such occasions," she mused with a little smile. "It had an elegantly barbed spike in the middle and an outside trough to catch the blood. Like a moat."

"I'd like his address, please," I said without a trace of humor. And then I remembered my secondary plot. "And I need your help deciphering this note. Have you paper and pen?"

She provided them, and I struggled to write in the damnable gloves. Four years of disuse combined with an annoying amount of kidskin between my fingers meant that my handwriting was barely legible, but she understood almost instantly.

"The tasseinist on Ruby Lane. Mr. Sweeting. You cannot go there. He is a fiend."

"But what is a tasseinist?"

Her skin rippled into mottled shades of lavender and sea green and brown. I'd seen a similar configuration when I'd found a long-dead Pinky on a hunt once. Bruise and rot. Whatever a tasseinist was, it scared her.

"It is horrid, what a tasseinist does. How do you say it? Like a taxidermist but for people."

"Who would want such things?"

"Scientists. Loved ones who can't let go. Sadists. Those who would preserve the flesh with hopes of reanimating it. It is a dark place, indeed. He is a daimon like me, but a very bad one who feeds on the basest of emotions. Do not go there. And where did you find this address?"

"I saw it somewhere," I said lightly.

If I told her that it was my body's original destination, I'd never find a way to get there. As it was, I barely had the stomach for it. But I knew that I needed whatever answers Mr. Sweeting might hold before I went up against the formidable Ravenna. And I had a disguise now, so my only concern was getting to Ruby Lane before Casper returned.

"I have work to do," Reve said. "Please make yourself at home. Keen has some blood for you in the sitting room, I believe."

She waved me toward another door, and I realized just how hungry I was. Growing up in the palace, I had never known hunger. It was difficult for a Bludman to grow fat, and my mother had always insisted that I be dainty and refined in my drinking and my killing. But the draining had left me utterly insatiable. I smacked my lips when I saw Keen standing by a bookshelf in the sitting room, her short hair showing a strip of her tender neck to delicious advantage.

"I've got only two vials for you." She laid them on a table. "And there's no cup, so you won't be able to stick your scaly pinkie in the air."

I watched her as I uncorked a vial and downed it in three gulps. It was clear that she hated me, whether because I was a Bludman, a rich Bludman, or just someone she was forced to talk to. But I wasn't about to broach that topic.

"Can you read?" I asked instead, seeing her glove brush the line of book spines.

She jerked her hand away guiltily. " 'Course I can. But nobody gives books to foundlings. It would just give us uppity ideas, wouldn't it?"

"So you're an orphan, then?"

"None of your bloody business."

"That again. Your rudeness is intolerable."

She snorted. "Just because you're the bitchiest blood-sucker in London doesn't mean you're my boss."

I sighed as I uncorked the next vial. Hidden hostility I was used to, but this sort of outspoken hatred was entirely new to me, as anyone in Freesia who spoke to me that way would have been on the dinner table within moments. Was this how all the Pinkies of Sangland felt about Blud-men, or did she have a problem with me in particular? I had to find a way to win her over if I wanted her help.

"Would you like some books of your own? When we've succeeded, I'll give you free run of the library of the Ice Palace, maybe even give you a few volumes for your own collection. I've always enjoyed a good novel. *Robertson Crusoe*, for example."

I plucked the novel off the shelf and admired the green leather cover and gold-leafed pages. Longing rippled briefly over her face, and she gulped. Then her eyes went shifty.

"What do you want in exchange?"

"You're a very wise child." I held out the book to her. "I just want to make a little detour before we leave. There's a shop I've been meaning to visit. Would you take me there?"

"Where is it?"

"I'm not sure. But I know it's on Ruby Lane."

"Ruby Lane? You want me to take you to Ruby Lane?" She threw back her head and laughed, hands on her skinny hips. "That's a good joke, lady. Casper would skin me whole if I took you there."

"What's so bad about it?"

"It's in the heart of Deep Darkside. Chock full of diabolists, bludwhores, opium dens, and the sort of daimon that does more than change color. We'd be lucky to get out alive."

I smiled, showing her my fangs, which I knew were stained with blood. "Keen, darling, I may be small and well mannered, but I assure you that I am a killing machine. There is nothing on Ruby Lane that you should fear more than my displeasure."

She leaned back against the bookshelf, biting her lip and staring at me. I met her eyes. Neither of us blinked. Normally, I was quite good at reading people. But I had no idea what was going on in that shaggy, ill-bred head of hers.

"Okay," she finally said. "But we leave now, without a word to Reve. Deal?"

"Deal." I grinned, feeling immensely pleased with myself.

After all, if things went as I hoped they would, she'd soon be too dead to read any books.

7

Escape was easier than anticipated, thanks to the overpowering cabaret tunes belting out of Reve's gramophone—and mouth—as she worked. The daimon had a lovely, husky voice that quavered with unexpected bitterness. We climbed out a back window and dropped into a filthy alley. The conveniently placed rubbish bin and Keen's mischievous smile told me that she had done this before.

Following her through the shadows of London was easier this time around, mostly because we stayed in the less-traveled areas. Every turn seemed to take us into a darker, more miserable alley. I got a closer look at the giant maroon rodents that had hissed at me on my way to Reve's workshop and realized that they weren't simply bludlemmings of a different color. These things were the size of Tommy Pain, who had decided to sit out this journey on a tufted footstool. Later I'd have to wonder how the cat knew exactly where things would be safer.

"What is that thing?" I whispered, tugging on Keen's jacket.

"Bludrat," she whispered back over her shoulder. "Just leave it alone."

I was happy to comply. Ugly was bad enough, but it was slick with grime, too. I preferred my predators to have some elegance about them. Although I was sure that the bludrats wouldn't be able to digest me, I didn't want proof.

When Keen finally stopped, I almost ran into her. She stood stock-still in front of the darkest alley I'd seen yet. A heavy archway of weeping stones framed the dismal shadows beyond. "Ruby Lane" was slashed over the arch in paint too red to be blood. An evil chuckle echoed from the unaccountably thick fog and rolled down the glistening cobblestones.

"How picturesque."

"They do it this way on purpose." Keen shrugged as if she was shaking a spider off her shoulder. "To keep the wrong sort of people out."

"And whom do they consider 'the wrong sort of people'?"

"The right sort of people."

"Then let's get this over with quickly." I pressed bravely into the gloom.

We walked side-by-side, and I could barely see her. The mist smelled of magic, and I wondered what sort of hag spent her days conjuring a cloud to hide the dark goings-on of Ruby Lane.

"Do you know where you're going, then?" Keen asked me.

"I'll know it when I see it."

We passed shivering bundles of clothing that must have been people. We passed small fires that stunk of magic and bones. We passed an old woman selling roasted bludrats on sticks, a sickening steam rising from their charred fur and twitching legs. We held our breath by the Dragon's Lair, where heady lavender smoke swirled along the ground, beckoning with the mystery of the East. We heard the mournful strains of an out-of-tune harpsichord drunkenly plunking from the Green Fairy's Sister, the sort of place where the absinthe most likely harbored something worse than wormwood. A two-headed dog followed us briefly, sniffing at my hand and growling before I kicked at it and hissed. It was altogether the most unpleasant place I'd ever seen, outside of my own palace's dungeon.

The next shop window stopped me in my tracks, though. Behind the clouded glass, hanging on a stark white wall and arrayed on a shelf, were a variety of monstrosities. Body parts, shiny skulls, deformed fetuses floating in large jars, a stuffed child covered in lizard scales, and a woman's head mounted on a plaque. Keen kept walking, but I stopped to stare. That woman—I knew her. Correction: *had known.*

She wasn't labeled. And I could tell that the eyes were made of glass, because the color was a little off. But the hair was real and arranged with care, and the earbobs dangling from her ears had surely been borrowed from my mother's boudoir without permission.

"See something you need?" Keen shivered and turned to the next shop.

I put a glove to the ice-cold glass. "Olgha," I said stiffly. "My sister."

"Sweet Jesus," she murmured. I didn't know who that was, and I had expected something snottier from her, but it didn't come.

I was mesmerized by the horror, unable to stop staring at features I'd known all my life. From Olgha's much-bemoaned, overly large nose, inherited straight from our father, to the scar under her right eye that I'd made with my own talons during a squabble over a bit of ribbon, she was trapped forever, mounted like the bludstags and wolf heads on the walls of the palace library. The only thing missing was the other sister. Me.

"You still want to do this?" Keen's voice was pitched low, one foot poised to run.

"I must. Now more than ever."

I steeled myself. Keen handed me a crusty handkerchief, and I wiped the place where tears would have been and settled the dark glasses more firmly on my button nose, which I had fortunately inherited from my mother or possibly, as many said, handsome King Charles of Sveden. Thanks to my unusually light hair, there had been much talk regarding my birth exactly nine months after my parents' diplomatic mission to Stockhelm. But of course, anyone caught calling me anything other than the true daughter of Tsar Nikolas would have been tortured to death. For the moment, staring through the window, it was a blessing to look nothing like my sister.

I stepped through the door with a meekness I didn't feel and pretended to fidget as I'd seen frightened humans do. I didn't want to appear a threat to this Mr. Sweeting. Not at first.

The room wasn't as dusty as it looked from outside. But it was crowded. An army of jars squatted on a bookshelf, each of their freakish inhabitants more grotesque than the last. An entire wall held nothing but heads on plaques, from the usual hunting trophies to more humans and Bludmen, their glass eyes too focused for comfort. A large black bear loomed in the corner, mouth open to show ivory teeth tipped in red. And the glass counter facing the door held anything that could be stuffed and even some things that didn't seem possible, such as a tiny Kraken that should have collapsed out of water, frozen in time and shiny with varnish. A clockwork fox trotted out from behind the counter and barked, copper wings folded at its sides.

Something stroked my shoulder with a serpent's impersonal coldness, and I bit back a hiss. It was a bookish-looking man in a stylish suit, with red skin, a black spade beard, and horns. He was the Pinky devil incarnate, despite his natty cravat, and I disliked him immediately.

"Can I help you, miss?" he said with a crocodile's smile.

"I was interested in the earbobs on that . . . er . . . lady's head in the window. Are they for sale?"

"You don't look like my usual customers." He hadn't blinked yet. Neither had I.

"You don't look like my usual tasseinist, and you didn't answer my question. The earbobs. Are they for sale or not?"

"I'm afraid not, miss. That piece is on reserve for a very important foreign client, half of a matched set, and I can't dismantle the merchandise. But I've got an entire case of trinkets over here, if you'd care to look."

I didn't care to do any such thing, but I couldn't think of a reasonable response to the contrary. He led me to a different case, shining under a single light. I was treated to the strange theatrics of his tail, which was red and long, with a forked end. It waved around behind him in a distracting sort of way, as if it had a mind of its own.

"If it's earbobs you're looking for, there are several sets in this case. But I must warn you, miss." He leaned over the glass, his eyes boring into mine. "These aren't ordinary goods. I'm not a milliner or a jeweler or even an antiques dealer. Everything in my shop has a price. Some pieces are cursed, some are lucky, most were taken off of dead bodies or stolen from the claws of skeletons. Touch not, lest ye be touched."

"I understand." My nod of dismissal didn't budge him. "Thank you for the warning."

As I considered the case of sparkling jewelry, he loomed over me. Did I imagine that leather wings curled around me, luring me closer to the magical objects within? Surely he had some sort of magic about him, for every object seemed brighter and more beautiful than the last. Gems, necklaces, bracelets, earbobs with silver clips, rings, a diadem, and a set of talons made of rubies all beckoned, whispering on the edge of hearing.

And then I saw it.

"That piddly little ring there, with the blue paste jewel. How much?"

His gloved hand snaked in and pulled it out.

"You have quite the eye, miss." He rolled the ring back and forth between satin gloves.

Somewhere in the back of my mind, I noticed that he had six fingers on each hand. But that wasn't important. What really mattered was that he was holding the Ring of Freesian Succession, the jewel that announced Olgha's claim to our matriarchal throne. Its very existence was a deeply kept family secret, or else it would have already been in Ravenna's lacquered claws, and he surely wouldn't have had it on display with the other baubles.

"But I assure you that this stone is not paste. This, my lady, is a midnight diamond, perfectly formed and flawless. The fifteen blue topazes circling it are cold as ice and said to have mesmerizing powers when wielded by a true witch. It is the finest piece in my collection."

"Bullshit."

I turned in surprise to find Keen standing there, her hands in fists at her sides.

"Excuse me, Miss Lorelei. I didn't see you there, especially as you've been forbidden to enter my shop. Perhaps you'd like to leave before I disembowel you?"

Mr. Sweeting's voice stayed calm and polite, but his tail twitched back and forth, stabbing the air. Something brushed my skirts, and I looked down to see the clockwork fox, wings raised and sharp as hatchets, mouth open and razor-sharp teeth vibrating. I took a step back.

"First of all, don't call me Lorelei, you devil bastard. Second, we both know there's nothing magical about that manky old trinket. Third of all, you owe me."

"I believe our bargain has been satisfied." He took a menacing step closer.

"Then I'll just go find a Copper, and we'll have a chat, yeah?" she said, her little chin jutting out.

"Just because you found me standing in an open grave doesn't mean I've done anything illegal, child."

"I'm pretty sure that's exactly what it means, daimon."

The tension grew as thick as London fog. I cleared my throat. "This is all very exciting, but I'd really just like to hear the price of that ring, assuming that it is indeed paste, as it appears." I held up my hands in what I hoped was a harmless fashion. I even remembered not to curl my fingers into talons.

The tasseinist turned to me with a double row of teeth drawn back in something like a smile. "Fine. Let us bargain."

"Not again," I said to myself, but he ignored it.

"You give me your true name, and I'll give you the ring."

"My true name? That's all you want?" I laughed. "But sir, surely it can't be worth that much to you."

"You look familiar to me." I could feel his eyes traveling over my face with the skittering invasiveness of insect feet. "And certainty is sometimes worth more than silver."

"Then we have a deal. That ring for my true name."

We shook. But when I tried to pull my hand back, he held it firmly between his own. His prehensile tail waved, the barbed point coming to rest over my heart, in a place where the leather corset couldn't protect me.

"Look into my eyes. I'll know if you're lying. And if you lie, I strike."

"I assure you I have no intention of lying." I shifted, his tail following me like a cobra. "But what would happen if you did strike me?"

"The poison is insidious. You would be numb but alive, watching and feeling and thinking but trapped within a useless body, mine, to do with whatever I chose. You might end up hacked into pieces, or floating in a jar, or nailed on the wall. Whatever I, and my customers, could imagine. But since you didn't ask about that bit before we struck our bargain, it's too late to back out."

"You are very cunning, Mr. Sweeting."

"I am among the darkest of daimons, miss, and I do what I must to feed. Now, look into my eyes, and tell me your true name."

Keen took a ragged breath, and I gave her a brief smile of reassurance. Then I looked into Mr. Sweeting's acid-yellow eyes and said, "My name is Anne Carol."

His tail quivered, the sharp barb wavering over my stuttering heart. I was almost sure it would work. His eyes narrowed, and his hands dropped mine and crushed my shoulders.

"You're not lying," he said, his voice deadly. "You're hiding something from me, but by the gods of hell, you're not lying."

He shook with rage, and I could hear his teeth grinding. His fingers pressed into my flesh, and I fought the urge to hiss and tear him to ribbons, monster to monster.

"Whoever you are, rest assured I won't forget this. You'd better pray that I never find you alone after dark. As for you, Lorelei, if I see you again, I'll hammer your ear to my door and let your head drip on the welcome mat."

"Thanks, but I've actually reserved her head for a pike." I snatched the ring off his palm and slipped it over my glove's thumb, for I knew from years of forbidden and secret practice that it was much too big for its rightful place on my fourth finger. "Come along, Keen." And with that, I walked out the door.

His roar rattled the wood at my back, and I finally took a breath. I paused in front of the window, and no matter how hard Keen tugged at my hand, I wouldn't budge. Not until I was ready.

"*Do svidaniya*," I said to the perpetually smiling head surrounded by her court of horror. "I promise I will avenge you, my sister. And thank you, Olgha, for the ring."

I had once asked to wear it, when I was very young. "You're a bastard and a cuckoo, and you'll wear it over my dead body!" she had shouted before shoving me into the pond. I had wanted revenge. I guess I finally had it.

It didn't feel as good as I thought it would.

8

By the time we slipped in through the back window, it was nearly dark. Reve was in an uproar, screeching so loud in a foreign language that Tommy Pain had scuttled under an ottoman. And then she saw us.

"Idiot children! Fools! Of all the ridiculous, dangerous, foolhardy adventures, did it have to be to Sweeting? I can smell him on you! You reek of death and broken promises and lies as sweet as poisoned caramel. And you have something. Of his."

"It was a fair bargain." I hid my hands behind my back. "And it's mine by rights."

"You I would believe it of," she spat at me. "But Keen, *chérie*. You know better. You know so much better."

Keen's only answer was a sulky glare.

"Why would you do it, child?"

"I didn't know where she wanted to go. She just said Ruby Lane. Seemed harmless enough."

"Everything poor Casper has done for you both, and you repay him with this, a trip into hell and an angry dark daimon who will track you back to my doorstep." She shook her head, her skin rippling through furious shades of burgundy and black.

At the mention of Casper, I watched her more carefully. What exactly had he done for us? He had a bargain with me, one that should provide a payout better than his wildest dreams. But what had he done for Keen? She was the filthiest, scrawniest, most pathetic creature I'd ever seen. What could she possibly have to repay anyone? For the first time in my life, I was curious about other people and their own machinations outside of what I could take from them.

"My ears were burning." Casper stepped from the antechamber with a grin. He had a satchel over one shoulder and pulled a wheeled trunk behind him.

"Your little bêtes noires have been out to play," Reve said sharply. She disappeared behind a screen to rustle around, leaving us to face Casper alone.

"Casper, we——" Keen started. But I held my tongue. I didn't have to explain myself to him, no matter what some feisty daimon might think.

"I don't want to hear it." He held up a gloved hand, and she sighed. "You don't belong to me. We have an arrangement, and what you do on your own time is your own business, just as what I do on my own time is my own business. You're alive and seemingly unharmed, and that's all I care about."

His face was like steel, as if the man inside was miles within and untouchable. Keen's breath hitched, and she stormed upstairs. His words had wounded her somehow. But he hadn't wounded me. I was untouchable, too.

"Now that that's behind us, what's the next step?" I asked.

"I've secured transport out of the city. We'll take a bus tank to Dover, then scout around. We'll find a steamboat or airship or coach, whatever will get us to the Continent and Muscovy."

"That's your plan?" I snorted most unroyally. "I could have planned a better strategy when I was seven. And a bank? A princess, a royal Bludwoman, on a filthy, smoke-belching monstrosity of public conveyance, surrounded by commoners who can't afford a coach? Are you mad?"

"I'm not mad, princess. I'm poor, and so, might I add, are you. I've never been to Dover before, and I don't know what sort of transport is available or what it costs. But I'm willing to bet my life that I can figure it out to our eventual satisfaction."

My hands made fists in the thick stuff of my skirt, and I could feel my ribs pressing against the leather corset with every breath. Being so near him made me angry and hungry and unsettled in a way I couldn't place.

"Besides," he added, grinning in the face of my fury, "it's not like you have any options."

"You tread on my patience."

He stepped dangerously close. "You're cute when you're angry. I like a girl with spirit."

I took a deep breath, hampered by the corset. I couldn't let him know how much he affected me. I had to look down. "I'm not a girl, Casper." My voice was softer than I meant it to be, softer than he'd heard it before. Whether I was reminding him that I was fully mature or that I was of a different species, I didn't know. Being near him made me muddled, as if I was always half-drained.

"So that's how it is," he said softly to himself. One hand crept up to touch my face, and I slapped it away, but gently.

"I will do whatever it takes to get back to my people, including putting up with you."

I stepped away, breathing out through my nose so I

wouldn't take in any more of his scent, so slightly wrong and yet so right. I needed to get out of the cluttered shop, where every move one of us made brought the other closer in proximity. London was definitely not a safe town for me, even if my suitcase coffin had never reached the tasseinist's clever hands.

"Good. Then get ready. Our bank leaves from the southern gate in two hours."

He opened the box he'd dragged in, a lady's traveling trunk. I expected to see gowns and boots and jewels, but instead, it was divided into two sections. One held clothes, papers, and books. The other side held a crate of blood vials, each snuggled in its own little niche.

"I traded my harpsichord for this," he said. But I couldn't take my eyes off all the blood. I was still hollow with hunger, the need for blood as annoying and constant as a hair caught in my corset. I licked my lips and reached out for a vial.

"Hey!"

He grabbed my shoulders, and I hissed and tried to pull away, but he wouldn't let go. His eyes clouded over, his teeth bared in fury, and his fingers dug into flesh that was still tender from my visit with Mr. Sweeting's claws. There was a ferocity in the lines of his body, in the growl of his musical voice, that made me see him as more than a meal, as more than just a human. His eyes reminded me of a frozen lake, of the deep darkness trapped in ice, and being so near him made my breath catch in my throat. But I had seen what happened to noble Bludwomen who used their humans for the needs of the flesh and grew too attached. Humiliation and heavy fines and, if they weren't careful and contrite, public disfigurement. I looked down. Would they accept me as queen, if I fell into such an entanglement?

"Look at me, Ahnastasia. You're not a princess now. And I'm not some lowly trash. I'm your only way out of here. The least you can do is acknowledge me when I'm telling you that I sold the last piece of my soul for a box of blood. For you."

"I didn't ask for your soul," I snapped. "I'm nearly drained. I need more——"

But his lips sealed over mine.

I gasped into his mouth and pushed against his chest with my hands, but I was still weak, and he was much stronger than I had imagined. His mouth was hot and spiced with wine, his lips soft but aggressive against mine. For a moment, the world stopped spinning, and I couldn't breathe. I realized my hands weren't resisting him anymore; they were curled into his shirt.

And then he shoved me roughly away.

"You're not the only one with needs," he said raggedly. "You might not be a girl, but don't forget that I'm a man."

I put a gloved hand to my mouth, to the place where his cheek had rasped against mine. He had stolen my first kiss, the bastard. Just another reason to make him pay. His hands hung at his sides as his eyes searched mine for something he didn't seem to find. I felt dizzy and weak, hungrier than ever.

"The only thing I need is blood." I was surprised at how tiny my voice could be.

"Keep telling yourself that. You kissed me back."

"I didn't."

Finally, his eyes released me, and the moment snapped like a snagged thread. I stepped back, my hands flying instinctively to smooth hair that was no longer there. He stepped away from me, too, his boot nudging his leather satchel. It clanked lightly, and my eyes were drawn to it.

"I can smell when you're lying." He gave me a crooked smile. "And I saw what you did to my room. Don't ever touch my things again, or I'll put you right back in that suitcase where I found you."

"The feather and the coin—" I started, but he cut me off with a finger in my face.

"Never speak of it again."

The words fell, heavy as boulders, to the ground. For all his threats and promises, they were the darkest words he'd spoken yet. And I found myself determined to discover what such an odd creature could hold so dear.

Since I had no belongings to pack and no preparations to make, I spent the next bit of time scratching Tommy Pain's belly and studying my sister's ring in the bright lights of Reve's mirror. Any Bludman could tell it wasn't paste; the dark diamond oozed power and rarity like a fine perfume. And Mr. Sweeting had been right about the topaz stones—they were colder than ice. But they weren't the seat of the ring's power and magic, other than the magic of inheriting a matriarchy that was currently in thrall to a monster.

A monster called Ravenna.

She had come to our country as a traveling mystic. With her ink-black curls and dusky skin and huge, almond-shaped eyes, she had seemed a harmless curiosity. From the villages of the Pinkies to the back doors of the Blud Barons to the gates of the Ice Palace she had gone, winning over everyone she met with charm, cleverness, and a low, sweet voice like winter wine.

The first time I saw her, I was but a pup, dancing through the gates of the Sugar Snow Festival. Children were allowed to enjoy the festivities and performers and treats on the palace grounds in the evening, but we were always herded back into the castle to lie in bed long before moonrise, ears straining to hear the first waltz of the Sugar Snow Ball. Later, after all the children were asleep, the adults danced a dance so beautiful and mysterious that no one ever spoke of it. But it was twilight when Ravenna found me there by the palace wall as I galloped around my nursemaid among the wagons of the caravan.

"Tell your fortune, ice princess," a low voice had murmured from behind the indigo silk of a star-strewn tent.

"Go ahead, little beauty," my maid had said. "See what the famous Ravenna can tell you of your future greatness."

Ravenna had been but a lapdog then and harmless. She had smiled at me, teeth bright against her honey-colored skin.

"Give me your hand," she had said, and I still remembered how my temper had flared, that this common foreigner would dare demand anything of me.

"You can't make me," I had answered, my pert little nose in the air.

And she had laughed a laugh like icicles chiming in the wind and said, "Then there is your fortune, princess."

I had stomped and shrieked and wailed and threatened, but after that, she had utterly refused to take my palm and tell me of my future.

My maid had comforted me and given me a cone of

bloody snow to suck on, saying, "The wildest things refuse to be tamed, sweet one."

Now, years later, after all I'd seen, I wondered which of us she had meant.

"Bonne chance, chérie," **Reve called** out the door after us, the black cat twining around her legs. "If you succeed, remember where to find the greatest costumer in the world, eh?"

I waved royally until Keen slapped my hand. "You're not in a parade. Tone it down."

When I let out a warning hiss, Casper stepped between us. "She's right. You've got to pretend you're nobody." And that's when I was given the bags to carry and the trunk to pull. I was so furious at being treated like a servant that my palpable rage probably scared off more potential attackers than Casper's walking cane and Keen's blade.

The walk to London's southern gate was dark and dirty. The streets were mostly empty at night, aside from some Pinkies and Bludmen too dull with drink to note the danger all around. Singing and shouting carried on the heavy air, surging out from under the doors of orange-lit bars and inns. Bludrats hissed from every shadow, and sometimes screams would ring out, followed by the sound of rending flesh.

We stuck to larger roads lit by an endless string of gas lamps. Most trouble avoided us, although Casper did have to club a scrawny old Bludman who staggered out from a dark alley, hands outstretched, muttering, "Oh, middlings. Dark and deep, dark and deep." He fell to the ground, bleeding from the temple and mumbling to himself with a toothless mouth. I had never seen anything more pathetic.

After that, Casper hummed forcefully to himself, the same tune he'd been playing when he'd found me, the one about "Hey, Jude." The song was becoming familiar to me, and I caught myself humming along once and quickly covered it up with a cough.

As we walked farther and farther downhill, an ominous form loomed over us. Of course, I had heard of the huge walls the Pinkies erected around their cities in Sangland, but it was another thing entirely to find myself dwarfed by the ugly, imposing structure of brick and barbed wire. These fortifications had been designed to keep the monsters out—the bludstags, the bludbunnies, the wolves that were always crying with hunger. And they kept the soft, edible creatures safe inside—the cows and chickens and pigs, not to mention the Pinkies themselves.

But it was hideous and unnatural, blotting out the stars like that, even if the sky was garbled with smoke and pollution from the factories and machinery. The celebrated city of London had shown me nothing but fear, repulsiveness, starvation, and horror, and I would not be sorry to leave it.

As we passed a cattle lot, the fool creatures screamed and bawled and rolled their eyes, skittering away from me and huddling in the shadows, wearing shawls of their own droppings. My prey in Freesia had always been so elegant, so pretty and poised, wild animals and carefully groomed servants. These dumb creatures had nothing to fear from me, no matter how hungry I might have been. I still had standards.

We finally entered the alley by the wall, and Casper led us along under its shadow.

"Here are the rules," he said. "For the bank and for whatever we find after that. Princess, you pretend to be a common Pinky. Deferential, meek, frightened even. Don't speak unless you have to. And don't stare too long at exposed skin, if anyone is stupid enough to have it. Do you have an alias?"

"How about Anne Carol?" I could hear the sneer in Keen's voice. I kept my face carefully blank and shrugged as if I didn't care what they called me.

Casper thought a moment. "That'll do. Anne Carol it is."

He stopped and spun Keen around, nudging her under a gas lamp and using her skinny back as a writing desk for a piece of worn brown paper. He scribbled something with a brass fountain pen and waved the page in the air to dry the ink.

"So that's done. I'll be posing as your uncle, since you look like you're eighteen and have hair a similar color to mine now. I'm chaperoning you en route to a job as a governess to a baron's house in Muscovy. I'm a musician. Keen is my servant. Everybody got that?"

"I don't like it," I said.

"Neither do I," Keen said, hard on my heels.

Casper didn't even turn around. "Tough."

We had reached the gate by then, a huge and rusty affair with a lamp-lit guard box to the side.

"Papers!" the guard shouted, his voice magnified by a speaker. I couldn't even see his face, just a tall brown hat and goggles. He might as well have been a brass clock-work, for all I could see. Which was probably the point.

Casper put a packet of brown papers into a metal box, which withdrew into the guard post with a ringing clank.

"Casper Sterling. Lorelei Keen. Anne Carol. Will you be returning to London?"

"Lorelei and I will. My niece is traveling to be a governess in Muscovy."

The box shot back out, and Casper took our papers.

"May Saint Ermenegilda have mercy on your soul, Miss Carol," the guard said.

Before I could ask what on earth he meant by that, Casper had me by the arm and propelled me and the trunk toward a large gray vehicle that shuddered, chugging in place against a dark and cloudy sky. We stepped up stairs mere inches away from the heavy treads, and Casper handed the driver our tickets.

"About time," the thick man muttered around a pipe before clomping outside to stow our trunk.

I ducked through the narrow door. The inside of the bus-tank didn't smell any better than the fuggy cloud around the begoggled driver. It was less than half full, and most of the other passengers looked to be of the low-class, seedy sort I'd only read about in newspapers. Traveling salesmen wore extra-tall top hats buttoned tightly under the chin, with enormous unfolding suitcases beside them on their seats. Young men who had likely sold their souls to the navy or something more piratical quivered fearfully in place, en route to sinking ships and sea monsters. One other woman, who looked more masculine than the driver, held a corncob pipe clenched in yellow-streaked teeth, squatting across two seats like a citadel over a river.

Casper led us to the back, pointing me toward the very last seat. He shoved our bags into the bins overhead. As Keen settled in front of me, Casper slid onto the bench, his leg pressing warm against mine.

"I brought you something to read."

He shoved a rolled-up tube of greasy newspapers into my hand. I felt something hard in the middle and sighed in relief. A corked vial of blood, wrapped with yet more newspaper and tied with twine. I untied it and held a section of newspaper in front of my face to hide the vial as I gulped, and Casper leaned over to block the view from the aisle. His face was so uncomfortably close that my eyes sought the newspaper, and that's when I noticed that it was the *London Observer,* and I was staring at a section labeled "News of Sang," including updates on "Victory in Freesia."

"Victory in Freesia? That does sound like a good read, uncle," I said.

He chuckled darkly and handed me a red handkerchief, which I stared at in confusion.

"I think you'll be disappointed, niece. Don't forget who writes the papers in London."

I expected him to leave me then, but he didn't budge from my side. As I scanned the story and finally understood the depth of my country's trouble, I put my head to his shoulder and wept.

9

When I pulled my face away from Casper's shoulder, the handkerchief between us was sticky with blud tears. Much to my surprise, his arm was around me, and even more to my surprise, I didn't care. The fall of my family may have seemed like a victory to the Pinkies of London, but for my people and my country, it was a tragedy.

Casper had told me the truth. Freesia was collapsing. My parents were recently executed, my sister and I had been missing for years, and my younger brother, Alex, was in thrall to Ravenna.

According to reports from Muscovy, the upstart gypsy witch had deposed or murdered several landed barons and hand-picked their replacements on the Blud Council, our token House of Lords. She had been declared prime minister and was absorbing several of the Tsarina's roles as she stood at Alex's side. And she was having a statue raised in honor of the lost Princess Olgha, whose ship had supposedly been sunk by her younger sister, the bastard half-Svede Ahnastasia. I was also presumed dead, but the price on my head had gone up even more.

Which I could handle. I no longer resembled the doe-eyed, long-haired ice angel in the newspaper image. What pained me the most were the rumors that my brother Alex was in love with Ravenna and on the verge of marrying her. The papers claimed that she fed him secret medicines and magic potions to combat his chronic ferocity, trying to tame the hot blood that made him little more than an animal and the only Feodor sibling incapable of taking the throne. No wonder he was the only one she had left alive—he was by far the most easily mastered.

I fought the urge to rip the paper to shreds with my teeth and then kill everyone on the bank. I had never felt so helpless, so far from home. I looked out the window, watching the endless green of the moors roll by, willing the bank to speed up. But the gears kept grinding, and the engine kept burning, and we plodded along at the speed of a fast trot. I had to lash out at something, so I kicked the seat in front of me with a growl.

Casper chuckled softly, a look of grim understanding in his eyes. "Makes you want to burn down the world, doesn't it? Knowing that what you want most is far away. That your old life is gone forever."

"My entire world." I stroked a finger down the thick, cloudy glass. "My family. My country. Gone in a heartbeat. Gone, while I slept." I wiped away another tear. "I'm completely alone."

The silence fell heavy between us. I could sense that he wanted me to look at him, that there was something he wanted to tell me. But I resisted. What I felt—it was too much. He couldn't possibly understand.

With a last, sorrowful sigh and a hand on my shoulder, he said, "You're not the only one who's ever lost a world, you know. And you're only as alone as you want to be."

He slipped back onto the bench in front of me. Keen

murmured in sleepy annoyance as he settled down beside her. I should have been exhausted myself, but I was caught between sorrow and uselessness and hunger, trapped on a slow, plodding bank with my listless, clueless prey. Had they known what I was, what I wanted to do to them, they would have hated me. It was an uncomfortable feeling, being hated by creatures who had all but worshipped me in my youth, even as I fed from them. The Pinkies of Sang were so different from the ones in Freesia.

I looked over at the nearest passenger, trying to see past his blood to the person below. It was a young man in a sailor's uniform sitting diagonally from me. His silly white hat extended down over his neck and buckled to his navy-blue jacket. His eyes glanced nervously around the bank, full of fear, and he panted as if he were losing a fight against his uniform's chin strap. Closing my eyes, I inhaled. I could smell his terror, as sure as a hawk could sense a baby bird in its nest. This boy had most likely chafed at being cooped up in London, probably bragged to his friends and his girl about joining the navy and seeing the exotic places of Sang. And now he was petrified of the outside world. He smelled of dead plants and cheap soap. Like a peasant.

But most of all, he smelled of blood. Sweet, warm, deep. I could scent it on his breath, see the tiny patch on his cheek that he'd sliced open shaving that morning. In my old life, he would have knelt before me, in his proper place, cleaned and dressed, his hair parted just so, and I would have taken my due with great care and restraint. Instead, I exhaled and pressed the grease-splotched newspaper against my nose, willing myself not to think about food. After four years of starvation and a few tiny vials, he was still more appetizer than equal.

At least Casper and Keen didn't smell so good to me. She was too filthy and covered up, and he had that strange stink. It reminded me of something I had read once about how wild animals would urinate around their dens, marking their territory as a warning. But who had marked him? And what in Sang had driven Casper to kiss me? And why was I more curious than angry about it?

Feelings warred inside me, sadness and loss and fury and hunger and the deep, pounding need for revenge. And something else, a softening warmth that seemed to radiate from the shoulder Casper had just squeezed. For a moment, I caught the soft glow of his hair over the edge of his seat, but he gave a dreamy sigh and shifted away. I turned my face to the window, trying to ignore the odd longing tugging at my heart where no longing had any right to be.

I watched the grasses roll by, the smooth darkness of the moor outside broken up only by the stars shining on an occasional copse or abandoned town or warren of bludbunnies. My eyes dipped closed. And eventually, I slept.

Movement woke me, and with it, the smell of food dangerously near. But I denied the beast inside and raised one eyelid, peeking underneath my arm, fully aware of where I was and what was at stake.

A man sat in the seat across from mine, which had previously been empty. He stank of wine. Leaning toward me, elbows on his knees, he hissed, "Oi, pretty little thing."

I quickly took stock of my environment. By the low lights of the bank, I could see Keen's head leaning on Casper's shoulder through the space between their seats, and if I focused, I could hear their slow, steady breathing. The world outside was as dark as a closet, not even a glint of light. The only sound I could hear on the entire bank was soft snoring, and the air was filled with the warm, cozy smell of pulsing blood.

"You awake, love?" The man hissed and made kissing noises through his teeth, a little louder this time. The cloth of his jacket whispered as his hand reached for my leg.

"Can I help you?" I sat up cautiously, crossing my arms and glaring at him.

He lurched back and fiddled with his watch chain as if trying to hide that he'd been on the verge of touching a strange woman's knee. He was young but wiry, cocky, and almost good-looking for a Pinky. But there was something wanting, a certain looseness of morals to be read in his narrow shoulders, too-short trousers, and cruel, yellowing grin. Had I been anyone else, this fellow would have been trouble.

As it was, *I* was the trouble.

"Just wanted to talk, love." He winked. "Everybody else is asleep, and I thought you might like some company, as they say."

"Really? I was fairly certain you were about to make free with my sleeping person, actually." I smiled, keeping my lips carefully pulled down over too-sharp teeth.

He had the absolute gall to look injured. "I would never make advances at an innocent young miss as such. Unless . . . hmm?" He waggled his eyebrows as high as his bowler would allow and held out a tarnished flask.

I glanced around, throwing out all of my senses. Everyone else was unconscious, which was probably why he'd sought me out in the first place.

"Come close, and I'll tell you a secret." I pursed my lips and batted my eyelashes.

His grin widened, and his eyes took on a predatory gleam that I unconsciously mirrored. It was a different kind of hunger that moved me to my next action, inappropriate and dangerous as it was.

I scooted into the corner and patted the space I'd just vacated, which was still warm from my sleeping body. He took a sip from his flask and sidled across the aisle to slide in beside me, leaving his salesman's valise in the other seat, where it advertised Stephanie's Superior Seamstress Salve to no one. His hand was working its way up my skirt before his weight had settled on the plush bench. I let his fingers wander, curious at the feelings it aroused.

As a young princess, I had been kept far away from most males, especially those my own age. Even at the Sugar Snow Ball, no one had dared to touch me improperly, much less tempt me into the shadows with my parents and all of the Freesian royalty watching. I had heard rumors and whispers of love play in the castle, and Olgha had told me some desperately ridiculous things about mating. Other than Casper's kiss, which I still didn't really understand, I knew very little of what passed between men and women. With the boy's forceful hand stroking up my calf, I was disgusted but curious.

With a knowing smile, I began pulling the laces under his chin to loosen his hat. So inconvenient, the way these Sanglish Pinkies kept themselves all laced up, their pulse points covered in smelly old leather.

"You're a dirty girl, you are," he said approvingly as his hand caressed my knee, only a thin stretch of stocking between his glove and my flesh.

Finally, I pulled out the last of the filthy laces and pushed back his hat. The smell of his hair underneath was nauseating—had he even heard of bathing? The stench probably did more to scare off local Bludmen than the leather shielding. But underneath the stink was the true smell. The blood, warm and inviting.

I ran a hand through his hair and nibbled his ear, and he sucked air in through his teeth. His hand jerked up to my thigh, digging into the flesh. For a few brief seconds, I let his hand angle farther upward. My legs were crossed tightly, but it was fun, defying his urgency to pry them open. I licked a line from his ear to the place where his jugular vein nearly touched the surface. My lips lingered there, prolonging the moment. He hummed, caught in my power.

And then I bit down.

Before he could make even the slightest groan, my glove was over his mouth, my other arm holding him tightly to my chest. If anyone had been awake to see it, they would have seen two young people fumbling with underclothes in the back of the bank, an occurrence that surely had some precedent in impolite society. Still, I slid down a little in my seat, in case the driver chose that exact moment to look up from his sleepy parade across the lonely moors.

The man struggled against me, but he was no match for a Bludman's strength, even a young and weakened little thing like me. I drank, deep and deeper, eyes rolled back in bliss. The liquor in his blood made me feel warm and dreamy. When I was so full that my belly swelled uncomfortably against the leather corset, I licked my lips and tugged the grubby handkerchief out of his pocket to wipe at the little tear my teeth had made in his neck.

"What a lovely conversation," I whispered into his grime-stained ear.

I stood, letting him slump to the seat. Everyone on the bank still slept. I had killed one of their fellows mere feet away, and their breathing hadn't even stuttered. I turned my back to the far-off and mostly hidden driver's box and opened the back door. It was a common occurrence for a lady to empty a chamberpot hidden under her voluminous skirts; I'd seen it happen several times myself, the scent of blood in their cheeks singing to me of their embarrassment and edibility. The banks stopped for nothing, especially not bladders, and I'd been careful to look away each time someone tossed something unmentionable out into the sea of grass. No wonder the back seats had been empty.

Using my wide skirts to block the aisle, I tossed the man's body outside and kicked his valise after him. The roaring of the motor and the grinding of the treads engulfed any sound he made when he hit the ground. I shut the door, wiped my hands off on my skirt, and sat back down in my seat.

Perhaps public transportation wasn't so horrid after all.

Oddly enough, I couldn't get back to sleep. As warm and dreamy and satisfied as I felt, there was something else plucking at my metaphorical sleeve. With so many worries, it was no surprise. As the other passengers woke up, I watched carefully to see if anyone would notice the missing salesman, but no one did. Not that he mattered to me—he was prey, and dangerous prey at that. Perhaps I'd even saved the virtue of some other, slightly more innocent traveler. As the sun rose bloodred on a gray sky the color of bruises, I tried to put the entire incident out of mind.

When a slight change in his breathing signaled Casper's return to consciousness, I pretended to be asleep.

"Anne?" he whispered around the edge of the seat.

"Hmph?"

"Did you sleep well?"

"Goodness, I suppose I did. The sound of the engines and the rumble of the treads are quite soporific, don't you think?"

"You look like the sleep did you good." He scanned my face but seemed hesitant to move closer. "I was worried that the night would be . . . difficult for you. Considering."

I gave him a winning smile and flicked my fingers. "Difficult? Gracious, no. I've had to practice self-control my entire life. This is nothing." I hoped he wouldn't notice the little droplets of blood on my sleeve.

"If you say so." He narrowed his eyes at me, and I shrugged innocently. "Still, take this. We can't have any accidents."

He handed me another vial swaddled in greasy newspaper. I wasn't hungry, but I managed to gulp it down anyway. With every drop of blood, my strength increased, and I was going to need all the power I could muster to face Ravenna.

Shortly after that, the bank rumbled to a halt, and we disembarked. I was the last one off. The driver hunched over the steering wheel, holding a clipboard and glaring at me. He was more heavily dressed than anyone I'd seen yet, as if wild Bludmen roamed the moors, waiting to attack. I imagined that he would have smelled like a shoe if he ever took off all that leather.

"You the last one off, miss?"

"Yes, sir," I said sweetly. "What a charming journey."

He blinked at me through his goggles, his mud-brown eyes utterly surprised.

"Oh, well, yes, thank you, miss," he mumbled. "You have a nice time in Dover." He trudged back onto the bank, muttering, "Bloody traveling salesmen. Lad's probably drunk under the seats."

"Let's get out of here." I tugged Casper's arm to follow the crowd toward the tall city gates of Dover. Keen gave me her sneaky, slit-eyed look, and I smiled, showing her my teeth.

The guard checked our papers at the wall, and we followed our fellow passengers into the port city as dawn lit the tired white buildings within. I stayed close to Casper, grateful for his hand on my elbow in the sea of strangers milling anxiously toward the docks. I grew accustomed to being jostled and having my feet trod upon, all while holding my nose, both for the stench and the blood. And then I felt a tug at my sleeve.

"You dropped this on the bank," Keen whispered, shoving something into my hand.

It was the salesman's grubby handkerchief, still wet with blood.

10

"This isn't mine, Keen."

"Never said it was . . . Anne."

I let the hankie fall, pausing to grind it into the filthy cobbles with my heel. Casper's fingers tugged against my elbow, urging me to keep up with the crowd. Sighing heavily, he pulled me closer, tucking my arm tightly to his chest. I was too surprised to fight him.

"Look, it's simple. Don't look at anyone. Don't speak to anyone. Don't stand out. Your job is to remain unnoticed. That's what shy Pinky girls do."

"I'm just going to pretend that you're my porter, and I've told you to arrange everything on my behalf." I patted his arm. "Porter, make it so!"

"I'm going to pretend that you're a child I'm babysitting and ignore most of what you say," Casper said as he led me along, but I could hear him fighting a chuckle.

"Oh, and if I disobey, what are you going to do?" I grinned. "Smack my hand or chain me up in the dungeon?"

"Is that an invitation?" The words were playful, but the tone was dark, and he squeezed my hand with more strength than I expected.

"You'd have to catch me first." It came out low and

breathy as I squeezed back, feeling the bones in his fingers rub together. He didn't flinch, but I had made my point. How many times did I have to remind him that I was a woman grown, not the child I so resembled?

Keen sighed dramatically behind us. I glanced back to find the little monster waving a now even grubbier bloody hankie at me. So she'd mastered the art of blackmail; I could only hope that her price wouldn't be too high. And apparently, she'd mastered the art of pickpocketing, too, as she was eating a shiny yellow apple of such beauty and quality that I knew she could never have afforded it, not even if she had possessed anything worth selling.

"Put that away," Casper hissed over his shoulder. "The Coppers will beat you bloody, girl."

"Like it matters." By the time Casper had turned around, the hankie had disappeared, and now the apple did, too. Instead, she took out the brass sphere I'd seen her juggling earlier. To me, it didn't look much different from the apple. She saw me watching her and waggled her eyebrows. She must have stolen that, too.

Even amid the crowd, Casper exuded a confidence and quiet strength that I had never seen before in a human. And I still wasn't sure if he even *was* a human. Maybe he was part daimon and kept his strangeness under wraps. A hidden tail, perhaps? I leaned back to check his posterior, but all was exactly where it was supposed to be. Or maybe he was something entirely new, something that hadn't been included in my nursemaid's lectures on the people of Sang.

I'd learned only the barest history of countries that weren't under the rule of Freesia or allied against us. Although I knew the ice folk of Sveden well, the other nations and races of the world were mostly bedtime stories for a princess whose sphere would be only the Snow Court or the castles of nearby kings. Sang was such a large place, and everything was so far apart, and travel was so dangerous and sea monsters so prevalent, that most people who crossed great distances either died or just stayed where they landed.

I'd heard of the daimons of Franchia, strange creatures like Reve and Mr. Sweeting who fed on the emotions of humans. I had heard fairy tales of lizard people, bird people, fish people, witches, ghosts, and even people whose blood made Bludmen crazy. And I knew of the beastfolk of Almanica who lived as barbarians and rode in chariots pulled by buffalo and bludstags.

Perhaps that was what Casper was—perhaps he could change into a wolf or a wild cat, if the feeling took him. It would certainly explain his odd accent, strangely animal smell, uncanny strength, and dislike of restrictive clothing. I'd have to provoke him and find out, one day, what he was capable of. I could have simply asked, but I was far too well bred for that sort of thing.

"Here we are," he whispered, startling me. I'd been unconsciously lingering on the way his silky copper-colored hair curled over his exposed ear, wondering how his skin would taste in comparison with the traveling salesman. With his hand still on my elbow, he led us to a low wall where people had stopped, piling up their trunks and valises as if waiting for something to happen.

I looked ahead, over the top hats and bonnets of the folks in the street. I had expected to see the masts of ships and the periscopes of submarines. Instead, I saw ropes dangling from the sky.

I gulped.

"Dear Aztarte. Surely you don't mean we're flying?"

He just chuckled darkly, as if he already knew I was terrified of heights.

My eyes traced the thick ropes up, up, and still farther up, to where a variety of airships hung suspended among the low clouds. I moaned and collapsed onto the wheeled trunk.

"Finally found a chink in your armor, eh?" Keen laughed. "Guess you Bluddies aren't so perfect, now, are you?"

"Being a Bludman's got nothing to do with fear of heights," I said, my voice barely a squeak. "It's just a deep personal flaw."

I could barely breathe, and my hands struggled to undo the brass clasps on my corset until gloved hands pulled them away gently and dropped them into my lap. Casper sat down beside me on the trunk, the wood creaking under his added weight.

"Look, it's not so bad. We'll find a larger one, something with a windowless cabin. Once you're on board, you won't even feel like you're up high."

"I still don't like it." I slumped over, boneless. "Not a bit. Can't we take a ship instead?"

"I thought about that." Casper scratched his chin under the leather strap of his hat. "But ships are dangerous for you. They're watched more carefully. There are navies and pirates and the possibility of being thrown overboard, which you couldn't survive. And the airships have a little more leeway for us to work for passage. I can probably find a place as a musician on a large one, and then you can hide in the cabin as my invalid niece." He looked down into my eyes, over the lenses of my dark glasses. "Besides, I'm terrified of the sea monsters. Aren't you?"

"The sea's the scary part." I shivered and scrunched my nose. "All that salt."

"See? And there's another reason to take to the air. Now, I did a bit of research, and here's what I know. The ones that are lowest to the ground—the gaudy ones? Those are simple hot-air balloons. They can only carry a few people, and they aren't very good for the crossing, due to wind issues. More for pleasure rides and lovers looking for a tryst."

And I could see exactly what he meant. A mauve balloon all hung over with ribbons and sashes and bloodred hearts played backdrop for a man in a top hat kissing a woman, her arm draped over the balloon's woven basket, a brass spyglass dangling forgotten from her hand.

"And there, the next biggest ones. Zeppelins." He pointed to a ship with a flat deck suspended from an oblong bladder that glowed like amber. "Those are mostly used for the crossing over to Callous. They're dangerous, since they're made of skin, but they're very fast. They use those mostly for shipping things they don't care much about, including the poorer people."

"I don't want to go on one of those." Blood rose in my throat. I didn't trust something as flimsy as skin to keep me in the air. And it didn't have a rail that I could see, either.

"We won't. We're going to find a nice metal-cladder, one of the bigger ones. Very expensive to own, so they take over lots of people at a time. Like banks, but for the air, and with actual rooms. Very slow but steady—and safer. Keen's off negotiating."

I hadn't even noticed that the unctuous ragamuffin was gone. But I thought again of that shiny golden apple and her run-in with Mr. Sweeting and had to assume that she was more competent than she appeared.

"What's her story?" I asked him. He gazed off into the distance with a sort of fond, confused sadness that reminded me of a falconer with no hawk on his arm. He sighed and shook his head.

"It's hers to tell."

"What about your story?" I said before I could stop myself. The brightness of his smile winked out, leaving again the dark mask.

"That's mine. And I don't give it away as easily as I used to."

Keen appeared, seemingly out of nowhere. They conversed in hurried whispers. She was excited about something, but he shook his head in annoyance. I fiddled with my dark glasses in an attempt to cover up my embarrassment. Not only had I asked a personal question and been denied, something I was entirely unaccustomed to, but now he knew that he had something I wanted. I hated being in someone else's power, and even more, I despised making tactical mistakes.

But what bothered me the most was that I genuinely wanted to know. I, who had never cared about anything but myself, now wanted to know more about this strange man who was neither a Bludman nor royalty. It was a troubling impulse, and I straightened my back with renewed purpose. Use him for my goals and then keep my promise regarding his head on a platter—that was the plan. And if he was lucky, let him play the royal harpsichord, just once, in the most beautiful palace in the world. Just enough to make good on our agreement. Just enough to hear the beauty he could coax from its ancient, magical keys.

He turned to me with a scowl, hands on slim hips. "Most of the ships are full. Keen's found us a metal-cladder, but I have to make the final arrangements. You two wait here. I'll only be a moment." He pinned Keen with a sharp glare. "If anything happens to her, it's over."

Keen wrinkled her nose and nodded sullenly as she

sat beside me on the trunk with an unladylike slump. I watched Casper disappear into the milling crowd of tourists and sailors and hawk-eyed vendors. With a sudden thump, Keen collapsed, curled up on the trunk like a puppy, and began to snore softly. Confused by the behavior but glad to be free of her company, I closed my eyes and let the scents of hundreds of Pinkies invade me, noting the foreign spices and overlying stink of the ignorant herd and, somewhere nearby, just a whiff of magic.

"Strange, isn't it?"

The voice was cultured, cool, and amused, and I looked up into the face of the first real Bludman I'd seen in Sangland. My heart leaped to see sharp features and a cloudy gaze, to know that I wasn't alone in playacting among the prey. And my heart stayed right where it was, heavy in my throat, when I saw what an attractive Bludman he was. Spare but powerful, with shadowy gray eyes dancing with excitement and smooth black hair pulled back under his hat. He could have been a prince, with a face like that. Oddly, a Pinky clung tightly to his arm, and her smell hung over him like a second skin.

"I imagine you're unaccustomed to the stink of rabble, my lady. And to think that they aren't even aware of two foxes in the henhouse. Or two snow foxes among the bludlemmings, perhaps." His mouth quirked up, and he winked.

I went on alert immediately and barely stopped myself from hissing as I stood to face him. Was I that easy to recognize? Was he an assassin? Would I have to kill him right here?

"You have me at a disadvantage," I said, my accent making my words all the colder.

"Honestly, Crim. You're going to give the poor girl a conniption." The Pinky smiled at me in an oddly kind fashion and stroked one gloved hand down his arm in the same manner I would use to calm an overexcited bludmare.

"Forgive me, then, princess. My name is Criminy Stain, and I'm at your service." He swept a practiced bow and rose with a bouquet of snow-white flowers in hand. "Your secret is safe with me."

I glanced around. The crowd was oblivious, as if they couldn't even see us. My eyes narrowed at him, but his smile was bright, and I couldn't sense a bit of aggression. Still, I didn't take the flowers.

"How did you guess?"

"I'm the proprietor of a traveling caravan, and my wife is a fortune-teller. Our train is stopped just outside of Dover, and a glance last night informed her that we would find you here. I couldn't miss a chance to meet you, my dear. I wish you only the best."

"What do you want? Money?"

He threw back his head and laughed. "What is money to me? No, pet. I wanted only to see you myself and give you a gift."

I raised one eyebrow. "Flowers?"

He shook his head and clapped his hands together. The bouquet of white blooms exploded in a shower of glittering snow. With a sudden jolt of homesickness, I reached out to catch the falling flakes, but they were neither cold nor wet and simply disappeared.

Criminy's hand swiftly clasped mine, and he wrapped my gloved fingers around something hard before I could pull away.

"You're going to need this, Ahnastasia," he whispered, leaning close. "More than you know. One day, it will be the only thing between you and a world of pain."

I looked down and opened my hand. It was a paper packet folded tightly and sealed with a wax stamp bearing a compass and an *S*. My instinct was to throw it onto the ground, but something stopped me.

"What is it? Why do I need it?"

Criminy looked at the Pinky on his arm, fierce warmth and love radiating from his eyes.

"I can't tell you, honey," the woman said. She looked as if she wanted to reach out and pat my arm but knew that I would rip it off if she tried. "Open it when you're at the final straw. That's all I can say."

Turning the packet over in my hands, I shivered. I hadn't dealt with magic since Ravenna and then Mr. Sweeting, and I didn't like the thought of more mystery, much less mysterious gifts from someone who knew who I was. How was I supposed to trust this strange pair?

"He's coming," the Bludman spat, and his Pinky nodded and said, "Tell Casper that Tish said hi."

"Good luck, my princess." Criminy bowed again and gave me a knowing, charming smile. "My lady wife is always right, and I assure you that all will turn out for the best, much as I hate to say it, for that undeserving bugger." He jerked his head toward the airships, and within seconds, he and his Pinky had disappeared into the crowd.

"Anne!"

My head spun in the opposite direction as Casper hurried toward me, worry written all over his face.

"I couldn't find you. Who were you talking to? Are you okay?"

"I don't know this 'okay,' but I am safe." I sat back down on the trunk, before my legs could collapse. "Tell me, what do you know of Criminy Stain?"

Casper stilled, eyes going hard as he took a deep breath through his nostrils. "Criminy Stain. Criminy Stain was here?" He searched the crowd, avid as a wolf. "Was he alone? What did he say?"

"He was here. He knew me. He had a pet Pinky with him, a fortune-teller, but she smelled strange. She said to tell you Tish said hi. And Criminy gave me this."

I held out the packet, but Casper didn't touch it. "If Tish saw something of the future and Criminy gave you that, it's important." He looked both furious and lost, and I slipped the folded paper into the top of my corset, next to the necklace from my valise.

"But who are they? Who is Tish?"

He shook his head as if trying to dislodge something painful. "Maybe I'll tell you someday. For now, we have to hurry. It's almost time to take off."

"Then you've secured passage?"

"I have."

"You don't look happy about it," I murmured. And he didn't. He looked irritated, and worried, and ever so slightly amused.

"The passenger ships are full and only take coin, so this is a trade situation. They need a musician, seeing as how the old one's too drunk to play. But we have to share a room, and you'll need to stay in it the entire time. Do you understand?"

"Indubitably. I don't want to be outside among Pinkies and ruffians." I salivated a little, thinking about all that blood, but caught myself before I licked my lips. "And it's only for the crossing. A day at most."

"Actually, our ride will take several days, all the way to Muscovy, with brief stops at Paris, Barlin, Warsaw, and

Minks. Stops for which you and Keen will remain locked in our room at all times."

"I am not accustomed to following orders." I stood and crossed my arms. Unfortunately, the top of my head barely came up to his broad chest, and with his top hat, he towered over me.

"If you expect me to get you to Muscovy in one pretty little piece, you're going to learn," he snapped. He shrugged his shoulders with a menacing creak of leather, and without thinking, I took a step back.

"Fine. Let's say I agree to this airship. Why are you so worried about it?"

He threw a look of stern annoyance at Keen, who was rising from her nap on the trunk with a look of groggy confusion.

"What happened?" she asked, her voice slurry with sleep.

"I'm filling Anne in on the fine accommodations you've secured."

Keen chuckled, stuck her hands in her pants pockets, and beamed that one, extraordinary smile. She looked far too proud of herself for any good to come of the situation.

Casper sighed and pointed into the clouds. I followed his finger to an enormous metal-clad behemoth of an airship—one of the biggest. The body was brass, shining dully with the lemon-yellow rays of the morning sun. Beneath it hung a large sort of box, which was painted with the gargantuan image of a mostly naked woman draped over a swoopy couch. Large, curlicued letters spelled "A.S. Maybuck."

"Is that woman . . . ?" I couldn't finish the sentence.

"Yes, she is. As are many of the passengers. The *Maybuck* is Sang's largest—and only—floating brothel. And we're expected on the deck in half an hour for launch."

11

They didn't have to carry me kicking and screaming—not until we were right under the *Maybuck*. I balked then, and Casper had to drag me firmly by the arm while Keen stayed close enough behind me that I couldn't run back down the long, narrow ramp that led to the docking platform. When it was our turn to embark, I stepped onto the lift and collapsed to the muddy planks with my eyes squeezed shut.

"Sit on me," I whispered.

Casper snorted. "Won't you have me beheaded for that?"

"Not this time." It came out as a whimper.

Keen had no such trepidations and planted her skinny rump right in the middle of my back. I exhaled gratefully, hugging the boards and moaning. Casper got down on his haunches and peered into my face.

"Care to explain your sudden collapse, niece?" He was trying not to laugh—but not trying too hard, I noticed.

"I don't want to fly away and fall down," I explained. "If the wind caught in my skirts, a fierce gale could send me over the edge to my death."

"There's a railing."

"I'm very small. I weigh practically nothing."

"Me, neither!" Keen shouted, bouncing up and down and leaving what I was sure were permanent corset-shaped indentations in my back.

"I won't be so helpless one day," I growled.

"Me, neither!" She stopped bouncing and all but ground me into the boards.

With a sudden lurch and a metallic squeal, our platform began to rise. I closed my eyes again.

"Hold my hand."

My voice came out tiny and plaintive, and Casper leaned closer. "Was that an order?"

"Hold my hand, please?"

He chuckled and sat on the boards near my head, curling both of his hands around one of mine. Even through the gloves, he was warm, and it was his calming touch more than Keen's insignificant weight that kept me in place.

In all my planning of revenge and ultimate victory, it somehow hadn't been clear to me that getting from Sangland to Muscovy was going to involve either sea or air. It would have been easier if I had still been unconscious and securely buckled inside a valise. At least I wouldn't have been this terrified and had my weaknesses broadcast to the world. I turned my head to the side and dashed away a red-tinged tear before anyone could see it. At least Reve had provided gloves of a deep, rusty brown, handy for concealing both today's tears and the stains from last night's snack.

Ascending to the airship proper took eons. Ages. Epochs. Dragons roamed Sangland again by the time the platform finally shuddered to a halt and I heard the sound of metal clipping into place as it was fastened to the airship deck.

Keen leaped up, and Casper helped me stand. The platform swayed slightly, and I clung to him, legs wobbling.

"My niece gets vertigo," he said to someone I couldn't see, since my eyes were still squeezed shut.

"Around here, we call that a case of the shits."

The new voice was loud and filled with lusty good humor. I looked up and nearly heaved all over her platform boots, narrowly avoiding unmasking myself in a splatter of blood and getting us all thrown overboard. It wasn't that she was ugly—far from it. The woman was past her bloom but holding steady in her prime, lush and flush and clearly the queen of the ship. She was a Pinky, but dressed with a Bludwoman's love of flesh—and she was smoking a pipe. She was just fine—more than fine, if I had been in any way hungry.

The problem was that we were surrounded by clouds.

"Welcome to the *Maybuck,* Maestro." She held out a lace-gloved hand to Casper. "Still can't believe it's you, although I've read about your exploits in the papers. You'll be fitting in right well, I think. And welcome to you, too, Miss . . . ?"

"My niece, Miss Anne Carol," Casper said. "My brother's daughter. From London."

"Miss Carol." She nodded in my direction. I smiled as best I could, mouth closed over teeth stained with blood from my near-retching. "Don't worry, my girl; you'll get your air legs about you soon enough. Looks like your little maid is already enjoying herself. She got a trade yet, that one?"

She narrowed her eyes at Keen's blindingly pretty smile. The girl had climbed partway up a rope and was dangling from the metal balloon, her hair whipping in the wind and her cheeks pink with excitement. The woman looked Keen's body up and down as if measuring future growth and meditatively chewed her pipe.

"I'm training her in harpsichord," Casper snapped.

"Pity." The woman shrugged sinuously, her flesh rippling. "She's going to bloom like a rose one day, and there's copper to be made among the clouds. I'm Madam Laurabelle May, by the way. But everyone calls me Miss May." She nudged Casper in the side and winked, adding, "Although certain lads with enough copper can call me Mother-May-I, then, can't they?"

"Pleasure to meet you, Miss May." He flashed a wolfish grin I hadn't seen before.

"Pleasure's all mine, I'm quite sure," she purred back.

"Stateroom?" I managed to groan, my head down and my mouth hidden behind my hand.

"Did she ask for a stateroom?" Miss May cackled. "Oh, yes, your highness. I'll have the palanquin fetch you to your gilded throne!" Once she'd gotten all the laughter out, she pointed at me with her pipe and said, "Small, windowless, as requested, and all three of you will share it. But I'll have someone take you there before you yark on my deck and put the boys off their feed."

I heard giggling and the slap of a bare hand on skin. I was grateful for the nausea, because I began to suspect that there was an overabundance of naked flesh on the *Maybuck*. Better to be ill than bloodhungry.

"Colette! Victoire! Please show the Maestro and his niece to the Velvet Room."

Two girls even younger than Keen ran up and curtsied. When I saw that they wore nothing but diaphanous white gowns, I covered my nose and mouth with my glove and tried to think about a much-decomposed and thoroughly unappetizing bear corpse I'd once come across on a hunt. Casper's hands on my shoulders steered me across the ship, and with my eyes still closed, I could almost imagine that we were on land. Almost.

"It's a very nice room," said one of the girls in a distinctly Sanglish accent. The Franchian names must have been part of the game, like the see-through gowns. I heard a door open, and Casper ushered me inside, thanked the girls, and slammed it behind us. I collapsed across the bed on my belly, burying my face in a pillow and tossing aside the smoky glasses.

"Ahnastasia, how are you holding up?"

He sat down beside me, not close enough to touch, but I felt the soft mattress indent beneath his weight. Another first: I was alone in a small room, arranged on a bed with a strange man of questionable background and species.

"I'm on a floating brothel surrounded by naked degenerates," I muttered into the soft pink velvet coverlet. It was so luxuriously deep that it reminded me of the lion's tongue I had once seen at the royal zoo. "I'm not well."

"Are you going to be sick?"

Out of the corner of my eye, I saw one of his gloved hands move toward my back and hover there, as if his impulse was to touch me but something held him back. The princess and the beast weren't the only instincts within me anymore, but I didn't know how to describe the new urge, the one that had awakened with his kiss, the one wanted to be touched. Instead, I slunk from under his hand and sat against the headboard, pulling a tasseled pillow to my chest.

"I think I can manage it now." I breathed in stale air

thick with Casper's scent and fanned myself with a hand. "Although there doesn't seem to be enough air in here."

"You wanted a cabin with no windows, and that's what you got."

We both looked around the small room. The walls were papered in red velvet damask, and the floor had fuzzy rugs that looked like entire scalped sheep. Tommy Pain would have loved lounging among them like an overfed sultan, and I realized that I missed the strange cat, who had been left behind with Reve. The bed took up most of the space and was quite large, but there was a small writing desk with a stool on one side and room for our trunk. Two smaller doors must have led to the bathroom and closet. I secretly smirked about Keen—wherever she slept, it was going to be uncomfortable. It was a hell she richly deserved for tricking me into traveling aboard a brothel.

It would be hell for me, too, if I didn't get enough blood. Who knew how long I would be trapped in this tiny, airless room with two people and nothing but a cask of vials? Casper's blood wasn't entirely perfect, but it was still nutritional enough to keep me sated, and killing Keen would be hard to resist, if only for the peace and quiet. I wondered exactly how many passengers were on the *Maybuck* and how well they were accounted for. If the promise of a hand under my skirt was all it took to lure some idiotic Pinky into serving himself up to me on a platter, I was definitely on the right boat—provided I could pitch his body overboard before anyone noticed.

And that reminded me of something.

"Do you think it's clean?" I asked. I sniffed the pillow in front of me but didn't pick up any odors that smelled . . . lascivious.

"You honestly haven't heard of the *Maybuck*?" Casper grinned at me with those damned dimples again.

"The care and feeding of princesses doesn't normally include discussions of prostitutes."

"Yes, but surely you've read about it? The *Maybuck* is Sang's only floating brothel. It's known for high-class courtesans who choose their own patrons and can only be bought by the wealthy and royal, many of whom are currently on board. If one of their customers ever found so much as a flea on this boat, Miss May's reputation would be shot."

I fingered the coverlet and had to admit to myself that it was fine stuff. The ermine tails on the fur-covered pillows were definitely real. And the Titian hanging over the bed had every appearance of being by the master himself. Even I had to admit that it was a terribly royal-looking brothel.

"And they let us on here for free?" I asked. It simply didn't add up.

He unlaced his hat and ran a hand through his sweaty hair. "You're the only person in Sang who hasn't heard of Casper Sterling, world-famous musician. I used to be in the papers even more than you. I was the biggest celebrity in London and toured all the major cities—Paris, Bruzzles, Stockhelm. That's why everyone calls me Maestro."

"What happened?" I had to know.

His expression darkened. He made dark look delicious. "I told you: my business is my business." He looked away, and I stared at his back. Sweat had streaked his hair the color of old copper, and the tiny cabin was filled with the scent of male. I inhaled despite myself. But his anger wasn't about to stop me. I was curious.

"We're stuck here in very close quarters, Maestro. We're going to have to trust each other, at least a little bit."

That didn't mean I was going to go spilling my heart out to him, but I wanted to know his mysterious past, and I was sick of having to ask. And sick of being denied.

"Don't call me that. Please."

"Casper, then," I said softly.

He pulled off his gloves and stuffed them into his top hat. His fingers flexed and popped, and he stared at them with the oddest mixture of love and hate. Then he pulled a copper coin out of his waistcoat and began flipping it over his knuckles, back and forth. It was hypnotic, and in the still, airless silence, I held my breath, waiting for what came next.

"Let's just say I had my heart broken one too many times and went looking for the pieces in the wrong bottle," he finally said, his voice raw. "And then, one day, I woke up in a third-rate Blud bar with a two-year hangover, playing tunes no one else had ever heard, unsure if they'd ever existed or I was losing my mind. No one recognized me anymore. And I didn't really recognize myself."

The coin rippled across his fingers, and I wondered what he would have played had there been a harpsichord at hand. Something loud and crashing and furious or something slow and painful, each note a blade's kiss, bleeding out the past?

"And then?" I said softly.

"And then a skinny little blond ice monster jumped out of a suitcase and tried to murder me."

He was smiling again, although something still roved, restless and dangerous, behind his eyes. The coin disappeared back to wherever he kept it. I knew it had to be the one from the box under his bed, and I wondered where its companion feather was hiding.

"A skinny little blond ice monster?" I said in mock indignation. "I'll have you know that my presentation ball was the most beautiful in Freesian history."

"I saw the sketches in the paper." He looked me up and down, and I sat up straighter, wishing for the frame of my hair and the hypnotic power of a beautiful dress. Brown would never be my color. "You were like a porcelain doll, before they drained you and left you for dead. But you must admit that it was quite the wake-up call. For both of us."

"I must have been very frightening." I looked down and fiddled with the tassels on the pillow.

"You were nothing but the beast," he said gently. "It wasn't your fault. I can't believe you were that close to drained and still able to come back at all."

"It was the music," I admitted. "That and the blood."

"You're a Beatles fan, huh?"

"What?"

"Inside joke. Between me and Keen."

"I like jokes," I said, trying not to sound as if it mattered.

"Sorry, princess," he said. "But your Mario is in another castle."

Before I could ask what that meant, Keen burst through the door. Casper and I jumped apart, although we hadn't been anywhere close to touching. The girl smirked and tossed a blood orange in the air.

"Dinner's in an hour, and we're expected to dine at the main table. I told Miss May that Anne's probably too pukey to show."

For reasons I couldn't yet contemplate, the thought of Casper walking into that room of half-clad women and a smiling Miss May made my ferocity override my fear.

"Dinner? Oh, I wouldn't dare miss it." I smiled sweetly at their matching expressions of surprise mixed with dread. "But at least I'll have a good reason not to eat, now that you've spread the word about what a horrible traveler I am."

"Do you really think it's safe for you to go?" Casper asked cautiously, as if I was going to attack him for questioning me. Which, I supposed, was a reasonable fear, considering my previous behavior.

"I don't know what sorts of tales the people of Sangland tell about Bludmen," I said, unbuttoning my hat and fluffing my short hair, "but so long as we're well fed, we have great control. Nearly all of our lower-ranked palace servants are Pinkies. My first memory is of having my hand smacked for trying to bite a maid's leg. My manners and self-control are impeccable."

"Except when you're attacking the Maestro or killing innocent people," Keen added, and my heart stuttered in horror.

"She couldn't help attacking me. And she hasn't killed anyone in at least four years." Casper shot her a disapproving look. "You know what they say about when you assume."

"I'm not the one who's an ass," Keen muttered, but she gave me a sly wink before she slunk back out the door.

"Get back in here, Keen. It's not safe for a girl like you—"

With admirable quickness, she shut the door before he could finish.

"I am cursed with unruly women," Casper said to himself.

But I was still staring at the door Keen had just slammed. That proved it—she'd seen me with the boy on the bank. But why hadn't she said anything? Did Casper have a clue? And, more important, what did she want from me as payment for her continued silence?

"Do you think you'll be able to get through dinner? Do you need another vial?"

Casper slid off the bed and rummaged in the trunk for a tube of blood.

"How many do we have?" I wasn't hungry, of course, but I needed to pretend that I hadn't utterly bloated myself last night while he was sleeping.

"Enough to get you home, I think."

I thought about counting the vials and doing the calculations in my head, but it just made me dizzier. For now, I'd be content to leave the mechanics of the journey to fate. If the worst came to pass, surely there was some nasty little cabin boy that could be spared. But I took the vial from Casper and drank it lustily to bolster my charade.

"Much better." I held out the empty vial with a tame smile. "Dinner should be a snap."

At the time, I utterly failed to understand his facial expression, an unflattering mix of amusement, horror, and impending disaster.

After dinner, I understood.

12

I would have dressed for the occasion, but I had only one dress. In a minor huff, I settled for pinning up what little hair I had left and doing my makeup in the Pinky style. To be honest, I was enjoying that part of the masquerade. I'd never pretended to be anything other than the willful brat that I was, and it was refreshing to be free from royal expectation. In a fit of rebellion, I unbuttoned my blouse and rolled up my sleeves, grateful for some air on my skin.

Casper stayed in the room while I went through my ministrations, reading a book he had pulled from the trunk. I was curious—was he staying because he didn't trust me, or was he just as worried about going to dinner as I was? I'd never been among whores and degenerates before. Still, it was oddly comforting to have him nearby, his steady breathing helping me to relax.

It was a short walk down the hallway to a closed door and a brass plaque announcing the captain's quarters. I kept my eyes shut and my hands clamped on his arm. Despite what I'd said of my control, the smell of human bodies was nearly overwhelming, not least of all Casper's. He had returned to the same open-necked costume he'd worn at the Seven Scars, and I realized I'd have to grow accustomed to seeing the blue veins pulse in his neck, wrists, and hands. I dared to peek at the arm I was holding, nothing but loose linen separating my teeth from his golden skin. Licking my lips, I took a deep breath to test my resolve, but all was well under control. I no longer wanted to rip out his throat. Thank heavens I'd snatched that boy on the bank.

Casper stopped me in front of the door and whispered into my ear. I froze.

"Listen."

His breath tickled the exposed curve of my neck, and a little thrill ran through me. I held very still, waiting to feel it again and shiver. I missed the first part of what he said and caught just the tail end.

"If you think you're going to lose control in here, just act like you're going to be sick and run out. I'll make your excuses. Niece."

"Thank you, Uncle Casper," I said sweetly and breathily in his ear.

He swallowed hard and stumbled toward the door.

I smiled. Two could play at this game.

The door swung open on a writhing mass of flesh. Feeling safe from the dangers of my kind, the whores and their customers were dressed to show as much skin as possible. One girl wore only a tight red corset and bloomers and boots, the bright scarlet plume from her tiny hat dipping all over the table as she laughed. The lady next to her had the tall white-powdered hair of the last century and was dressed in a gorgeous brocade gown fit for a queen—except for the fact that the front panel was missing, exposing her legs from ankle to thigh when she stood to reach for the wine. Another posed in an odd outfit of nothing but sleek black leather and shiny silver rings. Her hair was short and slicked back like a man's, and there was actually a small piece of metal through each of her ears. I unconsciously licked my lips.

Those three caught my eye, but the overall impression was of temptation, glamour, costume, delight, and a massive amount of wickedness. The men lounged and laughed and ogled in a state of undress that was outrageous, according to my conservative upbringing. Cravats untied, shirts unbuttoned, no hats, and one gentleman appeared to be wearing some sort of plaid skirt with a furry purse. I blushed and looked away.

Casper's hand tightened on my arm. We'd been standing in the doorway for all of three seconds, and no one had acknowledged us. I was sure my complexion was an unbecoming shade of mauve. Casper sighed and steered me to a chair in the far corner, placing himself between me and the fellow in the skirt. I looked around for Keen, but she was nowhere to be found.

"*Bonjour,* darling," trilled the girl dressed like a queen, who was sitting on the other side of my corner. She gracefully pulled her long legs out of a stodgy-looking old man's lap. "You aren't a new girl, are you?"

"This is my niece, Anne," Casper said. "A passenger. She's to be a governess in Freesia. And you're Jeanne."

"*Oui,*" she said with delight, holding out her bare, bejeweled hand for his kiss. "I see my reputation precedes me, even in the pious Sangland."

"I played for you once, in Paris." Casper released her hand with a distant smile. "We performed a Franchian lullaby together."

"Ah, yes. I remember now. We did other things, too." Jeanne dimpled behind her fan. "With my scarf and a horse whip, *non*?" And she laughed, a sound both carefree and practiced, like gilt-edged leaves dancing in the breeze.

Casper cleared his throat and grinned at me, shrugging. I gave him a withering glare. He met my eyes for a few seconds longer than was necessary, until the look became something else entirely. I cleared my throat and searched the table for a napkin. There wasn't one.

"I didn't know we were getting a new girl." An older woman leaned across the table. She was dressed smartly and in a modern fashion that I had to assume was very *de mode*, although her dress was hemmed above the knee.

"I'm just a passenger," I answered for myself. "But your hat is exquisite. Where did you get it?"

She smiled, not the fake smile of a prostitute but the genuine smile of a woman whose genius has been recognized. "Like it, do you? It's my own work, dear. I was a milliner before I took to the air."

Her voice was refined and high London, and her manner told me she'd been raised properly. How had she ended up on the *Maybuck*, I wondered? I liked her instantly, and not just because of her bonnet.

"If she is new, I'll take the first plunge," the man in the skirt said with a heavy brogue, leaning behind Casper to run a hand up my arm. "She looks juicy as a plum."

Casper leaned back, crushing the man's arm. "She's a passenger. Off limits."

The man withdrew his arm with a jerk, rubbing the velvet sleeve of his fine coat. "Look, laddie. You needn't be brash. I've a purse full of coin. There's a price for everything."

"She's my niece, my lord, en route to Freesia as a governess," Casper growled with barely contained rage. "And I've been charged with protecting her innocence. Surely a gentleman understands an oath of such magnitude?"

"Bonny, she is." The man ignored Casper to lean across the table. He was ruggedly handsome and knew it, probably a good fighter, with broad shoulders and huge hands. Another predator. I batted my eyelashes at him, feigning naive curiosity. His long lips curled into a knowing smile.

"Freesia's full of monsters, wee thing. You'll go there to watch a Blud Baron's spawn, and they'll eat you right up. Wouldn't you rather be a lord's mistress? Nice little cottage in Glasgow, weekly allowance, pretty dresses? I won't use ye too hard. Eh?"

I heard a cracking noise and looked over to find Casper's hands flexing, his teeth bared. Before I could decide how to extricate myself from my first proposal, Casper leaned over and whispered something into his ear.

"Perhaps another time, lass." The man scooted his chair back abruptly and found a different seat at the other end of the table.

"What did you say to him?" I whispered to Casper.

"None of your—"

"—goddamn business," I finished for him with a sigh.

"Exactly, yes," he said in a dignified voice as the table went quiet.

Miss May posed dramatically in the doorway. After slamming it shut, she swaggered into the room and to the head of the table. She was dressed as a lady pirate, with the most covering bits of her costume missing. She swung one booted foot up onto her chair, letting the fluttering petticoats drip from her knee and offering a view that made me cough and look away.

"Welcome, all, to the Airship *Maybuck*, the world's first and best floating pleasure ship. Everything on this boat is for sale, at a price. You know the rules, or you wouldn't have made it past the dock. Pay for what you take. Mind your manners. And no fighting. Break a rule, and you'll find yourself in the brig or thrown overboard. Until then, enjoy yourself. We're here for your pleasure."

Her grin made it very clear that it was somewhat for her pleasure, too. Everyone cheered, and the men managed somehow to untangle their limbs from the ladies long enough to raise a toast of wine to the ship's captain. She raised her glass in return, and the little girls in their white gowns filed in through the door with platters of food that I couldn't identify. It was all meat or trash to me, but there was a lot of it.

Just then, I noticed that the pretty girl carrying a smallish pig was none other than Keen. In a diaphanous white gown, with her hair and face washed, she was like an angel, all huge brown eyes and long lashes and that mischievous grin that made me want to drain her and then strangle her for being so foolish.

Casper stiffened beside me, grabbing her wrist as she set down the piglet with a chaste curtsy.

"What are you playing at?" he hissed.

She yanked her arm back. "I make my own choices. And you're not my dad." She offered him a blinding smile and scampered out the door. A hand from the crowd reached out to smack her on the rump, and I felt Casper shaking with anger beside me.

"What's a dad?" I whispered.

He put his head in his hands, speaking quickly and so low I had to lean close to hear him.

"Dad means father. She thinks I act too much like her father. But she forgets what a dangerous world this is. She's too young to be here. I shouldn't have brought her along."

"Where are her real parents? Why is it your business, what she does?"

"You have no idea what you're talking about."

"I know that if she's over fourteen, there's nothing you can do."

"There's always something I can do."

He reached into his waistcoat and pulled out a silver flask, which he slopped into his red wine in such a way as to obscure the contents. Stronger liquor, perhaps? Laudanum? A potion? But he didn't have the eyes of an opium addict—our old butler had had that look, shortly before my mother staked him for incompetence. There were so many smells in the room, so much skin scent in the air, that I didn't have a hope of puzzling out his secret ingredient.

"Oi, Maestro!" Miss May lounged back in her chair and grinned at Casper. She held up her own glass of deep burgundy wine. "To an excellent bargain."

He toasted her in return and drank deeply before pouring himself another glass.

Casper and I spent the rest of the meal in our own pool of silence, a tiny island of tension amid the great, lashing waves of flesh and gluttony. He finished his glass of wine and swirled the last drops of deep maroon around and around in his goblet.

He never ate a bite.

*   *   *

The dinner didn't come to an end so much as the food was sampled and abandoned for other needs. The wine still flowed, though, and the party only became more animated as Keen and the other girls carried platters out to make space. When an elderly gentleman with a curled mustache pulled one of the girls into his lap and yanked down the sheer fabric above her corset to expose pierced nipples, Casper bolted up from his seat.

"Leaving so soon?" Miss May murmured sweetly, her ruby lips against a flushed young man's ear.

"My niece is unaccustomed to such goings-on." Casper pulled me behind him, attempting to drag me around the table toward the door.

Without really thinking, I said, "But, Uncle, I think this could be quite educational."

Quite honestly, I was intrigued. I knew that my mother had had her pets, that her marriage to my father was mostly a political alliance. And of course, that he truly had been my father was in question, if you believed certain circles. But what sport occurred at the Ice Palace occurred behind firmly closed and locked doors. I'd never seen a live naked woman's body, other than my own. And I'd never seen what lay under a man's many layers of clothes.

The old man shifted the half-dressed, laughing girl and fussed with his buttons, and I leaned over in amazement, angling to see more. With a snarl, Casper lifted me around the waist and carried me out of the room past the giggling, moaning guests and their quickly disappearing clothing.

He slammed the door and dropped me to the deck, steering me down the hall by my arm.

"Well, that was a little awkward of you, Uncle." I tripped,

trying to keep up with him. "Things were just getting interesting."

"We may be hitching a ride on a floating whorehouse, but that doesn't mean I'm going to stand around and watch you be utterly . . ."

I watched him wince, fighting for the right word.

"Debased? Spoiled? Scandalized? Ruined?" I smirked. "Informed?"

"Let's just say that those men aren't used to being told no, and that room is going to get a lot worse." And then his face went totally white, and he ran a hand through his hair. "Keen. Dear God. I left the poor girl in there. We've got to go find her." He started to walk back down the hall, but I didn't move, and he soon turned back with worry in his eyes. "Ahna, come on. It will only be a moment."

"I'm going back to the room. I can take care of myself," I flashed my fangs and huffed. Being told what to do rankled, and I badly needed a vial of blood.

He stepped closer, one hand around my upper arm and his hair brushing my cheek. "That's the thing, though. If they find out what you are, who you are, the worst won't be getting thrown off this boat. They could ransom you, punish you, chain you up. Torture you." He shook his head. "Anything. Please just come with me now. Don't make me worry for you both."

"I'm . . . you . . ." It was hard to concentrate, being so close to him. "You don't have to worry for me. The men are all in that room and busy. There is nothing to fear out here."

"You're right . . . but you might be wrong. Just get back to the room and lock the door. I'll hurry."

He released me and stormed down the hall, already

intent on his next errand. I took the rare chance to admire his backside in the tight breeches and the way his coppery hair floated behind him, lit by the orange lamps. He really was a fine physical specimen, whatever he was. What had truly captured my attention, though, had been the look in his eyes and the purpose in his stride. He wasn't just protecting his meal ticket—he really was afraid for me, the predator who had promised to put his head on a pike. And the only reason he was willing to leave me alone was to go save the insolent young girl who had recently accused him of acting too much like her father. No matter what Casper's sharp words might have said, he honestly cared about us both. I was annoyed—but oddly touched.

I turned back to creep down the long hall, taking time to read the plaques by each door. The Leather Room. The Brocade Room. The Silk Room. The Damask Room. All fabrics, and lush ones. Did each girl have her own room, I wondered, or were they at the mercy of any wealthy passenger who beckoned? And who would normally have used our chamber, the Velvet Room?

I was so interested in my surroundings that I didn't notice the man waiting in the shadows until he was close enough to stroke my cheek.

"Are you lost, little snowbird?"

It took every ounce of self-control I had not to hiss, let my shaking hands curl into talons, and rip into him. Instead, I stepped back and put my hands in front of me in a gesture of supplication that I'd seen frightened maids use when my mother was on a rampage. I blinked, opening my eyes wide, and simpered at him.

My immediate impression was of an ermine in the summer, small and dark and deft. But his smile was after something more carnal than meat, and his sharp teeth matched my own. A Bludman—but for some reason, I couldn't smell him, and that scared me even more.

"Please, good sir. I am a maid and a passenger here, not one of . . . not a . . ." I stumbled over the word. What would a girl call a whore if she didn't know what a whore was?

"Not a lady of the night?" His snicker was teasing, but I could hear an accent under the words. I looked more closely.

He wasn't dressed like the other men on the boat, in clothes that showed status and wealth. Aside from eyes so light they were nearly white, everything about him was shadowy, down to the leather that held all of his weapons and the kohl ringing his eyes. He didn't seem to belong there at all, and that's what made unfamiliar fear trickle down my spine.

"Ah, but you are a different sort of lady, and it is the night, and we are alone. And I think you won't want to scream now."

One black-gloved finger moved toward my face, and I pursed my lips to keep from biting it. I was a roiling storm of emotions. My natural instincts to maim and kill and drink raged against my self-control with every thump of my hungry heart against the tight leather corset. And my ingrained behavior, the princess in me, was insulted that this man would dare to touch me and make pretty, lying words at me as if he was offering candy to an innocent Pinky child.

I began to understand the bone-deep fear of prey. This man wasn't a soft duke or an aging baron. He didn't belong on the *Maybuck,* which meant that no one knew he was there. Would it be anything close to a fair fight? He was bristling with weapons, and I was sorely hampered by leather and canvas and lace. Even if I managed to kill him, I would expose myself as a Bludwoman and follow him over the side to the sea far below.

So that left me in the position of any other young girl: I was in his power. I had to find a way to escape him before he hurt me or drove me to a killing fury. Or both.

He took a step toward me, a knowing smile on his lips. I took a step back, hands still up.

"Please," I said again. "My uncle will be back soon. He's the Maestro. He'll be most upset if my person is assaulted in any way."

"He's not your uncle, little flower. And whoever he is, if he brought you on the *Maybuck*, he didn't have much concern for your honor." Quick as a whip, he swung around, one hand on either side of my face, trapping me against the wall. So I played prey. I cowered.

"Besides, I'll return you in good shape," he whispered in my ear, the scent of blood and wine heavy on his breath. "I'll get you warmed up for your future husband. Do the hard work. You'll thank me for it. For warming you up."

I gulped and turned away as he nuzzled my neck where I'd unlaced the thick collar of my shirt. One of his hands fumbled with the cloth of my skirt, as the boy's had the night before. No wonder women wore so many layers of clothes. My hands slapped his away, but his fingers only dug harder into my flesh.

My breathing sped up, my chest straining against the corset. The more I fought him, and the more he fought the cloth hiding my scent, the more I realized that I was truly in danger. Even without unleashing his sharp teeth, he was besting me. His beast was stronger than my beast, and I began to push him away in earnest.

"I like it if you fight me a little, vixen," he murmured, his voice husky.

Left with little choice, I sighed and jerked away from his hand. And then I head-butted him.

I heard the *crack* and saw stars, but it bought me only a moment of mercy.

"You nasty little bitch." He touched the split skin on his forehead and snarled, snagging both of my gloved wrists and pinning them painfully against the wall over my head. He tucked his blud-covered forehead into my shoulder, beyond the reach of another head-butt. Shoving his hips hard against me, he said, "You owe me your maiden's blood now, little flower, and I'll have it."

His tongue darted out to slide up my face, until he pulled back in surprise.

"You! On this ship! How can—"

Before he could finish, he went completely stiff and shuddered, then vomited blood and wine all over my skirts. He dropped my wrists and fell to his knees, and I screeched and danced away from him, trying to fling the wine-soaked filth from the only dress I owned.

There was a loud *thud* as boot met face, and my attacker fell to the boards. When I looked up again, Casper stood like a vengeful god over the man's inert body, his face white with rage and his eyes promising murder. His hands were taut white fists at his sides, and he was panting in a way that made all his veins throb with a song as lovely as his music. Keen stood just behind him, her crafty glare and alert stance at odds with the frilly, diaphanous gown.

"Did he hurt you?" Casper's voice was soft, flat, deadly.

Rubbing my forehead, I gave a weak chuckle and said, "No, but I split his forehead open."

He gave a humorless snort and kicked the body over with a high black boot. When he saw the man's unusual dress, he inhaled through his teeth.

"Know what that is?" he asked.

"A Bludman. Not someone who belongs here."

"That's a pirate. An assassin or a scout, maybe. But you're right, he doesn't belong here. And we've got to get rid of him—fast."

Casper looked up and down the hall before picking the pirate up under his armpits and dragging him quickly away. Keen grabbed the man's soft black boots, and they were soon tossing him overboard from the empty deck. I grinned as I watched the body fall into the midnight clouds and noted that I didn't feel airsick at all.

"We tell no one." Casper scanned the hollow sky as if expecting a skull-plastered ship to be waiting nearby. "If Miss May hears of pirates, they'll search every crevice of the *Maybuck*. If they find what's hidden in our room, we'll be exposed and tossed out. We'll just have to hope he was alone." He rubbed his fist and cracked his knuckles. "God, that hurts. I must have punched him in a knife. Or a bone."

"You punched him?"

"Right in the kidney." His lopsided smile was full of pride and dimples. "I read somewhere that it can make you throw up, being punched in the kidney."

"You didn't read it. I told you," Keen muttered. "Learned it on the street."

"Effective, if messy." I smiled at Casper, caught off guard by our strange situation. "Well done."

He held out his arm, and I took it, careful not to get gore on his shirt as he guided me back to our room. I didn't read the plaques on the doors this time—the barely lit passages didn't feel as safe as they had before, and I wanted to be behind my own closed door. The fact of the matter was, I was shaken.

For the first time in my life. I didn't feel like a princess or a beast or a Bludman. Just a creature grateful to be alive. My first real taste of physical fear wasn't sitting well with me. I'd faced off with the largest, fiercest predators the tundra could produce. Ice bears, timber wolves, wolverines, and me armed with nothing but my own sharp teeth and nails and determination to master the enemy. I'd faced my mother in one of her world-famous dark moods. I'd floated into the clouds, shivering against wood boards and waiting for the moment the wind carried me overboard and into the sea.

But I'd never lacked confidence in my own abilities as a predator, not until a stronger Bludman's hands had pinned my wrists, finally showing me where I fit in the world. Whatever Casper was, he had saved me when I couldn't save myself. I wasn't the ultimate killing machine my mother had always told me I was.

Perhaps that wasn't such a bad thing after all.

13

Somehow we ended up back at our door, Casper's arm around my shivering shoulders. He withdrew with a gentle pat, hovering near, probably afraid I was going to fall over without him there to hold me up. For once, I wasn't angered by his attentiveness.

"I'll be in my bunk." Keen disappeared into the closet and slammed the door. Her next words were muffled by thick wood. "Enough bloody excitement for one night."

I looked down at my only dress, the thick, tawny cloth splattered with wine stains and blood.

"How am I supposed to clean this up? I have no wardrobe, no maid. Do we even have running water on this flying hatbox?"

Casper looked me up and down and flushed, then turned to dig through my trunk. He handed me a wad of soft white cloth.

"It's bedtime. Here's your nightgown. Just go to sleep, and we'll deal with it in the morning, when everyone is . . ."

"Less coital?" I offered.

"More clothed and sober."

"But what about you?"

"I'll go outside to keep watch. The other passengers

will just think I'm drunk. I'm possibly the only person besides you who isn't. So that's new."

He went for the door, and I panicked. "Wait."

"Yes?" His gaze was steady, roving over me as if hunting for sore places.

"Would you mind . . ." I took a deep breath, searching for the right words. I was accustomed to ordering people around, not asking favors.

Casper's face softened. "Shall I stay in the room until you're asleep?"

A small smile and a nod were all I could muster.

He pulled a book out of the trunk and began to read by the light of the wall sconce. After a contemplative look, I went into the bathroom to disrobe. It was the same size as the closet and very primitive, just a toilet, a spigot, and a mirror, but all I needed was the privacy. It felt wonderful to unbuckle the corset and peel the filthy layers from my skin. I'd never worn clothes so heavy and tight and binding. Or, for that matter, so smelly. I pulled on the light cotton nightgown Reve had packed for me and tiptoed to the bed, leaving my soiled clothes on the ground. Casper did me the courtesy of not looking up, and I turned on my side and pulled the velvet coverlet over my shoulder.

As I fell asleep, I couldn't help thinking about Casper, listening to him breathe as his bare fingers whispered over the pages of his book. I'd watched him drinking. He'd had glass after glass of wine, and he'd surreptitiously mixed in his own special brew from the flask with every refill. He should have been drunk. But he wasn't. Either that, or he was a good actor. And under the smell of red wine, filling the airless room, there was still something else, irritating me like an itch I couldn't quite scratch.

"Good night, Ahna," he whispered. As if I finally had permission, I slept.

I was trying to muddle through Casper's book when the door opened the next morning. I hadn't seen Casper or Keen since waking up, and I was bored already, sick of the small room and unaccustomed to being trapped. The book was dull, nothing but music theory and dizzying arrays of notes. Casper's company would be a welcome diversion, if only for the bickering. Maybe that was why there was something teasing in my tone when I said, "And where have you been?"

"Picking out the perfect gown to highlight your eyes."

The voice belonged to a woman, and I stifled my instinct to attack her as she emerged from behind the door with an impish smile. My nose registered that it was a stranger, a woman, and someone similar to Casper, in that she had that mild underlying stink.

"Can I help you?" My voice was frosty, my stare unforgiving.

She had short, smooth hair, black and shiny against creamy white skin that shone in the orange light. Her dress was in a loose, foreign style, with a flowing skirt and a fitted bodice, the entire garment almost see-through. One hand held folded blue cloth, and the other one stroked suggestively down her collarbone as she closed the door and leaned back against it.

"You're lovely, you know," she murmured in a cultured London accent. "I couldn't keep my eyes off you at dinner last night."

I didn't know what to say, so I said nothing, just glared.

"You could make a lot of money. I could teach you."

"Not interested."

"It's not all bad. I can make sure you enjoy it." She walked toward me, hips swaying and painted lips quirked up on one side.

The only thing I needed less than a half-dressed snack in my room was a prostitute in my bed. I drew a deep breath and opened my mouth as if to scream, and she drew back with a sigh.

"Oh, don't fuss. I'll stop."

"Where's Casper?"

"Playing harpsichord at breakfast, albeit very softly."

"Why are you really here?"

She grinned and winked, holding up a shimmery puddle of blue silk. "Miss May asked me to bring you something to wear while they clean your clothes. I thought this might suit."

I raised an eyebrow and reached for the dress. It would be a welcome change, wearing something pretty and light again. I could already imagine the silk sliding over my skin, whispering as I walked. But she yanked it back, her eyes glazing over with hunger.

"That's cheating, lovely. Off with the nightdress first."

"Get out. Now."

She held up the dress, letting the skirt tumble from her bare hands to dance in the air. I crossed my arms over my chest and barely stopped myself from hissing.

"You truly are a beauty," she said with a sigh. "Are you still a virgin? Miss May would set a price that would keep you in silks for life, you know."

"I'm not for sale at any price. You delivered the dress. Now, go."

"You've got to pay the price first, little pretty," she purred. "And everything on the *Maybuck* has a price."

She draped the dress over the foot of the bed, the light blue silk shining against the plush velvet. With a confident smile, she leaned close and placed one soft, white hand to my cheek as if to pull me closer. I froze as my beast roared inside. A glimmering curtain of red overlay everything I saw, and I lunged for her bare white throat.

My teeth met in the air, barely a whisper away from her jugular, her hands on either side of my face.

She actually laughed. "Not today, sweetheart," she said.

Soft bare fingers held my head away with a strength she should not have had. Her pulse hadn't even gone up. Before she could say anything else, I whipped my face out of her grasp and crawled hastily off the bed. I wouldn't underestimate her again.

"What are you," I said, making it a statement.

"Someone who wants to be like you."

Her eyes lingered on the low neck of my gown. I snatched Casper's coat off the desk and slung it around my shoulders, tucking it over my chest. "I don't know what you mean."

She jerked her chin toward my hands, and I realized they had been bare the whole time. "You're a Bludwoman in disguise, and that means each of us has something the other wants."

"Explain."

"I want your blud, and you want my silence. You give me what I want, I'll keep your secret."

"Are you blackmailing me?" I asked carefully.

A slow, dreamy, satisfied smile spread over her face.

She reclined on the bed as gracefully as water toppling over rocks and said, "As a matter of fact, I am. And now that I think of it, you have two things I want. And from what I hear, you're only going to enjoy one of them."

"What's that supposed to mean?"

"You give me your blud or your body, or I tell Miss May that a monster's hiding on her boat. She'll toss you overboard into the sea quicker than I can snap." She held up long, slender fingers and snapped. "Just like that."

"What do you want with my blud?" I asked. "What good will it do?"

Her eyes glittered as she bit her red-painted lip coyly. "Oh, honey. You can't be that naive. Did no one ever teach you how to blud someone?"

My nails dug into my palms. I hated admitting ignorance. But I had no earthly idea what she was talking about. And I could barely control myself from attacking her again, the way she had arrayed herself on my bed like food on a table. She was taunting me, and she was loving it.

"Guess not," she said to herself. She sat up and leaned toward me like a little girl sharing a secret. "See, Bludmen can turn humans into Bludmen. Drinking just a little bit of blud makes a human stronger and less attractive to Bludmen as prey. But once we start drinking blud, once we tip over from a dab to an addiction, we can't stop, or we go mad. Blud is rather expensive, and most of us half-bluds would sell our souls for the next sip. Being bludded would be much better, but your sort are so selfish." She shrugged, her slender shoulders rising in a practiced way that made her dress slide off one side, revealing a blue vein just underneath creamy skin. I licked my lips. "You would get to drink my blood, too, you know."

I snapped back to attention. "That's a lie. It can't be true. You can't just change your species by drinking someone's blud."

She rose sinuously from my bed and smoothed the coverlet, her gaze lingering on the bedside table, where an empty wine bottle sat.

"Ask the Maestro about it," she said with a secretive smile. "He'll tell you the truth. And then you come find me. Wear that dress, either way. I'll give you until midnight to decide. Body or blud."

She sashayed across the room with practiced grace, her slippers whispering over the boards. Turning at the door with a self-satisfied smirk, she added, "The name's Cora Pearl, by the way."

"You're a dead woman, Cora."

"Sure I am, honey."

I heard her laughing all the way down the hall. When the room was silent again, I slipped out of the nightdress and into the blue gown, with my back to the door and a blush hot in my cheeks. She had made me feel dirty and foolish, and the dress now seemed tawdry and revealing. Whatever I chose, she'd turned me into a traitor or a whore, and I couldn't even kill her for it. I locked the door and fluffed the pillows and buried myself under the blankets, wishing to hide for the first time in my life.

I had no idea what time it was, but midnight would come too soon.

14

When the doorknob jiggled, it might have been minutes later, or it might have been hours. I was no closer to making my decision.

"Go away!" I pulled the thick covers up to my chin.

"I can't."

It was Casper. I darted to the door, unlocked it, and dove back into bed.

Casper walked in looking sorely put-upon. When he saw me cowering under the blanket, he had to laugh.

"You're hiding from me now?"

"No, I'm hiding from the hordes of pirates and prostitutes who insist upon attacking me," I mumbled peevishly. I dropped the covers, then remembered how much my blue dress revealed and pulled them back up. He stifled another laugh in a cough. "If you're not here to attack me, are you here to feed me?"

"I'm not your manservant, princess. You can eat anytime you need to. The blood's been in the closet all along."

"Ah."

I slid out of bed and knelt to rummage in the box in the closet, painfully aware that half of my back was revealed by the flimsy blue dress. The glutted rush of the boy on the bank was long gone, and my run-ins with the pirate and Cora had left me ravenous. I popped the cork from a vial and stood. And then I froze.

His eyes reminded me of a wolf I'd once seen. I hadn't been hunting that day, and neither I nor the wolf had been paying particular attention to our surroundings. I rounded an outcropping, and there he was, ice-spangled white fur dancing around deep blue eyes.

In Casper, as in the wolf, there was neither desperation nor mercy. Only dead stillness and an odd, patient hunger. I couldn't look away. A strange little thrill quivered down my spine like the thrum of plucked strings, and I had to focus on my breathing to keep from betraying myself. *Never show weakness. Never blink first.*

He broke the tension, whipping out his dimpled smile like a dagger, saying, "So are you going to drink that or what?"

"Of course" was all I could manage.

But I kept my eyes locked on his as I drank. I imagined it was his blood on my tongue, hot and wet. He returned the stare with a dark grin that made me wish I could read his thoughts. Two gulps and the vial was empty, and he watched me lick my lips. Altogether, the scene lasted about twenty seconds and felt more intimate than draining the boy on the bus with his hand twitching against my thigh.

"I see Cora found you with the dress."

I almost fumbled the vial as I put it back in the box. With my back to Casper, I said, "She was very . . . persistent."

I wasn't quite sure how much to tell Casper. In my former life, I had confided only in my old nursemaid, Verusha. Had I met Casper on my own terms, I probably would have had him killed or beaten within moments. But now, trapped on the *Maybuck,* he was the closest thing I had to an ally. And if what Cora had said was true, there was a lot more to the world than I knew. In the dark room with no pocket watch, I had no idea how much time I had left until midnight, but there were things I needed to know—and fast.

The only thing to do was confess, and it came out in a rush.

"Cora wants me to blud her."

His gaze sharpened. "Really?"

"I didn't know it was possible. I don't know how to do it. But if I don't, she's going to tell Miss May what I am."

"Did she say why she wanted to be bludded?"

"She said she was a halfblud, and it made her nearly mad. And she said that my part in the process would be painful. Is it all true?"

I had once asked my mother the same question about fairies, and it didn't escape me that all the wrong things turned out to be real. His eyebrows were drawn down as if it hurt to speak.

"It's true." He glanced to the closet, where the box still showed dozens of blood-filled vials. "It's a nasty business. Whether halfbluds are born or made, most of them just want to be bludded and get on with life without the unbearable hunger and inevitable madness. Are there no halfbluds in Freesia?"

"Absolutely not," I snapped. "They would be seen as an abomination. Ever since the Bloodless Revolution, the lines between Bludmen and humans are very strict. In the palace, a nobleman would no sooner share blud with a human than you would serve a dog your lopped-off finger in a bowl."

"Interesting analogy."

"I didn't even know it was possible," I said, mostly to myself. Now, among all my other problems, I had to wonder what else had been purposefully omitted from my privileged education.

"It's not considered a polite topic of conversation." He leaned back against the wall and crossed his arms. I suddenly became aware that he was seeing altogether more skin than he'd ever seen on me. His eyes lingered on my collarbones, and goose bumps rose along my arms. I went back to rummage through the closet for . . . anything, really. I didn't have possessions, but I needed something to do with my hands and eyes while his voice filled the small room. In a nest of scraps and trash, I found Keen's brass sphere and rolled it between my palms as Casper deliberated. The thing was incised all over and heavy, but I had no idea what it was. I set it down and turned around to face him when he began talking again.

"In Sangland, the Bludmen are bad off, but the half-bluds have it worse. They try to keep what they are a secret, as Pinkies and Bludmen both consider them unpredictable and dangerous, but as it goes on, it's harder to hide. It's expensive to buy enough blud to keep from going mad. And even if you're lucky enough to find a Bludman willing to accept the pain of the bludding and give you his or her blud, it doesn't always take."

"So I could actually kill her?"

"For my sake and Keen's, let's hope you don't. I'd rather not walk the airship plank."

"But wouldn't Miss May know about her? Wouldn't

she be just as unwelcome on the *Maybuck* as I would be?"

"It's different," Casper said softly. "If Miss May knows what Cora is, and Cora makes enough to pay for the blud. She's probably considered exotic. So long as she's controlled, her price might even be higher. It's said that half-bluds have a sort of intoxicating charisma."

My head fell forward. "I hate having to hide who I am."

I heard his sigh, his bare feet whispering across the thick rugs. When had he taken off his boots? He stopped just behind me, and I paused, my arm on his coat in the closet, where I'd hung it once Cora had left.

"I know," he said. "It's not fair. But it's necessary if you want to get back home. And you're not alone."

He was so close that I could smell him, the hot scent of his skin, the sweet call of his blood, and a heady, musky cologne. Part of me ached to feel his hand on my shoulder, but I was scared, too. Scared to trust anyone, scared to be comforted when I was accustomed to putting up a smooth royal front. I almost told him about Cora's offer for my body, but I was too proud to let him see me blush.

"I am always alone," I whispered.

"You're only as alone as you wish to be."

I didn't know what to say, what to do with my hands. I wanted to cover up, and for the first time, I missed the rough, heavy material of my old dress. And Casper just stood there, still and steady, damn him. As if he had all the answers. But what did he know? He didn't have a midnight deadline to give up something he prized.

"What time is it?" I snapped.

He was silent for a moment, and I wondered if he was studying me as hard as I was studying his presence, trying to understand him as one animal does another. He didn't feel like prey anymore, and I didn't necessarily feel like a predator. I could read his face somehow but not his body, not his silence.

After a whisper of cloth and a metallic snap, he said, "It's afternoon. If you're going to blud her, you need to fill up. You'll nearly drain her of blud, but she'll nearly drain yours, over and over again—or something like that. And get some sleep, too, if you can." He sighed in annoyance. "I have to go play the harpsichord, not as if they even hear it. Will you be okay until then?"

"I guess I'll have to be."

He moved away as I knelt and fumbled around for two more vials. I was going through them faster than I had anticipated, and it would have been helpful to know more about our schedule, such as how long until we touched down in another big city and found enough blood to keep me docile.

"I'll let you know when it's eleven thirty, shall I?" he asked.

I couldn't bear to turn around. I felt like a string pulled taut, barely held together, and if his eyes had been too kind, I might have snapped. But he didn't move, and he didn't reach out. He was waiting for something, some signal I didn't know how to give.

"Thank you," I mumbled.

I would have sworn I heard him smile. It didn't occur to me until after he'd shut the door that I had already broken one rule.

Princesses weren't supposed to say thank you.

Even after three vials of blood, sleep eluded me. I had made my choice, and I was antsy, waiting for it to be over.

I pulled a book from the small bookshelf fitted into the wall and lost myself in the sort of novel I'd never known existed. It *was* a flying brothel, after all. And despite my foreboding, it was a very educational afternoon.

When Casper knocked, I leaped up, shoving the book under my pillow before he could open the door.

"Don't bother arguing. I'm escorting you there, at the very least."

I nodded, feeling the corner of my mouth quirk up and tremble.

My heart was beating so hard against my chest that I expected it to show through the blue silk. My corset and clothes had not been returned, and I wondered how much of that was Cora's doing. As I followed Casper through the halls, I was all too aware of the sounds on the other side of each door I passed. Moans, laughter, the slap of leather on flesh, and in one case, manly snores that recalled a dying bear.

Finally, we came to the Pearl Room. An engraved calling card was tucked into a slot below the plaque, with "Miss Cora Pearl" curling across the creamy paper in elegant script. With a deep breath, I straightened my dress and knocked.

"I'll be right here," Casper whispered.

"Please don't. I couldn't stand the thought—"

"Come in, darling," Cora called, her voice as sweet as bells in winter. It was meant to entice and charm, but it chilled my blood nonetheless. I didn't finish my sentence, but Casper walked backward away from me, his eyes crying helplessness and his mouth in a hard line.

I slipped inside, anxious to keep my shame hidden. I was willing to bet that no Freesian princess had ever knowingly entered a courtesan's chambers.

"Welcome, darling," she purred from the bed. "I've been expecting you. Have you made your choice, then?"

"I'm here, aren't I?"

My back was against the door, my arms crossed over my chest. Cora posed in a long, beautifully draped kimono that trailed over the ground. In one hand, she held a green crystal decanter, and in the other, a dainty glass goblet of dark red wine. Her hair was perfectly smooth, her lips bright red and perfect. Her smile spoke of power, of smug self-satisfaction. The room was much larger than mine and done in an elegant Eastern style, all cranes and chrysanthemums, and she was curled in the middle of it like a pearl nestled in velvet.

"Wine?" She held out the goblet.

"Of course not."

Her laugh rippled as she crossed the room to stand uncomfortably close.

"Darling, they really didn't tell you anything, did they? You must have come from an orphanage. You can drink wine, so long as it's mixed with blood. It'll help you relax."

I knew that, of course. Celebrations at the palace included tables laden with delicacies, blood mixed with candies and liquors and dainty tarts. But she didn't need to know that.

She took a sip, her throat rippling and her eyes closed in pleasure.

"It's not drugged, sugar. See?"

I reached for the wine as if it was a dare, taking the first sip with a rebellious glare at my blackmailer. Up close, I could see that her eyebrows had been filled in with some sort of paint and that her long dark eyelashes were drenched in kohl. The tiny lines at the corners of her eyes were hidden with white powder. No wonder she wanted my blud. When her beauty faded, so did her way of life. Here was a woman who couldn't do without her pearls and crystal.

The glass was cool against my lips, and the first sip was heady. Along with the usual warm, satisfying tang of blood, I welcomed the tart bite of wine and, deeper down, something sweet that numbed my lips. She must have seen my surprise, as she giggled like a little girl.

"You've never tasted blud before? I mixed that up just for us. Thought you might need some liquid courage."

I took another sip, savoring the velvety burn as I weighed my options. I'd never tasted the blud of my own people, had always thought it forbidden. But there it was, rolling over my tongue and sliding down my throat, fiery and exciting. I licked my lips and stared at her.

Allowing my body to be used was out of the question, and so was bludding her. I couldn't stand the thought of this horrid creature touching me, much less walking the earth with my own lifeblud in her veins. All day, I had thought on it. And still I had reached the same conclusion.

A clock chimed daintily, and she said, "It's midnight, and I can't wait to hear your choice, little pretty."

"Fine. Let's get this over with."

Her hands stroked the silk on my shoulders, and her breath tickled my ear, and she said, "What'll it be, doll?"

I took a deep breath and bared my fangs as my hands locked around her throat.

"Neither," I hissed.

"You . . ." she whispered, choking as she dangled in my grasp, feet kicking weakly. The empty goblet dropped from her hand and bounced on the thick rug.

"I'm not a pet." I squeezed, both thumbs on her trachea. "I'm not some tame thing."

Cora tried to swallow, her throat working under my fingers.

"I'll tell—"

"You'll tell no one. Because if you do, I'll find you and drain you dry and toss you over the rail."

I loosened my hold, curious to hear her reaction.

Each word was a gasp. "You wouldn't dare."

"Try me. I would relish it."

I dropped her, and she collapsed on the bed, one hand to her bruised neck. I stood with as much grace as I could muster, hoping the long skirt hid my shaking knees and wishing I'd just strangled her earlier in the afternoon. I had stalled and acquiesced, hoping for a better choice. But, as ever, a predator was a predator, and my only choice was the one I was willing to fight for. After straightening my dress, I turned to her. She looked pathetic and broken, lying there, lipstick smeared and creamy skin mottled with maroon splotches.

"You would make a terrible Bludwoman, Cora."

"This isn't over."

"I'll decide when it's over." I smoothed down my hair in the mirror by the door as she coughed. "But understand me when I say that this is my first act of mercy, and I'm liable to change my mind."

By the time I slammed the door, she was already pouring herself another glass of wine from the green crystal decanter.

15

I ran down the halls, my bare feet cold on the wood planks. I passed one couple grunting against the walls, and the man called, "Join us, sweeting? There's a silver in it for you."

I had to fight the urge to gut him on the spot. I was angry and scared and ashamed and deeply, ferociously hungry. Cora's wine had left me feeling strange. I didn't even pause as I turned the corner.

The door was open just the tiniest bit, and inside, Keen was crying. I peeked in through the doorway, unsure of how to approach. Casper glared at me over the girl's shaking shoulders, her head buried in his shirt and her back to me. Her white gown had an ugly rip at the neck that made my hackles rise.

"You should have been taking care of me. You should have been there!" she cried in a strange accent.

"I didn't know, honey," he murmured in the same accent, his eyes never leaving mine. "I had to help Ahna."

"She doesn't need you. She's a freakin' Dracula. But I'm people, Cas. And that bastard tried to grab me."

He winced. "I seem to recall you telling me to back off. That I'm not your dad."

Keen pushed away from him and stumbled. She was gasping, her shoulder blades heaving. She held the torn neck of the thin white chemise together as she said, "You're as stupid as he was. You think I don't see what's been happening? I'm not that naive. You're not the same as you were when you found me. You saved me. But I can't save you. Maybe she can. But you're going to lose me. God, this is so fucked up. Like a Disney movie or something. Stupid princesses."

She still hadn't seen me. Casper drew her back into his arms, and she broke into racking sobs. I couldn't fathom her age, but she had never seemed as small and lost and tender as she did now, curled against him, beating his chest weakly with white fists.

She looked up at his face and followed his line of sight straight to me.

"Of course, you're here," she said in her usual Sanglish accent. "Can't even let us have a moment's peace, can you?"

I went rigid. "I didn't ask to be here."

She snorted, and my pity for her disappeared. The crying child was gone, the stone-eyed urchin left to scowl at me. "Neither did we. But it's not like we're trying to drag you back to our world, are we?"

"My entire country is at stake." My fingers curled into claws at my sides as my teeth ground together with each word. "This is not a lark or a pleasure trip. The lives of thousands of people hang in the balance. Perhaps you're unfamiliar with responsibility. With politics. With family. Perhaps you forget my parents and sister were murdered?"

"You're going to talk to me about losing family? Really?"

She dropped the Sanglish accent entirely, advancing on me as if I wasn't a Bludman, as if I was just something standing in her way. "You have no idea who I am and what I've been through. You're the most selfish, superior, nasty bitch I've ever met, and I spent the last few years living in a place where toddlers will cut your throat for bread. You will not take the only thing I have left."

The beast in me stilled, considering her. Casper's eyes didn't leave me.

"I want—" I started.

"What? What do you want? To take what you need and damn the rest? Did you ever think about what it's like for us, about how—"

I hissed, long and low.

"That's enough, Keen." Casper pulled her back against his chest, where she gave in to another round of shuddering sobs. His accent was subtly changed, too. Rounder, softer. Mellow, like afternoon sunshine. Definitely not from Sangland.

I nodded at Keen's dress. "You're not the only one under attack. Cora was blackmailing me. She wants to be bludded."

"What?" Keen looked from me to Casper in shock.

Casper nodded. "I know."

"But I didn't tell you that she offered me a third choice. She could tell Miss May, I could blud her, or . . . I could give her my body."

They both stared at me. Keen's mouth hung open. Casper cocked his head, alert and considering.

"And you let her?" Keen finally asked.

I drew myself up, tall and proud. "I'd rather die than give my blud or my body to someone undeserving. So

I shook her by the neck and told her I'd kill her if she exposed me."

Keen sniffled and straightened. "Must be nice to be that dangerous."

"Not when you can't show your fangs." I grinned, showing them just to her. "But I witness and wait. No one needs to know what I can do now. Let them underestimate us both. We'll show them later what we're capable of."

She nodded, giving me a rare, shy smile. "I'm looking forward to later myself. And I'm going to Kitty's room for new duds."

"Are you sure that's safe?" Casper asked.

She rolled her eyes at him. "As long as I'm moving, I'm safe. It's when I hold still that things go to hell."

"What do you think, Ahna?" Casper asked once she had darted out the door. "Do we need to get off at Barlin?"

"If I thought Cora was going to tell, I would have gone ahead and killed her." I looked down at my bare feet, suddenly aware of how very little I was wearing and how very small the cabin was. "She struck me as a coward who valued her life."

"And what would you call someone who was the opposite of that?"

"Someone with courage and no love of life?" I thought about it for a second, tracing the wood grain with my big toe. "Lucky, I suppose. They've got nothing to lose."

He chuckled and scratched his beard stubble. "Aye, there's the rub," he said.

"What was Keen talking about earlier?" I asked. "She mentioned stupid princesses?"

His smile was sad and tired. "She was talking about fairy tales where we come from."

"Which ones?"

"The ones that end happily ever after, of course. Isn't that how they all end?"

"In Freesia, they mostly end with people having their hearts torn out and their blood drained through the hole into goblets."

That earned a real laugh out of him, the kind of laugh that kept going until tears ran down his cheeks.

"That's much more accurate," he said, "if a bit braggy."

"If you've actually done it, it's not bragging." I grinned at him, licking my lips.

He looked at me as if he'd seen a ghost—but a welcome one. I shrugged and, realizing I was starving, fetched another vial of blood.

Before I raised it to my lips, he excused himself to go play the harpsichord on the deck, although he didn't seem particularly happy about it. We were apparently hovering over Barlin.

"Miss May wants me front and center when the *Maybuck* stops in a new city. As if the new passengers are here for me." He shrugged into his glittering jacket and ran a hand through his hair with a sigh.

I didn't know whether his look of frustration was out of concern for my safety or his own longing for a soft bed and sleep, but I noted that he locked the door on his way out. As it was past midnight, I washed quickly with the ewer and cloth provided and crawled into bed, but sleep wouldn't come. I knew I would be on edge until we landed. Cora would always be waiting, somewhere, for more leverage.

To my vexation, I missed Casper's presence, if only for the comfort of not being alone. And where, for that matter, was Keen spending all her time? From what I could tell, she had been assaulted by one of the men, yet she had walked back out that door with her original confidence, never looking back. I had once dreaded sharing the tiny room with them both, but now the air grew cold and empty, humming with unanswered questions and my own conflicted emotions.

While I was still tossing and turning, Keen sneaked in, fluttered around in the closet, and eventually settled into childish snores. Still later, I heard Casper's boots on the boards and the whisper of his jacket hitting the desk. He paused there in the near darkness, and I gave my best imitation of sleep, curious if he could tell the difference—and if he could, anxious to see what we would have to say to each other. He cracked his fingers one at a time, as was his habit. And then I heard him sigh and slip to the floor. Even with the furs and rugs, it couldn't have been comfortable. But since I wasn't about to invite him into my large and comfortable bed, there didn't seem any point in feeling bad about it.

I listened to his breathing, even and deep in the shadows. I found myself unconsciously inhaling and exhaling in time with him, attuning myself to his body. And I was asleep before I could conclude what that might mean.

I woke up on my side in the dark, and the first thing I saw by the light of a glowing clock was Casper asleep on the floor. My arm hung over the edge of the bed, and his outstretched hand was almost close enough to touch. Dear Aztarte, had I sought him while asleep? I snatched my arm back so quickly that he startled awake.

"Ahna? What's wrong?"

I flopped back against the pillows, fumbling for something to say.

"Where'd the clock come from?" was the first thing that came to mind.

"Since you're trapped in here, I thought you might like a little light in the darkness and a way to tell if it was day or night. It must be confusing for you."

He sat up, rubbing his eyes and running a hand through sleep-tangled hair.

"I need fresh air," I grumbled. "I vastly underestimated how cramped and airless a windowless cabin would be. I can't breathe in here."

"Well, technically, you're not supposed to leave the room." He seemed bemused by my grouchiness, and it occurred to me that perhaps his hand had been the one to seek mine.

"Daylight should be safe enough for me. Won't they all be asleep?"

"No time is safe for you on the *Maybuck*," he said darkly. "But at least you have time to rest and get strong again before facing off with Ravenna. I've never heard of anyone surviving so long after being drained."

"My mother always said I was hard to kill." With a sigh, I touched my shorn hair. "You know, it's funny. I've missed four Sugar Snow Balls in Freesia by now. My beaux will have moved on. I'm past my prime, as princesses go." I sighed. "A spinster."

"Anne."

He stood, forcing me to look up at him.

I blushed at what I saw on his face. I was thankful that he didn't have a Bludman's eyes in the darkness to see my reaction.

"Ahna. You're not a princess anymore. You're a queen. You know you're lovely, don't you?"

"I don't feel like myself." I looked away, fiddling with the ermine tails on a pillow. "This isn't my hair. These aren't my clothes. I don't have a purpose here. I'm drifting."

"We're all drifting," he said. "You just have to get to where you don't mind so much."

"But I was raised to be someone special. To do something special. I used to be . . . extraordinary."

"Me, too. And tonight I'll be playing an out-of-tune harpsichord while rich men dance badly with prostitutes on a zeppelin. And worrying about two ladies who mostly hate me but are, for better or worse, in my care." He leaned over to turn on the light and look into my eyes. "Miss May is expecting me to play all night for the new passengers. Promise me you won't open the door for anyone."

"As Keen says, you are not my father." I sat up to glare at him with light-blind eyes.

"I know that. Of course, I know that," he snapped. "But you can't protect yourself without revealing what you are. Cora already knows. We don't need anyone else to. And we don't want to end up on our own in Barlin, either. Unless you speak Prussian?"

"*Nein.*"

"Exactly. We don't have any coppers. We're stuck on the *Maybuck,* for better or worse. Once we're on the ground in Freesia, you're in charge. Until then, you do what I say."

"Do I?" I stood and took a step toward him, my mouth curling in amusement.

"You do."

"And what if I don't behave?"

"You mean, if you go off on your own again? I'll truss you up and lock you in this room."

He shrugged off his shirt, and I tried not to stare at his well-muscled torso as he rummaged through the trunk for another.

"You wouldn't dare."

"I brought plenty of cravats. Try me."

He pulled on a new shirt and turned to face me, standing so close that I could see his eyelashes. They were white-blond at the roots and auburn at the tips. Pretty. And there was a gruffness in him, a power I hadn't seen before. Something he kept in check, lurking behind the sunshine and dimples.

"No one's ever threatened me before," I said.

"Except Cora."

"Right. Except her."

"And the pirate."

"Yes, and look what happened to him."

"It's a good thing I can't punch myself in the kidney."

And then, in perfect unison, we burst out laughing. I felt relief—and a strange giddiness, as though Cora's wine still rippled through my veins.

"But there has to be some way I can get a little fresh air. I'm practically swooning, Casper."

He smirked. "No one's allowed above deck right now. The servants are decorating it for a special dinner. But I can take you to the library, if you're not too worried about windows. Believe me when I say it's rarely used, as the gentlemen are far too busy elsewhere and the chairs aren't roomy enough for two. But it's got a great view."

He handed me my gloves and held out his arm. I slipped them on to disguise my hands, and he led me down the hall in the opposite direction from Cora's room. I added the new hallways to my mental map of the airship's interior, but I was still surprised when we came to a set of winding wooden stairs. I hadn't known that the ship had more than one level. When I should have been studying it from the ground, I had been cowering flat on my face.

Instead of rooms named after fine fabrics, we passed kitchens, pounding machinery, and a butcher's workshop filled with ice and hanging carcasses that smelled heavily of blood. Finally, Casper opened the door at the end of the hall, revealing a room filled with blessed light and fresh air. Two large stained-glass windows shaped like white roses gave everything a warm glow.

No. Strike that.

The windows were shaped like breasts. But one was open, letting in a crisp breeze and more sunshine than I'd seen in days. Cushy seats with plump pillows nestled under the windows, and the walls were solid with books. In the center of the room sat a table with a globe, several strange machines, a humidor, and a bottle of golden liquid that didn't have a bottom but rolled back and forth as the ship moved.

"You're not going to find Sang's greatest literature in here." Casper held a slim volume upside down, and a foldout tumbled from between the pages, showing a woman in a mask doing something unexpected with a parasol. I grimaced. "But there's probably something better than *Lady Gabriella's Clockwork Cobbler*."

I blushed and picked up the first thing that came to hand, one of the instruments on the table. So he'd noticed the book I'd hidden under the pillow. He chuckled, and I inspected the instrument further to hide my face.

It was a spyglass, but I couldn't find the mechanism to expand it. Casper took it gently from my hands and flicked a switch, and the thing elongated in a manner that would have seemed more scandalous had we not been on a flying brothel.

"There's a cradle for it here, by the window."

He set it up and beckoned me over, and I looked out onto one of the most stunning tableaus I'd ever seen. A village was built into the mountains below, with picturesque Prussian chalets as dainty as cuckoo clocks leaning precariously over the snow-dusted valley. The spyglass brought the image so close that I could see clothes drying on lines between the buildings and goats grazing among the crags.

"It's amazing." I held out the glass to him, and he swiveled it around and looked down.

"It's like a little Christmas village," he said with a surprised chuckle. "The tiny flags, the goats. I can even see buttons on that boy's jacket."

"What's a Christmas village?" I asked. He left the glass to inspect the books, his back to me.

"Oh. Just something from where I'm from."

"I don't think I've ever actually asked you where you're from originally. I had just assumed it was Sangland. But you don't always have the right accent. Almanica, perhaps?"

"That's right." He feigned interest in the bookshelves. "From the east coast. I don't like to talk about home."

"I don't know much about Almanica." I focused on

the village through the spyglass so I didn't have to look at him and feel clumsy. It was an awkward dance, trying to learn more about him. "My tutors always said it was a wild place, where people lived by different rules. Did you like it there?"

"Very much," he said softly.

"Maybe you'll go back one day."

The air went cold, and I looked up in confusion. I'd been on the verge of flirting with him, and now he was tense, his face unreadable as he looked out the window. I had definitely said the wrong thing.

"Enjoy the library for as long as you like," he said. "In fact, I'm locking you in to keep you out of trouble."

"I'm sorry—" I started, but he cut off my highly unusual apology.

"Don't be. You can't possibly know what I lost. I won't be going back."

He spun and stormed out the door, slamming it behind him. A key turned in the lock, and I knew that trying to force the doors would be useless. My anger only lasted until a fresh breeze blew in through the giant glass breast and some geese honked just outside. But my curiosity grew deeper still. I had to figure out where Casper had come from, and more important, why he couldn't return.

16

My nose was so deep in a book on Almanica that I was startled by the sound of the key scraping in the lock. Panicking, I threw the thick volume out the window and put my eye to the telescope, lest Casper think I was trying to study up on his home. Unfortunately, I hadn't learned anything that would help me understand him better.

"May I escort you to your prison, my lady?"

When I looked up at him, he smirked. He was wearing the same fancy outfit he had worn at the Seven Scars, the glittering tailcoat and tight breeches and high, polished boots. But the stubble had grown out on his cheeks, giving him a rakish air, and the cravat he was wearing was one of the ones I recalled from being tied up in his room.

I returned the smirk. "I suppose I'm bound to accept."

He chuckled darkly. "*Touché.*"

Down the hall and up the stairs, my hand felt oddly formal on his arm. The sequins on his jacket were cold and hard, and I was well aware that I was still in Cora's flimsy blue dress. When he deposited me in our empty room, I felt the way I had as a little princess, sent to bed as all the adults arrived in their fine carriages for a ball. It was clear that he was in a hurry to leave, but I wasn't ready to be alone.

"Is it pleasant?" I asked him. "Playing for them?"

Casper cocked his head at me. "I think you know well enough that nothing's fun when you're forced. No one wants to work at a party while other people dance. But at least I still have my music, even if the company's horrible. If it gets too bad, I can always jump ship."

He sounded all too much as if he meant it. As he took a sip from his flask, I flopped backward on the bed in a huff and stared at the constellations painted on the ceiling.

"How much longer until we're off this monstrosity?"

"We'll be over Warsaw tomorrow. Just a few more days. Can you handle it?"

"I can handle anything that will get me back to Freesia."

He leaned over me, upside down. "I bet you can. Just a little longer, darlin'."

I smiled. And then he was gone.

"Blast." I drummed my heels against the side of the bed, feeling cooped up and irritated and anxious to get off the airship and down to the business of killing Ravenna.

"Blast yourself."

I yanked up my bare feet in surprise. The words had come from under the bed, and fabric rustled against the wood as Keen crawled out into the lamplight.

"I thought you slept in the closet."

"I needed some elbow room."

She stood and stretched, and I noticed that she had traded the flimsy white dress for her old layers of ragamuffin gear.

"Back to your hoodlum ways?"

Her eyes narrowed at me, half angry and half desperate, like a starving dog.

"You saw my dress last night. One of those bastards ripped it when I said no. This seemed safer."

"Does Casper know?"

"About yesterday, but it happened again. That other girl, Milly—the one they call Colette. She likes it. They give her candy and coppers if she lets them touch her. She sent me over with the wine and watched him grope me and laughed when she caught me crying after I ran away."

"So what'd you do?"

"I punched her smug face."

She grinned, and I grinned back, glad to know she still had her pluck. Despite my general disdain for anything unbludded, I felt a rush of protectiveness for her. If there was one thing I'd learned in the last week, it was that life outside the palace wasn't easy for anyone. And I admired her for standing up for herself, refusing to be compromised for a few coins.

"Once I'm in my rightful place, you won't be at the mercy of such villains," I said.

"Oh, no. I'll just be a servant and a bludmule. Kept in a posh cage to fatten up."

I stared at her, aghast. "I don't know what you've been told, but royal servants are treasured and pampered. I give you my personal guarantee that no one will drink from you unless you wish it."

"Why the hell would I want to be food?"

"It's not being food. It's providing a service, and it's richly rewarded. Our servants are carefully bred and tended—"

She stabbed a finger in my face, and I very nearly bit it. "There! Hear that? Bred? Tended? That's not a person. That's cattle."

"But what else would humans do in Freesia? It's cold,

it's dangerous, and with a population dominated by Blud-men, there's no other need for food crops. We treasure our humans."

"Not enough to give them rights, apparently."

"I would think you'd be grateful." I gestured to her outfit. "You have nothing. You come from nothing. But I have much power, and when I'm reinstated, you'll have everything you've ever wished for."

"That's a goddamn lie, and you know it! I have a *life*, and I don't want the fake one you think I need. We had it good, me and the Maestro. Everything was fine before you showed up."

"Sorry to wake up mostly murdered and muck up your happy family," I shot back without thinking. I instantly regretted it.

"We weren't *happy*. I don't even remember what happy feels like. But we had a home, and we had each other. It was safe. And now you've got us running across the globe, sur-rounded by handsy jerks, and they keep trying to yank me into their laps, and I hate it." The last part came out as a des-perate growl, and I could see that under her tough mask, she was pushed to her limit, just as I was, by being cooped up.

"I never meant for any of this to happen, you know. I'm as much a victim as you. On the other side of this journey is a fight I might not win. And I'm not even allowed to leave this wretched little cube of a room."

She sat down on the stool, legs wide apart like a man in her grubby pants. "Says who?"

"Excuse me?"

"Who says you can't leave? You can walk out the door right now."

"Miss May made it quite clear. And Casper—"

"Casper ain't here. And he's not our boss."

Keen grinned an evil grin, and so did I. She was right. I would soon be the Tsarina of Freesia. The threats of a madam and a musician couldn't hold me.

"What do you propose?"

"I propose we crash dinner."

"I can't do it in this . . . scrap." I held out the whispery silk skirt of my dress.

Keen's grin widened. "You've never been to the costumer, have you? Come on."

She actually grabbed my gloved hand and dragged me out the door and down the hall. I was terrified that we'd see someone, but the halls were empty. Moments later, she shoved me through a nondescript door.

"Back so soon?" a woman said. She sat on a tuffet, dressed in high fashion and magnifying goggles as she sewed a button onto a ruffled skirt. A clockwork insect buzzed around her head, tied to a brooch on her shoulder. I realized it was the kindly ex-milliner with the beautiful hat whom I had met at dinner my first night on the ship.

"Can she borrow something, Kitty?" Keen asked. "Anne needs something more . . ."

"Substantial?" the woman said with a wink, and I nodded. "Help yourself, dear."

It was a pleasure to choose my own attire again. The room was lined in racks of clothing, and although most of the offerings were the sort of revealing costumes favored by the *Maybuck* girls, I found a collection of more modest gowns in the corner. I couldn't help wondering if these were the dresses women wore when they first set foot on the *Maybuck*, before they learned to show their skin.

Behind a folding screen, I squeezed into a new corset

and slipped on a simple dress of dark blue velvet. Kitty didn't budge from her work and kept her eyes down, to her credit. As I laced up the waist and tied a bow by the modest neckline, I was all the more aware of the low cut of the older woman's gown. Inhaling deeply, I caught the delicious, spicy scent of blood rising from her skin. As if sensing my attention, she looked up.

"That blue does lovely things for you. What creamy skin you have! Almost translucent. But you look so familiar. Have we met before?"

"At dinner the other night," I said firmly.

"No, before then. Perhaps in London? Or Manchester? I traveled as an actress for several years there and enjoyed a good bit of notoriety. Although that was probably before you were born, young as you are. Seventeen, by my guess?"

"Eighteen," I said quickly, grateful for the ageless face of a Bludman. I wouldn't have Kitty's wrinkles and soft chin until I was at least a hundred and fifty, if then.

She set down her sewing and stepped closer to arrange my dress just right. I tugged down my gloves and held my breath, and Keen skulked in a corner, fidgeting with that gold sphere of hers. Up close, I could see that Kitty's clockwork insect was a bumblebee, and it buzzed in lazy circles around her head, occasionally landing on her hat or shoulder. She reached down once to stroke it briefly, making its metal wings shiver.

"I remember being eighteen. Miss May and I came up together, you know," she said, retying my sash. "We met in Manchester. It was innocent back then. We just wanted to be onstage. But we learned that we could earn four times as much if we wore less clothing. We made enough money to keep a town house and a salon, and other girls joined us one by one. I was so young and naive. I didn't know what I was until the first one left a purse of silvers by my bedside, after. I thought he loved me, but he just wanted my maidenhead."

"That's horrid," I said without thinking.

"That's Manchester." She gave a rueful wink. "But what is lost is lost. We've never wanted for food or spending money. We've helped damaged girls get off the street. And now look at us, two old ladies on an airship, with more money than we can ever spend in one lifetime. It's not so bad."

I cocked my head. "Are you trying to convince me or yourself?"

She chuckled. "You're quicker than you look. It's just that I've dressed a thousand girls for dinner and more, and I can tell right off that you don't belong. And didn't Miss May tell you to stay in your room?"

"She's not our boss," Keen said.

"She is if you're on her ship without paying."

"Someone needs to stand up to her."

"I did once, and she stabbed me in the back."

"She betrayed you?" Keen asked.

"No, darling. She stabbed me in the back. With a knife. Said if I ever left her, she'd spend every copper she had hunting me down. So I try to enjoy my golden cage. Have you ever taken a bath in champagne? It's lovely."

She sighed, the gentle smile never leaving her face as she watched the bee twirl in circles at the end of its shining tether.

"That'll never be me," Keen muttered.

"Just don't do what I did and sell yourself too cheaply, darling." Kitty smoothed my hair and gave me a pointed look. "You're worth more than diamonds, no matter what anyone tells you."

But of course, I already knew that. And I wasn't planning on selling myself at all.

"Same goes to you, lass." She chucked Keen under her chin. "If they won't leave you alone, claim to have a stomachache and come find me. I'll keep you hidden. At the very least, keep busy with fetching food, and don't trust a single one of them."

"I never do," Keen said, her steely resolve winning a smile from me.

Kitty got up to open the door for us, but something made her pause. She stooped and rummaged under her dress, then held up a small dagger.

"Take this, and if anyone tries to force you, use it," she said to Keen. "But you didn't hear that from me."

Keen fit the dagger into the top of her boot.

"I didn't hear nothing," she said.

"Here we go." Keen paused at the bottom of the stairs. Beyond, I could see a razor's edge of the night sky. The last time I'd been up on deck, I'd been covered with blood and helping to dispose of an unconscious pirate. Quite frankly, I was more scared of the dinner party. I could hear Casper's music playing as backdrop to conversation and giggling and the clink of glasses. In an unusual show of solidarity, I linked my arm through Keen's and ascended the stairs to the windy deck.

For some reason, I had expected a banquet like the ones at the Ice Palace. That was foolish of me, of course. Dinner on the deck of the *Maybuck* was a messy, tawdry affair, and no amount of sequins would make it anything other than an excuse for brazen misbehavior.

"And so the Maestro's niece finally decides to join us." Miss

May ambushed us at the door, engulfing us in a lavender-scented and ample-bosomed squeeze. The leather cups of her corset dug into me painfully. "How are you enjoying your room, Miss Carol?"

After a moment of confusion, I remembered that she was speaking to me.

"I find myself wishing for more windows," I answered, pretending that I hadn't been caught breaking her main rule. "Although it's my maiden voyage by airship, I'm surprised to find it doesn't feel as if my feet have left the ground."

Miss May threw her head back and cackled. "Oh, bless you. Ain't nothin' maiden about this old boat, and never was. But the Maestro says he's shown you the library. If that's not enough freedom for you, you'll have to take on some passengers of your own, if you know what I mean."

"My niece is all booked up." Casper's arm clamped around me like an iron vise.

Miss May waggled her eyebrows at us. "Being on the *Maybuck* is sure to loosen her up a bit, one way or the other. Now, be sure to dance with some of the gents, girl, and maybe you'll get a tip or two." She waved a hand at the men sprawled around the deck.

"You're not dancing with any of them," Casper growled in my ear, his hand tightening over mine.

He swung me away from Miss May, and I took in the full view of the deck for the first time since we'd embarked. It was dressed like the stage for a play, with painted mermaids and sea monsters and coral hiding the rigging and forming niches to shield writhing bodies from prying eyes. Instead of one big table, there were a few small ones around the rails, leaving plenty of room for couples to entwine. And on the far side of the deck stood a long glass tank, about waist-high, filled with rocks and the flash of fins. Beside it, an aged gramophone played a wobbling waltz that didn't hold a candle to Casper's talents.

The deck was beautiful, but it seemed like a useless gesture when the wealthy customers were clearly just there for the women. As my mother often said, "Why buy the maid when you can get the blood for free?"

I was just about to ask Casper about it when a familiar voice said, "Enjoying yourself, Anne?"

Cora's cool hand slid down my shoulder and squeezed my arm. I recoiled with a snarl.

"I was."

Casper's arm cinched tighter around me as we faced her side by side.

"Can't afford the professionals, so you have to go for the free wares, eh, Maestro?" Leaning close, she whispered, "You get what you pay for, you know." She smoothed her black bob and ran her hands knowingly down her dress.

"Diamonds and glass look a lot alike, Miss Pearl," he said stiffly. "Fortunately, I can tell the difference."

"I can tell things, too, you know." With a significant glance at Miss May, she sashayed across the deck to the waiting gentleman who'd been eyeing her appreciatively. So she hadn't told. Yet.

"Playtime's over," Casper whispered, pulling me toward the door.

"No." I dug in my heels and snatched my hand back. "I'm sick of being pushed and pulled and moved around like a doll. I'm not leaving until I'm satisfied."

"There are plenty of gentlemen here who would be willing to accommodate you," he snapped. "It's for your own good. Please, Anne. Let me escort you back downstairs."

"Only after I have a glass of wine."

Standing close, facing me, he was a tempest, a wall, a statue. Implacable, hard, and angry. And yet, somewhere underneath, amused.

"Fine. One glass of wine," Casper said. "Lord knows I need it, and you need to explain to me exactly why you're up here, dressed like that."

There was an odd fire in his eyes as he bowed me toward the refreshment table. He walked just a shade too close, and I was aware of every minor movement of our bodies. The velvet of the dress clung to my skin, moving with me, vastly different from the complex and revealing costumes of all the other girls in the room. But no one was looking at me. They were all too busy with one another. Except for Casper.

At the table, I reached for a slender glass goblet and nearly knocked it over with a shaking hand. Casper caught it deftly and poured it half full of deep red wine. I fidgeted with the stem as he poured his own. Without blood mixed in, it didn't smell remotely appetizing, but I could pretend if it would buy me a few rare moments of fresh air.

"Wait." He reached for the flask in his waistcoat and poured a dollop of something red into both of our glasses. "Now you can actually drink it."

I took a sip, and that's when I finally realized what he was.

I couldn't believe it had taken me so long to figure it out, but the blud in my glass could mean only one thing.

Casper was a halfblud, too.

17

It finally made sense. His odd, musky smell, his strength, his recklessness, the way he stayed alive barely eating anything. And now I knew why he wasn't scared of me. And why he'd laughed when I'd tried to kill him in my first, desperate moments of rebirth.

He was a halfblud. Just like Cora.

Great Aztarte, how had I been so blind?

All this time, and he had never mentioned it. He must have wanted my blud as badly as Cora did, yet he'd said nothing. He hadn't really hidden his true self, but it had probably taken me much longer than it should have to understand.

I tried to ignore my shaking hand as I sipped the wine, tasting the blud of my own species for the second time. It was heady, thick, and deep. As it slipped down my throat, something in me untangled, like a knot unraveling and trailing ribbons down my spine. I relaxed a little, felt my mouth slide into a slow smile.

"How do you feel?" Casper asked me.

"Lovely," I said. And I meant it.

He watched me for a moment, then took a step closer. "Ahna—Anne—are you okay? Your eyes are strange."

"Mmm." I lifted the glass back to my lips. I needed more.

"Stop." When he tried to take the glass from me, I fought him.

"No. Want more."

"You've got to give me the goblet now." His whisper came in a rush, his breath hot on my neck. "You've got to stay on your toes here. We're surrounded by . . . people. And enemies. Now, give over."

"Shan't."

He took a deep breath through his nose. As I opened my mouth to say that he looked like an angry bludmare, he dashed the top of the goblet to the ground, leaving the jagged stem in my hand.

"Why did you do that?" I nearly shouted.

"It's for your own good, darlin'. And mine."

He took the stem from me and set it on the table, then whistled to Colette and Victoire. They ran over with cloths to mop up the mess as he put an arm around my shoulders to move me away from the thick red puddle.

"Anne, you mustn't drink that again."

"Oh, but I want to," I breathed, mesmerized by his smoldering blue eyes. Every detail of his face called to me, and I reached a finger toward his cheekbone.

"Oh, dear Lord." He sighed. "Not now."

"Now."

"Back to the cabin. And I'm locking you in, whether you like it or not."

As he turned to lead me back down the hatch and into the halls of the airship, Miss May's voice rang out over the burbling sound of water, calling, "Maestro! Our bargain!"

He rubbed a spot between his eyebrows and shook his

head as if trying to clear it. "Keen!" he shouted, and when she ran over, he said, "Take Anne to the cabin. Lock her in. Wait outside. If anyone asks, say she's ill. And if she wants something to drink, tell her no."

"Aye-aye, Maestro." She was clearly delighted to be escaping our adventure on the deck.

I balked against her tugging. I wanted to watch Casper play. With an impudent bow to Miss May on her throne, he walked to the harpsichord and sat, flipping out the tails on his coat. After cracking his fingers, he began to play a song I hadn't heard before, and people lined up to dance. Keen pulled on my arm, but I was entranced.

Not by the pageantry of the *Maybuck* in full swing.

By Casper.

Watching him play the harpsichord was magical. His posture. His single-minded focus on the keyboard. His boots pounding time on the ground, making his thighs flex in a fascinating sort of way. And most of all, his fingers, free of their gloves, flying over the keys with a sensuous familiarity that made me tingle in a way I'd never tingled. Both of Keen's shoving hands couldn't budge me from where I stood, watching Casper become an entirely different creature, transformed by his art.

"Ah, my dear. You're even more beautiful than the music. Glowing."

I tore my eyes away from Casper and gaped into the smoky-red glasses of a man I hadn't seen at our first dinner on the *Maybuck*. He must have come on in Barlin. I couldn't help staring at his odd burnished-leather waistcoat, which buckled twice under his neck and around his chest, almost like armor.

"You're too kind," I said, coming to my senses now that

I wasn't ogling Casper. I had been in a fog for a moment, mesmerized by his peculiar magic. But my thoughts sharpened, and I took a step back from the man, who stood just a little too close for my comfort.

"And are you enjoying the festivities?" The man's accent was thick, his voice cruel. He stepped closer. Even from behind the smoky lenses of his glasses, his eyes were piercing in their fervor.

"No. I'm feeling poorly and will be returning to my room." I tried to sidestep him and reached for Keen.

With the sparse movements of a fencer, he snagged my outstretched arm, tucking it into his, and propelled me across the deck. I couldn't exert my full force to escape him but resisted as much as I thought I could. He was as hard as stone, and I began to panic. My eyes flew to Casper, but he was focused on his harpsichord, utterly lost in his music. Behind us, Keen tugged on the man's coat, calling, "Sir! Sir! Beg pardon, sir!" over and over. He ignored her.

"Everything to your liking, Van Helsing?" Miss May called in her most obsequious voice. "Miss Anne is an obliging creature, ain't she?"

I heard the threat implicit in her little speech. One look at the decorated rail of the deck, one inhaled breath of cloud-crisp air, told me that I wasn't giving anyone any reason to find fault with me.

"Very," he answered genially, but I could hear the steel underneath.

He steered me toward the low glass tank. My steps grew short as my body instinctively shrank from the salt water within. What was he playing at?

"And do you know why you glow, my dear?" he said in my ear, his thick glove squeezing my arm hard enough to leave a bruise on a normal woman. I flinched for effect.

"It must be the fresh air," I answered, trying to play my part.

He leaned close. I saw one of the whores watching us from across the deck, her smile tilting up in the corner. She nodded knowingly, as if she knew what was happening. But she couldn't have imagined what he was saying to me.

"*Tsk.* That's not the reason. You glow because you're a Bludman. The glass of my spectacles was especially made to reveal your vile kind to my eyes. I'm a sort of trophy hunter, you see."

"You mistake me," I said, but I heard my own voice waver.

"I don't mistake you at all. Ahnastasia."

His hand tightened another notch. The pressure would have broken a Pinky's arm at that point, and I would surely have bruises for at least a few hours. I clenched my teeth and held in the hiss fighting to escape.

By then, we were standing over the tank. I could smell the horrid salt of it, and I turned my head and closed my eyes as the light spray from the fountain caught on the breeze and blew against my cheek. It burned.

"Do you know much about the creatures of the sea, princess?"

"I know nothing of the sea."

"This is a touch tank. Within are the golden jewels of the ocean. Bright corals, waving anemones, tiny crabs, toothless sharks, harmless fish, even a baby Kraken, if Miss May isn't lying, although she probably is. It's considered greatly sensual to touch the soft, fleshy body of a Kraken. Would you like to try?"

"I would not."

He took my hand and forcefully unclenched my fist, gently tugging at my satin glove. My fingers sprang closed like a trap.

"I want you to feel the Kraken, princess. Put your hand in the tank and touch it."

"And if I won't?"

"Everyone will know you for what you are. I'll kill you and collect the reward and your fangs. And you'll be the ninety-seventh bloodsucker I've destroyed."

My hand hovered over the water, shaking in his unforgiving grasp. Behind me, Keen gasped. Casper's playing didn't skip a beat. He had moved into a rousing quadrille, and everyone's feet were pounding on the floor.

Over the merry sounds of the dance, Miss May's voice rang out. "Don't be scared, Miss Carol. Van Helsing will take care of you. The Kraken doesn't bite!"

I looked at Keen. She knew what would happen if I touched the water. My skin would burn, and everyone would know what I was. Either way, I was doomed.

"Now, princess," Van Helsing hissed in my ear.

I took a deep breath and fought to keep the beast down. When the blud took me over, I was all brawn and no brains. And I needed an intelligent solution more than I needed a bloodbath.

"Let me go, and I'd be glad to touch the Kraken."

He released me. I pulled my glove back up over my wrist and shook my arm, trying to get the feeling to return to my fingertips. Taking a step back, he gave me a slow, vicious smile.

I scanned the deck, barely containing my panic but ready to take a desperate chance. No one was watching us. I reached for the edge of the tank, grabbed it with both hands, and pushed it as hard as I could. The glass rocked for a moment, the water spilling away from us and splattering over the deck. Then, in one fluid movement, I yanked the glass back toward us as hard as I could and leaped away. The tank fell in slow motion, the water sloshing in a graceful, slopping wave. Van Helsing was but a simple human, of course—he hadn't moved quickly enough and fell with the tank.

I was already halfway across the deck. I turned to watch as the tank shattered over the man's fallen form, raining broken shards of glass, bits of coral, and flapping fish all over the wood of the deck. Crabs skittered drunkenly over the boards, their claws snapping. Panic broke out, the women shrieking and the men running about drunkenly.

I was down the steps before the salt water could touch the hem of my dress.

18

I huddled in the closet, waiting for a flood of seawater or an angry Miss May to claim me. When the door banged open, I cringed only a little. The blud in my wine had sharpened my senses. I could tell by the smell that it was Casper, and he was alone.

"Ahna, where are you?"

I unfolded myself and crept out of the closet. "Are they coming for me?"

"No. Everyone's too busy cleaning up. No one saw what happened. Including me." He watched me, waiting for answers.

"He knew me." I checked the floor for seawater before slipping off my boots and gloves and curling up on the bed, my arms wrapped around my knees. "He knew what I was. Who I was. He called me Ahnastasia, and he tried to make me touch the water. So I pushed it over on him."

He nodded. "That worked out well, then."

I gaped at him, heart racing. "Well?" He shrugged. "It's a disaster. Van Helsing wants me dead! He tried to force me to touch salt water. He hunts my people. He's a monster."

"*Was* a monster," Casper said softly, crossing the room to sit on the foot of the bed.

"Surely the tank didn't kill him," I said, confused.

"Almost. Five hundred gallons of water and a ton of glass is a lot for one Pinky. But that didn't kill him. I did."

His gloved fingers unfurled to reveal the jagged stem from the goblet he'd broken earlier. Droplets of blood clung to it, and I unconsciously licked my lips. Casper placed it gently on the bedside table, just out of my reach.

"I've never killed anyone before. And he probably would have died on his own before the night was over. But he was trying to say your name. To say 'Ahnastasia.'"

Hearing my name on his lips drew my attention away from the bloody glass and back to his face. He seemed different to me somehow.

We stared into each other's eyes for a long moment.

"How do you feel?" he finally asked.

I took inventory and rubbed the place on my arm where Van Helsing had held me. "I feel shaken. A little bruised. You?"

"I need a drink." He reached for the bottle on the bedside table, knocking the goblet stem to the ground with a growl. Sitting back, he uncorked it and took a long swig as his eyes captured mine. I held out a hand for the bottle.

"Are you sure you want more?" he asked. "It had a strange effect on you earlier."

"It made me feel relaxed. I just had a big scare. I could use some relaxation."

He handed it over, his fingers reluctant to leave the bottle until I tugged. "Have you never had bludwine before?"

I took several swallows and passed the bottle back. "Cora gave me a sip. And I've had bloodwine, with human blood. But not this."

"It seemed a little like you were drunk, the way you were behaving on deck."

"Then let's get drunk." I could already feel the warm, pleasant uncoiling in the pit of my stomach. I licked my lips and smiled, slow and wide. The world grew fuzzy around the edges. For someone as tightly in control as I normally was, it was a delicious sort of release. Before he could stop me, I snagged the bottle back and had another sip.

"Slow down, there, speed demon." He tried to take the bottle back. But the taste was growing on me. I craved it. It was richer than the richest blood I'd ever had. If normal blood was a tributary, this was the river.

"I'm not a daimon, silly," I said with a giggle.

I covered my mouth to burp, and he snagged the bottle, tipped it back, and drained it.

"That was mine!" I said.

"You're a hungry little thing." His voice slurred, just a little.

"Always."

The slow smile on his face matched mine as he pushed back to sit against the bed's headboard, just a few feet away from me. He crossed his boots on the velvet coverlet and leaned back contentedly.

"You're right," he said, eyes on the ceiling. "This is much better. I've never drunk so much at once. I'm going to feel like hell in the morning. Prolly go mad. But I just killed a guy, so I guess I deserve a little oblivion."

I rolled my head over to look at him, and the room spun with me. I could barely move, but I managed to maneuver onto my side, smoothing his long hair out of my way. Up close, it was the color of burnished maple and smelled impossibly of fir trees.

"You've never killed anyone before?" I absentmindedly twirled a lock of his hair around my finger.

"'Course not." He rolled over likewise to face me. I felt his knees graze mine but was too melty and fuzzy to react. Our eyes met with a sizzle, and part of me woke up a little bit, just enough to appreciate the fine blue of his irises, the knowing curve of his lips.

"Where I come from, killing is a serious crime. I've punched a few guys, but I've never drawn blood." He paused to move a sand-colored curl that had fallen over my cheek. His fingers barely grazed my skin, but I felt his touch like trails of fire. It took everything I had not to purr under his fingers like the cat, yearning shamelessly toward his touch. Instead, I shook my head just the tiniest bit, to see if another curl would oblige.

It did. He moved that one, too, this time more slowly. I grinned at him, and he echoed it, complete with dimples. Somewhere inside me, the beast stirred. But instead of rising in a fury, hissing and spitting and fighting from the dark depths, it seemed to curl and stretch and unfurl, as Tommy Pain did when he found a nice sunbeam.

For the first time in my life, my beast didn't want blood.

"You good, sugarplum?" Casper drew a finger down my cheek.

"Do we have more wine?" I asked, trying to cover my confusion.

"One more bottle." He rolled over to rummage in his bag. "That's all I have to hold me until Minks. But you can have another sip if you need it. Considering the current circumstances."

He popped out the cork and handed me the full bottle. I took a moment to sniff it, drawing in the strange combination of aged fruit and blud. I took a deep whiff, trying to detect what might have gone into the brew, whether it held the blud of one Bludman or many. I wanted to know how he had found it, how much it cost, whether the blud had been obtained by fair trade or stolen. But I wanted the oblivion more. I wanted the lack of control, a liquor I'd never before tasted.

Knowing that it was precious to him, still I drank deeply, wanted to drink it forever. But he gently took it from me, recorked it, and stowed it back in his bag. I could feel his eyes on my face, his gaze sharper than usual but also warm. Was he actually looking at me as if I was the prey?

"What is it I see in your eyes?" I murmured.

"Long enough have I dreamed contemptible dreams," he replied softly, as if reciting something. "You are a dazzle of light, darlin'."

Faster than I could follow, his hand cupped my jaw as his thumb stroked under my lip. I shut my eyes and let the effects of the bludwine wash over me in a haze of red velvet and sweetness. When I opened them again, he was biting his lip, and I saw that his teeth were sharper than I had thought, almost fangs like mine.

"Was that a song?" I asked, but he shook his head.

"Ahna," he said, his voice husky and rough.

"Yes?" Lips parted, I held my breath.

His face angled toward me, and I closed my eyes, waiting. The kiss never came.

"Ahna. I should probably go. I've never had this much bludwine, and I can't . . . I can't control it. It's like there's some mad beast inside me, trying to take over. I should lock myself in the library and sleep it off."

"No." I leaned forward to put my hand on his sleeve. "I mean, you don't have to go. I don't mind."

"I feel like I'm half panther, half drunk." He looked down. His fingers idly stroked my own where they lay on his blood-spattered shirt, making me shiver. "I'm not fit for company."

"How do you think I feel?" I said softly.

He looked up from our hands, gazing into my eyes as if searching for something there. "I don't know how you feel," he said. "You never speak of your feelings."

"I feel the same as you. Muddled and drunk and not sure whether or not to let the beast out. It's not a bad thing."

"You have a beast?"

I snorted. "You've met my beast. She tried to kill you once. I think you laughed at her before you sliced her open. Tasted her."

"Mm. I remember." He reached out to touch my wrist. A thin pink scar crossed the white skin, and he lifted my arm to kiss it. "She tasted good. But I'll make amends."

When his lips touched my skin, I nearly melted. But not like ice. No, like mercury, like metal sizzling, as if my veins were filled with molten fire. I gasped and closed my eyes, and I felt him smile against my skin, kissing his way up my arm, every touch burned into memory with a hot iron.

"I can smell your blud now," he said, his voice dark. "Right here, so close to the skin, beating like a tiny bird thrashing against a cage."

His tongue shot out, and a little thrill rippled through me. It was a struggle to hold still, to keep the beast from attacking him in a thousand different ways that I myself didn't understand. For just a split second, his teeth scraped against the tender skin there, and I felt a thrum of fear and indignation and furious demand, but then his kisses turned harmless again and moved down to my hand, and I relaxed.

He kissed my palm and each finger, then released me. For a moment, my hand hovered in midair, my eyes closed. Then I went boneless and let my hand drop to the bed, the little thrills still running up and down, echoes of his touch. I opened my eyes and licked my lips. My breath was coming fast, the same feeling I would get on a hunt, watching the prey, waiting for the right moment to pounce.

But I wasn't the hunter this time. My eyes met his, and I saw his beast there, roiling beneath the surface, dark and hungry. I could see the tension in his broad shoulders, his hands curling and uncurling against the blanket as if testing claws.

"Come on, beast," I whispered.

His lips crashed against mine, his body driving me back into the soft pillows with a passion just one notch above fury.

I had never imagined that a kiss could be like that, like a live thing, like lightning. The hasty, awkward fumbling of the salesman on the tank and the press of the pirate, even that earlier searing brand from Casper himself, were as different from this as a drop of rain was from a hurricane. His mouth moved against mine, hungry and seeking and offering no quarter, no escape. As he parted my lips with his tongue, I tangled my hands in his hair, pinning him to me and daring him to leave me wanting.

In response, he pressed his body against mine, cupping my jaw and settling over me possessively. It was delicious, the strength and purpose in him, the tension in his muscles against the thick velvet of my dress. Barely knowing what I was doing, I growled softly into his kiss and hooked a leg over one of his boots. Heedless of all my training as a predator and a princess, I wanted him right where he was, and damn the rest.

He pulled away to chuckle against my mouth, and I nipped his lip, tasting just the tiniest hint of blood. He growled as I sucked his lip and moaned, trying to draw in more of the marvelous, wild taste of him. No wonder I'd tried to kill him when I'd first woken up. Under that odd, musky odor, he was just a step below the bludwine. Casper was intoxicating.

He pulled back, eyes afire. Trailing a finger down my face, he ran his thumb between my lips. Remembering the sensual dance of his fingers over the harpsichord's keys, I wrapped my mouth around his thumb and sucked until he pulled it out with a tortured groan.

"No more blood," he said, his voice as ragged as I'd ever heard.

"Tit for tat," I said with a brazen smile. Now that I'd had a taste of him, I wanted more.

"Is that how it works? You try to kill me, so I cut you; I make amends and you kiss me until I bleed?"

"I could do without the first two parts," I purred.

"Could you, now?"

I just smiled, my eyes focused on his lip and the single bead of blood there. I shifted under him a little, noticing his weight now that we weren't kissing, wanting more kisses. When I tried to move my leg, he caught it against his side. "Oh, no you don't," he muttered, stopping my wiggling by pressing up against me in a way that made me gasp and then settling his lips over my open mouth.

My heart was thumping against my corset, and I lost myself in the kiss. I didn't know where I ended and he began, whose tongue was whose, how much of the beast took me over. I wrapped my other leg around him, and he pressed against me with the rhythm of a spring river crashing against rocks. I found myself moving with him, my hands fumbling with his cravat.

He caught my throat in one hand, and I hissed on principle. He laughed and kissed his way down my neck, making me squirm and pant. He paused between kisses, and the hunger when his hot mouth wasn't on my skin was interminable. When his teeth grazed my jaw, I leaned my head farther back. My beast didn't care if my throat was ripped out, so long as his hands stayed on me.

I was lost in sensation, feeling things I'd never felt, never considered. The fire arcing down my spine, settling in my belly like lava, trickling deeper to a need I'd never known, a deep ache between my legs worse than any hunger for blood. I wasn't sure what I wanted, but I'd never wanted anything so badly. When he reached down to unlace the front of my dress, I caught his ear in my teeth and whispered, "Don't stop."

"I don't plan to." He unpicked the ribbons with nimble fingers. I surged toward him, needing his hands on my skin, responding to his body on instinct.

He jerked my dress open and found the corset instead.

"Fucking corsets!" he growled.

I went for the first hook and eye, to show him how it was done. Instead, he caught my hands and pinned them over my head, running his tongue down my neck and over the tops of my breasts, crushed as they were against the corset. I moaned and bucked, and he ran one hand down my side and over my hip, to the place where my dress and petticoats puddled in velvet and lace. As his hand plunged into the mess of fabric, hunting for my skin, he caught my mouth again in a kiss barely less fierce and somehow more intimate for its control.

I pressed myself against him, ablaze inside as his hand stroked closer and closer to the place where I knew I truly wanted him. I kissed him as if he was air, as if there was nothing but him and me and blood and blud and tongues and claiming.

He finally stroked me in a place I hadn't dared to think about, a single finger slicked between my thighs, and I cried out in amazement and passion and fierce joy.

And that's when I heard the door open and Keen howl, "Goddammit!"

19

Her boots clomped away down the hall as I sat up, trying to put my skirts to rights, my face flushed to have been seen in such a state. Was it so wrong, what we had done? Did Casper hate me now that Keen had seen? I pulled up my knees, tucking my skirts tightly under my legs. I was looking down, but I could hear Casper putting himself to rights, too.

"This isn't over," he said, his voice half growl and half whisper.

When I didn't look up, he put a gentle hand under my chin and forced me to meet his gaze.

"Don't blush," he said, as serious as I'd ever seen him. "Don't you dare be ashamed."

"Are you telling me what to do?" I said, trying to muster my usual arrogance. The quiver in my lip betrayed me.

"Yeah, maybe I am." He sat down on the bed beside me.

Everything was hazy, like the dregs of a dream. The bludwine, what had passed between us—it was like waking up suddenly, cold and confused in harsh daylight, not sure what was real. I fidgeted, not knowing what to do with my hands. A single, shiny chestnut hair was caught in one of my fingernails. I picked it out and watched it fall to the ground.

"Aren't you going after her?" I finally asked.

He smiled sadly. "She doesn't want to be chased. She needs to sulk alone. She'll come back when she's ready. Believe me—it's happened plenty of times before."

"It's—I mean—oh," I said, feeling more silly and pathetic than ever.

Of course, I was just one in a long line of girls he'd seduced. No wonder Keen was always angry at me. She seemed to think of Casper as a father; she must have felt about his women the same way I felt about my mother's string of disposable lovers. Disgusted and hateful.

What little rapport I had recently found with the girl would be gone. Strangely enough, that made me . . . sad. Thousands of miles from home, surrounded by strangers, it had been nice to talk to someone who didn't want me dead.

Casper paced the small room, his fingers drumming hard against his thighs. I couldn't imagine what the song might be, but it was hard and pounding. His breathing was fast, and when he stopped to look at me, his pupils were pinpricks in the darkened blue of his eyes. As much as I had liked meeting his beast, what I saw in him now was madness of a different sort, and it worried me.

"Ahna." It came out ragged, harsh. Tortured.

"Maybe you should go," I said. I realized that my dress was unlaced, showing the white corset underneath. I held the velvet together over my chest and struggled to lace it, sure that my face was redder than blood.

"Maybe I don't want to go."

I turned my back, hiding my shame and the damning tears that I couldn't stop.

"Ahnastasia, please—"

"Just call me Anne," I answered quietly. "It will be easier that way."

For one long moment, he stood there. I imagined his hand held out, something holding him back from touching me, comforting me. But I didn't let myself look to see if it was true. Maybe he was counting his money to see if he could afford one of the courtesans tonight instead. Maybe he had a deal with Miss May. I just wanted him to leave so I could cry in peace.

"Just go, Casper."

He sighed sadly, and I heard his boot turn on the wood. Just then, the airship shuddered, throwing him onto the bed with me. I stifled my protest with a hand over my mouth at my sudden nausea. Screams erupted overhead, and the *Maybuck* bucked again.

"What is it?" I croaked, bloody bile rising in my throat.

Casper went into a defensive crouch. "I don't know, but it's wrong."

Feet thundered above us, and I stared at the ceiling, quite positive that there shouldn't have been that many heavy boots on the ship. Casper opened the door to look out, and the sounds of screams and clashing metal rang down the hall.

"Stay here." He tossed something onto the bed, and I picked it up. A dagger, barely more than a letter opener. "I don't know what's happening, but lock the door, and be ready. I've got to find Keen."

I turned the blade over in my hands and slipped it beneath my leg. Casper held the empty bottle like a club and staggered toward the hallway as the ship tilted again. Something dark flew through the open door and thunked heavily against his bare head, and he crumpled to the ground. The form that filled the doorway was wild, with matted hair and a single eye that gleamed in the lamplight like Tommy Pain's.

With a hiss, I was on my feet on the bed, Casper's knife clutched in hand.

"You're holding that all wrong, missy," the man said with unexpected humor.

"I've got other weapons."

"It ain't your weapons I'm wanting to see."

As the pirate stepped closer, somehow both menacing and tentative, my predator's eyes scanned his every detail. His hair was dark and fell in long, tangled locks down his back, wrapped with bits of rope and shell and bone. He was built like a bear, with huge arms and callused paws. One of his eyes was the color of honey, and the other was covered with a black leather patch. Weapons hung from every inch of him, swaying with each step. A strange C-shaped piece of wood was in his hand, matching the one that had clattered to the floor beside Casper.

"What do you want?" I asked, voice low.

In answer, he smiled slowly, showing a mouth filled with metal. "This here's the *Maybuck*," he said before spitting on the plush rug. "What do you think I'm here for, poppet?"

I started to whimper and turned it into a growl. He chuckled and stepped closer, and two more figures shoved each other through the door like pups on the heels of a big dog, hoping for his leftovers.

"You try to touch me, and I'll rip your throat out, I swear it." I had to raise my voice to be heard over the shouting, stamping, and fighting from overhead and spilling down from the deck. A quick glance at Casper proved that he was still unconscious and breathing but unable to save me yet again. Not that I needed to be saved.

"What's this, eh?" one of the new pirates asked, his voice high and excited. He was small and as twitchy as a mad bludlemming.

The third man was silent and slight, holding a crossbow and wearing a Freesian coat with a high, funnel-like neck and a bowler pulled down low over leather goggles. Something about him tugged at my memory. I breathed deep, hoping for clues.

"McHale, you fool. Shut the door." I'd barely noticed the big pirate getting close, but he was near enough that his thick legs pressed against the bed frame with a creak. "Gandy, get ready to catch her if she bolts."

I squeezed my back against the wall, waving my knife, seconds away from showing my teeth and revealing myself as a Bludwoman.

The door shut gently, and the air went still. While I studied McHale, the first pirate reached for my ankle and yanked me down hard. I landed on my back on the bed, the air bursting from my lungs. One of his big hands plucked the knife from mine as if it were a child's toy, and I realized that I wasn't wearing my gloves, but he didn't seem to notice or care. With a shriek of fury, I twisted away from him, trying to claw my way off my back and out of a helpless position. The big pirate laughed and pulled me back with sure hands, inch by inch toward him.

"Stop!" It was McHale, his hand on his crossbow.

"You forget yourself, Bluddy," the big pirate barked. "You'll get thirds and be glad of it."

"Can't you see she's not a whore? She's terrified, man."

With one meaty mitt wrapped around my ankle, the big pirate slowly turned to face McHale.

"I ain't in here because she's a whore. I'm in here because she's a woman. You want in on this, or you and Gandy want to go belowdecks and blow each other's bilges?"

"I ain't a poof!" Gandy shouted, unbuckling his belt and trying to shove himself closer to me. "Let me in, and I'll prove it! I'm smaller than you, anyway. I'll get her started for you."

With a leisurely swing of his fist, the big pirate sent Gandy into the wall and to the ground beside Casper.

"This one"—he pulled lips back over teeth of glinting gold—"is mine."

With animal quickness, McHale launched himself at the big pirate, driving him into the bed across my legs. I smelled the blood before I saw it, and the beast took me over. I had slipped my legs out from under the big pirate's body and pressed my face to his wrist before I noticed McHale poised over the pirate's red-splattered neck. The body danced beneath us as the big man screamed and fought for his life. Together, we held him easily.

"You," I growled.

"Eat first," he said with just a hint of a Freesian accent. "Then we'll talk."

My eyes held him for one moment, not trusting my good luck. My savior was a Bludman, and one more than willing to share, which was a prize rarer than rubies.

"You're generous."

"I am honored to share the kill." He took one long pull and bowed his head to me, blood dripping from the corner of his mouth. "My princess."

20

It was oddly intimate, sharing someone's kill for the first time. The room was a warm cocoon of comforting sounds. The polite slurping of blood rose gently over the rhythmic breaths of the still-living men, and I sighed in contentment to feel my hunger sated for the first time in days. The big pirate was fantastically full of blood.

I left the last pull for my host, as it seemed the polite thing to do. But he sat back, too.

"Please, my lady. It's yours."

I paused, considering. But the princess in me won out, and I drew the last of the hot blood down my throat and wiped my mouth off on the dead pirate's sleeve.

With a nod, McHale tidily looted the big pirate's body. When he held out a handful of coins, trinkets, gems, and pearls to me, I shook my head. Not because I didn't need money but because now that he was dead and bloodless, everything about him struck me as disgusting.

Kneeling across from each other over the deflated body of the pirate, we were both seized by a sudden awkward shyness. McHale flipped the goggles on top of his head to gaze at me with ice-blue eyes and concerned curiosity. I was at a loss for how to behave. He knew who I was and showed proper respect. Did I address him as I would address a Bludman in my country, with total majesty and arrogance? Or did I respect the fact that he had just protected me from a larger predator and shared his meal with me, putting us on more equal footing?

Yet again, he swooped in with perfect courtesy. "My princess, you are weak. Have they been keeping you on this filthy tub for long?" His Freesian accent was more pronounced now that we were alone, and his eyes were anxious. But that didn't mean he could be trusted. He could easily be a spy or someone under Ravenna's power.

"I am not here against my will."

"But you are not . . . one of the . . . *Maybuck*'s offerings?"

"No."

He exhaled and ran a hand down the sparse dark stubble of a beard. "Then I don't have to kill everyone. That's a relief." I chuckled, and he added, "Except these two, I suppose." He stood and curled his gloves into fists, eyes latching onto Casper.

"No!"

His eyes darted to me. "My princess?"

"Kill the pirate, if you wish, but leave the other."

He nudged Casper with a toe, contemplating the fineness of his coat and watch chain, I suppose, and the careful shine on his boots.

"Are you sure? He would be the cleanest thing I've eaten in weeks. And you need blood, my liege. As much as possible." He shook his head sadly. "So thin. So wan."

"That man is my servant, and I'll not have him harmed." The mantle of royalty fell back over me, my spine going sharp and straight at his slight insult. "The other I will allow you."

He bowed briefly before kneeling over Gandy with a formal sort of precision lacking in his attack on the bigger pirate. Rolling down the man's collar, he wrinkled his nose. "I won't be sorry to see this one go."

He ripped the jugular gently, as if trying to show me his good breeding. With a question in his eyes, he held up Gandy's arm, and I gladly took it. Together, we held the body down as it fought senselessly against oblivion. This time, I insisted he take the last pull and went to check on Casper.

I crouched beside his unconscious form, picking up the weapon that had knocked him out.

"Boomerang," McHale said, taking it from my hand. "He should be unharmed."

I traced the purple bruise on Casper's temple, where the burnished wood had slammed into him. It was strange, seeing my black-scaled hands and white talons against his golden skin. He was halfway between Bludman and Pinky, predator and prey, and I was curious to know what would happen to his hands were he ever bludded. Was the transition sudden, or would the fine fingers slowly fade to dark? At least he would still have the harpsichord, if it came to that. So long as the talons were kept trimmed, a Bludman could play just as well as any Pinky, if not faster and better.

Without meaning to, I found myself brushing the hair back from his sleeping face, remembering the feeling of copper-colored tendrils curling around my fingers like unanswered question marks. If only he had more bludwine in his bottle. I wanted to taste it again. I had enjoyed that looseness, that release, more than I wanted to admit.

Tall, buckled boots stepped close, and I pulled my hand back guiltily.

"He should be awake soon," McHale said. He nudged Casper in the side with the toe of his boot, and Casper's eyes jerked open.

"Ahna!"

He scrambled upright and shoved me behind him. Still dizzy and wobbling, it struck me to the heart that his instinct, even damaged and uncertain, was to protect me. McHale just laughed, a distinctly Freesian sound, and clapped him on the shoulder as if he was an unruly hound.

"That's a good servant, your highness. Jumping in front of you like that."

Casper shrugged off the pirate's hand and bristled as he took in the room. Two dead bodies, a minimum of blood spilled. And me, standing behind him, one step away from fretting, my cheeks pink with blood and feeling bad for a reason I couldn't name.

"You okay, Ah—" He swallowed. "Anne. Did he hurt you?"

"He saved me. The big one on the bed knocked you out and came after me, but McHale stopped him."

Casper looked from my mouth to McHale's, both stained with red. "I see."

I pushed past Casper to stand between them. The air was cloudy with the scent of blood, and I could sense each man's hackles rising as if they both wanted nothing more than a fight. It was an awfully small room for two bristling males, and it was left to me to defuse the tension before I lost one or more of my allies.

"McHale, you've been so kind. Can you tell us what's happening on the ship?"

With a chuckle, the pirate's stance relaxed. "Please call me Mikhail, princess. And what's happening is an act of piracy. Captain Corvus of the *Bludeagle* has invaded the *Maybuck*."

"Then all the girls are being . . ." I gulped. What the big pirate had planned for me might have been their usual way of business, but I hated the thought of all the women on board being forced.

But Mikhail shook his head. "The *Maybuck* is famous, and not for the coin. I suspect my captain and your Miss May had a deal that would benefit both parties. We sent a scout several days ago to make the arrangements. Although he didn't return, Miss May must have accepted. It was far too easy, the way your ship sat, waiting for us. You were unlucky that Big Gar found you first."

"And why do you move among these barbarians?" I asked, for he seemed polite, cultured, and clean for a pirate.

Mikhail's eyes narrowed at Casper. "Can this one be trusted?"

I nodded once. "I trust him with my life."

"Very well. Ravenna needed room on the Blud Council for her pawns, so many of the ancient barons were deposed or executed. I am a bastard son, and when my father was thrown out, I had nothing left. We formed a group and fought against her, and we lost. With Ravenna's mark, there's no way to prosper in what's become of Freesia." He pulled back his glove to show a stark red symbol burned into his wrist, an X inside a circle.

"So this mark means . . ."

"No succor. No blood. No trade. In a grand feat of irony, she has turned Freesia's own royal sons into gypsies. Piracy seemed a safe enough option. There's plenty of blood, in any case."

"And your captain doesn't mind?" Casper asked.

"It's all the rage among air pirates, keeping pet Bludmen. Like dogs on a chain. I brought a few of my fellows with me, but they're always careful to break us up on little runs like this. I won't miss Big Gar." He spat, and the red glob clung to the big pirate's sunken cheek.

As I watched it slowly slide to the carpet, Casper exhaled in a burst and grabbed Mikhail by the arm, taking us all by surprise.

"We have to get off this boat before Ahna is discovered. Three of us. In Minks."

Mikhail jerked his arm out of Casper's grasp and gave him a look of grudging measure. "We're a day away, at this pace. But the captain will want to know what happened to Gar and Gandy. He'll blame me. If he finds you, you won't live to see Minks at all."

"Then how can we get to the ground?"

Mikhail's eyes sharpened as he looked us over. "Parachutes, if you know where they are. The princess must be protected at all costs. Where is the third person?"

I looked to Casper and saw my own desperation mirrored. We two had been lucky, but what had become of Keen? The screaming above deck had stopped, and I could only hope that meant the girls had found a way to calm their new clients.

"I'll have to go look for her," Casper said.

"Don't go unarmed. You look enough like a woman from the back, and the pirates are animals."

Casper grimaced, and I scoffed. There was nothing remotely feminine about him, except possibly his hair, and even that was wilder than any woman's hair had a right to be. He stretched his shoulders and stooped to pluck a wicked machete off the big pirate.

"I had hoped I wouldn't ever have to find out how bad I am with a knife."

"Then hurry. Your only hope is to find your friend while the men are still busy with swiving."

"Where could she be? Where would she run?" I would have paced, but the already small room was cluttered with bodies, their stench rising in the tight space. My heart jolted with an uncomfortable tightness as I thought of Big Gar reaching for his pants. What would a man like him do to a tiny thing like Keen?

"Someone's coming," Mikhail said, and then I heard the boots pounding down the hall.

"C'mon, girly," a man shouted just outside, and Keen bolted into the room with a pirate grabbing for her jacket. With a casual flick of his arm, Mikhail drove a knife into the old man's belly.

Keen hid behind Casper, shivering and panting as another dead pirate fell to the ground.

"That's one problem solved, then," Mikhail said, absorbing Keen's appearance with ease, his head to one side.

"Pirates," Keen panted, eyes wide with terror.

"We were just leaving," I added, holding out my hand to her.

Much to my surprise, she actually came to me, nervous as a colt. I held her close as she shivered.

"What about the . . ." I gulped. I couldn't say it.

"Parachutes," Casper supplied.

I shot him a dark look.

"I know where they are. I can be there and back in a few minutes." With Keen returned, his attitude went from worried to confident, as if jumping off an airship was nothing. For once, I envied his recklessness.

He quickly stripped the long duster from Gandy's body and buckled it across his chest, before tucking his hair up under the dead pirate's disreputable-looking bowler. The coat was too small and tugged across the shoulders, but Casper looked piratical enough.

"As long as you don't talk to anyone and they don't look too closely, that should do," Mikhail said. "I'll keep the princess safe."

"Be sure that you do."

Casper looked at me, and the strangest feeling took me over. There was possession there, and concern, and warning, and I found myself stepping forward, saying, "It's fine. We'll be fine. Go."

Not until he was out the door did it occur to me to wish him luck.

Not until Mikhail turned to me, his smile wide and sharp and his eyes fever-bright, did it occur to me that we might not, in fact, be fine.

Mikhail turned to Keen where she sat on the bed. I went on alert as he reached into his coat, but he withdrew a fist, not a weapon. His arm snapped out, dusting Keen with powder, and he muttered, "Sleep, child."

Keen's eyes drooped closed, her head falling gently to the side and her mouth going slack. I hissed. Magic set my teeth on edge after Ravenna, but now I knew how Criminy Stain had arranged our private meeting in Dover.

Mikhail turned back to me, lit with energy and stepping too close. "You've nothing to fear from me, princess. I want the same thing you do."

"And what's that?"

"The safety of our people. The return of the land to her ancient rulers. A world free of *them,* except as cattle." He glared at Keen's sleeping form, so childlike and soft. His eyes shone feverishly when he looked at me, and I leaned back against the closet door, trying to get my bearings. In a heartbeat, he was on his knees, my bare hand clutched to his lips.

"My princess. My queen. The throne is yours for the taking. Come back with me to Freesia. Together we can gather the deposed barons, the forgotten sons, the dukes shivering in the forest. They'll rally to our cause, to *your* cause. My queen, we can take it back. We can make it better."

The message was more than welcome, and yet his words, his fervor, his magic repelled me. It was my mission, to be sure. Everything I'd done, from visiting the tasseinist to enlisting Casper and Keen to ignoring fear of heights and impropriety to board the *Maybuck,* had been in service to that goal. I had decided from the very first that nothing would stop me, that I would use every advantage to attain my throne.

And yet.

There was something in his disdain for Keen, something cruel behind his eyes, that twisted my stomach.

He was a zealot, and zealots were dangerous.

As gently as I could, I extricated my hand. Mikhail moved just a fraction of an inch, tilting his head in a way that was cold and calculating, like a snake I'd seen once at the zoo. He was all sharp lines and warning as he stood.

With great control, I pulled my lip back to expose a single fang and let out a soft hiss of warning.

"Is this not what you wish?" Hearing the threat in his words, I showed more fang.

"I have my own plans." I clutched the ring of succession where it rested, hidden in a pocket of my dress.

"Are they . . . soft plans?" He glanced at Keen, one eyebrow cutting upward. "Because Freesia is not a land of softness."

With a speed even he couldn't match, I slapped Mikhail hard across the face, my fingers curled just so. He held perfectly still, unflinching at the perfectly parallel cuts I'd left on his cheek. My mother had slapped me like that once, and I had worn the shame of it for a week before I'd been allowed to drink enough blood to heal it smoothly.

"It is not yours to choose what Freesia will be, little half-baron," I said in Sanguine, the words falling as heavy as icicles from my chilled lips. I could taste the sharp, sweet bite of the winter wind in every word, and he must have felt it, too. Mikhail dropped to his knees before me and kissed the hem of my dress, a display my mother had always enjoyed but that had always made me squirm.

"Your word, my life," he muttered, the traditional pledge of fealty, but it didn't feel as if his heart was in it.

He stood and inspected Keen with impersonal curiosity.

"How do you stand it, my queen? Trapped in these tight quarters with such tender prey. She smells as pure as the first snow. A delicacy. Have you tasted her?"

My stomach, so heavy with blood, rebelled at the thought of hurting Keen after what we'd been through together on the *Maybuck*.

"She's my servant. I forbid you to touch her."

"So exotic," he murmured, sniffing the air. "I wouldn't hurt her. I'll just have a taste. I would say you owe me, wouldn't you?" He gave a significant glance to the hulking corpse of Big Gar.

"Owe you?" I felt the anger rising, the beast and princess in me demanding his blud. But I heard my mother's voice in memory, reminding me that the best punishment was turning an enemy into a tool. "Very well. Allow me to repay you." I reached for the ring of succession, sliding it onto the correct finger. The fervor lit his eyes again when he looked on it, for the thing had a certain magic even for those who didn't know of its legend. "You want a true ruler? Give me your wrist."

He held out the same arm he'd shown me earlier, the one Ravenna had branded. Grasping his wrist in one hand, I pressed the ring firmly into Ravenna's mark, and Mikhail hissed as a cloud of cold steam rose from his skin.

"That is the Tsarina's Crest. You are sworn."

I pulled the ring away, and my first subject inspected his new sigil. Dark red patches marked the large center stone and the crown of topaz around it. Ravenna's brand had disappeared.

Mikhail's eyes shone with respect and awe, a correct and natural result of the ceremony.

"It's true, then," he breathed, and I nodded solemnly.

"You're a knight of the crown now. Betray me, and you buy your own death. But know that I'm taking Freesia back at the first snow."

"Your word, my life—my queen," he said again, more sure this time. "I am yours to command."

I smiled, cold and certain. "You always were."

"What first?"

"Get me off this ship. I can't be discovered. Where is Casper?"

Mikhail shrugged with a wry smile. "He is late."

I stared at him, silent and unblinking, until he bowed his head and said, "So it begins. I will find him for you or die trying."

He slipped out the door before I could respond. His quick acceptance of my rule was gratifying but strange. The enormity of taking control of my country from Ravenna started to sink in. Whether or not I wanted the heavy mantle of responsibility, seeking it was the only acceptable choice. And Mikhail had taught me that even those who professed to be on my side would need to be gathered, rallied, dominated, and commanded.

On the bed, Keen mumbled and yawned, sitting up and looking around in confusion. "What the hell?"

"We're about to go. If you have valuables, stow them."

Keen had to nudge Gandy aside to open the closet, but she must have seen enough of the pirates by then not to resent his fate. I knew where she hid her golden ball, but I didn't know what else she might have that she cared about.

Taking my own advice, I made sure that the ring, the necklace, and the mysterious paper packet from Criminy were all firmly lodged in my corset. I tightened the laces even further and checked the mirror and smoothed down my hair. By the time male laughter sounded in the hall, I had decided that there was nothing more I needed from the *Maybuck*.

Keen sidled into the blind corner behind the door, Kitty's knife in hand. Mikhail entered first, looking vexed. Behind him, Casper appeared with his arm around another man, a pirate and a stranger.

"What about pizza? And chicken wings?" the man said.

Casper laughed, an easy and mellow sound. "Oh, law. You could just pick up the phone, and they would deliver it to your door. With Coke and those little cheesy things and cinnamon bread. And what about TV game shows?"

"Jesus, man. I don't miss that a bit. My girlfriend loved that shi—" His eyes met my disapproving glare, and the man dropped his arm off Casper and nodded warily. "Ma'am."

His accent was even more golden and mellow than Casper's. He was smaller and older, with shaggy blond hair graying at the temples, his face leathery with sun except for white rings around his eyes that matched the shape of the goggles perched on his hat.

I nodded primly, and Casper said, "This is my niece, Anne. And that's Keen. Y'all—I mean, ladies—this is Teddy. He's from Almanica, too."

"Land of the free and home of the brave," Teddy said genially, pantomiming the tip of a hat without actually moving his hat.

"How long?" Keen asked anxiously, and Teddy answered, "Twenty years, little lady."

"Then you don't even know about Google, do you?"

"Goggles, yes. Googles, no. But I miss Def Leppard most of all."

Keen wrinkled her nose and said, "Lame."

The three of them all laughed together, and Mikhail and I shared a skeptical look. I had always heard that things were strange in the wild country across the ocean, but there was something definitely off about these Almanicans.

"Where?" Keen asked.

"San Antonio. You?"

"Raleigh."

"Then we're all from the right side of the Mason-Dixon, at least." Teddy held out his hand, and Keen shook it. Then they just all stood there like idiots, grinning.

"The parachutes?" I barked, and Keen rolled her eyes.

"My bad," Teddy said. He clapped Casper on the shoulder and went for the door. "Back in two shakes, friends."

"I don't approve." Mikhail sneered at the door. "That man is wrong."

"Lot of that going around," Keen said, returning Mikhail's sneer.

Casper chuckled to himself. "Oh, man. I thought I was a goner. I was grabbing the parachutes, and the door opened. I knew I was caught."

"Then what happened?" I asked.

He smiled, dimples and all. "Then he said 'y'all.'"

"I take it that's Almanican?"

"That's Southern."

Teddy barged in through the door with three large packs. Dumping them onto the floor at my feet, he said, "Good luck, y'all. I've got to skedaddle before the captain wonders where I got off to, but good luck with whatever you're up to." He looked pointedly at the parachutes. "I'd count to ten and start praying, folks."

Casper jerked him into a hug, and they beat each other on the back like brothers.

"Good to see you, man," Casper said. "It's been too long since I've seen a face from home."

Keen cleared her throat loudly, and Casper rumpled her hair affectionately.

"Not many make it," Teddy agreed, pumping Casper's

hand again. "At least you got her. I had a kid about that age. Samantha. She's grown by now, I guess. You're a lucky man." He dashed tears out of his eyes, rubbing the network of wrinkles at their corners tiredly. "Take care of that girl, you hear me?"

Casper put an arm around the shorter man's shoulders. "Be careful out there, Ted."

It was one of the longest good-byes I'd ever seen, and they had just met.

"Baseball. Harleys. Convertibles," Teddy said wistfully at the door.

"Movie theaters. Reese's Peanut Butter Cups," Casper answered.

"Cell phones and french fries and prom," Keen muttered, and Casper pulled her into a hug and said, "You would have hated it, kid," into the top of her head. She sniffled and hugged him back for just a second before pushing away from him and picking up one of the parachutes.

"Are you sure these things are functional?" I asked.

Casper wiped at his eyes. Without a word, he went to the closet and put on his leather traveling coat and his sturdiest top hat. He handed me one parachute and pulled the other one over his shoulders, tightening and buckling the straps across his chest.

"Too late to worry about that, darlin'. If it comes down to getting thrown off or jumping, I'll jump every time."

21

The last thing Mikhail said to me was, "We'll be ready."

All I could answer was, "Pray that you are," in Sanguine and hope that he wouldn't do anything rash in his fervor to serve me. And then he was gone, whispering with Teddy in unexpected camaraderie as they planned the disruption that would cover our escape.

We waited a few moments, nervous and alert in the doorway. A loud boom rocked the ship with a sickening lurch, followed by shouting. Casper held up a finger to his lips and ran. Keen followed, and I took the rear.

The straps of the parachute dug into my corset, the string that would open it bouncing against my stomach. I could taste the blood seeping up my throat, Big Gar and Gandy going sour in my belly. Getting onto the airship had taken every ounce of courage I possessed, but getting off of it was going to be exponentially worse.

The route Casper took was a familiar one, and I wasn't surprised when he led us into the library and locked the door from the inside.

As he unlatched the breast-shaped window, I groaned. "Please, not that."

"It's a big window off the back of the ship. It's the best

shot we have of getting out of here alive and not in chains. How much do you want to win?"

"Enough to jump through a nipple."

"Thought so."

He opened the window all the way, and a chill breeze rustled the pages of a book left open on the seat. I breathed in deeply, grateful to find no taste of salt on the air. With a sudden bout of inspiration, Casper took down a coiled rope, a long satin thing with tassels. I didn't really want to think about why it was resting on a shelf in the library, but he didn't offer me the chance to reject it. After stepping up onto the window seat, he helped me and Keen up and threaded the rope through the harness of first his parachute and then each of ours. He knotted the ends together and pulled it tight, forcing us into closer quarters than was comfortable or safe.

My nose was buried in his chest, and Keen's cheek was turned to my shoulder. Hunger trilled in the back of my throat, but I was still full enough of pirate blood that being so near didn't send me into a frenzy.

"Is this really necessary?" With every word, I took in a lungful of Keen's young, innocent edibility and Casper's scent, masculine and spiced with sweat.

"Seriously," Keen said, her voice muffled by my shoulder. "She smells like hot pennies."

"If we get separated in the forest, you'll think it's pretty necessary," he said.

For a moment, we simply stood there, breathing fresh air and feeling the slight, sucking breeze. It was early morning, the clouds a sickly purple rimmed with red. At least it wasn't raining.

"On three?" Casper asked.

"What?"

But he'd already leaned backward out the round window, curling his arms around us like a shield and carrying us with him into the emptiness of the sky. My mouth opened in a scream as we tumbled, weightless, but Casper's hand sealed my lips, and the sound died. Everything was happening both too quickly and with infinite slowness as the wind rushed around us. Up and down had no meaning, and my heart thumped against my corset. I fought to keep the blood down and the scream in and the tears at bay. We spun, and I caught a brief glimpse of the airship, her bronze balloon reflecting the morning sun with a fierce vengeance. The reclining woman on the gondola, which I now recognized as an optimistic portrayal of Miss May, seemed to be winking at me upside down.

And then Casper was laughing, and despite my terror and fear and utter confusion, I managed to glare at him. His face gave me something to focus on, as opposed to the nothingness of the sky, and the manic joy and wonder I saw there was startling.

"Woooooooohooooo!" he yelled, throwing his arms into the air. After a moment, Keen followed suit.

"Aren't we supposed to pull the string and not die?" I shouted.

"Hold on, baby! It's gonna be a bumpy ride!"

I clutched the front of his jacket with one hand, curling my head against his chest and trying to prepare myself for something for which one couldn't really prepare.

"One . . . two . . . three!"

I pulled my string and nearly bit my tongue off as our bodies jolted against the tight straps of the parachutes. When I dared to pull my face away and look up, I saw two white pillows poofed out against the violet clouds.

"Casper! It didn't go! Mine didn't go!"

Keen pulled frantically at the string, but her pack was still contained. Although we'd slowed down a great deal, it felt as if we were moving too fast. With an ominous creak, the silky rope lashing us together slipped a few inches, and Keen grabbed Casper's coat and my sleeve in a death grip.

Casper looked down, his face going ashen. "Just hold on, girl," he said. "Keen, look at me. Hold on. You can do this. You've done worse. We're going to get through it."

The rope creaked again, a few more inches sneaking out past Casper's careful knot. Keen screamed and clawed at us as if she could climb our bodies and get to a safer place. Casper wrapped both arms around her waist and held her close with visible effort, the sweat starting to bead up on his forehead.

I looked down. A sea of dark green trees rose to meet us, fast and furious. Crows exploded from the pines just below us, their feathers left to drift in the air. One floated past my face, and I reached up in wonder to grab it, but we were falling too swiftly, and I knew it.

"Ahna!"

I looked up, startled out of my reverie by the urgency of Casper's voice.

"You can take the most damage. Can you slow our fall somehow? I have to hold Keen."

The words ripped past my ears, stolen by the wind. I looked down, flexing my toes. There wasn't much time before we tumbled into the trees. From high up, they had looked like moss or the cover on a bed, but as we got closer, the danger was thrown in stark relief. Sharp black branches, broken and ragged, reached toward us. It was so surreal, the falling, that I had forgotten to be afraid. But he was right—my body was much harder to injure and easier to heal than theirs were. My fear of heights was considered unusual among Bludmen.

"I don't know—" I started, and he edged an arm up around Keen's ears and shouted, "Then figure it out!"

I tugged at the rope lashing us together, but it refused to slip any farther. With a sigh of frustration, I felt around the inside of Casper's coat. He twitched away at first, but he understood as soon as my fingers wrapped around the hilt of the knife on his belt. I pulled it out, yelled, "Hold her!" and slit the slender cord with one upward thrust.

Keen squealed as her body jerked downward, but Casper caught her up. I quickly handed myself down, crawling along his body until my arms were wrapped around his knees and my skirts were free and billowing upward. The trees were mere seconds away as I aimed for a sturdy-looking branch and braced myself for impact.

My boots struck wood, the shock reverberating throughout my body. I tried to buffer Casper and Keen with my arms and save them the worst of the hit. They knocked me sideways, and my heels skidded off the bark, and we were falling again, Keen's scream heavy in my ears. I fell into a trunk sideways, smashed in by Casper, and then we all tumbled downward in a confusing, bruising jumble of parachute strings, leather, and limbs.

I hit the ground first. Someone's foot found my head, and I slumped over gratefully into the dew-wet pine scree. It was an old forest with a thick floor of needles, and I sank in, breathing the sharp sap and rich black dirt. It wasn't my home, but it was close enough.

Groaning and grunting, Casper and Keen rolled off my aching, battered body. Keen bolted off into the forest, her parachute unopened on her back, calling "Bathroom!" over her shoulder. Casper and I were tangled together, my parachute caught in the trees and his flopped low on the ground. He gently unwound my fingers from the knife I still held, forgotten, in a white-knuckle grip. Thank Aztarte I hadn't cut anyone on the way down.

But wait. I smelled it. Casper's blood, on the knife and beading a small slash in the thigh of his pants. I leaned toward him, avid, mouth open, already imagining the hot press of it on my tongue. Fear always made me hungry afterward.

"Ahna." The words were loaded with exhaustion and warning.

"I only need a little." I swallowed, feeling desperate. "You're already losing the blood. You might as well put it to good use."

He flopped onto his back, slicing the parachute off his chest. "Fine. I don't care anymore. No teeth."

Still caught by my chute, I had enough room to kneel and shift his leather coat aside, settling my mouth over the slice in his breeches. It wasn't bad or deep, just a graze. But blood was blood, and I gently pressed the wound open and ran my tongue along it. He twitched and moaned, and I savored the strange taste of his blood. At first, the smell had repelled me, but now it called to me, an acquired taste.

"Jesus Christ on the cross!" Keen shouted.

She stood, half behind a tree, her face frozen in disgust and hatred and her shirt speckled with vomit.

"Enough of the act, Keen," Casper said tiredly without sitting up. "You know very well how things are headed for me, even if you try to ignore it. This isn't the most horrible thing you've seen this week, and it's bound to get a lot worse. She needs to eat if we're going to get her home."

"Screw getting her home! Screw things getting worse!

I don't even know why we're doing this. It's a suicide mission. You've lasted this long. Don't give in now."

"You're out of line." He rubbed his eyes in that way he had, when he was tired of thinking. "Nobody made you come along. I gave you a choice, and you made it."

She stomped, but her foot just sank into the needles. "I didn't think you were serious. I didn't think you'd actually see it through. I didn't think you'd let her . . . let her drink from you like a fricking Renfield!"

"This ain't a movie, kid. This is life or death. She's not Dracula; she's just a lost girl. We've still got to get through the forest, into Minks, and onto a train. If letting Ahna drink from an already open wound will give us a leg up, I'll take it."

She looked at my hands pressing around his thigh, and we all suddenly noticed the effect it was having on his body. I jerked back. He sat up and flipped his coat over his lap, but she was already stomping into the forest, muttering to herself, her breath hitching.

"You like it, you asshole. You're just like the rest of them. You effing like it!"

I sat back on my heels and wiped my lips on the back of my hand. His blood didn't drive me to a frenzy, but seeing it and smelling it had temporarily clouded my judgment. I was mortified, not that I had drunk from him but that I had done so from such a tender, personal place on his body.

"I didn't mean to . . ." I trailed off. There was no good way to end that sentence.

Casper scooted back, settling against a tree trunk. The morning sun backlit him, limning his hair like liquid gold. "Can you keep a secret?"

It was the last thing I had imagined him saying, and I

managed to shrug. "Whom would I tell? You know my secret, and you've kept it well enough."

"Keen and I aren't from Almanica." He took a deep breath and gazed into the branches overhead. "We're Strangers, and we're from America, which is like Almanica in another world."

I snorted and shook my head. "Did you hit your head on the way down? That's not a secret; it's a myth."

He smiled, all dimples and madness. "Let's look at the facts. I know things you can't know. I can play songs you've never heard of, things way more complicated than anything I could ever compose." He held out his arm and rolled up the sleeve to show me the black mark I remembered on his forearm. A raven holding a key.

"I have a tattoo. You ever seen a Pinky who would let a needle pierce his skin again and again and then walk around with an open wound for a week? Did you know what I was talking about with Teddy and Keen? This is not the world I was born in, darlin', and it ain't been kind to me."

I stared at the mark on his arm. It was true—I'd never seen anything like it except in pictures of Bludmen from exotic lands. When he held out his earlobe and wiggled it back and forth, showing a tiny hole, I just shook my head.

"Why are you telling me this?" I finally asked.

"Because I need you to understand Keen. She's a Stranger, too. I found her in London, living on the streets, eating trash and bludrats and singing for coins. She's got a decent enough voice, but she didn't remember all the words to 'Yellow Submarine,' so I started singing, too. I took her under my wing. I was already in a downward spiral by then, but I hid my life from her. I had gotten too deep into the bludwine, but no one ever told me that it would take me over, drive me mad. I kept her safe and fed but always held her at arm's length, because I knew one day I'd either die or get bludded. I'm realizing now that I did her a disservice. I never really saw her as she was; I just saw a helpless kid from my homeland. And now she's doing what all teenagers do in America—she's rebelling."

"That's what teenagers do in Freesia, too," I said, cocking my head as I studied him. There were certain things about him that had always seemed foreign and exotic. The shade of his skin, the shape of his face. His strange accent, which he was using now instead of the cultured, clipped tones of Sangland. Could he really be from another world? Of course, I'd heard stories of Strangers, who supposedly showed up out of nowhere, naked and helpless. But they weren't as common in Freesia as they were in Sangland, and I'd never actually seen one. What Strangers were to us, unicorns were to them—charming tales that were nothing like the reality, apparently.

"So she's rebelling. So she doesn't like me. So what?"

"It's not just you. It's me. I've mostly kept it from her, the fact that I'm a halfblud and starting to suffer from it. I've hidden the bludwine, kept her from following me when I went to Darkside to buy vials of blud or have my own drawn in exchange. Whenever I've been close to going into a rage, I've locked myself in my room and gotten drunk. Only now that we've been forced into that tiny cabin on the ship and since she talked to the other girls on the *Maybuck* has she realized what it means."

"What does it mean?"

"You know what it means. You heard Cora. It means that soon I'll either have to be bludded or go mad."

I snorted and flicked my fingers. "And that's so bad?"

"Imagine it. You wake up naked in another world where everything is different. You're just a kid, you're scared, you're almost eaten by giant red rats. You manage to cobble together a life on the streets, just this side of starvation, and then a rich and glamorous countryman takes you under his wing, becomes your only attachment to the life you loved. And then that person grows distant, dangerous, unpredictable. Starts making bad decisions, choices that feel like betrayals. What does that kid have in the entire world but me? And again and again, I've chosen blud over her, shoved her aside, given her the bare minimum."

He drove a fist into the soft ground. When he knocked his hat back and ran a hand through his hair, he left clods of dirt and leaf mold among the sweat-streaked copper.

"And now?" My voice trembled.

"In my daydreams, she found a place in your magnificent castle. She had her own room, fine clothes, healthy food. I made her so happy that she didn't need me anymore. And that's the worst betrayal of all."

"Wanting to take care of someone, wanting the best for them, isn't a betrayal."

He was across the space in seconds, so close I could see his eyes jumping madly. "Ahna, I don't want the best for her. I want the best for me."

"And what's wrong with that?"

"I owe her. Don't you see? She's my responsibility. I don't know how to keep her safe without giving up my own needs, and I'm no longer willing to make that trade." He reached into his coat and pulled out the feather I'd found in the box under his bed. It felt like a lifetime ago, and the princess scrabbling cheerfully and viciously for a stranger's treasures had been invariably altered.

"This feather. It fell off a turban. A fortune-teller's turban in a caravan. She was a Stranger, too, and I thought I loved her. I thought she was going to save me."

"And she betrayed you."

"She chose a Bludman over me, took the fortune she saw when she held his hand. I know there was something more than what she told me. I saw her face, and I know she held something back." He stroked the feather back and forth over my hand as if painting a secret message there. "'Your loss will be your salvation,' she told me. Well, I lost her, and it didn't save me. I lost my riches and fame, and it didn't save me. So what's the next loss? Keen? My humanity? My mind?" He stared straight into my eyes, and I swallowed at his bald desperation. "Is it you?"

I looked down, taking the feather from him and twirling it back and forth between my fingers. "My mother once told me that fortune-tellers see what they want to see and tell what they want to tell." I watched the feather, considering how very carefully I had to choose my next words. "I was always told that the fortune I chose for myself was the truest one."

"And what fortune did you choose after that?"

"That I wouldn't be forced into doing anything ever again."

"Yet here you are. Are we all just victims, then, Ahna? Just puppets?"

I stood and shook my head defiantly, letting pine bits flutter to the earth. "Only if we allow ourselves to become so. I choose to meet life as a powerful conquerer. Nothing will ever take command of me again."

"But what if—"

A scream cut through the woods, silencing us both.

22

Casper was up and running beside me faster than I would have expected him to move. He must have been right about becoming more like a Bludman and less like a Pinky. After a few short steps, the strings of my chute trapped me like a spider in a web, and I howled in animal frustration, ripping through the heavy lines with my teeth and pounding through the trees in Casper's wake.

The forest was thick and heavy, old and cold. I dashed through the branches, flinging them out of my way in pieces when necessary. I threw out my senses but didn't hear Keen. The scream—it hadn't actually sounded like her. The scent of bludbears clung to the earth and trees, but that was expected. This part of the country was known for the shaggy monsters, which grew large and lazy on bludlemmings and the foolish pioneers perpetually tromping into the woods, expecting to make new Pinky cities outside the harsh blud rule of Minks and Muscovy. But bludbears weren't the problem. Something else was wrong. The forest was too quiet.

Another scream echoed through the air, and I put on a burst of speed as I recognized its source. I had to hurry, before they lured her closer.

Scrabbling under branches and past fans of sharp green needles, I let the beast go free, abandoning all pretense of royalty. In a fierce gallop, I caught up with Casper and pulled ahead, my nose aimed straight for Keen.

We burst into a small clearing, the sort of green-lit hollow my mother had called a fairy dun. Keen stood there, a look of wonder and joy on her face. Her hand stretched out toward a magnificent peacock, a male in full splendor. His tail was set wide, shivering back and forth and throwing sunlight off the vibrant feathers. His head cocked to the side as he danced closer to her, and she laughed.

Looking beyond her into the forest, I saw what I feared: the red spark of an eye.

"Drag her into the underbrush," I whispered to Casper. "Have your knife ready."

"What?"

But I had already launched myself across the clearing, darting past Keen and diving into the shadows of the forest. The creature had already seen me and wheeled to escape, but I dug my talons into its flanks and ripped a gash in the dingy white fur of its rump.

Fear for Keen melted into fierce joy. I had always loved unicorn blood.

The beast bucked, trying to throw me off and keep me from tearing the wound bigger. Without weapons or hunting partners, I couldn't take it down, but I held on as long as I could. I would teach this creature to tangle with virgins.

As I lapped up as much blood as I could, feeling it shift into my throat like sunshine, the unicorn snorted and squealed, its hooves knocking against the ground and trees as it tried to fight me off. Somewhere far away, the peacock screamed again and again, warning the unicorn that danger was near. Its pure call finally ended in a gurgle and silence, the scavenger dying before its master.

Spinning on two hooves, the unicorn tried to skewer me, but I dodged its gnarled horn easily and leaped away, sliding behind a thick tree. I licked my lips, sated, as the unicorn blew air through its lips and galloped off into the forest. Its blood spread through me, leaving me warm and satisfied like nothing else.

"Ahna!" Casper called, his voice high and frantic.

"I'm here!" I struggled to compose myself and tried not to skip on my way back to the clearing.

I saw Keen first; she was trembling, eyes huge, with rips down her sleeves. Her arms were wrapped around her skinny middle as she breathed through her nose like a spooked bludmare. The peacock lay battered and bloody on the ground, and Casper soon appeared from between the trees with a dead pirate's machete in his hand. He dropped it when he saw me.

"Ahna. Thank God. Are you hurt?" He rushed to take my shoulders in firm hands as he checked me up and down. With unicorn blood in my belly, it was hard not to giggle at his unnecessary concern.

"I saw it," Keen said, barely an awed whisper. "The unicorn."

Casper gazed down at me in confusion. "A unicorn?"

I shrugged. "He won't be back. Let's go."

"So they're real?" Keen breathed.

I snorted. "They're just animals. Big, bloodthirsty monsters. But animals. Welcome to my world." Seeing their dropped jaws and the mist of magic still swirling in Keen's eyes, I sighed. "Unicorns aren't magical and beautiful. They're just predatory horses that have horns and love to eat virgins." Casper pointed at the peacock carcass and raised his eyebrows, and I nodded. "Unicorns and peacocks work together. The peacocks are bludded scavengers that scout for prey. While the peacock dances, the unicorn is sneaking up behind you to run you through with his horn. And then they gorge and drag your carcass home to their harems."

"This place," Keen said slowly, shaking her head, "is wack."

Casper knelt to run a finger along the peacock's sharp beak.

"Jesus. It's like one big tooth."

I grinned. "They're the only bludded birds in all of Sang, and they originate in Freesia. The Mad Tsar bludded them centuries ago, and they escaped the Ice Palace and managed to breed in the wild. No one knows the source of their partnership with the unicorns. An elegant friendship, don't you think?"

I reached down to pluck a plume from the dead peacock's tail and stuck it through the band of Casper's hat. It didn't escape me that we'd dropped his old feather in the forest when we heard the peacock's scream. A jay called, and another bird answered, and then the forest finally came back to life, with the unicorn out of range.

"I can't believe I was almost eaten by a unicorn," Keen muttered. She shook her head as if the magic had finally fled, and her hands went to her pockets. "Donatello! He's gone."

She fell to her knees and rustled through the leaf litter, and Casper gave me a pained look.

"That gold ball she's always playing with. It's . . . the

only thing she really cares about, but she won't tell me why."

"I'm right here, asshole, and I'm not deaf. I'm not leaving until we find him."

I spun slowly in a circle, breathing deep until I caught a scent that stood out from the ancient greenery and earth. I followed the metallic tang and dug around in the forest floor near the peacock until I found it—the brass sphere I'd seen Keen playing with again and again. I turned, holding it out to her, and her face lit up with that brilliant smile.

"Donatello!" She snatched it from me and nuzzled it.

"What is that thing?" I asked, trying to rub the oily scent of clockwork off on my skirt.

Keen held the sphere up to the light with a radiant grin. "I guess we're far enough away now that I can show y'all. Not like anyone in London is ever going to find me, right?"

Casper shrugged, and I watched her little fingers reach in to turn a nearly invisible brass switch. The sphere opened up smoothly, the parts unfolding and twisting until a brass tortoise sat on her hand with the subtle whisper of ticking gears.

"I get it," Casper said, stepping closer with a smile. "Teenage Mutant Ninja Turtles."

"It's actually a tortoise," I started, and she cut me off.

"Shut up. There's no cool names for tortoises."

"So when did you pickpocket that little gem?" Casper asked.

"Nicked him from Sweeting," she said with a shrug. "He owed me."

Casper groaned and rubbed his eyes. "You're suicidal, girl."

"Whatever. You're the one who just yanked me out of a window with a broken parachute."

With things somewhat back to normal, I scanned our surroundings, but the forest all looked the same to me. Although I had been taught to hunt, no one had ever bothered to teach me how to survive outside of the Ice Palace and its grounds. I knew geography but not how to navigate. My entire life had been meant to unfold in the halls of grand castles.

"We need to get to Minks," I said. "Then we can take the train directly into Muscovy."

"And then?" Keen's attitude and accent were back, and I tried to hide my smile.

"And then we find an old acquaintance of mine and decide the best way to approach the palace."

"But if you're in disguise and we have no money, how do you think we're going to get on the train? They don't need famous pianists to drive a steam engine," Casper said with a bitter shake of his leaf-strewn hair.

The cold, manipulative smile curled across my features, familiar and welcome. It felt good, having some power again. Surprising someone. Showing my cunning.

"I've been keeping a little secret of my own," I said.

23

With a wink, I plunged a hand down the front of my corset to draw out the necklace I'd been carrying, warm and heavy, since London. The silver links were tarnished, but the stones danced in the dappled light of morning. The birds went still in the trees, and I imagined their wise and hungry eyes captured by the glittering diamonds and topazes that so resembled the heart of the glacier that was rumored to have spat it forth like the will of the ice gods.

"Where the hell did you get that?"

"Shut your mouth before a crow flies in, darling. It's a necklace." I smiled, showing Keen the sharpness of my fangs. It was gratifying, giving her yet another reminder that while I'd been tame enough on the ship, we were in my world now.

"How long have you had that?" Casper asked quietly.

"I pulled it out of the suitcase on the way to Reve's."

"And when were you going to tell us?"

"When I had to."

In a flash, he was across the clearing and in my face, lips pulled back and exposed teeth mirroring mine. "All this time. All these stupid risks. We could have bought our berth on a safer ship. We could have kept Keen away from those lechers and you away from danger and me . . ." He ran a hand through his hair, and I noticed that his nails were sharp and going narrow. "Dammit, Ahna! I sold my harpsichord for you. I played an out-of-tune box on a ship while old men nailed whores beside me on the bench. You could have fixed it with one damn stone off your fancy-ass necklace."

"It was a last resort," I said through gritted teeth.

"Maybe for you." One finger poked me in the chest, right over my heart. "Maybe the rest of us already gave everything we had. You wouldn't be here without us. And you've never apologized for any of it. Not once."

"I . . ."

I faltered. What could I say to that? He was right, of course. Part of me wanted to screech at him, the spoiled princess so sure of herself and her place. The necklace was mine, my birthright. What was the point of risking it before absolutely necessary? And wasn't it the saving grace now, the one sure thing we had left? And who was he to judge me? Every step toward Minks, whichever direction it was, was a step further into my world and closer to the country I planned to rule.

And yet.

I shifted uncomfortably. In my hand, the necklace was too heavy, and I let my arm drop to my side. Without really meaning to, I let the chain slip from my fingers to dangle in the air above the ground.

Dear Aztarte. This feeling. This awful, heavy, suffocating feeling. This sensation that made me want to run, to hide, to crawl away. Could it be . . . guilt?

"I'm sorry." The unfamiliar words tasted heavy in my mouth.

"Sorry doesn't begin to cover it," Casper said.

I held up my hands with a bitter laugh, one harsh note. "I'll only say it once. Look around you, Casper. We're in a forest, surrounded by hidden enemies, creatures of blud and monsters on two feet. We can't tarry here. We must march, my darling. To Muscovy and to Ravenna's blud. The faster the better."

He stilled, as he sometimes did, as if gears were turning in his head. "How do you do that?" he muttered. "Just when I think I'm going to tell you off, you go and say something extraordinary."

I could read him now. The way he was rubbing his eyes, his sigh. I was winning him over, so I pressed harder. "What's done is done. We have what we need now. Can we just put all that behind us and start from here?" I pulled the necklace back up and let it run through my fingers, the big stones catching the sun and sending sparkles over the tree trunks. "I bet one of the little stones could get us separate sleeping cars on the train to Muscovy."

Keen watched, her eyes gone sharp. I could almost see her tallying figures as she thought of what even the daintiest gems could buy for us now. Here in the forest, surrounded by giant trees and bloodthirsty unicorns, we were still closer than we'd ever been to our main goal.

"I get my own room, a new shirt, and all the hot food I can eat," she finally said. "And when you're the queen, I get a pony."

"Deal." I held out my hand and was glad when she shook it without wincing.

Before I knew what had happened, Casper had swept us both into a tight, messy hug. The swoop in my heart wasn't all that different from the one I'd felt the last time we'd been this close—when we'd jumped out of a moving airship. I realized he had let go of Keen and was hugging me even closer. I surged toward the crush of skin, the press of cloth, and a mouthful of his unruly hair.

"Are you guys done?" Keen asked, voice flat.

I pulled away, breathless. My eyes met Casper's, and I could sense his response, so similar to mine, in the dancing fire of his blue eyes. We were on the ground, we were alive, and we were on the road to victory.

"Let's go, then," I said, turning to hide the blush in my cheeks. I supposed that meant I was forgiven, and my heart felt oddly lighter for it.

Casper took the lead, and we hurried to match his stride.

"I saw Minks when we were in the air, and I'm pretty sure we can make it there in a couple of hours."

I looked from tree to identical tree. "How can you possibly know where it is? Where we are?"

"I'm not completely incompetent, you know." He held up a compass with a grin.

"There go my dreams of wandering the woods until you and Keen collapse from exhaustion so I could drain you without complaint." I tried to put some of my old viciousness into the words, but even I could hear that I'd failed. It was strange, liking Pinkies for reasons other than the availability of their blood. I hoped the train and our arrival in Muscovy would reignite the predator within. This soft, this easily affected, I'd never be able to face off with Ravenna and survive.

"Cheer up, princess. There are worse things than not eating your friends."

He nudged my shoulder with a dimpled grin, keeping pace with me as we wove among the old trees. Keen had disappeared from sight, but I could still smell her, lingering behind us. The unicorn fight and its heady blood had worn off, and I was on edge. It made me excited but nervous, being near the blud world and my people. I couldn't help getting in at least a little bit of teeth.

"Do you two have any idea what we're walking into? Minks and then Muscovy?"

"I've seen all of Sangland, a bit of Franchia, and the big cities of the mainland. But never this far east."

The low chuckle I gave then was meant to warn. "In Sangland, there's balance between Bludman and human. In Franchia and the mainland, the daimons keep things light and playful. But over here, once things get cold . . . you'll be nothing more than at best a servant and at worst a midnight snack. Outside the palace, your kind has less footing than pet hounds. Staying on my good side is your only hope for getting out of here alive."

"But won't it help that I'm a halfblud?"

"You're an abomination. They'll want to murder you in ugly ways before they eat you. Out of spite."

"And Keen?"

"She's an appetizer. Hardly enough for two to share. But that won't stop them."

I could feel the anger rising in him, smell the heat of his blood boiling. I smiled. Finally, he was taking me seriously.

"Funny that you failed to mention any of these circumstances when we were planning this trip," he said. "Never once did you say, 'Oh, hey, by the way? You're going into a very dangerous country where unicorns will stab you and barons will suck your blood.'"

"You never asked. And you never requested permission to bring Keen along. She wasn't part of the deal, you know. Besides, I assumed that everyone has had lessons in history and geography."

"Yeah, but my lessons were on Russia and the USSR," he growled.

I caught the smell of meat and spun around. Keen ambled behind us on the trail, chewing on a shred of dried animal flesh.

"Put that away. The smell carries."

She grinned, bits of brown stuff stuck in her teeth. "Can't you just kill anything that comes after us? Even the unicorn was scared of you."

I snatched the meat out of her hand and stuffed it into her jacket with a stern look. There was so much that these two soft little Pinkies didn't know about my world, and I wanted them to come out on the other side mostly alive.

"We need to get out of the forest and into the city in time to catch the train at dusk. Fighting bludbears takes up valuable time. That food of yours reeks."

"And what if we don't make it by nightfall?" Casper asked.

"Then *you* won't make it," I answered. "Something worse than unicorns will find us, if we don't freeze to death first. This is an unforgiving land."

Casper took the lead of our party, checking the compass every so often. There were no paths, just thick trees that barely let in golden fingers of sunshine. Keen was already shivering, and it wasn't even noon yet by my counting. I was grateful for my natural resistance to cold, and I supposed Casper felt something similar, as he shrugged out of his big coat and wrapped it around her.

She was far too short, and the hem scraped the ground, but at least she stopped trembling and throwing off more scent than was necessary.

We didn't speak much, and I was grateful for the silence. Noise would draw undue attention, and I was too confused in my own feelings to stay alert to our surroundings. I couldn't get over Casper's admission about the fairy-tale land from which they had come. Could it be true that there were other worlds than Sang? That Casper wasn't just a debauched musician and a halfblud fallen to ruin but also a traveler from another world entirely? I was growing used to the idea. My curiosity was piqued by the thought that he could be something more than he seemed. I had been taught to look for value in others only as related to politics, court intrigue, and the price of a throne or a favor. Liking him was the worst kind of rebellion.

I grinned to myself. I'd always liked rebellion.

We trudged along for hours. For the longest time, nothing changed. The same trees, the same brief snatches of sky or patches of brittle brown grass. Whatever blud creatures might have been hiding scented me and took off, and I grinned whenever I heard branches breaking or hooves pounding through the woods ahead of us. The animals of the forest knew well enough when a bigger predator was about, and I basked in the return of myself. I was born to be dangerous, to rule, and holding myself in check on the airship had cost me deeply.

I smelled the tundra before I saw it, the thick, syrupy sting of the pines interwoven with the faintest breath of frosted, faded grasses and wild winds. I sighed and smiled. That same scent clung to the Ice Palace, where we held the forest at bay with wide fields that would leave our enemies exposed should they ever attempt to come for us. There was very little that could threaten me in a field.

Not so for Casper and Keen. They huddled closer together, looking all around as if unicorns might burst from the knee-high grasses and spear them through. Casper looked back at me once, but seeing the grin of avid triumph and confidence on my face, he seemed reassured that I could take care of myself.

He checked his compass again and again, slightly correcting our path. Not that we needed it, not really. I could already smell Minks, a grand city spread out over an old river heavy with ice and majesty. Unlike the crowded filth and tumbling randomness of London, Minks was a Blud city ruled with careful planning, beauty, and thoughtful regard for the needs of Bludmen. I remembered seeing drawings of the broad parks, the statuary gardens, and the grand church of Aztarte, which rose, airy and beautiful, to settle over the city like the wings of a grand black swan. Provided I could successfully sell some of the stones from my necklace, life would get much easier and more comfortable quite soon.

A low grumble drew our attention to a conveyance rumbling down a wide dirt road, a plume of grayish-green smoke in its wake. Casper threw an arm across Keen in an entirely useless gesture of protection, and I pushed past them both, saying only, "Follow my lead. We're on dangerous ground here."

I changed our angle and sped up, aiming for just the right place to meet the slowly trundling wagon, its bed piled high with green things from the Pinky farms. When I planted myself in the road, one black-scaled hand held out, talons splayed, I was gratified to see the machine slow and roll to a stop almost close enough for me to touch.

We were in luck. A wary Pinky sat in the contained driver's cabin, and I grinned wickedly when I saw him check the lock on his door. Bludmen had no need of vegetables and other Pinky foodstuffs, other than to keep our food source as healthy and robust as possible. It was a common practice, using humans to tend our farms according to carefully drawn plans by their superiors. This wagon would be headed straight to Minks.

"Mistress, I am at your service, but please forgive me. I am on a timetable," the man said through a speaker, his voice tinny and heavily accented with the broad strokes of the country.

Raising my voice and injecting it with the proper amount of authority, I mimicked his accent. "I and my servants will require conveyance to the city proper."

"The back is filled with cabbages, but you are more than welcome to ride there," the man said. I could hear the fear in his voice; the country Pinkies never really felt safe around their masters. Even though it was at my command, he was aghast at offering a highly placed Bludwoman a seat among rotting foodstuffs.

"That will suffice," I said with a firm nod, and the conveyance chugged in place as we walked around back. The smell nearly gagged me, as my sensitive nose could detect the moment a plant stopped living and began dying, and all of his cabbages were dying. Casper helped me up, gave Keen a boost, and leaped up to sit on the edge, his legs dangling over the metal lip. I knocked a fist on the metal, and with a belch of green smoke, the conveyance scraped and scuttled toward the city on treads much like those of the bank we'd taken to Dover. A short ride later, the wagon stopped at the city gates, where we slid from the truck and waited our turn in the road.

"Get behind me, and look properly awed," I hissed, and Casper and Keen obeyed.

They had probably never seen a Blud city, and it was made to impress. The shining white wall was well maintained, the guards friendly and obsequious when they saw my hands. They bowed me through the gates and kindly gave directions to the train station without asking a single question about my name or plans. A Bludwoman didn't need papers to enter, and neither did her chosen servants. It was so very unlike the cities of Sangland, and I was glad to have my feet firmly on carefully bricked roads, surrounded by smiling faces and polite nods.

As we moved into the city, Keen sidled close, skittish and wild, saying, "Want me to sell a stone? I know my way around a city's back streets, no mistake."

"This isn't London, darling," I said, patting her on the head and making her scowl. "I'm the only one with whom anyone here will do business. You they'd probably kill on principle."

She was right, though—we did have to sell a few stones if we wanted to get on the train. I could see the station a few streets over, the façade shining like sunlight on snow. I pulled the necklace back out of my corset and used my pinkie talon to pry out a smaller stone, a diamond. It hurt my heart to see the setting empty, the prongs clutching for riches lost, but I could always have it fixed if I succeeded. If I didn't succeed, a faulty necklace would be the least of my problems, as I would most likely be without a neck to hang it on.

I pried out two more stones for good measure, leaving twelve behind. Jiggling them in my hand like the bone dice the Pinkies used for their betting games, I scanned the street for the right sort of place before remembering that I didn't have to hide anymore.

"Pardon me," I said, approaching a dapper old Bludman on the street, "but could you be so kind as to point me toward a jewelry shop?" After a polite but curious look askance, he bowed and sent us to a reputable dealer who offered me a fine price with no questions asked.

When I stopped outside a dressmaker's shop, Casper sighed and Keen snorted. "Stopping to get gussied up, eh? Figures."

"I don't know if you've noticed, but my people would never be caught dead in such a get-up." I brushed hands down my skirt, ragged now with pine sap and blood droplets. "The object is to blend in, and as it stands, I'm attracting undue attention. Oh, and put up that clockwork before someone sees it and drains you for theft. I'll just be a moment."

With that, I slipped into the store and shut the door in Keen's surprised face. If she thought I was being cruel and haughty now, it was going to get a lot worse. Let her stew on the sidewalk for a while, awaiting her mistress like a dog tied to a post. Casper was silent and stoic, facing some interior struggle that I couldn't comprehend.

When I walked back outside a half hour later, I handed Keen a paper-wrapped package and couldn't help curtsying to Casper. Even with my hair still short and mousy, I knew well enough that I was back in my element. The fashionable gown of subdued rose was as splashy as I could risk, not too bright but just bright enough, and had luckily fit with no alterations. I had also purchased a hat with a discreet veil, but even hidden, I felt more like Princess Ahnastasia than I had since that long-ago ill-fated day by the fountain behind the castle.

Casper had rebuckled his top hat and dusted off his coat, and he almost looked genteel for a Pinky. Still, there was something wild about his eyes that made me peer close. He was right on the edge of something, alert and frantic but trying to hide it. I put the back of my hand to his cheek and found it strikingly hot.

"Are you well?" I murmured.

He leaned closer, much closer than a Pinky servant was allowed. "I've gone too long without blud." He licked his lips nervously, his eyes darting about the everyday bustle of the orderly street. "It's getting to me. I can smell them."

"Where's your bottle?"

"Gone."

Something would have to be done, and soon, if blud madness was anything like blood madness. Misbehavior wasn't tolerated in Blud cities, and he could get us all in trouble if his beast rose to the surface.

"Can you make it to the train?"

"You'll have to lock me in when we get there, I think. I'm losing it."

"Welcome to my world," I whispered.

24

After placing my train ticket on the bedside table, I held my arms out wide and flopped backward onto the bed. It billowed underneath me like a cloud, and I rolled around and giggled. The most expensive cars had been booked in advance, but I couldn't summon a single complaint about this room, purchased with the proceeds of one stone with plenty left over. The bed was my own, soft and luxurious. Two vials were soon to be delivered by the carhop, and all was well with the world for the next sixteen hours. Once we arrived in Muscovy, things were bound to get more complicated, but I would relish comfort for as long as I could.

Keen and Casper had to share a tiny servants' room with two bunks, unfortunately. We had barely made it to the station in time, and it was either that or the common car, which was impossible. Without my presence, they would have been gobbled up by the general populace in mere moments. Keen had been furious, but it wasn't as if they would have allowed her to enjoy a Bludman's room, anyway. She had made me well aware that I still owed her from our earlier bargain.

I had been fascinated by trains as a child and had even

seen this very one arrive in Muscovy from the other side of the iron gates. I remembered well the strange color of the locomotive's clouds as they puffed backward in a greenish-gray haze, melding the power of steam with some strange liquid a scientist had dreamed up. I had been told that trains were for the rabble, for simple folk visiting families or seeking a greater fortune elsewhere, perpetually believing that the blood was redder on the other side of the wall. Royals were meant to travel in state in great conveyances or velvet-appointed carriages pulled by the grandest of snow-white bludmares with long plumes bobbing back from high brows. To sleep in a bed where strangers had slept before, in a bed where one's ancestors hadn't died or given birth—that was not the way I had been reared.

So this would be another of my rebellions, then. I would sleep alone in this narrow room, all of its appointments carefully screwed to the polished wood walls. I lay back and stared up at the elegant black chandelier, its red crystals catching and reflecting the warm orange light of the lamps. When the train lurched suddenly forward, I laughed, my heart light.

I had pulled it off.

I had come back from the brink of death and befriended the most unlikely of creatures. Disguised as my enemy, I had traveled from the smoky alleys of London's Darkside, across the channel and over the Continent beneath a giant metal envelope of gas. I had jumped out of a breast-shaped window and into the great unknown and floated down into a frozen forest and tasted a unicorn. And now here I was, spread out in a second-rate room on Sang's third-best train, chugging faster and faster toward my destiny. In a few short days, I would hold Ravenna's slender neck in my talons. I would set my people free.

When the knock sounded at my door, I didn't think twice.

"Come in. Leave it on the table."

"Leave what?"

I sat up quickly and readjusted my skirts as Casper walked in, his fingers drumming nervously against his hips. Casper's eyes were even more bright and desperate than before, with a mad sort of glitter about them. On the airship, sipping and even gulping his wine, I hadn't seriously considered how pressing his problem had become. The way he was looking at me now—for the first time, I began to feel uneasy.

"Blood. I ordered some blood. Did you order food? You can, you know."

He wasn't looking at me, though. He was staring around the room with twitchy curiosity, as if he could hear someone speaking just out of reach and kept trying to find the source of the voice.

"Not hungry." When he did focus on me, it was like staring into a black pit. Or an oubliette. His eyes shone with madness, the color of twilight and deep water, hungry and soul-sucking, but the intelligence lurked still, under the hunger. "Honestly. Have you ever seen me eat? There's only one thing I need right now. And I can't get it."

"How did it start?" I asked, anxious to keep him distracted.

He chuckled ruefully and paced the tiny room. "It started out—it was innocent. I didn't know any better. I was a Stranger. I thought I was goddamn brilliant. Criminy mentioned once that if a human drank a Bludman's blud, even a drop, that Bludman wouldn't want to feed on him. It was the gloves, you see." He held up his bare hands, which were shaded just the slightest gray, as if with dust. "I couldn't stand playing the harpsichord in gloves. It was so impersonal. So cold. So I asked him for a drop of his blud. He gave it to me, of course. Thought it was pretty funny, because he thought everything was funny. As I moved through the caravan, I persuaded each of the Bludmen to give me a drop. It made their lives that much easier, not seeing me as food. And I got to swagger around, gloves off and shirt open and barefoot, the smart lad who'd bested the Bludmen." He cracked each finger, as I'd seen him do before. "He called me a clever boots. I thought it was a compliment."

"He never told you that it would . . ."

"Addict me? Engulf me? Take me over until food tasted like dirt and my vision swirled with red?" He clinched his fists and stared hard into my eyes as if pleading. "He never told me, the bastard. As if he knew Tish was going to show up and choose him and leave me on the precipice of a downward fucking spiral. As if he was the one who could see the future."

"Did you ever ask anyone about it?"

"No! No, I never thought to ask someone, 'Oh, say, if I drink your blud, will I start to go insane and dream about ripping out a pretty girl's throat? Will I see spots dancing on the walls and hear cold hearts pumping across the room and compose songs about the vein I can see fluttering against your collarbone?'" He reached out one finger, so quick, and stroked the exposed edge of my neck, and I shivered and pulled away from him. "No, darlin', no one ever mentioned that part. Unfortunately."

"When did you find out?"

"After it was too late to save myself. After I was too far

gone, addicted and debauched and drunk in London. It's all the rage in some of the cabarets. Absinthe is the Green Fairy. Bludwine is the Red Siren. You wouldn't believe the things girls will do for a sip."

"I suppose not," I said with a frosty glare.

"Look, Ahna. If I can forgive you for hiding the diamonds and throwing that dead kid off the bank, you can forgive me for trying to lose myself in a string of girls I never cared about. We've both had our vices."

"I . . ."

"You?"

I swallowed hard and looked down. "I suppose you're right."

With a feral growl that surprised even me with its ferocity, he threw himself onto the bed and wrapped his arms around a pillow as if it were a life vest and he were about to drown in a river.

"I've never been so far from myself," he said wonderingly. He scooted back against the cloth-covered headboard, hugging the pillow to his chest. He looked so lost and hopeless and wild that I sat down beside him, close enough to feel the warmth of his body.

"Do you have to have wine?" I asked softly.

"The wine's no good without the blud, but the blud's no good without the wine. At least, it didn't used to be."

When he looked up at me again, the lines of his face had gone rigid, as if he barely kept himself from flying apart at the seams. He breathed in deep and breathed out a long, slow, painful sound halfway between a groan and a growl. That sound—it was as if it had been designed just for me, and I leaned forward, avid and intense.

"I can't believe I'm going to do this," I said to myself.

"Do wha—?"

I didn't let him finish. The act was as swift and strange as the impulse. I grabbed his head with both hands and pulled him close while biting my tongue with sharp fangs. As the hot blud filled my mouth, I kissed him.

His body thudded in shock, but his mouth knew what to do well enough. His tongue lapped at mine, pulling hard at the wound as if he would swallow all of me in one fell swoop. I made to pull away, but his hands caught my face, hard but tender. His thumbs made a token stroke down my jaw, and he looped one arm around my waist and dragged me into his lap.

The bite on my tongue was already healing, but I couldn't pull away from him. He was strong, and I was surprised when the struggle turned real. With one concentrated push, I wrested my face away from his, panting in the sudden silence. We were both breathless, and his pupils were pinpricks in a much lighter shade of blue than they'd been before. He absentmindedly wiped a dribble of blud off his cheek with one finger and licked it clean. I was stunned, fascinated, and caught by his gaze. He was himself again.

Perhaps I should have feared him then. But I had seen his beast, and something in me had liked it, and I couldn't make myself move a single inch farther away from him.

"Why'd you do that?" He chuckled in that familiar way of his. "Not that I mind."

I couldn't blink, couldn't find words. I'd had enough of pretending to be human. Fragile, soft, lying with pretty words. I would tell him the truth, and his response would determine whether or not the die had been cast. Did he see me as what I was or what I had been?

"I did it because I wanted to."

"I wouldn't have pegged you as merciful."

"It wasn't mercy. It was selfish. I wanted to kiss you, so I did. I wanted you to be one step closer to me. I understand the beast in you better than the human."

I held his gaze as I said it, the words spiced with ferocity as if daring him to question me. With a simple turn of his head, he seemed more focused and Bluddish.

"You're different since we landed here," he said carefully. "More yourself."

"Of course. I don't have to pretend. It's not in a Bludman to hide. I know you can feel it taking you over. So why do you persist in pretending?"

"Because I've been human my whole life. It's frightening, becoming something else."

"Maybe you're not becoming something new. Maybe you're becoming what you've been all along." I grinned, knowing that my teeth would be shining with warm light. "Is the beast really so bad? Were you ever really fit for a conventional life? All these things you've done before—were you happy?"

He sat forward, elbows on his knees. "I wanted to be. I tried. But it never felt right."

"Then you've got nothing to lose."

"There's Keen."

"Does she know the bit about how if you're not bludded, you'll go mad? Because someone who truly cares for you will want what's best for you, even if it means that things change."

"When did you get so wise?"

"When there was something worth knowing. I was well trained in diplomacy, you see. And the beast is wise.

The beast is placid and self-contained. It doesn't whine or think of sin. I'd rather make peace with my beast. Wouldn't you?"

He smiled for real, then, dimples and all. "You're not what I expected in a murderous princess."

"We didn't meet under the best circumstances."

"At least we know you fit in a suitcase."

It caught me off guard, and I laughed brightly. The train had reached its speed, and the movement was soothing and exciting at the same time. I felt on track, as if I was where I was supposed to be for the first time in forever. And I realized that it felt right, having Casper with me. I had been raised to trust no one, and yet here I was—trusting someone.

"You're not what I expected, either," I said.

After an awkward pause, he leaned toward me. "Want to play Truth or Dare?"

"Is that a Pinky game?"

"It's a Stranger game. You have to choose whether you want to be asked a question you have to answer or whether you'd rather take a dare. But whatever it is, you have to do it."

I scooted to sit beside him, my back against the headboard and my legs stretched out before me under the shimmering ripples of my dress.

"Truth," I said.

"Why did you tell Mr. Sweeting that your name was Anne Carol?"

"You sneaky little creature!" I smacked his arm. I had taken the game for fun, but now he'd all but bound me to reveal secrets I wasn't ready to share. I'd underestimated him again. But I had my honor.

"Anne is the Sanglish version of Ahnastasia, so that part is true. As for Carol, it's the Sanglish version of Charles, which is the name of the Svedish king. Many people in my home country say that I'm his bastard daughter through my mother, who spent much time with the king in Stockhelm on a diplomatic mission that lasted longer than expected. As I'm the only person in my family with this coloring and without the Tsar's trademark nose, I have always wondered if it was true."

"Sweeting would have killed you if you had been wrong. I guess you have your answer now."

My eyebrows went up. "You've dealt with him?"

He looked away. "Selling blud is the tamest of his pastimes."

"Your turn."

"Dare."

"I dare you to kiss me." I licked my lips and waited.

"You don't play around, do you?"

"No. Why should I have to?"

"Well, then. I guess I've got no choice, do I, darlin'?"

He leaned toward me with infinite slowness, his mouth curling in a smile and his eyes falling closed with a sweep of auburn lashes. I breathed him in, contented to find that my scent was highest in his blood, as if I'd marked him as my own. Long ago, when I'd first smelled him, I'd recognized the blud of other predators. Now I smelled only him and me, and it was a pleasant and heady mix. Just before his lips found mine, I leaned over to meet him.

It was agonizing, the slowness with which he took my mouth. The ferocity of him roiled underneath, waiting. I parted my lips, wanting more, and his hand came up to cup my jaw and hold me in place. I was surely caught, but not by his hand, and I sighed when his tongue finally found mine, sweetly seeking and intense.

I had little experience with kissing, but he had plenty, and he used it well. Hot and sweet, firm and unyielding, he tasted me and teased me and made me hungry for more. He kissed me so carefully that my beast never rose; I felt all of the power with none of the frenzy, and, like a banked fire, the heat only grew the deeper it got. When he finally pulled away, I realized that I'd slid down the bed onto my back, my talons sunk in the pillowy coverlet and shredding the fluffy white.

"Your turn," he said, his voice dusky with promise.

"Dare."

The grin he gave me was so masculine, so confident, so seductive, that I stopped breathing. "Now you kiss me."

I smiled coquettishly and licked my lips. Bolstering myself on an elbow, I leaned over with the same casual slowness he had used to torture me and licked a searing line up his jugular vein, ending with a chaste kiss behind his ear.

"Oh, you little minx," he growled.

"You didn't say what kind of kiss or where," I said blithely, putting my hands behind my head and my elbows out as I leaned back against the pillows. "Your turn."

"Truth."

"What do you want to do right this moment, Casper?"

"So many things, darlin'. So many things." The look he gave me then—it burned right through me.

"That answer doesn't count."

He sat up, leaning possessively over me. "Then I guess we're even."

"I don't think we are."

He caught my chin in deft fingers, his lips so close I could feel their warmth against mine. "Are you trying to make me crazy, woman?"

"I was trying to stop that from happening, but I think I've changed my mind. I like you better wild."

Something twisted in the air between us, a breathless pause that reminded me of that moment when the first snowflake falls, giving the sky permission to erupt in flurries of blinding white. He was kissing me before I'd even noticed him moving, and I took it as permission to let go of the control I'd kept around him until then. My hands caught in his hair, and he pressed me back, deep into white blankets that billowed around us like clouds.

I laughed fiercely into his mouth, and he whispered, "This is serious, girl," and licked a searing trail up my neck to the same place where I'd kissed him earlier, right behind my ear. It ran tingles of fire down my spine, and I gasped and made fists in his hair. No wonder he'd called me a minx. That place was like liquid gold. He was halfway on top of me, and I curled one leg over his leg, keeping him there. He made me feel small and dainty, and I liked the weight of him, pressing against me in the most wonderful ways.

He took my mouth again, his tongue dipping between my lips with ferocious purpose. I was learning, and I kissed him back, loving the taste of him. Pulling away and licking my lips, he murmured, "I want more."

Grabbing me around the waist, he pulled me down until I was stretched out the full length of the bed. He placed one hand on my neck, trailing it down my chest and stomach.

"And your very flesh will be a great poem," he said.

"You have me laid out before you, and you speak of poetry?" I couldn't help laughing. "Is that how things are done in your world?"

"You make me remember things I thought were lost forever," he whispered. "Things I needed. Things I'm glad to have back."

"Maybe one day you can scrawl poems on me with a brush," I purred. "Starting at my ankles, with black ink winding ever upward."

"Oh, woman. It's like you want to kill what's left of the gentleman inside me."

"I don't want him dead. Just quiet. Kiss me again."

I pulled him down to me and nipped his lip. Words were pretty, but I didn't want words. I wanted his body, his mouth, his growls. I wanted the fire behind his eyes to consume us both. I wanted the flame he had kindled in me to catch and burn. I wanted him to make me forget everything else.

He kissed down my neck and along my collarbone, his lips and tongue searing against my skin. It was as if I'd never felt anything before, as if every inch of my body was waking up, and waking up hungry. He kissed along the neckline of my gown, following it to the V and licking deep in the line between my breasts. I moaned underneath him, pressing upward, aching to rub against him as I'd once seen a cat do.

His hand slipped under me to fiddle with the buttons down my back, and I rolled to my side to accommodate him. If his deftness with buttons was any indication, those nimble fingers were going to be delicious on my skin.

He was running his tongue across the tops of my breasts when the lights winked out, leaving us in complete darkness. I gasped and pulled back, for there wasn't even the faintest hint of light to see by. I was lost without all my senses.

"There's a tunnel," Casper murmured into my skin. "Under the mountains."

I felt the kiss of skin on my back and sighed as he pulled the strings of my corset, releasing the bow. His mouth was still busy with the mounds of my breasts pushed up by the corset, and he found one nipple and teased it with his tongue.

"But, Casper, the lights . . . ?"

"The shadows will fall behind you."

When his lips slanted again over mine, messy and rough in the dark, I thought perhaps he kissed me just to shut me up, and I obliged him by unbuttoning his collar, down and down, until his chest was laid bare to my hands.

Just then, a sound rang out over the throbbing hum of the train. Metal scraping against metal—in the door's lock. With a hiss and reflexes long honed by the threat of assassins, I grabbed Casper's shirt and yanked him to me, rolling us both onto the ground beside the bed. Before he could ask me why, I put a hand over his mouth. Even without a Bludman's perfect hearing, he should have recognized the sound of a heavy boot on the floor of my room.

25

The door opened on silent hinges. Casper froze for the barest moment before lurching to his feet and springing away. I couldn't see anything, but I heard a strange man's yelp of surprise. After a quick tussle, liquid splashed over the ground, and I crawled up on the bed before the salt-reeking water could reach me. The smell was sharp and painful, biting at my nose. The fight continued, and an unfamiliar voice shrieked in wordless fury. The scent of burning flesh filled the room, and Casper called, "Are you hurt? Did the bastard get you?"

"I'm unharmed. What's happening? I can't see anything!"

Three quick thumps, then the heavy smack of a big form landing on the ground, all of it overlaid with shrieking and growling and an unsettling hiss.

"How do you kill a Bludman?" Casper grunted with effort. "Quick!"

"You can't kill him yet. We have to question him first."

"Screw questioning him!" Casper shouted between the sounds of a struggle. "He's big, and he's already been hit with his own seawater, and he's still not cooperating."

"Little bitch, I hear you!" the man called between grunts.

He had a thick Svedish accent, and I breathed in deeply, trying to get a sense of him. A Bludman, and one strong enough to fight while soaked in seawater.

And then I knew the answer to Casper's question about killing him.

Without saying a word, I crept forward, one hand out in front of me and my boots splashing in the puddle.

"Where are you, Casper?"

"On the ground. I'm on top of him. But stay back; he's covered with salt water."

I scooted one foot ahead of me until I nudged a heavy boot. It struck out at my leg, and I jerked back before he could bruise me. Carefully and quietly, I nudged my way up his body. He tried to grab my boot at one point, and I stepped on his hand and ground the bones under my heel.

"I can see you, ice bitch," he growled.

"And I can smell you, fool. Who sent you?"

He chuckled, low and deep. "Your father."

I reached out until I found Casper and traced down his arm until I found his hand on the assassin's shoulder, pinning the larger man down. Before he could ask me what I was up to, I felt down Casper's half-dressed torso for the knife he wore always on his hip. Once I had it in hand, I knocked him off and straddled the man in his place, ignoring the damp water that stung my knees.

"Here's a message for my father," I said in Sanguine, and I plunged the knife into his chest, right where I could hear his heart beating. He struggled for just a moment, but the strike was swift and sure, the knife lodged firmly in his breast.

"What did you do?" Casper asked.

"What I had to."

The man shuddered and bucked under me for a moment longer before going still and cold.

"Get me a light," I said, suddenly overcome with a grand idea. "And a cup or a bottle. Hurry."

Casper sighed and stood. "Do I even want to know what you're doing now?"

"What I have to," I said. He left the room before he could hear me whisper, "For you."

He returned with an antiquated lantern, a teacup, and an empty wine bottle.

"They'll have the lights back on soon. He took out the whole car, and everyone's raising a big stink over it. The carhop was handing out lanterns." He reached into his waistcoat, now smooth again over his buttoned shirt. "And he sent these, with his apologies."

The two vials of blood were heavy and cool in my hand, but I had other priorities. We had to hurry.

"Drag him into the bathroom. There's a narrow tub." Because I'd paid extra for it, of course.

In the light, the man was revealed to be tall but wiry and wrapped entirely in black leather. He wore strange goggles and carried dozens of knives and an instrument that squirted seawater when a trigger was pulled. Together we dumped the body into the tub. Casper didn't understand what was happening until I sliced the assassin's black sleeve with his own knife and slit the crease in his elbow by the sparse light of the lantern.

"Oh, Ahna. God. Do we have to . . ."

And then he smelled the blud. His eyes went to pinpricks, his breathing speeding up.

"So much of it. I've never seen so much at once."

I handed him the assassin's arm and quickly tipped the full teacup into the wine bottle. Casper's mouth sealed over the wound in the man's elbow. When I couldn't pry him off that cut, I made a new cut in the other elbow and kept going until the flow got sluggish and the wine bottle was half full. Between his feeding and my tidiness, we hadn't spilled a drip of blud.

Casper finally dropped the arm in the assassin's lap, licking his lips in bliss. I held up the bottle, and he whooped and grabbed me up into a hug.

"You beautiful, clever girl."

"Can't have you going mad when we're this close to Freesia, now, can we?"

The lights buzzed back on just as he was about to kiss me, and the previously shadow-hidden form of the mercenary in the bathtub was suddenly the biggest thing in the tiny closet of a room.

"Out the window, do you think?" Casper asked, and I nodded.

"We'll need to . . . how would Keen say it? Loot him first. But why is he wearing dark goggles?"

"Night vision," Casper said with a shrug. "So he could see once the lights were out."

I handed him the bottle and gingerly unbuttoned the assassin's jacket. The fellow was dressed for dastardly deeds, his leathers the color of shadows. I pulled off his cap and goggles to reveal ice-white hair and eyes the same color as mine. The knife, it turned out, was lodged so deeply that the hilt had sunk into his flesh, which made it difficult to search his jacket. Still, I took a fierce pride in the evidence of my strength and righteous anger.

Finally, I found what I was looking for. I slipped the

packet of papers out of his pocket and opened the little book with trembling hands.

"These are fake."

"How can you tell?" Casper leaned close to inspect the aged papers with their proper seals and signatures.

"Because I was raised to topple kings, and an assassin never carries his true papers. I don't even know what I was hoping to find. I already know the truth. The Swedish king wants me dead and most likely has a network of spies and assassins spread all over the Blud world, hoping to catch a glimpse of me."

"But why? If he's your father, why would he want you dead?"

I gave him a wry smile. "I may be his daughter, but he can't claim me or use me. Ravenna's Freesia is a weak thing, and Charles would love nothing more than to march on Muscovy and claim her for Sveden. I'm his only real impediment."

"Does this sort of thing happen often?"

"They plague the palace like bludlemmings, but it's rare that one makes it so close to royalty. It's fortunate you're still immune to seawater. There's nothing more to gain from him. Help me get him out the window, will you?"

With the determination and quiet strength I'd come to expect from him, Casper tugged open the window and leaned out to make sure no one else happened to be looking about at the same time. It was pitch black outside, the light from our lantern the only thing flashing on the rock wall of the tunnel. Together we hefted the rubbery body out the window and dropped it into the darkness, and the train chugged on as if nothing had happened.

I kept my head out of the window for a moment,

enjoying the smell of ice-frosted stone deep within the mountain. Revenge felt good.

Casper pulled me back from the window and into his arms.

"At first, I thought it was impossible. But now I'm starting to think you can do it. You're just full of surprises, aren't you?"

In answer, I buried my head in his shirt. Breathing in, I could smell the change the blud had wrought in him. If I looked at his hands in the sunlight, I was sure they would be duller and a shade grayer. As little as I knew about half-bluds now, I could only assume that the more blud he drank, the closer he came to being like me. With the assassin's blud corked in the bottle, he could stave off madness a while longer, but we both knew that every sip brought him one step closer to the bludding he so feared. I wanted him for my own purposes, and I wanted him soon, but I knew that I would have to wait until he was ready. I only hoped he wouldn't hate me once the deed was done.

Keen knocked on the door shortly thereafter to tell him their food had been delivered. He was still pretending to eat in front of her. She threw me a dark look before the door closed, and I realized my dress was still mostly unbuttoned. With businesslike tenderness, Casper rebuttoned me, dropping one warm kiss between my shoulder blades.

"Always an interruption," he murmured.

"No one knocks on the queen's door when it's locked."

"Your door doesn't lock anymore, thanks to Captain Clumsy Assassin. Will you be safe? I need to go, and I don't know much about political intrigue. Are there more of them?"

I could tell he didn't want to leave me, but I understood now that Keen was his family, his tie to the part of himself that was slipping away. If I wanted him, I would have to share him with her. And so I would let him go. For now.

"It's safe. If there were two assassins on this train, we would probably be dead."

"That's . . . not very comforting."

I gave him a gentle smile. "Sleep well, Casper."

"You, too, darlin'."

I was more than sorry to see him go. Not only because I had grown used to his company but also because I wanted to see what would happen if we continued our little game. Truth or Dare. What charming inventions they had in his world! The things that could be accomplished with such a game were limitless.

I leaned against the shut door, imagining the way he had kissed me, the touch of his hands. They were just as clever as I'd imagined but warmer. What a vast difference between the boy on the bank, the pirate, and the Maestro, yet they'd all approached me with the same goal in mind. If only the assassin hadn't intervened. I stepped in the puddle of seawater as I crossed to the bed and pinched my nose at the smell. I would have killed anyone who had interrupted us just then. Finally, a head that deserved a platter, and I'd just tossed him off the train.

I unlaced my boots and curled up in bed. What had happened with Casper had left me cross and anxious. Unfinished. But I was too proud to call him back, and I didn't have the words to say what I wanted anyway.

I thought of the dozens of knives that had fallen into the darkness with the assassin, wishing I had thought to keep at least one. After his intrusion, I didn't feel safe any-more. With a huff of annoyance, I rolled out of bed and went to the bathroom to see if I'd missed anything, but the only thing left was his goggles, which made every-thing glow a spooky green. Between this "night vision," as Casper had called it, and the goggles that Van Helsing said revealed Bludmen, I would never trust eyewear again. The artificers were getting too good. And I needed one in the palace, on my side and working for the Bludmen.

I tossed and turned, growling at the uncomfortable buttons up the back of my dress and wishing for some-thing, anything, to soothe me. Not until I smelled Casper on the other side of my door and heard him singing that song about Jude did I relax enough to let sleep finally take me, knowing that he would keep me safe.

If only I had been brave enough to invite him back in.

The train's brakes squealed, and I jerked awake. We were slowing down. That meant we were finally back in my homeland. I was at the window in seconds, gazing out at the ice-glazed city of Muscovy, the gem-shaped turrets rising into the deep blue sky to pierce the clouds. A rush of joy washed over me, little ripples swirling over my skin and making the tiny hairs rise on my arms. I was home. I was still far from the Ice Palace, but I was at least in a city that I knew and loved. One step closer to my goal.

I went into the water closet to freshen up and couldn't help noticing a few drops of blud on the tub. I washed them away with the strangest feeling, the copper cold under my fingers. So Charles of Sveden was my father, and I was worth more to him dead. The man who had raised me was gone, killed at my mother's side by Ravenna herself. He had loved me as much as a king was allowed, although he had probably known the truth. Palace politics were strange, and I would be sure to bear no bastards when I was queen. Of course, that meant I would need to distance myself from Casper, even if it pained me. Duty to country came first, and dealing with Ravenna came before that. No matter how I longed for him in the night, no matter how I loved the heat of his lips, my feet would soon be in Muscovy, and playtime would be over.

But not quite yet.

I fluffed my hair and smoothed down my dress before slipping outside and counting the cars and doors to the one I'd reserved for Casper and Keen. Before I could talk myself out of it, I knocked. The door opened just wide enough to show me Casper's bare chest.

"Just a minute," he said, slamming the door in my face.

He was back shortly in proper attire, with a blush riding his cheeks. I smiled at the warm, lazy hunger I felt, which I blamed on his embarrassment.

"Did you need something?"

"I . . . need to talk to someone. About something."

"Is that someone me, by any chance?" His teasing smile made me blush in return.

He held the door open for me, and I slipped in with a frisson of mischief. Whatever noble Bludwomen did on trains, entering the quarters of their Pinky servants probably wasn't considered conventional.

Their room was a little shabby, compared with mine, but not shameful. Two bunks nestled one over the other by a low table and a lamp. Casper's wine bottle sat on the table, and the journal I'd seen in his room at the Seven Scars lay open on the lower bed beside a pencil. The pages were covered in feverish scrawling, much as I remembered seeing before, but fewer lines were angrily crossed out.

"What are you working on?" I asked, realizing as I said it how very rude it was.

And yet a grin lit up his face, and he flopped onto the bed and started reading. "What is it that you express in your eyes? It seems to me more than all the print I have read in my life."

Something fluttered in my stomach. "Oh. That's . . . quite pretty."

"I discover myself on the verge of a usual mistake."

"That's . . . insulting?"

"I sound my barbaric yawp over the roofs of the world."

"That's flat-out bizarre. Is it supposed to be poetry?"

"I had a favorite book in my old world. I was obsessed with it, really. Owned several copies of it, one of them very special and expensive, a gift to myself. It was called *Leaves of Grass,* and it was written by a man named Walt Whitman. It didn't always make sense, but most of the time it did, especially one poem called *Song of Myself.* And while lots of books from my old world are in your world, if slightly different, I've never found evidence that there's anything like *Leaves of Grass* or *Song of Myself.*"

"So you have Bolstoy, and Dostoevskin and the other major writers?"

"Close enough. But it doesn't appear that there was ever a version of Walt Whitman writing in Sang."

"And so you're . . . trying to write the book yourself?"

He rolled over onto his back and laughed, a wild sound that marked how close he was to my world. "Exactly that. Something about you helps me remember. It's all coming back to me. I'll never have all of it, but I'm starting to think I might have enough." His smile was warm and dimpled. "You're becoming my muse. Or Walt's."

"Oh." I feigned interest in a painting on the wall to cover how very much it sounded as if we were flirting, despite the fact that I knew I needed to distance myself from him. It was odd that the dance of bodies should feel primal and natural but compliments from him were hard for me to swallow. And yet I liked all the things his mouth did, and so I had to learn this dance, too. "I'm glad that you're . . ."

"Finding the unfound?"

"Yes."

He scribbled something in his book, his face alight. I looked more closely at his wine bottle and found that its level was lower than I would have expected. He must have been busy last night.

"So was there something you wanted to talk about?" he asked.

"Maybe. Where's Keen?" I leaned against the wall, opposite him but close enough to touch, for it was a very narrow room.

"She's annoyed with me. Well, she's always annoyed with me. But more than usual just now. Said she would hang about the dining car and see if she could pick up any gossip from the local Pinkies. What did you need?"

My mouth fell open as I searched for an answer. "I . . ."

I had never felt so helpless and caught out. Why had I come to him? It was an impulse, one that I hadn't given much consideration. All my thoughts on assassins, Muscovy, Sveden, and Ravenna, all my determination to distance myself—and yet here I was. He stood and took a single step to my side. His arm went around me, and I was helpless to keep myself from leaning into him, savoring the warm bulk of his body.

"How can I help?"

I fidgeted with the laces on my dress. "It's just that . . . once my feet touch down in Muscovy, everything changes. I must be hard and cruel and merciless. I must focus on my goal."

"I know. And I want to help you."

"But how . . ."

"Ahna, honey, are you scared?" he asked softly.

"I just wish I was stronger."

He squeezed my hand. "You're strong enough," he said. "You got us this far."

"I had a lot of help."

His dimples came out in full force, and he brushed my hair back behind my ears, sending shivers all over me. "I thought you wanted my head on a platter?"

"I think it's more useful to me where it is."

"Do you, now?"

It was a short distance from his lips to mine, and I relished the soft tug of his hand behind my neck as he pulled me close. This time, I met him with open lips and a feverish wanting. He fell back onto the bed, taking me with him and holding me tighter as I squirmed sinuously against him. I couldn't tell him how I felt, that I was scared for me, for him and Keen. That I felt guilty for putting them in danger and even guiltier for knowing that I would have to put him aside later. That I was selfish and had wanted, all along, for him to touch me again like this and make me forget everything else.

One of his hands went back to my buttons as if it had

never left, and I pulled away just far enough to murmur into his mouth, "You can't undress me now. The train is stopped. We must go."

"This is nowhere close to finished," he murmured back into my mouth.

"I hope not," I whispered. "Although I can be hard to catch. Keep trying."

He pulled back with a grin. "Failing to fetch me at first, keep encouraged. Missing me one place, search another. I stop somewhere waiting for you."

With a wild laugh, he tumbled me onto my back, kissed my nose, and leaped up to scribble in his book. I sighed and hitched myself up on an elbow.

"Your priorities," I said slowly, "could use some work."

"I'm an artist, darlin', and the muse is a fickle bitch. I'll make it up to you later."

"I'll consider that a promise," I whispered in his ear as he scribbled.

I could hear the crowd outside, the doors opening and closing, and voices raised in laughter, annoyance, and greeting. As I stood to smooth my dress again, Keen burst in through the door and gave me a dirty look that I more or less deserved.

"I stopped by your room, but you were gone," she said. "Been busy again?"

"I've had enough," Casper started, standing to glower at her. "Keen, you need to remember that we're consenting adults, and what we do is our own business. I'm not your dad, as you keep reminding me. But I'm your friend, and any feelings I might have for Ahna don't change that." He looked from her to me, his eyes pleading.

Deadly assassins I could handle with aplomb, but the

drama of teenage girls was beyond me. And Casper had just admitted to having feelings for me. I was a mess of emotions, all of them distracting me from our goal.

"I want us to be friends, Keen," I finally said, realizing that, oddly enough, I meant it.

"Well, friend, would you like to explain why I found night-vision goggles on your bed?"

Casper rubbed his eyes, smearing ink across his forehead. "We were attacked by an assassin last night. We took care of it."

"I bet you took care of *it*," Keen said, and it was easy to see that the "it" in question wasn't the assassin.

I held up a hand, done with her games. "I extend my friendship to you, but I also give a warning. We're in Muscovy now. Do you know what they say in my country about nosy bludlemmings?"

"Do I care?"

"They lose their noses. Followed by their lives. Be careful in Freesia, little lemming, or you'll never get that pony."

She actually had the gall to stick her tongue out at me, and I nearly smiled. She had heart and guts, as my father would say of his best hounds. I was actually starting to admire the creature. To imagine a child waking up naked and alone in Sang and managing to live long enough to find food and clothes—it was impressive. And I suspected she would soon have much more vitriol to lay at my feet, and for genuine reasons.

Over her head, Casper mouthed the words *Thank you*, and I smiled and nodded.

He would have little reason to thank me once we were in the city.

26

As soon as my feet hit the streets, I was filled with purpose. Finally, things were familiar. The grand façade of the train station sparkled in a thousand shades of white and blue, the edges of every window picked out in solid gold. The city of Muscovy was the jewel of the Freesian empire, a hub of history and energy and art. From the beautifully laid-out parks with their ice sculptures and topiaries to the grand library to the museums and theaters, everything had been planned to impress and delight. I still remembered my first trip there as a child, how I had kept my hands hidden in a white fur muff for fear that I would get in trouble for touching something and smudging its magnificence.

I had to stop and wait for Keen and Casper. They were so fascinated by their surroundings that they were acting more like country-bred food slaves and less like respectable servants.

"My little snacks, do keep up," I said in my most cultured voice. One of the *militsiya* was approaching, tapping his billy club against the many medals on his elegant uniform jacket. "It's their first time in our grand city," I said to him coquettishly, as if we shared a great joke. "Can you imagine?"

"Leashes might be preferable, my lady," he said politely, eyeing Keen's scruffy outfit.

"I'll look into that, thank you."

I probably enjoyed myself too much, hauling her off by her collar and *tsk*ing in her ear.

"Behave, or they'll impound you," I said, and the look on her face was priceless. It was a very real threat, but only for free Pinkies, of course, and only on the more elegant streets.

I moved faster after that, urging them to hurry as well. It had been too long since I had looked at a Freesian calendar, and I didn't know how close we might be to the Sugar Snow Ball. We hadn't missed it yet, as the air didn't smell properly of snow and the streets were dry and still warm under my boots. But it was close, and one never knew how the weather would go. The sooner I found my old nursemaid, the better. Verusha saw and heard more than anyone alive.

It was difficult following the grand avenues without indulging in the many beauties of the White City. We had spent the summers there most years, and I knew well which shops kept the prettiest hats in stock and the softest dancing shoes and the finest feathered hair combs. Outside one of my favorite boutiques, we passed a grand lady with a precious little Pinky girl on a jeweled leash, pretty as could be, and I took in a deep and appreciative breath. Cleanliness, good breeding, and an understanding of one's place were hallmarks of a royal servant.

But when I looked closer, I saw the leash's collar digging into the child's tender white neck, leaving a red mark behind. It should have inspired hunger, but now I just felt pity. I could see in the child a reflection of Keen, but broken and tamed. The child's smile faded when her mistress turned her away from the sparkling window of a toy store, where she'd been gazing as if in a dream. Scurrying behind the grand dame's skirt, I saw the child for what she was: a slave and a prisoner, held against her will.

"Faster," I muttered, turning down the staircase to the underground trains that connected all of Muscovy with minimal grit and ugliness. I would have once considered the walk to Verusha's flat a pleasure, but I was too concerned about encountering something that would cause Keen to say the wrong thing to the wrong Bludman or Casper to release his beast in a suicidal fashion. Time was of the essence.

Once we were down the marble staircase and in the station, I turned into a corner to fetch the coins and necklace from my corset. The coins were there. The necklace was gone.

"Looking for this?" Keen held out the glistening trinket with a smug smirk, and I snatched it from her before anyone in the crowd noticed a Pinky carrying something so valuable.

"You could be staked for touching that, little fool."

As I smoothed out the chain to tuck it back into hiding, I noticed that there were five gems missing instead of the three I'd removed myself.

"You vile little thief!" I hissed.

"I figure you owe me," she said, putting her gloved hands in her pockets and rocking back on her heels. I began to see why she caused Casper such problems—just when I thought I was getting anywhere with her, she went and did something so ridiculous that I wanted her head right back on that platter. One step forward, two steps back, and now she was in deeper water than she knew.

"Give them back now, and I'll try not to drain you." I fought for composure, and Casper's hand subtly brushed my waist, a reminder of the slender wire I walked.

"Only got one left, but I'll make it up to you by paying for the tube." She held out a hand brimming with coins, and I cursed myself for leaving her alone outside the dress shop. She was lucky she hadn't been arrested. But we'd already attracted enough attention, so I just said, "Fine," and picked three coins out of her glove, careful not to touch the stained leather.

We were silent through the turnstiles and onto the car, aside from Keen's whispered "Holy crow!" as we sat on the tufted velvet bench seat. I'd been impressed the first time I'd seen it, too. The tunnels looked like catacombs, old brick and stone with skulls and bones mortared into complex patterns. But the train itself was as elegant as the one that had brought us from Minks, with beautiful details and glittering glass edged in gilt. A violinist in the corner took up her bow, swaying with the music, and Casper went still all over as plaintive music filled the air.

"That's brilliant," he said under his breath.

"Welcome to Muscovy," I murmured back.

We sped through several stops, changed trains at a grand station with soaring skylights, enormous chandeliers, and glittering mosaics, and disembarked at the stop where Verusha had lived ever since retiring as my maid.

"I will die here, darlink," she had told me once, settling back into her favorite chaise, surrounded by rich silks and soft furs, "but I think there will be many years before that happens."

She had been well over two hundred then. And yet something told me that she still reclined in the same divan, doing the needlepoint for which she was so famous, ordering around a fleet of daughters-in-law and grandchildren. If not—well, I would cross that bridge when I came to it.

I was blinded for a moment by the noon sun reflected on the marble outside the station. Shielding my eyes with a hand, I soon understood why so few people had gotten off the train with us. The once-grand block of retirement flats had become something I had been taught to dread: a tenement. Lines strung between the buildings carried all manner of unmentionable laundry, and small children and dogs ran about uncontained. Trash blew along the avenues, something I'd never seen before, mainly because my people ate nothing that required wrapping. The graffiti on the grimy walls was the nail in the coffin of my dreams of finding Verusha easily and swiftly.

Pinko District

Get your blud off our streets!

The people will rise!

And so I wasn't surprised when the first stone stung against my back. I spun, but there was no way to know where it had come from. The children had disappeared, and the dogs were on alert, hackles up and tails stiff. How had my city fallen so far in just four years? And why had Ravenna allowed it?

"Come." I walked back toward the station as quickly as I could without showing fear. "She's not here."

"Hey, friend! You don't have to bow to her no more!" someone called from behind closed shutters, and Casper subtly moved to cover my retreat.

"Sounds like they got the right idea around here," Keen muttered.

"If you like them, you're welcome to stay." I didn't look back, but I could hear her boots scraping along the stones behind me. The girl had a fantastic survival instinct, if nothing else. She slipped three more coins into my hand at the train-station gates.

Back on the train, Casper said, "I hate to say it, but humans can ruin anything."

"I must agree. It used to be so beautiful."

"Freedom's prettier than fancy marble," Keen said.

"Not if you're starving to death."

She just shrugged, and I let it go. As we moved away from the newly claimed Pinky district and back into the familiar areas of parks and walks near the central Basilica of Aztarte, the train car began to fill, and my nerves calmed. I understood how my people functioned, according to thoughtful rules, years of superiority, and wealth. I knew what to expect among Bludmen. But humans— they were unpredictable, wild, dangerous. I found myself taking an interest in them for the first time in my life. Perhaps the people throwing garbage at me had once been that little girl in the collar. Perhaps they were her parents.

At the correct station, I watched carefully to be sure that many well-dressed passengers also disembarked. Surely this part of the city still belonged to the upper crust.

"Stay close," I whispered to Casper and Keen, and we plunged into the colorful and cheerful crowd.

The stop had always been a popular one, as the area around the Tsarina's Park included public gardens, statuary, fountains, the ballet, and several prominent museums. There was also a fantastic clockwork carousel that I'd loved since I was a child. I had heard that the Magistrate of Sangland had commissioned a similar one in London, but it had malfunctioned on opening day and nearly killed people. I turned to ask Casper about it before remembering that women of my status wouldn't be seen arm in arm with their servants, discussing carousels.

Much to my satisfaction, the park was just as beautiful as ever, clean and bright and glowing in the sun. A large crowd had collected around a gazebo, and I could see flashes of the famous Bolshoi ballerinas practicing in feathery white swan costumes. I scurried around the edges of the crowd, keeping my face down and hoping no one would recognize me through my new hat's veil. We skirted the shadows around to the servants' entrance of the Tsarina's Palace, where my family stayed during the uncomfortable warmth of summer. A fleet of Pinkies worked outside, trimming bushes into careful spirals and washing already-sparkling windows, and royal peacocks danced on the brick wall and called from the trees. Keen shuddered, but I felt a glad rush of pride and familiarity.

Instead of going through the front door, as would have been my right, I sneaked around the corner and hid behind a topiary in the shape of a bludmare.

"Casper, go knock on that door. Tell them you need to find Lady Verusha. Tell them nothing else, even if they pry. Keep a straight face, and do not back down, but above all, be polite."

I stood on tiptoe to dust off his shoulders and straighten his hat. He grinned at me, all dimples and dancing eyes, and I tightened the laces that connected his hat to his collar. It was a gamble, sending a halfblud to the door of the royal family, but I trusted him more than I trusted Keen. When I nodded my approval, he walked briskly to the door and knocked.

After a few moments, the door opened just a crack, and I had never been happier to be in hiding. The housekeeper had never liked me to begin with and had probably danced when she heard of my disappearance and supposed demise. Her eyes narrowed at Casper, and she looked him up and down with an air of superiority that had been cultivated at my mother's right hand. I couldn't hear what was said between them, and I held my breath. It was the royal housekeeper's right to absorb local servants at her request, and I could only hope she found him good enough to dispense information to and shabby enough to send away.

He finally bowed, the door slamming inches from the top of his hat.

"Well?" I said, and he grinned.

"She's living with a daughter-in-law on Belila Avenue, running a groomery. Do I even want to know what that is?"

"You'll see soon enough. Come along."

Moments later, we stood before a grand storefront filled with ribbons and giant wheels of soap. I could smell the lavender and clementines and cloves even from the street, the familiar work of the Tsarina's former maid. A bell tinkled over the door as we entered, and a young girl in a fancy dress minced forward to meet me.

"My lady, welcome. Have you an appointment?" She looked Keen over with professional disdain, probably calculating what it would take to make the child presentable.

"I have a standing appointment with Verusha. Please tell her the pup has returned."

Her nose wrinkled up in confusion, but she knew better than to contradict a customer, which was a wise practice in a city as big and small as Muscovy. She curtsied and scurried through a filmy curtain and into the back room, and I smiled to see her hair done in the fancy braids that I remembered from my own childhood at Verusha's patient but implacable claws.

"What is this? Who dares to come into my groomery and claim—!"

She pushed the curtain aside and stopped mid-rant. I put back my veil. She looked me up and down before holding out her arms, dripping with suds, her eyes rimmed with blud tears.

"My little ermine pup, you are returned?"

I threw myself into her embrace. She had always been shorter than me and twice as wide, and it was like hugging a boulder.

She pulled away and caught a twisted claw in my curls. "Oh, tut, darleenk! Your hair. What have you done?"

"I think you know a disguise when you see it. I need your help."

She drew back to inspect me and murmured, "Oh, I see that you do. Much help. But come back into the parlor for a dram, and we will discuss. Do they need grooming, those two?" She stared skeptically at Casper and Keen and clicked her tongue. Keen put a hand on her hip as if daring the old Bludwoman to say anything else, and Verusha barked out a laugh. "That one needs to be dipped for fleas, I think, maybe left under a bit too long, eh?"

We laughed together, the wild laugh of Bludmen, and the world began to turn as it should. I was home, I was understood, and now I had a friend.

We didn't talk of important things at first, of course. That would have been terribly impolite. Against her protests, I handed Keen off to Verusha's daughter-in-law for a good grooming, but Casper I kept with me. My excuse was that he was actually capable of keeping himself clean and relatively dapper, but in reality, I wanted him close.

And I hoped Verusha would break the news to him that I myself had been dreading.

Verusha put a chunk of bread in Casper's hands and patted him on top of his hat. He couldn't eat it, of course, but he thanked her with tolerant bemusement. I could only imagine how Keen would react to the treatment of Freesia's Bludmen toward a messy and rebellious servant. If she wasn't careful, she would find herself trussed up and dangling upside down while they shaved her head for nits.

I sat in one of the indulgently cushioned chairs that Verusha had always favored, glad to sink back into the embroidered pillows. She put a dainty teacup in my hands, the porcelain so thin that it glowed pink with the blood within.

Sitting across from me and settled likewise with her matching cup, she took a sip and said, "Now, darleenk, my pup, tell old Verusha what you have done."

"What I've done?" I resisted the urge to throw the cup at her head like the spoiled child I'd been when last under her care. "I'm the victim here, old woman! I was kidnapped, nearly drained, and shipped all over Sang in a used valise."

She nodded slowly and said, "There were suspicions, of course. Your sister, too?"

My head dropped. "I found her in London. Her head, at least. We were both shipped to the same destination, but she actually arrived there."

"And you?" She sipped her tea as if I hadn't just announced Olgha's murder.

"I woke up in a blud bar because of him." I nodded at Casper.

Verusha's sharp eyes narrowed at Casper, who was busily turning the bread over and over in his hands as if trying to remember its purpose.

"You were the one who found the lost . . ." She cleared her throat. "Young lady?"

"He knows who I am, Verusha."

"Tut, darleenk! Will you tell all the world your secrets?"

"Not all the world. Just him. And the other one, the girl. They brought me here, all the way from London."

Her eyes narrowed to slits. "And what are they wanting as a reward, eh?"

"When I am queen, Casper will be court composer." I took a slow sip, feeling the strength of the blood seep in, daring Verusha to contradict me.

She cackled, just as she had when I had been small and made wild assertions about riding a bludbear or running away to join the caravan.

"And what a miracle that will take, my pup! That Ravenna, she is a demon." She turned her head, gathering her cheeks to spit blood. When she couldn't find a square inch of her own floor not dominated by expensive carpets, she cleared her throat and swallowed it back down. "Your poor mother and father, executed. My little Alex, ensorcelled. The barons thrown out and hungry as the humans riot in my old home." She rose and came to me, taking my empty cup and setting it on a table. Holding both of my hands in her twisted talons, she looked square into my eyes and said, "Darleenk, you are our only hope."

"I was hoping you would say that. But I need your help."

She smiled, showing sharp teeth. "I was hoping *you* would say *that*. What can Verusha do for you, princess?"

"I must kill Ravenna. At the Sugar Snow Ball. It's our only chance. Casper will go with me. We must blend in completely with the nobles. And when she begins the dance, I'll take her."

"A bold plan, my pup, a bold plan." She sat back down, leaning deep into the pillows, with a crafty look on her face. "My invitation to the ball is yours, of course. But there is one other problem, and well you know it." She pointed one claw at Casper.

"I'm the problem?" Casper asked, setting the bread down to lean forward in warning.

"In many ways, I think." She jabbed a claw at him knowingly. "Pinkies are not allowed at the Sugar Snow Ball, not unless they are on the table. And I suspect that she is not so ready to give you up."

I swallowed and took back my cup, gazing into the streaks of blood swirling around the porcelain. She was all too sharp, my old nursemaid.

Verusha stood, not that she was much taller standing. Walking close to Casper, she put her cheek almost against his forehead and inhaled deeply. When she exhaled again, it came out as a growl.

"You would take an abomination to the most holy and secret rite of your people? I raised you better than that, Ahnastasia!" She sat, trembling with fury. "How dare you put royal blud in the veins of a . . . a . . . whatever he is!" This time, she did spit, and it left a splatter of red on the cream-colored carpet, almost blending in with the woven roses.

"Don't blame her. She didn't do this. I did this to myself in ignorance, and believe me when I say I regret it more every day," he said quietly.

"At least you have the good sense to be ashamed," she snapped. "But do not lie to me. I know the smell of her lineage, and it sings to me from your skin."

"What would happen if I went to the ball?" he asked. "Would they notice?"

"Without the fetters of Pinky clothes, younger noses and sharper teeth would notice, my boy, and you would quickly become the scapegrace for everyone's fury. Staked out at four points and eaten whole by the company of dancers. It would be a long, slow death and not one that would help my poor pup regain her throne."

The silence was ungainly, and they both looked to me. For once, I didn't feel bold. I sipped at the distasteful dregs of my cup, keeping my face carefully blank.

"Then what do we do?" Casper finally asked.

"She can't go alone. We must find another patriot to accompany her. One of my sons might have a friend who can be trusted." Casper bristled, his posture changing subtly to indicate a threat.

"Or?" he asked.

"Or you ascend to a grander life, my boy. You're halfway there already. One might think it would be a relief, after the blud madness."

Casper went still with rage. "So I either send her into danger with another man, or I give up my humanity completely?"

"Exactly that, yes," Verusha said, settling back into the cushions to sip her blood thoughtfully. "Is not so bad, eh?"

"I can't imagine how it could be worse," he growled.

"Easy, little snack. The Sugar Snow Ball is in two days. So there is enough time to decide."

"Two days," he said to himself.

I shifted against the cushion, dress suddenly feeling too tight, and his head snapped to me.

"Did you know?" he asked simply. "Ahna, did you know all along?"

"I . . ."

"Well?"

"I had suspicions."

"And yet you never mentioned it?"

"I didn't see the point in worrying you unduly. It would end the same either way. The future is no more uncertain than the present."

Head in his hands, he chuckled, on the verge of tears. "My God, woman. How do you keep doing that?"

"Doing what?"

"Taking everything from me and giving it back in one breath?"

"I don't know how to be sorry, Casper. For a princess, I'm not a bit tamed." Nothing I said or did could change that.

He was on the verge of laughing, on the verge of crying, as if he were standing at the edge of a great precipice and deciding whether to jump or not. Which, I had to suppose, was exactly what was happening in his heart.

"You're untranslatable, you mean."

"That she is, lad, that she is," Verusha said, pulling out the little Turkish cigarettes she favored and lighting one with a clockwork lighter. The silence spread out, broken only by Casper's mad giggles and the puffing of Verusha's smoke rings.

"What will you do, then?" I asked.

"Sound my barbaric yawp, I suppose," he answered. With sudden violence, he stood and yelled, "Goddammit!" before lunging out the door and slamming it in his wake.

"Is he always this mad?" Verusha asked.

I shrugged. "Aren't we all?"

27

When I couldn't hide among the cushions anymore, I followed Casper's scent into the alley outside. Verusha didn't have to say a word. Her heavy silence, her disappointed glare, was sufficient. She hadn't raised me to cower from anyone, especially not halfblud abominations. I thought I heard her chuckle behind the closed door, but I was too embarrassed to check.

I was half terrified that Casper had run out into the streets alone, where he would surely have caused trouble of one kind or another. According to the laws of Muscovy, a lone servant could suffer anything from the merciless teasing of children to impounding or corporal punishment. Fortunately, he was simply sitting against the brick wall of the lane behind the shop, his hat still firmly laced under his chin.

"Do you hate me?" I asked. If the words were to be said, I wanted them to be mine and not his.

He snorted. "I want to. But I can't. I did this to myself. The universe is pointing me to the answer, and I don't like it. I can't blame you for that. It's a journey, I suppose. I can't stay in the same place forever."

I couldn't sit beside him on the ground, where someone might see. So I slumped against the wall, my gown's shoulder catching on the bricks.

"What's so bad about this life?" I gestured to the grand city around us and, more subtly, to myself.

"Would you want to become a Pinky, Ahna?"

I couldn't help but shudder. "Ugh. No."

"Okay, so that's how I feel about becoming a Bludman."

"But don't you see? Your position is untenable. You can't be human anymore. You can't be a halfblud for much longer. Why not accept what's inevitable? Why not choose it before something else chooses for you? It's better to be curious than judgmental. Compare this place with London. The dark streets, the fear riding the wind, the bludrats and Coppers. There's an elegance, a simplicity, to life as a predator. It's well ordered, calm. We celebrate the arts as the humans cannot and care for the individual as they won't. The only strife you've seen in this city was caused by the Pinkies."

"It's not a case of who is better or who is right. It's a case of giving up who I am, *what* I am. I exist as I am; that is enough."

"It very well is not. You're in the midst of a metamorphosis, and hiding from it is flat-out cowardly. Butterflies don't hide in cocoons; they bite their way out."

"Butterflies are extinct."

"You're not."

He stood in one fluid motion that was more predatorial than he would have cared to know. Towering a foot over me, he forced me to look up at him, and warmth rushed over my cheeks as I realized how very close we were standing and how very incorrect it was for us to be looking at each other that way in the alley behind a prominent groomery.

"You think I'm a coward, Ahna?"

I poked him in the chest with a talon. "Only on this topic. The one that matters most."

"Say I went through with it, then. How would it work?"

"I have no idea. But I'll find out. And I'll do it myself." I didn't realize the truth of it until I said it, but I couldn't imagine allowing anyone else to share so intimate an experience with him.

"You know it's painful. I don't want to cause you pain."

I shook my head at him. "Silly boy. It doesn't matter if it hurts. Agonies are one of my changes of garment."

He chuckled and shook his head. "Do you believe in destiny and reincarnation and . . . No, don't answer. It doesn't matter." His smile was gentle, tentative. He traced a line along my jaw with one finger and murmured, "You're a mystic, baffling wonder, woman."

I beamed. "I'll take that as a compliment."

He kissed me, gentle and swift.

"If I'm going to be a great poet, at least I have a great audience."

Back inside, Verusha shooed him into the groomery proper to wash off the grime of our long journey. I bristled momentarily, watching two pretty girls lead him off, petting him and offering him cookies, but I quickly remember that to them, he wasn't a man, much less an equal. He was a lapdog, a mindless creature to be cosseted and primped and displayed. After the bludding, I suspected I would be much more possessive of him.

"Show me what you have, darleenk," Verusha said,

motioning me over to an open window where the sun puddled through filmy curtains.

I had already plucked out a stone, the tear-shaped aquamarine heavy in my hand and as warm as a beating heart. When I held it in the sunlight, it winked as if snow-flakes danced within. I tipped it into Verusha's claws, and it rattled around as she inspected it.

"Will it buy everything we need?" I asked.

"Maybe yes. Maybe no." She prodded it with a clipped white talon. "Hard to say, these days."

"I want the best. I want to be beautiful when I kill Ravenna. And he needs to match."

"I know these things." She raised one eyebrow at me, but I didn't blink or apologize. The trick with Verusha was showing respect but not obedience or doubt. "There is also a charm you might want. It makes the bludding easier. For you both. But very, very expensive and hard to find."

Without a second thought, I pried another stone from the necklace, a diamond. It was cold in my hand, as sharp and hard as the ice it resembled.

"That, too, then."

She curled her hand around the stones, and they disappeared. The old woman nodded once, sharply, and withdrew a folded note from her shawl. The paper was thick and creamy, sealed with Verusha's crest, the bastard signet of the House of Muscovy.

"Go read it. Prepare yourself as much as you can. It's an ugly business, to be sure, but he's worth more bludded than dead or mad, yes?"

My face carefully blank, I said, "Yes. But where should it happen?"

Her lips pursed, wrinkling under the bright red paint. "Somewhere noisy," she finally said. "Not here."

After a pointed look at the ravaged necklace in my hand, she turned and hobbled back toward the parlor and the sunny prospect of business as usual. For just a moment, I thought about Keen, wondering if she had survived her grooming without embarrassing restraints and, if so, how she was enjoying the waiting room, where the polite servants of local Blud families would spend their afternoons sitting contentedly on benches, eating sweets and waiting to be retrieved. The little creature was probably inciting a rebellion.

I settled myself in the big chair. With my feet up and a belly full of blood that tasted like home, I was as ready as I could be for bad news. I broke Verusha's wax seal, slipped the note open, unfolded it, and began to read. Halfway through, I took a hard look at the remains of my necklace and popped out three more small diamonds. We were going to need them to pay off whichever unfortunate innkeeper ended up scrubbing away the bloodstains and losing custom on account of the screaming.

28

I decided upon the Moravian district. Not only because it was far from Verusha's shop and my family's ancient palace but also because the Moravians were known for being loud, messy, and mysterious. Their wild parties to celebrate the coming snow started early and ended late. And their traditional costume was handy, too. No one looked twice at us as we slipped down the avenue wrapped in long shawls and turbans, all but our eyes well hidden.

I'd never been to this part of Muscovy, as my parents had been prejudiced against anyone not of proven, pure-blud stock. I hadn't seen any of the other foreign districts, either, although our carriage had passed by a New Year's parade in the Dragon district when I was little, and I had sworn I'd seen a real dragon billowing white smoke into the sky. Once we had crossed under the exotically arched sign with "Little Moravia" picked out in bloodred and gilt, it was almost as if we were in another country.

The lights were gold like the sun, rather than the orange that my folk favored. The stone was white and creamy, with accents in vibrant jewel tones that recalled the sea and palm trees and exotic fruits I'd only seen in paintings. Brightly colored cloth flags and pennants fluttered on strings strung between the buildings, giving everything a festive look that made me feel as if I was on an adventure instead of skulking around in disguise to all but kill a man for my own sinister purposes.

The first inn we passed looked too shoddy, and the second was far too rich for the stones I'd chosen to part with. Fortunately, the third one seemed both reasonable and pretty, with a large mosaic of a camel picked out in glittering tile.

"La Jamala," Casper said, rolling the word around in his mouth. "I like it."

I nodded. "Camels are fascinating creatures. They can travel great distances, surviving on the blud stored in their humps. And when that runs out, they find another camel and eat its hump. Very resourceful creatures, camels."

I walked through the arched door ahead of Casper and secured a room, paying extra for "privacy and considerations." The way the old Bludman at the desk waggled his tangled eyebrows at me, I had to assume he thought we would be indulging in the most sordid brand of perversion. He saw nothing of me but my eyes swathed in burgundy cloth. To him, I was a twisted Bludwoman indulging myself with a lowly servant, but I had paid him well not to care. He put the skeleton key in my hand, the room number dangling from a faded leather tassel. I grabbed Casper's hand and pulled him into the inn, unsurprised to feel him trembling.

The stairs blended perfectly with the walls and had no handholds, and we went up and up in strange diamond patterns until I feared we would topple off the roof into the streets below. But no. Our room was at the very top, a converted attic garret. That was good—the floor would be thick, and there were no neighbors to either side, separated from our fracas by mere wood. The extra gems had served their purpose. I unlocked the door and pressed the button inside. A sky's worth of star-shaped lanterns buzzed into light, glowing with the glimmer of sun on desert sand.

I set down the bag I'd been carrying under my cloak with a clank. Casper pressed the door closed and locked it, his eyes on the bag.

"That what I think it is?"

"Believe me. We're going to need it." I pulled out the bottle and handed it to him.

He uncorked it and breathed it in. "Essence of assassin," he murmured, and with a shrug, he took a swig. I liked the fact that he was feeling bold. It would make the night easier for us both. After a couple of swallows, he grimaced. "Strong stuff."

"I added some extra ingredients."

Verusha had been unable to find the charm she had mentioned, the one that would make the bludding easier for us both. As an apology, she had given me a bottle of her finest bloodwine, from the same winery the royal family used. But I wasn't going to tell him that. I had a feeling he was going to have enough problems drinking human blood once he had no other options. What he didn't know now wouldn't kill him.

That was my job.

Bottle in hand, Casper pushed the shawl off his head and shook out his hair. He walked across the room, ducking under the star-shaped lanterns and stepping over the sultan's pillows and sheepskins. When he pushed open the door to the next chamber, he whistled low, an eerie sound that vibrated like some strange, free bird.

"What is it?" I asked, and he turned back with a warm smile.

"Come see."

I knew a little of Moravian culture, thanks to my tutors, and so I unlaced my boots and left them by the door before picking my way across the pillows to where he stood. The room on the other side was dark except for one brilliant rectangle of light, a stained-glass window that threw shimmering squares of color to glitter all over the floor. A wide, flat bed hung in the shifting rainbow, a rope at each corner tethering it to the ceiling and a pile of pillows waiting beside a single tasseled blanket, its corner turned back invitingly. Another thing about the Moravians—they liked to sleep off the ground.

I cleared my throat and looked away. "We should probably stick to the outer room. You're going to want to be on the floor for this." I unwrapped my shawl and let it drop to the tile in a puddle of rusty red.

He snorted and set down the bottle, its contents noticeably depleted. As he shucked off his knee-high boots, I took a few gulps myself, trying to pick apart the strange mélange of flavors as it went down. Blood, blud, wine, and the secret ingredients of the palace sommelier tickled the back of my throat and set my fingers and toes tingling.

"So it's going to hurt?" he asked.

I smiled grimly. "It's going to be 'a whole new world of pain,' to quote Verusha."

He slipped off his stockings and took a step toward me before hissing and holding up his foot. I could smell the drop of blood on his skin as he plucked something out and tossed it to the floor with a wry chuckle.

"Straw. Of course. Our inn is bedeviled with straw. The straw that broke the jamala's back."

"Wait!"

Everything that had just happened—I'd heard it before. I rummaged in my bag for the mysterious packet I'd carried all the way from the docks of Dover. The folded paper still wore Criminy's seal, although the ends were battered from being carried in my corset for so long. I held it up to my nose, breathing deep.

"What is it?" Casper asked, leaning close.

I broke the wax and unfolded the paper, careful not to spill the contents. The powder inside was the deep red of dried blood yet iridescent, as fine as ash. Written on the paper was, "Mix with the wine. It'll hurt less. Love, Criminy and Tish."

"Do you trust him?" I asked.

"Hell, no. But I trust her. Add it."

I folded the paper and tipped the powder into the remaining wine, putting a thumb over the bottle to mix it. As I was more invulnerable, I took the first swig to test it. The wine, already heavy and deep, now carried the airy tang of magic.

I felt lighter after that and offered him the bottle. With his usual recklessness, he drank deeply before handing it back. I sipped again, watching as he took off his coat, folded it, and set it aside. After a moment of contemplation, he lost his waistcoat and shirt, too. When he turned to me, hair loose and wild and wearing nothing but breeches, his torso outlined by the glittering sun dancing through the glass, I took another long gulp and felt the magic coat my lips.

My body was sending me so many signals that I couldn't tease them apart, and it seemed only natural to set down the empty bottle, launch myself at him, and push him to the ground, hunger surging and humming in my veins. I licked a long swath from his shoulder to his ear.

"Whoa, now," he said, and the tinge of fear in his voice was intoxicating.

"Too late for that." I straddled him, pinned his arms down, and nicked the vein pulsing in his neck. The first taste of his blood, straight from the source and drenched in wine and magic, sent a jolt of heat through my body. In between gulps, I murmured, "I thought it would be easier this way. Without deliberation."

He moaned and whimpered, then gritted his teeth and said, "Do it, then."

It was a simple process, from the outside, and almost exactly what Casper himself had said would have to happen in order to transform a human or halfblud into a full-on Bludman. There wasn't much new in the world, after all. I had to drink him nearly dry, then get enough of my blud into him to keep him going while he nearly drained *me* dry. We would go, give and take, back and forth, until the deed was complete. The hardest part was finding equilibrium between the two of us, each one controlling the predator within to keep from ripping the other apart or drinking too deeply, unto death.

The main ingredient may have been the mixture of blood and blud, but the secondary ingredient was trust, and I thought it better to hope for the best than to share my fears. My feelings toward him were muddled, as I suspected his were toward me, a push and pull of what the animal, mind, and heart wanted and needed and were willing to risk. Soon we would know the true balance between us, come what may.

For the moment, it was enough finally, finally, after so many weeks, to be sunk to the corners of my smile in his neck, gulping down the warm lifeblood of him, tasting him as no one else had. He trembled beneath me, muscles taut and hands curled into fists.

"It's okay," I whispered, "if you want to touch me."

His hands ran up and down my legs and hips, then gripped my ankles, grinding the bones together, and I pulled hard on his neck, drinking and drinking and drinking. When his hands finally fell from my legs, I woke up enough to know that for me, the easy part was over.

I pulled back and wiped my mouth with the back of my hand. "Casper? Casper, come along. It's your turn now. Drink. I'll help you."

His eyes were open and unfocused, glazed and staring. I traced his cheekbones, wishing for dimples that weren't there.

"C'mon. What is it you call me? Darlin'. Darlin', wake up now. You have to drink."

But I couldn't rouse him. I hadn't paid enough attention to his state and had drunk too deeply. I panicked, grabbing the bottle and slopping its contents into his mouth, hoping that what was left of the mixture would wake him up enough to take the blud I was more than ready to give him. There was barely any wine left. At first, the thick red stuff just dribbled down the side of his face and onto the black sheepskin beneath him. When almost all of the bottle was gone, though, I saw his throat move, his eyes blinking and focusing with a sudden ferocity I recognized all too well.

I shoved up the sleeve of my dress, rubbing the thin skin of my wrist over his lips. His eyes caught me, mad and desperate, but he didn't even try to bite me.

"I said, come on!" I growled. "Wake up! Take it! Rip me open, damn you!"

He shook his head and turned away from me, and with a feral howl, I shoved a finger into his mouth and caught it on one of his incisors, hoping the tiny nick would be enough to call him to task.

"Don't want to," he muttered around my finger. "Trying so hard not to."

"You must." After a few moments of him refusing the tiny bit of blud he might get before my finger healed, I said, "Please. I'm waiting for you."

His teeth bit down, testing just the tiniest bit, and he sighed. When I was one step away from ripping a hole in my own neck with a talon, I felt his teeth scissor sharply, opening up the cut again. He sucked my finger, and shivers raced down to my toes. His body came awake beneath me, bucking as he clamped down around my ankles once more. I could feel the thread of blud connecting us, feel his breathing speed up as the chest beneath me pumped harder and harder, sucking. When I didn't think I could take another moment of waiting for him to really drink, he groaned, a long and drawn-out sound. His leg snaked around my calf, and he rolled me over suddenly, the insistent suction on my finger never lessening.

His face rose over me, a sharp moon framed by wild hair and fading rays of sunlight. He released my finger with one last lick and bit his lip, panting.

"Oh, God, Ahna. You smell like . . ."

"Everything."

"The only thing."

"That's how it is."

"I can't stop myself."

With one talon, I scratched a line along my neck, right in the place where I had bitten him before.

"I wouldn't want you to," I whispered, turning my face away.

With a tortured breath, he bent over me, the wings of his hair tickling over my skin in deceptively sweet anticipation. It began as a kiss, tender and warm, and then, at the last possible moment, there were teeth. One sharp nip, and his lips settled around my throat with a moan of bliss. It was much gentler than I had expected, much gentler than I could have been, than I had been. His teeth weren't yet as sharp as mine.

His hand came up to stroke my face and draw my hair back, and it was my turn to clench my fists and buck and writhe, doing my pitiful best not to fight him off when he was still so new and weak.

It was a tender time, and the least little mistake could have been the end of either of us. I felt every heartbeat, every pump of blud flowing from me into him. The magic still glittered in me, the headiness of the wine making it somewhat easier to let him drain my life out through the thinnest skin of my body.

And then it hit me, for one perfect, clear moment.

This must be what it felt like to be a Pinky. To spend your life hiding your true desires and feelings, feigning politeness and manners, always waiting for the moment when your neck either bent for your master or was snapped in her hand with one flick of angry fingers. For the first time in my entire life, ever, I realized that the threat of death from blud loss was a very real thing, that I wasn't invincible. The euphoria turned into panic.

I started flailing and bucking, and Casper's hands moved

from cupping my jaw to pinning down my arms so I couldn't scrabble at him. His weight held me to the rugs and sheepskins, his mouth working against my throat and his ankles heavy on my legs. I whimpered softly, but I had no hope that he heard me.

"Casper?" I rasped, but he didn't respond.

I couldn't move, but I had to get his attention, and I didn't have long. My thoughts went back to the book I had found under his bed, long before I knew him and even before I learned that the sentiments weren't his own. But I couldn't remember the words written there, only scribbles and scratches. I was getting weaker and weaker, my mind growing sluggish. My mouth opened and closed wordlessly, until I finally recalled the first sound I had heard from him, even before I had seen him.

"Hey, Jude," I whispered, voice cracking. I went through as many lyrics as I could scrape together, certain that the song made no sense. And yet it was there in my subconscious, as if it had become a part of me and I couldn't quite escape it. I told him not to be afraid, to make things better. When I got to the part about skin, he pulled back, and I felt his breath whistle cold over the rip in my throat.

"Ahna? What . . . ?"

He moved to my side, touching my face. I could feel blud puddled in my hair, sticking it to my neck and ear. He had fed like a child, fast and messy, and I myself felt very much like a broken doll forgotten on the floor. I tried to move my arm and couldn't. My mouth opened, but I was finished singing.

"What do I do? Oh, God, Ahna. I can't believe I . . . what do I do?"

I moaned and rolled my eyes toward the scrap of paper

that had fallen from my hand to the floor. He didn't understand at first, but then he picked it up and scanned it. I knew he'd found the right part when he sighed and said, "Is there no end to it?"

In response, I mewled like a kitten, my entire being focused on his wrist, where the tiny blue veins fluttered like leaves in a chill autumn wind. He grimaced and looked at his arm.

"I don't think I can. I mean, not my wrist. Try this."

He picked me up, one arm under my knees and one around my shoulder. Emptied of blud, I weighed no more than an empty dress, and he carried me over to the wall and slid down until he sat with his back against a pillow. My mouth opened and closed uselessly, inches away from his neck. He pulled me close, cradling me as he smoothed back his hair with one hand to expose the golden skin underneath.

"Can you bite?" he asked. "Are you strong enough?"

"Closer," I managed to whisper, and when he obliged, I used every bit of strength I had to scrape him with a fang, just enough to start a dribble of red. As full as he was, it didn't take much to get the wound flowing and me drinking. Within moments, I was strong enough to wrap my arms around his neck and latch on for real. The more I drank, the tighter he held me. But this time, it didn't take so much. I was able to stop long before there was any danger to him. That had to mean it was working.

I pulled away, licking my lips and feeling suddenly ladylike. It was one thing being taken over by the beast, especially when on the verge of draining. But it had always been important among my people to show control and restraint whenever possible. My hair was plastered to the nape of my neck, the back of my gown sodden and sticky.

"I brought towels and rose water," I said, suddenly self-conscious. "For after."

His face was dark, shadowed with a beard and dominated by eyes gone cloudy and glittering like crushed sapphires. "How much longer?" he whispered. "How much more?"

"Until it's done." I looked him up and down, as much as I could see from within the cage of his arms. "I don't think we're there yet. You're still hungry?"

"It's the strangest hunger I've ever felt. Not in my stomach . . ."

"More like in your heart?"

He nodded, brow drawn down.

"That's how it is. Because what you need now isn't food." He stared past me, focusing on the sparkling Moravian lamps. In the darkness of the windowless room, they held their glow close, the deep indigo of the corners as fathomless as the night sky. It was a beautiful scene, peaceful and magical, a moment stolen out of time. I moved my hair aside and bent my head, saying only, "Go on, then."

"I don't want to hurt you."

"I volunteered. And it's getting easier, isn't it?"

"I feel strange. Not weak, like I did before." His voice was ragged and deeper than it had been. He swallowed hard and went still, and I knew that he had noticed the vein in my neck, thumping so close that there was no way he could avoid smelling it, no way he could stop the hunger.

"When will I want blood? Instead of you?"

"I can't say. What do you want now?"

"Only you."

"Then have me."

29

He sighed, a long and heartbreaking sound. His lips found my neck, kissing first, almost nibbling, as if he didn't quite know how to break the skin or was trying to fight the beast within. Then, as I had, he nipped just the tiniest bit. I jerked in his arms, surprised by the feeling it woke in me. His lips, the bite. The way he was sucking gently. It felt . . . good.

There was a primal rhythm to it, to the warm, wet pull of his mouth. I was still in his lap. One of his hands was splayed across my lower back, his other cupping my jaw and holding me in place. He moaned and shifted underneath me, and I realized that he felt it, too. He felt it and liked it . . . very much. Tingles shot down my spine, and I let my head fall back a little more. The blud he was taking—it made me feel lightheaded and weightless, as if I were floating. When he pulled away, a whimper escaped me. Before I could even open my eyes, his lips were sealed over mine.

His mouth tasted of home and hunger and wine and the spice of lingering magic. I kissed him back, my body uncaring whether I craved his blood or his blud or his hot, probing tongue. He tasted me, drank me in, growled into my mouth as if upset that he couldn't eat me in one big bite. I could feel the sharpness of his fangs with the tip of my tongue, and I reveled in the fact that he was no longer some weak prey animal, waiting for a tragedy or a stupid mistake to take him away, possibly at my hands. He was more substantial now, more real, more solid, tethering me to my body and the moment with the surety of the moon acting on the tides.

I felt him pulling away from me, and I sucked on his lip as he left, reluctant to be without him.

"Ahna, I feel so . . ." He trailed off, and I nipped his lip again.

"You feel?"

"Strange. Hungry but full. Powerful."

His arms held me loosely, and I liked how light I felt, how empty and malleable and open. Carefree and drunk on what little blud I had left, I swooned a little, and he caught me tighter against his bare chest, his skin so hot it felt like liquid flame.

"Kiss me, Casper."

"I can't kiss you. You need blood. And I can't control myself."

"Don't. You don't have to. I don't want you to." My voice slurred a little.

"The things I want to do . . . they scare me. It's like everything's washed over in red."

"Give in to it, Maestro."

"I don't know how."

"You'll learn."

I tried to kiss him again, but he held back as if afraid he might break me. The beast in me rose to the surface, furious at being denied. With that extra burst of ferocity, I pulled myself to his neck and latched on to the same place where I'd bitten him before. He was almost bludded but not quite finished, and he hadn't healed yet. I sucked hard, blissful at the heated rush of satisfaction, of blud and blood perfectly mixed. Old Verusha had never hinted that it would be anything like this. Bloody and messy and hideously painful for us both, yes, but delicious and sweet? I could not have imagined it. The charm was strong, the spell well cast. Whoever that Criminy fellow was, we had cause to thank him.

As I drank, savoring the rhythm of his heartbeat, his wide palm made circles on the small of my back. I couldn't escape knowing that he was enjoying it, too, his body's readiness apparent under the tangle of my dress. But it wasn't enough, being gathered in his lap like a child or a favorite dog. I had told him to give in to it, and bit by bit, as his hand inched around to caress the curve of my hip, I found that I couldn't escape giving in myself. With one last swallow, I pulled myself away from the blud, its call dampened by new urges. I licked my way up his neck, found his lips, and kissed him the way I wanted to be kissed. When his hands fastened around my waist, I turned to straddle him, my knees on either side of his legs.

"You need more," he murmured into my mouth, and I answered, "I'll take what I need."

When he tried to pull back again, I settled my hips against him, rocking from side to side as I kissed him, hard and demanding. His grip on my waist slid down, settling possessively on my hipbones. He jerked me closer and pulled up his knees behind my back. We were lined up in the most primal way, and I found that in this sense, at least, I liked being trapped.

"I need more," he whispered in my ear, and I turned

my neck for him, anxious for the sharp pain that pre-ceded the strange euphoria of him feeding on me.

He bit down harder this time, as if testing his fangs. I gasped as he latched on, and he moved against me, hip to hip, rubbing sensuously through the layers of fabric to reach the most secret part of me. Tentatively at first, then more pointedly, I moved with him, his thrusts match-ing the pulse of his lips sucking at my neck. It all moved together like the waves I'd seen at the ocean and never, ever dared touch. They were dangerous, those swells and crests, and I knew that they held the power to destroy me instantly. But this—these waves—they felt right, and if there was any threat of me flying apart, it was from plea-sure.

The rhythm was timeless, and I caught on fast, my breath-ing and heartbeat a high counterpoint. I wanted something, something more, something I couldn't describe. My hands found his bare shoulders, broad and muscled and warm, my nails digging in with urgency. I began to understand what could inevitably unfold between two people, but at the same time, I was somewhere else entirely, floating again. And hun-gry, so hungry. For him.

With one last, wild lick, he pulled back from me, his hips still moving, his mouth wet with my blud.

"Do you need more?"

"I'm . . . I need . . . I don't know." And I didn't.

"Do you want me, Ahnastasia?"

"I don't know what I want, but if I don't get it, I'm going to rip you to shreds."

"No," he barked, and when he stopped moving against me, I hissed and focused on him, our eyes but inches away. He chuckled and drew back, holding my face in both hands as if daring me to look away, his smile kind and dimpled but his eyes stern. "No, darlin'. No. We're way past that adorable little vicious act of yours. If we're doing this, we're doing it as equals. I'm not your pet anymore."

I whimpered and tried to kiss him, but he was stronger than he had been and kept me at arm's length.

"Why does it matter?" I said. "Don't you need it, too?"

"I need you, not it. And I'm done being used. If you're going to take from me, you're going to start giving back, and I'll start with your heart."

For that second, I swear my heart stopped beating. All the want and hunger and desperation faded in the face of his demand. Could it be possible that Casper . . . loved me?

I had been raised in wealth and coldness, receiving more warmth from Verusha than from my own family. Personal greetings were mannerly and swift, a polite peck on the cheek. Hugs were almost unknown, for how could my mother draw me close when her dress was encrusted with diamonds and weighed more than she did? Love and affection were things you felt for your country, for your favorite hat, for the wolfhound that greeted you without fail at the door. But to expect love from a royal match—it was laughable. Almost unheard of. I had never considered, in all my life, if my parents loved each other. I knew for a fact that they didn't.

And here we were, tangled up and blood-spattered on the floor of a Moravian inn, and this man, this Stranger, wanted my heart. He wanted my mouth to say words I had never heard spoken. He wanted me to declare myself just for the privilege of rutting with him as I'd seen the passengers of the *Maybuck* meet, flesh to flesh. The day before my final stand, before I planned to murder a dictator at a holy rite in front of my people, he wanted me to make a commitment that no princess, no Tsarina, could make. A Tsarina's heart belonged to her country.

The feelings he had awakened in me were tempting, and I was curious. But those feelings, that satisfaction—they weren't worth lying to him, making promises I couldn't keep. Maybe the intimacy I felt was part of the bludding process, part of the powder's magic. Maybe I had to admit to myself that my beast had desires, and blood was apparently not the only one.

Or maybe . . .

I swallowed hard and sought my answer in his eyes.

It hit me like an arrow, thudding in my chest. In Casper's eyes, I saw more than pleas and lust. I found recognition, acceptance, and dedication. It was all written there for me to read, in the shadows dancing against the blue. This man, this new Bludman, had feelings for me. Fierce ones that couldn't be denied. And he was no longer confused, lost within himself. He was strong like me, powerful like me. And he wanted me, he loved me, as sure as his blood beat in my veins.

In that moment, it went from impossible to simple.

He hadn't asked for a commitment, hadn't asked me to love him or marry him or pledge myself to him eternally. He wanted my heart, but he hadn't demanded it. He had asked me, quite simply, if I wanted him. And that was an easy question to answer.

"I want you," I said, and a wicked smile lit his face.

In one smooth swoop, he stood, holding me tight against his bare chest, his hands under my thighs. I wrapped my arms around his neck, and he carried me as if I weighed nothing. Before I knew what had happened, he had shoved through the door into the next room and spread me out on the bed. It swung under me slightly, the ropes that tied it to the ceiling creaking. I felt more weightless, more pure and groundless and free, than ever. Even though it was past the last rays of sunset, the lantern light from outside was bright enough to shimmer through the stained-glass window and paint me in a rainbow of colors.

Casper walked around the bed. Stalking me. I stretched and arched my back for him, lifting one leg to let the silk dress slide up one calf.

"Everything about you is just so . . . delicious."

I grinned, showing him my teeth. "Taste me, then."

He wrapped long fingers around the rope, his eyes tracing it to the ceiling in curiosity. Apparently satisfied by what he saw, he leaped lightly onto the bed, which barely swayed, thanks to his newfound dexterity, the balance and litheness of a predator already taking root. With the same care I'd seen Tommy Pain use when the cat walked a ledge, Casper prowled around the outside of the bed, drinking in every inch of me. When he wound around the ropes and stepped over my feet, his shadow blocked the window, and for just a moment, he looked rampant and wild as a timber wolf, his eyes glowing in the darkness.

There was a new confidence there, too, whether because of my admission or the fundamental change in his body. He appeared by my side on his knees, so quick and smooth that it seemed as if he'd melted, the bed barely swaying. The squares of light flowed over his bare shoulders like liquid, lighting his hair like the halos I'd seen in old-fashioned Pinky paintings of saints and angels.

"I have wanted you since the first moment I saw you. Even half-dead, you were more alive than any woman I've ever met." He stretched out, half beside me, half on me, one hand tugging my curls. "And that hair. It's like I can still see it sometimes, the color of butter. Like I can feel it pulling through my fingers when I'm asleep and dreaming of you."

"It'll grow back," I said, almost apologetically, and he chuckled.

"Hush, sugarplum," he said, his accent strange and mellow.

He kissed me, long and slow, taking his time. The anticipation built, my body crying for his touch and rabid for satisfaction as he refused to hurry. The wine had made it easy the first time. Sharing blud had made it even easier, the excuse of feeding and hunger melding with the physical desire for the body around the need for sustenance. But now there was only him and me and the knowledge that we wanted each other, whatever that meant.

"It's easier to kiss you now that I don't want to eat you," I murmured.

"For me, it's harder. Because now I want to eat you, too."

I gasped as he kissed down my jaw, tracing a line along the vulnerable skin there, the veins close to the surface where he'd already bitten. When he found the hollow of my throat, I moaned and ran my nails down the back of his neck, his hair soft on my wrist. He kept going, sliding his tongue along my collarbones and into the V of my silk dress. With a growl of frustration, he grasped the sides of the bodice as if to rip it in half, and I covered his hands with my own.

"Patience, Maestro." I slid his hands to my hips. "You've waited this long."

"If you insist."

I rolled over onto my stomach, and he gently bit the nape of my neck. Kissing down my spine, he unbuttoned the dress, one flick of fabric at a time. His lips followed his fingers, and I quivered as he hit the spot that was usually covered in corset. I had left it with Verusha, knowing that we were in for a messy and painful business. But now its absence gave me cause to purr, feeling the soft heat of Casper's lips trailing on skin tender with unaccustomed freedom. He undid the final button and ran his tongue all the way up my back, and something inside me melted, heavy and sweet as puddled wax.

He rolled me onto my back again, rough and slightly playful, the bed swaying. One after the other, he slid my arms from the fitted sleeves, kissing the curves of my shoulders, the tender insides of my elbows, and the pale white dip of each wrist. I closed my eyes, savoring the anticipation, wanting him to get back to kissing me or feeding on me or something less ticklish, more real, more demanding.

"I will never get used to all this damn fabric," he murmured into the curve of my neck.

He kissed me hard as his hands slid the gown down to my waist, and I pressed against him, skin to skin and hotter than the sun. When he pushed it down farther, past my hips, I arched up against him, glad to be free of the blood-soaked silk. My foamy petticoats and his breeches were the only things left between us once he tossed my dress onto the floor, and I wanted more than ever to be completely unfettered.

The bed creaked and swayed as he rolled onto his side,

taking me with him. One hand traced the swoops and valleys down my side, which had matured while I slept in the suitcase and filled out further with a week of good blood. When he found the swell of my hip, he groaned and pulled me closer, right up against him.

I couldn't wait any longer. I growled, slipping out of my petticoats and tossing them off the bed, finally free.

His hands were suddenly everywhere, hot and greedy and grasping. On my hips, pulling me closer against the swell in his breeches. Scratching lightly up my spine, making me squirm and bare my teeth. Cupping my breasts, teasing the nipples with his thumbs, squeezing and gently pinching. Eyes closed, I felt everything, my entire body awake and open and willing.

He rolled me onto my back, his cheek rasping as his lips found my nipple and sucked. I moaned, unprepared for the hunger it would raise in me. My back arched, my other breast crying out to be touched, and his hand obliged, the fingers as nimble and skilled as I had imagined. Every time I'd watched him play the harpsichord, whether I knew it or not, I had thought of this, or something like it, of cunning fingers and warmth and that same cocky ease applied to coaxing music from my body.

The way his hands and mouth roved over me—it was intoxicating, better than the bludwine. I couldn't tell where one hand touched and another stroked, where his mouth would go next with wet tongue and clever lips. He kissed between my breasts and licked a line down my ribs, dipping briefly into my navel and making me quiver. When he went farther down, I thought about stopping him, asking what, exactly, he was doing. Because surely he wasn't going to . . .

Oh, holy mother. He was.

Tongue wide and wet, he licked a long swath right where I wanted it most, right where I'd been aching for his touch, and I bucked and moaned as he found other ways to lick and taste. He seemed to savor it, and as I had no basis for comparison, I just closed my eyes, arched my back, and loved every second of it. The sweetest, warmest feeling started to bloom deep in my middle, and when he slid one finger in gently, moving it in time with his tongue, I thought I was going to die on the spot.

This feeling was better than the blud, better than anything I'd ever known. I didn't know how his harpsichord kept from bursting into flames under his hands. The loveliest sensation was building in me, and I could barely breathe, barely stop myself from screaming. One hand twisted in the bed sheets, one caught in his hair, I was riding a wave that I could barely contain.

With one last, deep taste, he pulled away. I wanted to rip his neck open in frustrated fury. He caught my open mouth with his before I could protest, all but swallowing my tongue with the same rhythm he'd used far below. One finger continued rubbing me, gentle and unceasing, and he kissed me deeply and unsnapped his breeches with his other hand. Somewhere far off, I heard his pants hit the ground, and then his body pressed against me from shoulder to foot, hot silk that smelled of pride and hunger and triumphant alpha male.

Aztarte help me, I purred and rubbed against him, shameless to resist my own nature.

His—I didn't even know what to call it, and I wasn't about to stop kissing him to look down—pressed against me, rubbing in the wetness he'd created and all but driving me into madness.

"Go on," I whimpered.

He pressed tighter, just the tip inside, one finger circling my flesh just above.

"It's your first time, isn't it?" He kissed me gently. "Then we should go slow, make sure you're—"

With a rugged growl, I rolled over on top of him and settled down, taking all of him and claiming what was mine in a savage thrust. There was a quick burst of pain, but it didn't stop me, and it didn't last. He sighed and groaned, hands grasping my hips firmly. Oh, it was lovely, so satisfying, and I moved up and down experimentally until I found what felt best. He obliged, guiding my hips until I had the rhythm just right and then finding that lovely spot again with a finger and rubbing and rubbing, faster and perfectly.

It was like dancing, but better, better than anything I'd ever known, moving together with him, feeling the delicious fullness and pressure building. I ran my hands through his hair, down over the muscles of his shoulders, and spread my fingers wide over his chest, which was lightly dusted with auburn hair that matched his eyelashes. When I sat up, I saw that a line of similar hair trailed down his flat belly.

With the angle changed, so did the feeling, and I rocked back with a little sigh of pleasure. One of his hands found my nipple, pinching and rolling it, and I let my head fall back, one hand on his stomach for balance. He surged underneath me, moving in delectable circles, his finger never ceasing, caressing me again and again. As I moved faster, breathing in frantic gulps between moans and sighs, he moved with me, making the most deliciously masculine noises deep in his throat. I was so close, so close, and I looked down into his eyes, and they were full of love and wonder and murder and the deep blue of the sapphire in my ring, mysterious as the night sky and dark and warm as the stars, and then it struck me, that feeling, radiating from the place where we joined out through my heart and blud and bones and body, and I arched and bucked and screamed, an animal howl of triumph and joy that must have surely shaken the world.

He kept with me, stroke for stroke, and just as I began to melt and fall, he caught me close and rolled me over to my back and battered against me, harder and harder and deeper than deep. I took it, teeth bared, swallowing down the little echoes of my release as his own trembling howl built and erupted. Heat and silk and sweetness filled me, and I went stiff and taut as the last notes held, a song unending.

Rolling sideways, he ran one sweaty hand over me, a companionable and possessive gesture that ended with the scratch of a fingernail already growing sharp.

"Oh, darlin'," he said, voice as sweet as blood oranges. "You're going to be the death of me."

"I already was," I answered, one hand likewise claiming, splayed over his thigh. "Now you start living for real."

"I love——" he began, but before he could finish, someone knocked on the door in the outer room. Casper lurched to his feet, naked, and charged the door with the full fury of a Bludman's beast unchained.

"Wait!" I shouted. But I was too late.

30

I held my breath as the bed jerked beneath me, the sturdy ropes creaking in protest. Casper ripped the door open with a growl, and I smirked at his naked back, knowing what was on the doorstep. His entire posture and energy went from murderous and bestial to baffled and embarrassed. By the light of the star-shaped lanterns, I admired his bum as he knelt to get something off the ground.

"Blood?"

"It's an inn," I called. "Room fees include two vials a day. It's customary."

He stared at the tray and shook his head, bemused. "If the knock had come five minutes earlier, that would be one dead innkeeper."

His feet slapped the tile briefly between the two rooms, his gait easy and confident. Setting the tray on the bed, he held out a vial to me, and I popped the cork and poured it into one of the two teacups. Casper fumbled with his cork, trying to pop it out with his thumb as I had. I smiled indulgently as I traced the skillfully painted Moravian designs in bright red and light blue on the thin porcelain. One of my geography tutors had been a world traveler, and I recalled her story of how

Moravians used paint to reimagine the spray of fresh blood against the desert sky.

Casper finally managed to dislodge the cork, blood spattering his chest lightly. I had forgotten we were naked.

"Better than ruining your waistcoat, eh?" I caught the blood on a finger and sucked it off.

"I've got a lot to learn, it seems." He poured the remaining blood into the other teacup and swirled it around, fascinated and bemused.

"Drink it fast, or it will coagulate. If you must take your time, keep swirling it. In warmer places, it stays fresh longer, but in Muscovy, with the cold, it thickens quickly when exposed to air." I took a dainty sip from my cup.

He tried a sip, rolling the blood around in his mouth. "Damn. That's bizarre. Salty and sweet. Almost syrupy. But with cinnamon."

I shrugged. "Local flavor."

As the blood slid down my throat, I couldn't help wondering what it would be like to try it for the first time, when one had no catalog of tastes to help recognize the flavors. Human food came in so many varieties, with different textures and shapes and colors. Blood mostly looked the same, no matter what the outside package had looked like. And yet everyone had a different palate, most Bludmen enjoying whatever blood had been most handy when they were young. I'd had Moravian before, although I was more accustomed to the stolid, hearty taste of well-bred Freesian servants. I hadn't tasted a Stranger or an Almanican before, so far as I knew, and I couldn't help being curious about what Casper had tasted like, before the blud had seeped into his body and started changing him. Now I would never know.

That made me think of Keen, and I almost asked about her. I hadn't seen her since handing her over to the groomers. Had they discussed his transition, or would he ask her forgiveness later? She was sure to hate me either way, but I hoped there would be some way to find resolution. Even if I didn't want to talk about her just then, I was forced to admit that I cared for the little urchin. She would have a place in the palace no matter what—that much I promised myself.

He placed his empty cup back on the enameled tray carefully, as if worried that he might smash it. I set mine down, too, unwrapping one of the swan-folded napkins to dab daintily at my lips, even though I knew very well that I hadn't spilled a drop. The mess from the bludding was still sticky in my hair, but my mouth was spotless.

"I feel so strange," Casper said, holding out his hands and flexing the long fingers. "Like I'm tight all over, like I'm ready to run."

"You're a predator now. You *are* ready to run. Did you feel how the beast carried you to the door when you sensed a threat? Your entire body is constantly waiting for exactly that. It's important that you drink two vials of blood a day, or that'll happen more and more easily. Your body wants to feed, and control takes time to develop."

He pulled on his breeches and walked over to an ornate mirror that hung on the plaster wall.

"Do I look different? Am I . . . I don't know. Prettier? Paler?"

I considered him. "Your eyes are different. Your smell is different. You move differently. But it isn't like going to the groomery a complete mess and coming out fixed up with a new hairstyle." Watching him stare at his hands by lantern light, I added, "And your hands, I think, will take some time to darken fully. We'll have to think of a way to hide them at the ball."

"The ball." He sighed, staring intently into his own eyes as if looking for something that had fled. "That gives me a day to learn everything I need to know."

"About being a Bludman?" I snorted. "You already know everything. Drink blood, be proud, fight to the death, and laugh loudly."

"About Freesia. About your people and family and customs. About why this Sugar Snow Ball is so damned important. About how to speak to people, how to bow. How to fake an accent. How to kill Ravenna if she murders you in front of everyone."

I stretched luxuriously and flicked my fingers at his reflection.

"Psh. You can learn all that in the carriage. So long as you know how to dance and be quiet, you'll do fine."

His posture changed, and in an instant, he was elegantly waltzing around the room with his shadow, shoulders back and feet nimble, elegantly muscled arms locked in a cage that held nothing. "I think you'll find me a more than adequate dance partner. Being quiet, though—I find myself more outspoken than ever. I don't know if silence is an option anymore. I feel like nothing and no one can hold me back. It's freeing, really." With a final spin, he dipped his invisible partner. His hair fell forward, glimmering in the rainbow light from the stained-glass window, and I couldn't stop staring. He was the most attractive creature I'd ever encountered, and it was somewhat unsettling to see him so different and yet unchanged.

When he stood up, laughing and pushing his hair back,

I realized how very well his dimples went with his pointier smile. I looked down when I felt myself blushing.

"So what do we do now?" he asked.

I shifted uncomfortably, finding that the aftereffects of our lovemaking were a bit disconcerting and messy. "It's an inn. We've paid through the night. So we'll stay the night, have a vial in the morning, and return to Verusha's to prepare."

"A pleasant night of sleep and a makeover," he said with another chuckle. "Fair enough. I guess that somewhere under the power and hunger and elation, I'm dog-tired."

"The process is supposed to be very taxing. I think sleep will be good for us both."

I stood, my feet a little wobbly, keeping the sheet wrapped around my body. In the heat of the moment, clothes had seemed very inconvenient indeed, and I had come close to ripping them off myself at a few points. But now, with him staring at me with a mixture of curiosity, tenderness, and, somehow, still more hunger, the sheet was a blessing. It trailed behind me to the narrow door in the far wall.

"So we still have to . . . use the . . . um . . ."

I burst out laughing. "We're predators, you fool. Not statues."

The look on his face as I dropped the sheet and slammed the door was utterly priceless.

When I was done in the bathroom, I found him relaxing in the bed, which had been tidied up, the covers straightened and pillows added to make a cozy nest. He'd pulled the curtain across the stained glass, and the room was mostly shadows. The darkness was warm and velvety, with Casper at its heart. Forgetting my sheet, I padded across the room and climbed onto the bed.

"The swaying reminds me of the *Maybuck* a little," Casper said, stretching one arm out invitingly. I slid in beside him, turning to face him. His arm curled around me, his hair brushing my collarbone. I nestled against him, breathing in his scent, which no longer sang to me of food. He reminded me of a summer day in the fields, of golden grass and heavy trees swaying in the breeze and sweet flowers and the manly odor of sweat and strength. Like sleeping in the sunshine, a brief respite.

"What do I smell like to you?" I asked suddenly.

He buried his cheek in my hair. I felt his chest expand beneath me, his breath warm against my ear. "Frozen flowers. Wind and ice. Something purple and beautiful, a bloom unfurling under the moon, in the snow."

I shivered and sighed and settled myself more firmly against him. It felt . . . right. As if I was exactly where I was supposed to be. I had no map for where I was going with him, no history for understanding how a man and a woman shared themselves. My parents had been the king and queen in a game of chess, always apart and moving in separate, incalculable ways. No wonder I didn't miss them more. I'd never seen a relationship built on trust and attraction, never seen passing touches and two creatures curled around each other in sleep. But my beast understood that Casper was powerful now and would defend me with his life and that I could do much worse for myself than settle close in his arms and find some peace before everything went to hell.

But something was bothering Casper. He shifted against

me as if he couldn't get comfortable and exhaled into my shoulder, and I turned to put a hand on his cheek.

"What's wrong? What could possibly be wrong?"

"It's just . . . it would just be an inconvenient time for you to . . ." He sighed deeply and swallowed. "For you to be with child. I wasn't thinking. I'm sorry."

When he trailed off, I kissed him lightly and chuckled. "That's what troubles you? Never fear. Now's not the time."

"How do you know?"

"I have a body. I always know when it's time."

"Is that a Bludman thing?"

"It's a Bludwoman thing. Any other concerns?"

He rubbed my back, sleepy and warm, and I relaxed a little. "We were together. I forget the rest," he said.

Contented, I fell asleep, swaying gently in his arms.

The next morning was filled with tiny awkwardnesses. I woke up with his body tangled sweetly around me, except for the bit that was unintentionally prodding me. When I shot out of the bed in sleepy surprise, Casper tried to roll out while it was swaying, and he landed on the floor in a lump of blankets. It was challenging, finding all of our clothes and catching sneaky glances at each other, little snippets of bodies we'd already seen in all their glory but couldn't help being curious about. He almost murdered the vial delivery boy again, but at least he was clothed this time.

Once we were dressed and fed, he was as suave and collected as any Bludman I'd ever seen. Confidence was key for a predator—lesser creatures were naturally suspicious. He had been cocky before, but now he was dangerously dauntless. If he wasn't careful, he was going to come across as a threat. A tricky line to walk, to be sure.

"How do you feel?" I asked, straightening my Moravian shawl in the mirror.

"Like I could take down a moose and drink it dry." He bounced on the balls of his feet, radiating energy.

"That's because you've never tasted one." I turned to face him, looking him up and down. He cut a fine figure, to be sure, and for a brief moment, I thought about launching myself at him and kissing him until he threw me back onto the bed. But no. I had a country to save. I picked up his shawl and draped it over him, hiding his long hair, his broad shoulders, everything but the toes of his boots. His old Pinky hat would go into a rubbish bin. "Most blud animals are gamey and thin compared with humans. Unless you take one in a fight to flavor it with victory, you'd find the taste repellent." I watched him move for a moment and added, "You might want to tone it down a bit, though. You'll attract unwanted attention from dangerous males, walking like that."

"It's not my fault I have vampire swagger," he said.

I raised one eyebrow at him, and he raised one back at me, and then he broke out in loud laughter. It was a welcome sound. After all our time together, I'd seen him drunk, conflicted, angry, scared, lusty, and nearly suicidal. But I'd never seen him happy. Not before just now.

My boots waited by the door, and I savored how easy it was to lace them when not wearing a corset. At home in the palace, I had never laced my own boots, and therefore the order of corsetry had never mattered. But I had learned on the *Maybuck* that smart girls put on shoes, then corset, then took off corset, then shoes. The first few times lacing either item by myself had been nearly impossible, but now I'd gotten used to it.

My mother would have fainted, to think of me tying my own boots or fixing my own hair. She had been well over a hundred and had never cut her own hair. The mass of it had fallen nearly to the floor, and the servants had always complained behind her back about the trouble it took to wash it, dry it, and put it up in ever more complicated styles that would set the fashion for all of Freesia. It was painful, thinking of how Ravenna must have defiled the Tsarina's beloved hair, not to mention her body.

My mother's idea of good leadership had been just like her hair—ornamental and vexing. I had been raised to rule, but ruling mostly meant dwelling in various palaces, reclining, complaining, and being vicious. It seemed quite petty, from where I stood now. And even if I didn't agree with her outdated and overly cruel style of monarchy, she had been better than Ravenna. The upstart gypsy snake had begun her reign with murder, deposed the barons, and let the Pinkies run unchecked. Although I didn't understand her ultimate goal, from what I could see, she wanted to destroy everything that Freesia stood for.

And what had become of poor Alex, my nearly feral younger brother? He had been born growling and nipping and hadn't really stopped since. While everyone else in the palace drank two or three vials a day or sometimes a few measured gulps from a willing servant, Alex was ravenous and required ten times as much blood to keep from going mad. When he had enough blood and was in a good patch, he was overly polite and given to intelligent pursuits. He wrote rambling letters to pen pals in Constantinoble and Melburn, took great interest in the hounds, and enjoyed falconry. We played chess together and planned imaginary trips. Olgha and I had always been rivals, but Alex and I got on fine, so long as he was fed. Without enough blood, he became dangerously savage and had to be chained up and forced to guzzle animal blood until he quit screaming. Chirurgeons and herbalists and mystics had been called in to cure him, but none had succeeded.

If Ravenna had found an ally in Alex, if she had found a way to calm him, if not cure him, then it was easy enough to see how she had won her way into the palace. A son who couldn't make an advantageous match for the royal house—a son who, much worse, couldn't even be taken out in public and might attack newspaper reporters—was a liability and a tragedy. My mother had first coddled him, then sent him away, then kept him close like a muzzled bludmare, hoping every day that a solution would present itself.

If what Casper had told me and what I had read in the newspapers was correct, Ravenna had found a way to subdue Alex. And that was one more problem with killing her. What if she was the only one who knew the secret to a normal life for my brother?

A hand landed on my shoulder. "Ahna? You're a thousand miles away. What's wrong?"

My fists were clenched around my bootlaces, which were tied in triple knots. I let go of the laces and stood, flexing my fingers to get the blud flowing through them once more.

"I was thinking about Freesia. About my brother. There are just so many variables."

He chucked me under the chin, and I wrenched my face away in annoyance. "A glancer once told me that I would have a happily ever after. I think that means we're going to succeed."

"I told you—I don't believe in omens." I picked up my bag and stood by the door, not yet ready to leave the comfort of our little aerie. "I was taught to believe that fortune-telling was the lowest form of chicanery, people telling you what you want, what you need to hear."

"I might have thought so once, if the fortune-teller hadn't broken my heart. Everything she said has come true so far. Why can't the good part be as true as the bad?"

He stepped close enough that had he been anyone else, it would have raised my hackles. Instead, I felt a strange ripple shimmy down my body. It reminded me of the way my father's favorite wolfhound had always greeted him, wiggling as if she were so full of joy she could shake it off like water. I cocked my head at him, considering. Was this lust? Or love? Or just fellow feeling tangled up with a hunger for his body? Before I could consider further, his lips brushed over mine, warm and swift as a breeze in summer.

Would there be time to understand these feelings fully by the time I stood before Ravenna, my entire country's future riding on my shoulders? There was no way to know. Maybe she would kill one or both of us, and I would never have to consider it further. With a sudden urgency, I leaned forward to kiss him back, my lips firm against his.

"Let's go take over this cold-ass country," he said with a dimpled grin. We pulled up the hoods of our Moravian disguises and disappeared among the morning crowd, two Bludmen in something a little like love.

31

When we arrived at the groomery, Verusha looked Casper up and down through her monocle and nodded, as close as she would come to congratulations. As for Keen, she had escaped after her grooming and hadn't been seen since. Casper was worried, especially since he hadn't had a chance to warn her of our grim outing, but he knew her well enough to know that looking for her would be futile. I was worried, too, and I realized that we needed a diversion to keep us from going crazy as we waited for tomorrow and the Sugar Snow Ball. All of my plans were about to come to fruition, but for the next few hours, there was nothing to do but fret, which Verusha wouldn't tolerate. I borrowed a clean dress from Verusha's daughter-in-law and returned to the parlor to find an entirely new version of Casper.

As a Pinky, Casper had been a major liability to me, and the slightest wrong word or gesture from him toward me—or anyone on the street—might have ended in him being impounded or beaten. Dressed in appropriate clothing, with his hair brushed and his cravat hanging loose, he was a fitting companion. I wanted him to see my homeland with a Bludman's eyes, and we left the groomery arm-in-arm as if we hadn't a care.

I took him first to the park where the ballerinas practiced, and we caught them at their midmorning encore, stretching toward the sun like bright flowers. Casper strolled over to the quartet playing in full parade dress on the bandstand, inspecting the instruments with a polite smile. I could see the calculations in his eyes as he realized that Blud musicians could play faster than Pinkies, their movements sharper and more complex. His gloved fingers flexed against his breeches, and I grinned to myself. I couldn't wait to see him at a harpsichord, discovering the true breadth of his skills.

Next we walked the topiary gardens, remarking on the impossible shapes carved into the bushes. He recognized several of the more famous statues, murmuring the names of the artists in his world who had created them and telling me their subtle differences, such as the fact that a reclining nude wasn't crushing a tiger's throat where he came from but was just, in fact, lying there.

At the Natural History Museum, he marveled at the stuffed exhibits of animals he'd never seen alive. The dodo, the roc, the sea goats, and the unicorn especially drew him close, and I found that I savored his amazement. I had not spent much time around children, and surely this was how a parent felt, watching a young creature reel at the possibilities of the wide world. When he stood under the dragon's yellowed skeleton, gawking, I outright laughed at him.

"But it's huge!" He held his arms out wide but was still dwarfed by its wingspan.

"I've seen bigger," I said with a smirk.

He grew quiet in the art museum, tears springing to his eyes as he stood before a strange little painting that I'd never really given any thought. The poor woman had no eyebrows, but her smile was rather enigmatic.

"I always wanted to see it, in my world. But I never got

around to it. I had a tour planned for Paris for the next summer, and the *Mona Lisa* was at the top of my list."

He leaned close, and the docent in the corner cleared her throat and wagged a finger. I grabbed his arm and pulled him away before they investigated us too closely. As different as I looked, this was my home country. Being recognized was all too real a possibility, and I had been careless to let him call attention to us.

"When I'm Tsarina," I whispered, leaning close, "I'll shut down the museum and send the guards home. You can lick it to taste the paint, if you wish."

He shook his head at me as if I were silly and adorable, a child playing make-believe. Anger rippled over me. Did he think I was telling idle lies? I latched my arm more firmly around his and dragged him down the long hallway under the glittering curves of giant crystal chandeliers shaped like Krakens. Up a spiraling staircase we went, our boots hushed by thick carpets woven with designs of snowflakes and icicles. He went along with me as he had all morning, bemused and indulgent, and I growled under my breath. What I was about to show him—he needed to see it, and now.

We passed door after door down the long hallway, not stopping to admire the world-renowned collection of decorative enameled emu and ostrich eggs. When I darted through the last door on the right, he followed. I moved to the side, and he stopped and muttered, "Jesus Christ," under his breath.

"There," I said. "Do you see now?"

The room was decorated in white and blue and dominated by a giant painting, twice as large as life. The artist had captured me perfectly, seventeen forever. I gazed out of the gilt frame, somehow both haughty and innocent. My face still held the vaguest curve of childhood, but my neck was already graceful and long. My hair was piled high in the fashion of the time, except for one long elegant braid that trailed over my shoulder and down to my waist, tied with a velvet ribbon and sprinkled with dark gray pearls. My dress was in a style already abandoned, heavy with beading in the shape of iridescent peacock feathers. I still remembered the thrill of trying it on, how heavy and adult it felt, the train sweeping the floor. I had spun in place and then hugged Verusha for giving the dressmaker instructions to let the neckline dip perfectly, just like my mother's.

It was clearly me, and I clearly sat in a throne, wearing a heavy crown set with a sapphire the size of my fist. The necklace draped around my neck was currently in Verusha's care, missing half of the stones that glittered larger than life in the painting. The engraved plaque screwed into the painting read, "Princess Ahnastasia Feodor."

The way he looked at me then—it was as if he finally realized that I wasn't just some foundling from a suitcase. He might have believed it, in theory, before then. We might have been working toward the same goal, moving together among my people. He called me Ahna, and princess, though only to tease. And my story may have added up. But in that moment, I saw it strike him in the heart, the enormity of who I was and what we were up against.

It may have also been a little unsettling to realize he had recently made love to a national treasure.

"It's a beautiful painting," he said carefully.

"I was considered a great beauty back then. Very promising. I was receiving marriage proposals by age twelve, but none was good enough."

"You were breathtaking then, it's true." He squeezed my arm. "But I like you even better now."

I felt the warmth rush into my cheeks, a little thrill rippling over me. He pulled me close, a firm hand on my back, and kissed me gently. I stood on my tiptoes to kiss him back, my fingers light on his shoulders and my hips pressed against him in a way that would have been innocent just yesterday. He deepened the kiss, and things were just starting to get good when a docent I hadn't noticed cleared his throat. We broke apart, and I hid my face in Casper's shoulder.

"Show some respect to the Blud Princess," the old Bludman said gruffly, his hat in his hand.

I risked a glance at the old man, peeking through Casper's hair. I couldn't ignore the bald sadness in his eyes.

"Do you think they'll ever find her?" Casper asked.

"I pray every day that it will happen," the docent said. "Poor girl."

Casper nodded, his face grave. "May your hope be answered," he said formally, with the respect one would expect of a born Bludman. We left the room quietly, his arm shielding my face. I heard the old man's sigh, long and sad. When I turned back briefly at the door, the docent stood before the painting of me, wiping away a blud tear.

We were silent as we walked slowly down the hall. Casper glanced briefly through the other doors, taking in the paintings of Olgha, Alex, and my parents, captured in a rare and planned moment together, stiff and wooden even considering the kindness of the artist's brush. Mounds of tiny crystal vials rested on every flat surface of the room—one blud tear in each, the formal show of mourning. My eyes squeezed shut in pain. I should have brought a vial and left a tear of my own, one drop of royal blud among thousands.

As if reading my mind, he squeezed my arm. "We're going to kick that bitch's ass," he said.

"That we are," I answered, squeezing back.

32

Our afternoon passed in the sweet haze of stolen indulgence. Browsing in shops, strolling down streets lined with tinkling snowdrops, visiting the world's largest collection of blud creatures in the Muscovy Zoo and laughing at the camels. We kissed in the highest belfry of the Basilica of Aztarte as I sat in a window, my hair rustled by a breeze that smelled of the coming snow. I found that I was no longer frightened of heights. Afterward, Casper stood in the window himself, leaning outward over the whole city, and yelled something barbaric that sounded very much like "Yawp." It brought him such strange joy that I found it bizarrely endearing.

Remembering Verusha's favorite treat, I stopped at a vendor in the Franchian district and bought a painted box of sugared liver. What were a few more coppers when soon I would be either dead or the reigning monarch? And it was worth it, seeing her face light up when we walked through the door of the groomery.

"Ah, darleenk, you remembered!" She snatched the box and popped a sliver into her mouth, sucking blissfully as she ushered us into her sitting room. Casper moved toward the divan, but she plucked at his jacket and tugged him into the last rays of afternoon sun by the window. She walked around him, old eyes narrow and calculating. "Tell me, now. Was it as horrible as they say?"

Casper managed to keep a straight face, and I merely inclined my head and said, "We managed to survive."

Verusha slapped Casper in the ribs, and he stood up straighter. She ran his hair through her talons and slid a hand down his arm, squeezing his muscles. She held his fingers up to the light, saying, "Interesting. It's coming on quite fast. But I can smell it on you, the vestiges of your humanity. You'll need a good bathing."

"Another grooming?" He grimaced and glanced at the door to the groomery.

Verusha drew back, one hand to her chest in affront. "A Bludman? In my groomery? How obscene."

"We might as well drag you out to the trough with the bludmares," I added with a grin. I swiped a bit of liver from the open box and savored the tartness of the sour sugar against the rich tang of blood.

"So I'm just suddenly . . . different to you?" Casper asked. His face was guarded, a strange mixture of anger and bemusement.

"My boy, you have gone from stew to stud," Verusha said, popping another bit of candy into her mouth. "It is not often one changes species overnight. We should celebrate. You are hungry?"

He nodded silently, as if it pained him to admit it. Verusha opened the warming cube that hummed gently on a shelf and withdrew two vials of blood. She took down two teacups, poured for us, and served, bowing her head slightly to him and greatly to me in the proper show of deference.

Casper sat, rigid, on the edge of the sofa. He took a sip of blood, tentative and with great concentration, as if every time he tasted it, he was afraid to find it repellent. After a few more sips, he relaxed all over and settled back against the cushions.

"I told you hunger would make you peevish," I said, and he chuckled.

"Funny how it loosens you up a little. Almost like alcohol but without the fuzziness. I feel just as sharp, just not like everything you say is a challenge. Much better."

He leaned back, one boot on his knee, savoring his blood as if trying to puzzle out a rare vintage.

"I would swear it tastes like butter," he said between sips. "How is that possible?"

"Verusha prefers good country stock," I supplied. "These Pinkies would have access to fresh dairy and butter, and perhaps that's what you're tasting. I sense cream and sunshine and freshness. Quite round and full-bodied."

Verusha settled back into her pillows with a handful of liver candy perched on her prodigious bosom. An easy life indoors, extra vials of country blood, and plenty of sweetmeats had made her cushy, and she was enjoying it.

"Good for the constitution," she said.

"And what's that, in the box?" Casper asked, setting down his empty teacup and leaning forward to pluck a bit of liver from the box on the table.

She hissed and made as if to swat him. "Stay out of an old woman's sweets," she muttered. "It's too expensive to waste on someone with no taste for riches."

He dodged her hand and sniffed the bit of deep red liver, coated with crystallized sugar and resembling a bright jewel. He had just opened his mouth when the door swung in to reveal a cleaner-than-usual Keen, her hair pulled back under the traditional kerchief of low-ranking Pinky servants.

"Is that candy?" She grinned as if she'd never been gone, skittering to his side and plunking herself down on the divan. "All the food here is dull. No salt. What's the point?" Before she could dig her gloved fingers into the box, he snapped it shut.

"It belongs to Verusha," he said. "Please try to have some manners."

"What the hell, Maestro? Who died and made you God?" She slung her booted feet up onto the small table and took out her clockwork tortoise, still in sphere form, tossing it from hand to hand. Casper quivered beside her and began breathing through his mouth, and I realized that it was the first time he'd been trapped in a small, airless room with a Pinky since being bludded.

"We should go." I stood and held out a hand to Casper, unsure of what I would do if he rejected the offer. But he took my hand and hurried around the table, away from Keen, who smelled less repulsive after a good grooming.

"Where are we going?" she said, clearly puzzled. "And where were you guys last night? And where have you been all day?" Her eyes narrowed as she looked at the open neck of Casper's shirt, and then she looked him up and down. "Smile," she commanded, glaring.

"I don't think I can."

She threw her tortoise down and rounded on me, hands balled into fists, as vicious and small as the bludweasel we'd seen at the zoo. "What did you do?" She stepped close enough for me to smell the scent of violets from Verusha's shampoo. "What did you do to him?"

"What had to be done," Casper said tiredly, pulling her back by the shoulders while keeping his face firmly turned away. "We didn't have a choice. I'm sorry."

"You're sorry? You're frigging sorry?" Keen backed away from us, one step after another toward the door. She was fighting tears, shoulders heaving. "You were fine, Casper. Why'd you have to ruin everything?"

"I didn't tell you. I couldn't. But it was getting bad in London. Worse on the *Maybuck*. I was starting to lose it. You don't understand—"

"I don't understand? Why you'd let her turn you into one of *them*? Jesus, Casper. You're not even a person anymore. You're a monster." She whipped the kerchief off her head and wiped her eyes angrily. "I read your frigging journal, you whiny sack. I can't believe that after that chick at the caravan chose a Blud over you, you kept drinking. You're such a goddamn addict. You're so sad. And weak. You're just like . . ."

"Like what, Keen?" A deadly calm had come over him. "Like whom?"

"It doesn't matter. I just expected better from you."

"I was lost long before you showed up. There was no escaping my past. You can't undo that much bludwine. It was this or madness."

She snorted and leaned back against the wall beside the door. "Don't you get it? This *is* madness. You're totally bugshit. You're always supposed to fight it, Casper. Dracula, the bad guys in *Blade,* the Lost Boys. Even Colin Farrell. They're bad guys. They kill people. You're *always* supposed to fight the vampires!"

"But vampires are cool. I thought it was zombies that you were always supposed to fight?" The corner of his mouth quirked up hopefully, his dimples flashing with a Bludman's killer charm, and she shut her eyes and beat her fist against Verusha's damask wallpaper.

"You think this is a joke? Awesome. I guess I'm the punch line." She pointed at me, right at my heart. "And I hope that gypsy bitch rips you in half. You'd make a suck-ass queen, anyway, considering you don't care about any-one but yourself."

One hand on the doorknob, she glared at him. He looked away, and she was gone. When the door slammed behind her, Casper finally inhaled. Verusha was already fetching another vial for him. He took the teacup and drank it down in several gulps, desperately and without testing or savoring it this time.

"She'll be back," he said quietly. "She always is."

Verusha and I nodded, but I wasn't so sure. That last look she'd given us had burned like a slap across the face. Somewhere deep inside me, the old version of Ahnasta-sia snarled and envisioned a slender head on a pike in the snow, the short brown hair dark against the hills and drip-ping blood. But the new version of me ached painfully and wished there had been some way to make her see the truth of it.

I picked the brass sphere off the couch and turned it over in my hands.

"She wanted a pet," Casper said. "I always said I would buy her a clockwork, but I just never got around to it. She'd be hanged for stealing that. I guess I didn't realize how much she needed . . ."

"A friend," I whispered.

When I looked down, I found Casper's hand in mine, but I couldn't recall when it had happened or who had reached for whom. I squeezed back anyway. I couldn't explain it, but I had lost something, too, and I already missed the little urchin. I could only hope that we all survived long enough for me to find her and fix the mess I'd made of a fellow victim's life.

I'd never had friends before, either.

We sat in silence for some time. Verusha finally broke the dark pall of the room by standing up and exclaiming, "This. This is why we don't allow Pinkies to think for themselves. Poor little fool!" She hurried out the door as if anxious to be away from us, calling, "There are beds made upstairs, the open doors. My darleenk, it is not silk and gold, but it is better than a valise. Sleep well. Tomorrow morning, we begin."

"What does that mean?" Casper's hand left mine, and he settled back to watch me. He looked haggard but handsome, the lines of his face sharper than they had been, as if an artist had gone over a sketch with a firmer hand, perfecting it.

"The Sugar Snow Ball is tomorrow night. Tomorrow morning, we'll prepare and dress. We'll board the carriage at dusk and ride through the forest to the Ice Palace. We'll dance to bring down the snow, and then I'll kill Ravenna."

"And after that?"

I chuckled, sinister and sweet. "After that, I make the rules."

"And what will you do?"

"So many things, darling. So many things."

I breathed in deeply, dreamily. I would fix things. I would clean up Ravenna's mess. I would send some very precious valises to the Svedish king with the heads of his ambassadors and spies tied up like holiday gifts inside. I would send dangerous men to visit Mr. Sweeting on Ruby Lane and fetch my sister's remains home. I would even put Keen's picture in the papers and see if we could find her with a reward large enough that she would come claim it herself.

"I'm talking about me, Ahna. What will you do about me?'

"You'll be the court composer for all of Muscovy. I keep my promises."

"That's not what I mean."

The turn of his head, the way his throat moved—he was all Bludman now. And I might have been able to wiggle out of his clutches before, but I could already feel the sharpened force of him. Before, I could have run. Now he could catch me. He was stronger, and it didn't matter that I was royal, a princess. I couldn't escape the reality of his physical presence, and especially not its pull on me. Especially not when he demanded it.

He waited, quiet but alert, as the emotions roiled in me. He was bigger, stronger, and the beast in me wanted to submit, to roll belly up and lick his throat as wolves did in the wild. I liked him. I cared about him. But I didn't know if we would survive tomorrow night and, if we did, if he would survive a single day in the Snow Court. He wasn't the only one who would wish to stand by my side, although the others would do it for political power. Was it kinder to tell him now or later that the only way we could ever be together during my reign was with me as the stoic, married royal and him as the court composer who warmed my bed in secret?

"Ahna. Ahnastasia."

He tried to touch my face, but I pulled back with a hiss and a blush. He smiled, lazy and slow. Leaning back with his arm across the sofa behind my head, he said, "I've never seen you running scared before, darlin'."

He could sense it, the bastard! I had been so eager to turn him into an ally I could use, someone like me, that I had forgotten the powers of an alpha-male Bludman in his prime.

"I'm not scared." I stood, smoothing down my dress and hunting for something more useful to do. I couldn't sit on the sofa beside him just then, with him so attuned to my feelings. I couldn't find the words for how I felt, and the longer and closer I lingered, the faster he would decide for himself. What I wanted to say to him would be my choice, and I wouldn't let his blud take that away from me. "But Verusha is right. We need sleep. Tomorrow will be long. Sleep well."

I didn't look back as I slipped into the hall and scurried up the stairs. The first open room was done up in burgundy, but the second room was appointed in sky blue and antiqued gold, as if Verusha had kept it waiting for me all these years. Once inside behind the locked door, I undressed quickly to slip into a bed firmly rooted to the floor, neither rolling nor floating over the ground.

His eyes in that last moment had been warm and sure and filled with dancing shadows. He had seen me, seen right through me. And he had let me go, although we both knew he could have kept me there. Whether with his body or his words, I would have been helpless if he had truly wanted me to stay. I had taken him, bribed him, turned him, kept him for my own uses. It had all been for one purpose: to save Freesia and be queen, powerful over all.

I couldn't admit to myself that one man now had power over me.

Tomorrow would be bad enough without admitting how much I had to lose.

33

I woke up to the sound of Verusha humming. Always the same song, since I had first left my mother's bed to sleep, cold and alone, in the nursery. I smiled and muttered, "You're off key, old woman."

"And you're an ungrateful little creature who deserves to be drowned in the river," she said in turn. "Sleeping past noon. Lazy beast!"

The warm familiarity of the ritual was soothing, but only until I realized that today was the day that would determine everything. Life or death, queen or pawn. Casper or . . . the emptiness where he should have been by my side.

I sat up as Verusha plumped the pillows behind my back and put a teacup of warm blood and bludmare's milk in my hands. As I sipped it, I was flooded with memories. The first time I'd been beaten for showing weakness. All the times Olgha had locked me in a trunk or smeared my face in the snow, telling me I would never be anything but a pretty brood mare. The time I had stolen into the Pinky kitchens and played with the children there, trying their food and spitting it out to our mutual amusement, and later, when I'd been punished. My mother had forced me to drink from one of the children, a little boy. She had held him rigid, his black hair in one hand and his shoulder pinched in the other.

"Never forget what they are to us," she had said as I paused, conflicted, clumsy teeth scraping his neck. "They are food. Servants. Chattel. To be used and bred and thrown away as we will it. Once they have laughed at you, they will always wait for their next chance."

The tears had slid down my cheeks and blurred with the boy's blood to smear across my lips. I had never returned to the kitchens, and that boy had avoided me for the rest of my time at the palace.

I hadn't thought about him for years, but now I wondered where he was and how my future would run. Would I change everything or nothing? Would I drive the Pinkies from their stolen district in the city proper or allow them to flourish? Did I really want to continue treating people the way Keen and Casper had been treated, as less than bludmares and hunting dogs? And if I chose not to do that, how would my people react? I'd seen evidence in print and in real life that Ravenna was letting the humans run wild. Before, I had hated her for it. But now, with my feelings changing, I couldn't help wondering how it would look when I deposed her and showed further sympathy to the Pinkies.

"I see you fussing, my darleenk," Verusha said. "Perhaps this will soothe you." She opened the closet and brought out a magnificent dress that was more than familiar to me, although its color was changed from the original cream to a cool aquamarine. I could imagine Verusha stealing it from the summer palace and dyeing it in secret, looking at it wistfully from time to time, as if she had known that I would one day return to claim it.

"Do you think that will still fit? I'm taller."

"But thinner. We'll make it work."

The beaded peacock feathers cascaded to the floor, shimmering iridescent against the heavy silk like the diamonds they were. Aquamarines and sapphires winked in the eyes of the feathers, and I was already anxious to feel the rich fabric slide over my skin. Wearing that dress to sit for the painting had made me feel queenly at seventeen; what would it do for me now?

"The bath is ready." She tipped her head to the door in the corner. "Soak a while, and Verusha will make you as beautiful as ever."

I'd always loved relaxing in big copper tubs full of perfumed water and rose-tinged mare's milk. But I'd never had cares before, never had problems weighing me down. I wanted to leap out onto the tile floor, dripping pinkish liquid, and rush out into the streets to fight or conquer something or at least get into an argument with someone of lesser wit. But I could hear Verusha in the outer room, humming lullabies to herself as she prepared to dress me as she had always wished, as the crowning beauty of the Feodor family, the future Tsarina. Even had I wanted to run away, she could have stopped me with one harsh word and a reminder of my destiny.

I slid down into the dark, warm silence of the tub, and brown swirled into the milky water. I closed my eyes and scrubbed soap into my scalp, wishing to wash out the dye along with the dirt of the last week's journey. I wasn't the same girl who had burst from the suitcase—that much was true. In some ways, I'd become harder. But in others, I was already too soft. First Casper and Keen and now even Verusha—they had all gotten to me. I would have to find my backbone as the carriage bumped through the forest toward the palace, or I'd end up pledging my allegiance to Ravenna and being married off or murdered within a fortnight.

"Dry off now, leetle fish," Verusha called, and I obeyed, my mind too busy planning rebellion to actually rebel.

She was fussing with me before I was out of my towel, rubbing rich creams into my skin. I let her bend me and move me as necessary, just as she always had. I was nearly hairless, and much of my youth had been spent holding back screams as she spread me with wax and ripped the bits of paper off in cruel jerks. She must have been thinking about the same thing, as she nodded with great authority and said, "You see? I told you it would be worth it. Smooth as glass, you are."

I just sighed. The fire that had kept me running for so long was burning low, buffeted by too many other emotions to flare brightly. Casper had been right last night; I was scared. Scared to tell him how I felt and scared to feel that way at all. And yet I couldn't wait to see him, kept looking at the closed door as if he might swagger in and grin at me with his new fangs.

Verusha helped me into an embroidered chemise and sat me gently on a stool before the vanity mirror, picking up a brush and running it through my wet curls. My hair was drying lighter than it had been, much of the dye having swirled out of the tub along with the bludmilk and water. It wasn't back to ice-white yet, more of a warm gold. But it was enough. I smiled as she arranged my curls, stabbing silver pins in to hold it tightly in place.

"You are bothered, little lemming. Verusha can tell. Do you worry that you will not best Ravenna?"

"Of course not." I looked up into the mirror, pulling back my lips to show sharp teeth.

"What is it, then? Your parents? Or Alex?"

I snorted. "My parents are gone. I can handle Alex. And I have plans for the king of Sveden as well."

She threw her head back and laughed, bosom heaving. "You are my same little princess, all teeth and pride. And yet something is changed. Have you recovered fully from your draining? Do you feel weak or muddled?"

"Muddled perhaps." I paused meaningfully, meeting her dark eyes in the mirror. She had always known whatever troubled me, even the things I didn't know myself. I had to hope that she could offer guidance now, when I needed it most and could speak it least.

"Did you know they had planned to marry you off to a Swedish prince?" she said blandly, and I flinched. "It's true, darleenk. The papers were almost drawn up when you disappeared. At first, they thought you had run away, but a Pinky in the stables swore a blood oath that he saw you snatched by terrifying figures in bear cloaks, stolen away into the woods behind the castle. That little one from the kitchen, with the black hair, you recall." I shuddered. In the back of my throat, I could still taste his blood and my own childish terror and shame. "In any case, when they realized Olgha had also been taken, the betrothal papers were lost. Your parents were executed. And then the rumors began that you had killed your own sister. But I knew they were false."

"Why Sveden?" I asked, once I had found my voice. "They've always been peaceful."

"King Charles wanted to cement an alliance, and he has so many bastards littering the palace that it made sense. That man—he is insatiable, they say. After you disappeared, once he couldn't use you for his own ends, he swore you an enemy. Assassins waiting everywhere."

I grinned. "There's one fewer now."

She patted my head. "And your mother was hot for the union, of course. It has been many years since the Feodors had outside blud. Some have said your father . . . is not the hot-bludded sort. He always preferred the hunt to the throne."

"So they say."

"You have more of your mother in you, of course. You may not take after her in looks, but your heart, many have said, beats with the glacier's heart of Freesia. An ice princess, a throwback to better times. The winters have been uneasy these past few years. Many of the people say the dance and the music have not been up to expectation, a proper offering to Aztarte and Hades. There are shrines to you in secret places, snowdrops and white roses and little cups of blud mixed with milk and pomegranate seeds and, of course, the tears. Some are calling you Proserpina, saying you're waiting in the darkness to lead us back into a proper winter."

"The rabble are fools."

"The rabble are your reason for existing, darleenk. They are the earth that supports your feet."

My hair was twisted back in braids and pin curls in a way that led the eye down my cheekbones to my lips, which she'd painted the traditional bright red. With dark kohl and glittering silver around my eyes, my face was foreign to me. In bright light, clean and fresh and no longer framed by dirt-colored waves, I saw a living doll, a creature of lines and curves fashioned of frozen milk, with eyes the color of aquamarines. I blinked, and the face blinked back.

"It's a shame you must hide."

Before I could ask her what she meant, what she knew, she held a porcelain mask over my face, hiding everything but eyes and lips. It was white and silver, a stylized peacock's face, the nose a dainty beak. White plumes erupted from the top. I couldn't help thinking of the peacocks at the Ice Palace, calling to one another with the sound of dying children. Although the wild peacocks were rarely seen without unicorns, the birds of the palace were proud things fed blood from dishes of hammered silver. The ruling family of birds were all white, and their more colorful brethren bowed to them or hung limply from sharp beaks. It was fitting, this mask, and I wondered how she would dress Casper to walk beside me.

Verusha held out a hand, and I stood, waiting. First, she brought layers of petticoats, filmy with lace. Then dancing slippers. Then the corset from Kitty's shop, and I took a few last deep breaths before my old maid worked her magic with the laces. The dress wasn't as heavy as I remembered, or maybe I was stronger. I stepped into it, and Verusha helped lift it onto my shoulders. The thick silk skimmed my curves and clung in all the right places, the deeply cut neck perfectly accenting flesh that had bloomed in four years of maturity and a week of good feeding.

Standing before the full-length mirror beside a very smug groomer, I did indeed look like some magical, mythical bird goddess. When I cocked my head to the side, the illusion was complete. My only sadness was that the matching necklace was destroyed, a plain twist of metal with a few lone stones still winking from tarnished silver.

My painted nails brushed my collarbone, and Verusha nodded sadly in understanding. "You couldn't take it, anyway, my sweet. Too recognizable."

"And the dress isn't?"

She smiled. "The peacock has changed its spots, darleenk. They will think it a clever forgery. They will laugh before you destroy them."

I dropped my hand and wished for some occupation, something to do besides be beautiful and wait and worry. The carriage ride was starting to feel more terrifying than the ascent to the *Maybuck* had been, but there was no hope of throwing myself onto the ground and begging someone to sit on me. From here on out, my chin was up, my eyes were open, and my claws were clenched to fight.

"I'm ready," I said, more to myself than anyone else.

Verusha nodded, her eyes narrowing to slits. "Good girl. If anyone can triumph, my darleenk, my princess, it is you. And if you go to Hades, take that gypsy cur with you, yes? For me."

"I'm going to rip her throat out."

"Good. Blud in the first snow is a happy omen. Aztarte will be pleased."

I turned back, stalling. "Do you actually believe in her, Verusha?"

Her wizened hand went to a pendant that disappeared into her cleavage. I knew well enough that it held a tiny splinter of bone, supposedly from Aztarte, the Bludman's goddess. I had never really believed in her, at least as a divine ruler. Not any more than I believed in Proserpina and Hades and all the old pagan relics that predated the monarchy at the heart of Freesia. We were supposedly descended from Aztarte herself, although there hadn't been red hair in the royal family in ten generations. The ferocity was telling enough, they said.

"If I didn't believe, my girl, I would never be foolish enough to admit it out loud."

Weighed down as I was by the mask, I couldn't throw back my head. But I did laugh, my lips pressing against the cold porcelain.

"You have always been wise," I said.

"That is why I am still alive—diplomacy and the ability to keep secrets." She sniffed. "Also, I am good with hair."

My hand was glued to the doorknob, the scales dark against the bright brass. And yet I couldn't turn it.

"Verusha. Can I do this?" I asked quietly.

"If you can't, no one else can. No one else will. And Freesia will fade into legend, as forgotten as melted snow."

I wanted to believe her. I wanted to believe I could do it. But in that moment, in all my finery, I couldn't even open the door.

"The first step is always the hardest," Verusha said with a slightly impish grin. "But I don't think it's Ravenna who worries you now. Go to him, darleenk."

She reached past me to turn the knob, and the door swung open.

34

Casper was waiting for me in the parlor, just as I knew he would be. But the former man looked like a god, and I was thrown off kilter by the look in his eyes as he regarded me in turn.

Verusha had done her work well, kitting him out as the peacock to my hen. His tailcoat was a brilliant teal, shimmering with embroidered feathers. A hint of gold brocade waistcoat and snowy jabot peeked out, making me wish to flick the heavy buttons and see what else lay beneath. His breeches were molded to his body in a most beguiling way, his boots high and shiny.

But his face, to me, was even more beautiful than his costume. He looked the part of a royal Bludman, his face shaved smooth and his eyes outlined in kohl as was the Freesian tradition, dating back to a time when hunters cut down on the snow glare by rubbing ashes under their eyes. It made the blue pop, bright as sapphires and snapping like flame on a windy day. His hair was down, framing sharper features with a golden glow. There was something exotic and rare about him, something different. Perhaps it was his hands, which were finally dark, as a Bludman's should be. Or perhaps it was the way he was looking at me, like I was the most edible thing in the city.

He knew how good he looked; I could read it in his proud posture and cocky grin. I subtly shifted, angling out a hip, unable to resist responding to the signals he sent. When I had first met him, he'd given off an air of suicidal amusement, a drunkard's bravado mixed with a thinking man's awareness of inescapable doom. There had always been a bit of intriguing madness about him, an insidious consequence of his blud habit.

But now I realized that all the versions of Casper I'd seen before had been incomplete, shades of who he truly was. This creature before me, this fine predator of such proud bearing—this was who he was meant to be. And I wondered what he saw in me now. Was I a Bludwoman in her prime, a queen ready to fight cunningly and viciously for her bludright? Or was I still the lost princess, a little girl with kitten teeth playing dress-up and hiding behind the safety of a mask? It was damned uncomfortable, not knowing.

So instead of asking him, I made the decision myself. I drew up taller, raised my chin, took a slinky step closer to him, and said, "Maestro, where is your mask?"

"That's all you have to say?" He smirked, beautifully.

Verusha rushed forward to hand him a half-mask with a pointed beak over the nose, muttering, "Do you know how hard it is to find such things the day before the ball? Ah, but you two make a troublesome pair. Old Verusha will be glad to see the backs of you, that is certain."

He tied the mask on and turned back to me, and I was startled anew by his eyes. Their blue was lighter than the shimmering indigo of the mask, and with the black kohl, he was otherworldly. We regarded each other, bird to bird, solemn and silent. I ached to kiss him, but it was impossible. Both in front of Verusha and with two beaks in the way. The only problem with looking so mutually ravishing was that we couldn't do a damned thing about it.

"Ungrateful creatures," Verusha muttered, dusting his coat off in a way that was transparently all about getting her hands on his rump. "Not a single thank you. Not a word about how lovely anyone looks. What is the world coming to?"

"Thank you, madam," Casper said, tossing out the tails of his coat and cutting a grand bow. His hair slid down around his mask, and Verusha simpered like a girl when he kissed her hand.

"And what of you, my little ermine pup?"

"Queens don't thank their servants," I said, my voice frosty.

She dabbed at her eyes with a handkerchief. "I have never been prouder, my Ahnastasia. You are everything I ever hoped you would be. The day you thank me is the day I will stop serving you."

"She's the strangest old woman I've ever met," Casper said, and she swatted him in faux annoyance.

"A queen does not thank servants, boy. You have much to learn about a world that runs on blood. You must teach him, darleenk. In the carriage. He cannot go thanking the servants at the ball, or they'll know him for what he is."

"And what, exactly, am I? An abomination?"

Her eyes narrowed at him impishly. "A secret weapon. Your senses will be just a little sharper, your vision just a little clearer. As if nature knows you need advantages as you adjust. You will help my Ahnastasia take what is hers."

"For a bumbling old fool, you haven't utterly failed," I said, and Verusha beamed with pride.

"The carriage is waiting, and time is short. You know the rest. Now go, my dear. Save us all."

"And have fun?" Casper added.

"Harrumph. Fun is for later, once the snow falls on Ravenna's corpse," Verusha said.

"The fun begins once I'm Tsarina."

I laid a careful hand along Casper's arm, and Verusha followed us to the front door of the shop. Two white blud-mares danced in place outside, red froth dripping from their mouths where the harsh bits cut into their lips, giv-ing them wicked smiles. A footman opened the carriage door for us, and Casper helped me up.

I let down the curtains and removed my mask, grateful finally to feel air on my face. Verusha had done well with the carriage. It wasn't so large or so small that it would draw attention, nor was it the newest or the oldest. It had been recently painted outside, with bright blue appoint-ments and gilt where gilt should be. And the comfort-able and roomy interior could have easily fit four people. I tried to settle my dress under me comfortably, but it seemed an impossible task. No matter where I put my weight, the tiny beads dug into my flesh. I remembered now that I had sat on the fluffiest of down pillows for the painting in the museum. Sugar Snow Ball dresses were for dancing, not sitting.

Across from me on an identical cushion, Casper fidg-eted and leaned, likewise uncomfortable. Living at the palace, I had never considered the misfortune of the city barons riding to the ball in what should have been grand comfort. It was but a short walk from the palace, through the field and into the forest and the ancient clearing where snow fell but didn't stick. I attended my first dance at age sixteen and had never once sat down in one of the specially made gowns, nor had I felt the heels of my dancing slippers catch in the carpet of a carriage.

Remembering my responsibilities and suddenly aware of the press of time, I rapped on the plush ceiling. Outside, leather reins slapped against curried flanks, and the bludmares screamed and leaped into a run. Casper lurched out of his seat and barely missed landing on me.

"I wasn't expecting that." He settled back onto the bench, hands clutching the velvet, and I laughed.

I'd heard that long ago, the horses had been as benign and harmless as Pinkies, great prey animals that could be coaxed into various gaits besides balk and gallop. Now every Bludman grew up knowing that carriages started with a jerk, and there were even handles built into the walls for those who needed extra bolstering. Verusha had been right; Casper did indeed have a lot to learn.

"It'll be twisty in the city, so you might want to hold on." I pointed to the handle. "But once we're on the road to the palace, things will be rather boring for a while. It takes several hours, and we may be hampered by other carriages and various mishaps."

"Mishaps?"

I waved a hand and leaned with the carriage as we went around a corner. "Broken axles, mired wheels, raging horses, random bears. The usual."

With a huff of annoyance, he took off his fine jacket and folded it, showing the brilliant gold within that very nearly matched his hair. I was just about to point out the hook on the wall when he hung the jacket neatly from it and slumped down into the seat, his waistcoat rumpling.

"I'll get the hang of it," he said peevishly, sitting up again to pull back the curtain and look out.

"You're rather twitchy."

"So?"

"Bludmen aren't, generally."

He stared at me, and I smiled with great calm, letting the carriage sway me and generally exhibiting the smug grace and tranquility of a sated predator.

I expected his usual saucy, dimpled riposte. Instead, he put his elbows on his knees and his head in his hands. "I can't stop worrying about Keen. Like maybe if I stare out the window at just the right time, I'll see her dart by. Or maybe she's riding on the roof of the carriage, playing at being a stowaway."

"The footmen would truss her up for a snack," I muttered.

"That's just it. She's got this fantastic survival instinct. She managed okay in our world, and she was scraping by in London. But in Muscovy . . ." He heaved a deep breath.

"There's nowhere to hide," I finished.

"I never got to explain it to her, how I didn't know what the bludwine would do until it was too late. I was so afraid to disappoint her. It was bad enough that she thought I was a drunk womanizer, and maybe I was. But I kept her safe, at least. And she deserves an explanation. She deserves to hear me say I'm sorry."

I crossed my arms and met his eyes. He was looking for

forgiveness, but he'd come to the wrong person. "Never be sorry."

He sat up and stared at me, half angry and half curious. "Aren't you?" he asked.

I considered him. He was slumped over, dark hands running through his hair with a very un-Bludman sort of melancholy. It was time for his lessons to begin. "Here is the heart of it, Casper. I'm sorry that she chose to run away instead of listening to sense, and I'm sorry that she didn't come back so that you would rest easier. But that's all I'm sorry for. You can apologize for how things happened. You can apologize for how she feels. But you should never apologize for being what you are. At the core of you, in your secret heart, you are an animal. Feelings will not change what is. Do not contradict what you are."

He chuckled ruefully, fell to his side, and rolled over onto his back, lying on the long bench with his hair falling over the edge. But he didn't see me; he was looking beyond, fighting with himself.

Finally, he exhaled.

"Do I contradict myself? Fine. Then I contradict myself. I am large. I contain multitudes." And then he burst out laughing, one fist beating the side of the bench as if it were the funniest thing he'd ever heard. "Damn, woman. The things you drag out of me."

"This is serious. I think perhaps you misunderstand—" I started, but he interrupted.

"I think perhaps I'm finally starting to understand. The thing is, you've only ever been one thing. You might have pretended to be human for a while on that airship, but you didn't really know how, and you didn't really try to understand. But I've been a lot of things, and I'm on my third life now, and I'm starting to realize that the rules are different for me."

"The rules of Bludmen are unyielding."

He leaned close, intent and sharp. "You keep saying that, but you keep forgetting you're about to be the queen of the goddamn Bludmen. Doesn't the queen make the unyielding rules? Isn't that the whole point of having a queen?"

My mouth dropped open, and my mind spun. In all my wisdom and ferocity, I'd never stopped to consider that once Ravenna was dead, I would have complete control—in all things. I had been so worried that someone would smell my blud in Casper's veins or disgrace me for keeping a commoner close at hand that it hadn't occurred to me that I could elevate him myself. I could give him land, make him a baron, or spin a tale of his mysterious beginnings. Just as I was what I had made of myself on this journey, he could also be whatever I wished him to be.

The people couldn't stop me if they tried.

My parents and tutors had raised me to believe that our family had been chosen by the gods, by Aztarte herself, to rule. They had raised me to be bloodthirsty, proud, and intractable. They had promised to keep me safe, and they had failed. I was alive only because Casper had saved me, again and again. He had, in effect, become my family.

From that moment on, I refused to worry further about being accepted by my own people. In bludding Casper, I had given myself more than a servant or a companion. I had given myself an equal and a partner. Whatever he had been when he was born and when he had found me, the blud of Freesian royalty now flowed in his veins.

I swallowed, on the verge of a great understanding.

"Casper, your book. The poem. What is it called again?"

"'Leaves of Grass'?"

"No, the other thing."

"'Song of Myself'?"

I laughed. Just a chuckle at first, but it built to a crescendo. He watched me, charmed and amused but confused.

"That's it. 'Song of Myself.' I write my own song. The words, and the music. We all do. Every one of us. Bludmen and Pinkies. And I will write the rules."

He nodded. "Whatever satisfies the soul is truth."

I snorted and wiped my eyes. "In philosophy, perhaps. But we have to best Ravenna before I can start writing that song. Until she's gone, your truth will get you staked and drained amid laughter and the trills of a harpsichord, and then all our dreams are lost. You'll have to learn the rules and play by them tonight."

"Tell me your rules, then, darlin', and I'll see if I want to play."

I sat back to consider him, the beads and buttons digging into my shoulders. How to distill thousands of years of heritage into one lecture?

"For one thing, Bludmen of the court are rarely silly. You must give no one any reason to single you out, to bait you, or to fight you. Think of a pack of hunting dogs or a pack of wolves. With posture and words, the men will jockey for position in the pack. They may try to goad you away, but don't rise to it. I need you at my back. Strong, silent, serious. That's what you must be until the deed is done. After that, be as loose of limits and artificial lines as you wish."

"I want to follow you around with a pen and paper and just write down every word you say."

"Shh. Stop staring at me like I'm edible. This is important."

"So's poetry."

I rolled my eyes at him and went on. "Don't take off your mask, even if someone tells you to. And most important of all, once the Dance of the Sugar Snow has started, don't stop dancing for any reason."

"That's more important than killing Ravenna? A dance?"

I pinched the bridge of my nose. "This is not just a ball. This is a holy rite of the goddess Aztarte, a ritual that ensures the prosperity of the blud monarchy of Freesia. The playing of the music and the grace of the dancers will determine the course of the next year. Should the musicians' fingers stutter or the dancers stumble, the snow might not fall. At the very, very least, word would spread that something had gone amiss, and the people of the city would begin to search for faults in their world. Verusha told us that the snow had not fallen heavily last year, and that means that the people are already suspecting that something is wrong in the palace. In the 1700s, two couples collided and knocked over a punch bowl of bludwine. That summer, there was a drought, and the crops wilted, and the Pinkies died, and blood became scarce. The people of Muscovy rioted outside the summer palace, dragged out the Tsarina, and disemboweled her in the square to appease the goddess. This dance is very, very serious."

Casper sat up, his playfulness fled, and thank heavens. "You didn't mention that when you offered me the job of court composer," he said.

"What, that if you didn't play perfectly once a year, you'd be drained into the fountain? Oops."

"Oops?"

I sighed and shifted uncomfortably in my dress. "To be quite honest, I didn't think we would make it this far. It was the sort of dream that starts optimistic, far off and beautiful. I also thought that I would eventually lose patience and murder you in your bed."

He flicked the hair out of his face, and when his eyes met mine, something in my middle flipped sweetly. "It's endearing how often you threaten to kill me. That's practically flirting to you, isn't it, darlin'?"

I leaned closer, wiggling just a little and lowering my lashes.

"I'll threaten anyone. But I only bite the pretty boys."

There suddenly wasn't enough air in the carriage, and I knew before he had even moved that he was going to attack me in the loveliest way. I jerked back out of reach.

"You can't kiss me. You can't touch me. I have to look perfect."

He hissed for the first time, long and low, shifting in his seat. "Only from the neck up," he said.

"But my dress—"

"Isn't necessary for what I'm going to do to you."

35

"Casper—"

"Turn around."

Something inside me thrilled to hear him say it, to hear him taking control, using his power. He was giving off heat and heaven only knows what else, and the beast inside me wanted to roll naked at his feet, belly up and arms stretched over head, begging for his mouth. I wanted to make myself open and pliant for him, let him take me over with the fury of a storm.

And I realized that he was right. No one would see the vast territories of flesh that stayed hidden under my heavy dress. We had at least two hours of privacy. Before I knew it, I had my back to him, my fingers digging into the top of the bench as he carefully but quickly undid the row of buttons down my back.

I turned my head and met the hungry fire of his eyes over my shoulder. He looked down at my mouth, his intention clear.

"You can't muss my lipstick."

"Open your mouth."

His eyes held me, stealing my breath. Ever so slowly, I opened my mouth. With one hand on the smooth plane of my back just above my corset, he leaned closer. His tongue darted in to caress mine, sweet and wet and hot, and it was all I could do to stay still. Part of me wanted to attack him, to drive him back into the cushioned bench. But my beast knew who held the power, who was in charge. I squirmed in place, wishing to press against him, begging him to press against me. But instead of answering my unspoken plea, he said, "Take it off."

I pushed the dress carefully down over my arms and slipped them one by one from under the long, heavy sleeves.

I stood, bent over awkwardly, and he sat back like a king and watched me step out of the dress, the fabric whispering as it slid to the carriage floor. I folded it reverently and draped it across the other bench. Before I could shift to a more attractive and comfortable position, his hands grasped the waist of my corset and dragged me to my knees. I gasped as he buried his mouth in the cleft between my breasts, his teeth scraping lightly as if he still wasn't accustomed to their sharpness. He settled me between his knees, and I ran my hands up the hard planes of his thighs.

"You're going to rumple your waistcoat," I whispered breathily in his ear.

"Good," he growled into my skin.

His tongue found my nipple with a searing heat, lapping hungrily under the edge of my corset. I moaned into his hair and ran my hands up the taut suede of his thighs. Careful not to muss my lipstick, I licked the edge of his ear, slow and breathy, until he shivered.

"That's about enough out of you, princess."

He moved faster than I had expected, catching my

wrists and transferring them both into one hand. I caught my breath, feeling dainty and exposed and highly anticipating what he would do next, with me completely in his power. It was highly erotic, not being the most dangerous creature in the very small room. When he snatched a twisted silk tassel from the curtains, I smiled, slow and sweet, and tugged experimentally at my wrists. It was gratifying, the strength of his grip.

"Front or back?" he asked.

"Do with me what you will," I whispered.

He held my captured wrists against my back and nibbled my neck as he tied them together with the rope and tested the knot. I could feel the tassels hanging lower, dusting my ankles where they peeked out from the long petticoats. I entwined my fingers and gave myself up to him completely.

He slipped off the bench and behind me, his knees just outside mine and his hips pressed urgently against me.

"Bend over," he said in my ear, and I turned my face and set my cheek against the satin cushion of the bench. A little shiver ran over me, followed by his hands. He started at the nape of my neck, raising the hairs along my spine as he brushed down my shoulders, down the sides of my corset, down my hips, feeling the curves of me like a painter sketching. One finger slipped under the edge of my corset, tracing a line across my hips. I caught my breath as he tugged down my petticoats, just enough to run his tongue along the strip of revealed skin and make me moan. With another savage tug, the layers of ruffles fell to the ground around my knees, and his breeches pressed up against the skin of my rump. Hot and wanting and wet, I pressed back, ready for more.

I had just started to rub against him when he pulled away.

"What——?" I started.

He smacked my bottom lightly, making me gasp. "Hush. I've been told not to ruin my costume."

Buttons hurriedly whispered through fabric, and then he pressed against me, skin to skin. With my hands bound and my face against the cushion, I had never been so vulnerable in my entire life, at least not while I was awake and outside the suitcase. I was very well aware that he could do anything to me, hurt me in a thousand ways only a Bludman could devise, or take me in a hundred ways that a man could imagine. It only made me want him all the more, and I bit my lip to hold in a whimper.

Hot and hard, he pressed against the cleft of me, testing, rubbing. I wiggled shamelessly, aching for more, and he pulled away and slapped my rump again, a little harder this time, making me squeal.

"Do you have any idea how long I've wanted to rule you?"

"Tell me," I whispered.

"Since the beginning. Since I tasted your blud. It was the sweetest thing I've ever known."

"You hid it well." He smacked me again, the sting heating my skin and making me bite my painted lip. My entire body was alive, alert, thrilling, tingling. I arched my spine, reaching for him, opening for him.

"You didn't truly see me until now, Ahnastasia. I was just prey before. But I'm beginning to understand. The need to dominate. I never did before, but now . . ."

"Now you have teeth."

He leaned over my back, his lips warm against my ear. "You may be a princess, but you belong to me."

My insides quivered, a flare of heat below where a finger dipped in to tease me. I could barely breathe. I was helpless against my body, against my senses, against the knowledge that the mad human had become an alpha Bludman commanding physical strength and power that I couldn't possess. My beast purred for him, longed to touch him, stroke him, hold him close. I flexed my hands and tested the rope, but it was tied tightly. Seeing me struggle, he chuckled low, pressed his finger lazily in and out as I strained to meet him.

"You're trapped, darlin'. I can do any damn thing I want to you."

His teeth dragged across the nape of my neck, and I shivered. He bit down just a little, just enough to make me pant and gnash my teeth, too.

His lips brushing my spine, he muttered, "I could snap your neck if I wanted to. I could rip you to pretty ribbons. You're still the best thing I've ever tasted, you know."

He pulled away, and I quivered, waiting, knowing, until he dragged his tongue up my cleft, deep and slow, just to prove he could.

In response, I whimpered and struggled for more. He straightened and chuckled his mastery, and I backed up to press my rump more firmly against the hard ridge of him, nothing left of me but a beggar, a beast. I wanted it, so badly. And everything he'd said was true. No matter what happened at the ball, no matter what happened tomorrow, at that moment, we were nothing more than animals, and I was completely in his power, and it was exquisite.

He grabbed my hips, pulling me hard against him with a grunt. I shoved forward a little on the bench, but he pulled me back again. As the carriage rattled along the mostly smooth road, a gentle swaying friction moved between us, a subtle rumble that added to the tension. We were always moving. I panted, unquiet and yearning, knowing what a fine line I rode between the ferocity and hunger of the heart and flesh.

One hand caught my neck, my skin still wet from his teeth. I arched my back and spread my legs further, unembarrassed by my eagerness. He rubbed against me, teasing me, nudging me gently open, out and in just the littlest bit, holding back, holding me in place with the beginnings of claws on my nape. But he didn't fully take me, not yet. I wanted so much more, and I whimpered and tried to toss my head.

"What do you want, princess?" His voice was dark and heavy, commanding. He withdrew, and I ached for more.

"Do it," I hissed.

"Tell me, Ahnastasia. Tell me what you want."

I didn't hesitate. "Take me now. Do it, Casper."

He chuckled and nudged me again, just the tip pushing in, hot and sweet. "I didn't expect you to give in so easily, darlin'. I wanted to torture you for a while, like you've been torturing me all along. I want to make you ache like your heart's going to burst in your chest. I want to be the only thing in the goddamn world for you."

"You are. It does. Oh, goddess, just claim what's yours!" I thrashed and pulled against the ropes on my wrists, and he pulled back. "Casper!" I growled, and in answer, he grabbed my hips with both hands and plunged in, hard and sure.

I felt him so deep, sliding in and out with a furious pounding that matched my heart. There was something exquisite about my helplessness, about being the object, the lesser of the beasts. I was hot and slippery, and he struck some place deep inside that felt sweeter than blood, sweeter than anything else I'd ever known. I wanted to move with him, to grasp and grapple and growl, but all I could do was turn my cheek to the cushion and take what he gave me.

With every thrust, my breasts pressed into the bench, the velvet raking my hard nipples, making each breath a gasp. When Casper grasped my corset strings and pulled them tighter, I went dizzy for a moment, my eyes rolling up and stars dancing in my vision. I reeled from the pull, the push, his thrusting, the velvet, the wheels grinding below us. I felt like a bludmare running away with the reins pulled taut by a masterly rider.

I turned my head to the other side, and the glittering fall of my dress filled my vision. I was lightheaded, furious, hungry, dizzy, pulsing with sweetness inside, and building again to that same tumultuous crescendo we had found the last time. For a moment, my eyes saw beyond to a snow-covered hill glittering in the moonlight, and I imagined Casper by my side, taking me on the blood altar in the clearing, the most ancient and primal rite of my people and the way it was said the strongest Tsarinas were spawned. For the space of a few frantic heartbeats, I smelled victory, the sugar snow falling like stars, cold and sparkling against the velvet darkness, and then I was there, hot and wet and desperate, taken over with the sweetness, thrumming deep inside, crying out, pulsing in time with Casper's ferocious thrusts as I shuddered beneath him.

His hand clutched my wrists where they lay limp, pressing them possessively and intimately into my back as he growled and bucked along with my release. When he finally exhaled and fell across me, I was breathing deep, heavy, and slow, my eyes glazed over as I tried to float back to earth. I felt sated and limp and tranquil. And he was damned heavy.

"Let me get that for you," he said, and I sighed as he untied the knot and freed my hands.

I sat up on my knees, still reeling, and flexed the feeling back into my fingers. With a shy smile, he handed me a fine handkerchief that matched his coat, and I felt only a little guilty as I cleaned myself off and let it flutter out the carriage window. My necklace had bought it, after all.

"Do you need help with your dress?" I turned to look at him. He sat on the opposite bench, his pants back to rights. It was a little fascinating, how he was an entirely different creature from what he had been a few short moments ago. The tenderness and humor had returned to his eyes, the dimples back in his smile. He was still powerful and confident—that would never go away. But there was just something lazy and calm about a sated hunter. One can't hold on to the ferocity forever. I slipped my petticoats on and settled back into the cushion to put my feet in his lap.

"I don't care to put it on yet." I stretched as far as the carriage would allow. "What's the point? There's time enough."

He leaned back, one hand on my ankle. "I like the way you think, sugarplum."

I grinned lazily and looked down, and that's when I noticed that my white corset was covered all over in black smears. I found similar stains on my wrists and hips.

"What . . . have you done to me?"

He bit his lip and tried really hard not to laugh, and I felt my first rumble of anger.

"It was Verusha's idea. She said my hands weren't dark enough, that someone might notice. So she rubbed ink into them. And I guess, with the sweat, it . . . rubbed off."

"Ink. I'm on the way to the Sugar Snow Ball covered in ink?"

He covered a snort of laughter, badly, in a cough. "Isn't there some way to clean it off? I don't have another handkerchief. Maybe some snow?"

I shook his hand off my foot and gave him a halfhearted kick. "Idiot. There's no snow. The first snow comes tonight. That's the whole point." I spat on my finger and rubbed at the stains that might actually show, the ones on my wrists. "Ink on your hands. Ink that will rub off. Fools. This is too important to mess up. This is—"

He caught my wrist. I hissed and tried to yank it away, but his grip was stronger than I remembered. His voice was soft and deadly. "I may not have you tied up and whimpering, but that doesn't mean I'm your subject, princess."

I went still all over. I had to. Damn him.

I swallowed hard and snatched my hand away, but we both knew it was only because he let me. We glared at each other, the air still between us, the crunching of stones under the carriage wheels the only sound. I rubbed my wrist and narrowed my eyes at him.

"You're turning into a damned fine Bludman," I finally said.

He grinned again, ruining the image. "I've got a good teacher," he said.

36

The next time I pulled back the carriage's curtain, I was surprised to see that it was dark and we were nearly to our destination. It was odd, how it seemed as if we'd been riding together forever, but also as if we'd had only a few stolen minutes. The forest was the last step of the journey. We'd be there soon, provided nothing tragic happened. There was a carriage ahead of us and another behind, so at least we would arrive in a crowd. The less we stood out, the better. Which meant, I supposed, that I needed to put on my dress.

"It's almost time." I checked my wrists for more of his damnable ink and started hitching up my dress to step in. "Don't you dare touch your coat. Do you know any magic?"

He wiggled his black-streaked hands. "Only with the piano and your body."

I rolled my eyes as I stepped into my gown and gently pulled it over my arms. The long sleeves would cover most of his mess, thank heavens. I tried to think about what I remembered of the Sugar Snow Ball, of the accommodations made for the city guests. There would have to be toilets, of course, and someplace with mirrors and water.

I also knew that there was a way for couples to disappear discreetly, so at least we would have excuses if our behavior was strange or conspiratorial. Still . . .

"We have to do something about your hands." I wiggled in my dress, unable to reach the tiny buttons running up my spine. "And quickly."

He grinned, a perfect merging of his old recklessness and his new self-possessed smugness. "I took a lesson from my old rival and stocked my waistcoat." Barely brushing the fabric, he pulled a bit of cloth from the pocket of his vest, a pair of black kid gloves that I remembered from his room at the Seven Scars. "I hate the damn things, but at least they're the right color."

"Try to keep your hands hidden, then. A country rube in gloves is better than an abomination with dirty hands."

He stilled, his eyes searing me. "I'm not an abomination. I'm a Bludman."

I inclined my head. "Just so."

He pulled on the gloves, and I turned my back to him. With a minimum of fumbling, he buttoned up my dress, ending with a searing kiss on the nape of my neck. And it was a good thing, too, as the carriage jolted to a stop, knocking us both over. Casper pulled on his peacock jacket as the bludmares outside screamed in greeting and challenge, their calls answered from nearby rivals. Peeking past the curtains, I was met with the curious face of an unfamiliar girl just a few feet away, leaning out her own lamplit carriage window. With a gasp, she popped back behind her curtain. It had to be her first ball, and I smiled to myself, remembering how excited I had been finally to see what it was that made the adults' eyes twinkle every year when the air began to turn cold and smell like excitement.

"Your mask," Casper said, and I growled to myself for being so foolish. I hoped the girl was too young to be as obsessed with my family as the old Muscovy barons had been. I slipped the cool porcelain back over my face and adjusted the feathers above. My best strategy was not to take it off again until I needed my teeth for murder.

Before I could likewise remind Casper, he hissed. He reached beyond me, his arm brushing the heavy beading of my dress with the sound of rustling leaves as he held out his own peacock mask, broken into three pieces.

"You can't yell at me," he said with a rueful chuckle. "After all, you were on this bench, so it's your fault, not mine."

With a finger under his chin, I turned his head this way and that. "Do you look different now to yourself?" I asked. "Would someone remember your face?"

"I can't tell. I stopped looking about a year ago. Every time I did, I saw a new person there whom I hated with various levels of regret."

"And now? Do you hate yourself now?"

He shook my finger off, pretending to snap at it. "Nope. Feels good. Do I look different to you?"

"Always and never the same. I would know better if I'd been awake for the last four years."

The pieces of ceramic dropped from his gloved hands, and my fingers roved to my own mask, feeling the impersonal smoothness. I had never been one to hide, and I almost envied him his sudden but unwelcome freedom. It was unheard of to arrive at the Sugar Snow Ball without a mask, even if some of the revelers favored dainty lace strips or modified eye patches. We would have to find something before he made a fool of himself or was refused entry.

"My lord, my lady! Will you descend?"

The voice from outside startled us, and in a fit of inspiration, I said, "Quick. Rub the ink over your eyes where a mask would go. It will have to do. You can't be seen with your face fully bare. It's tradition."

He took off his gloves, licked his fingers, and grimaced at the taste. Rubbing across his temples, over his eyes, and over the top of his nose produced a raw, primitive mask shape in dark hunter green. It made his blue eyes pop, brighter, wilder, and more shadowy than ever.

"Well?" he asked.

I fought the urge to kiss him again and unlocked the carriage door. "It'll have to do," I said.

It was easy enough to blend in with the crowd that strolled leisurely down the paved path and into the shadow of the Ice Forest. The women rustled like birds, their dresses reflecting the shining lanterns and moonlight in startling shimmers that left spots dancing in my eyes. The men were likewise resplendent, if more tame, their waistcoats and cravats shouting with color from staid jackets and breeches of chocolate, navy, and olive. Casper was one of a few dandies, outshone in brightness and glitter only by a tall, thin pair of gentlemen with dashing tailcoats and carefully tended facial hair under their half-masks. I recognized them from past balls, as they were much-celebrated dancers and fashion trendsetters in the city. Feeling their black-painted eyes on me, I turned my mask to Casper, clutching his arm harder than I meant to. It was a credit to him that he didn't complain.

I had never walked this walk, had never heard the women chatting and gossiping about last year's ball and how Ravenna's gown had taken half a year to embroider. If the whispers were correct, Ravenna's mask had been tatted from a unicorn's tail hairs, and my brother, Alex, was well enough to attend, which had never happened during my time in the palace. Casper tried to speak to me, but I shushed him and tried not to breathe. Every word I heard was another weapon in my arsenal, another tiny talon to take down my prey. These bright creatures would know things the papers did not.

The forest closed overhead, the ancient trees climbing as tall as the basilica in the city where we'd kissed yesterday, back when things had been easy and before we had lost Keen. The way Casper was scanning the crowd, I could tell he was thinking about her, too. As if maybe she was still trailing us, as she always had, skulking in the shadows and waiting to accost us with her strange accent and odder words. But had she been there, we would have smelled her, as every other Bludman would have. The girl would have been a moment's work to drain as fortification before the party, much as the gentlemen on the *Maybuck* had taken a shot of whiskey before claiming their women.

The night was even darker under the canopy of boughs. Lanterns hung from the trees, providing an ethereal, bobbing light that reminded me of childhood fairy tales. Some of them were pierced tin, some paper globes, some little braziers on chains. There were even a few Moravian stars that made me smile to myself, thinking of my time with Casper in the inn. I would never look at a glowing star the same way again. He squeezed my arm, and I realized that we shared that memory, that it might possibly mean as much to him as it did to me. It had been his rebirth, sure. But it had changed me, too, which I came to realize more and more. As if in taking in so much of his blood, I had taken in part of his humanity. My lack of fury at being an object of change was itself telling. His smile told me that perhaps he didn't regret it so much as he had before.

Ahead, the trail forked, the ladies taking the lefthand route and the gentlemen carrying on to the right. I had only a moment to glance desperately at Casper before we were forced apart around a stone fountain bubbling with blood-tinged champagne. I was caught in a group of about twenty other ladies, but it felt twice as crowded because of the giant bell-like skirts that were fashionable just then. I didn't see another dress in the clingy fishtail style I wore. Even if they didn't recognize me immediately, they would one day remember my dress, were I successful.

"Do you think the snow will even fall this year?" a tall lady clad in wine red asked a matron in indigo.

The grand dame bit her lip and sighed, eyes rolled heavenward. "We can only hope Aztarte hears our prayers," she answered ambiguously, leaving the woman in red sorely vexed.

"If you ask me, there's something underhanded going on," a dark-skinned girl in canary yellow said, nudging her skirts aside to walk side-by-side with the tall girl in red. "Nothing adds up. Someone should speak up and ask."

"Why don't you, then?"

The girl in yellow let loose a bright, high laugh as fake as the diamonds in her earbobs. "I'm suspicious, not suicidal." She patted her companion's hand and moved away, deeper into the crowd.

I looked from face to face, searching for someone familiar. The masks could only hide so much, and I had danced among the Freesian court for years. But I saw very few faces I knew, and I lost track of the mental list of acquaintances who should have been there but weren't. Mikhail had been telling the truth on the *Maybuck*; Ravenna had chased the old blood out and brought new faces to the Sugar Snow Ball. That meant that I was less likely to be recognized but also that I would have fewer allies. My only sworn follower was Mikhail, and there was no way to know when I would see him again. He had pledged himself and promised to help me, but with a parachute on my back and pirates on my tail, I hadn't bothered to ask how.

The walkway under my slippers was formed of the same smooth, carefully cut and fitted stone as the clearing where the Sugar Snow Ball took place. It had been crafted thousands of years ago—no one knew by whom or how they had made the stone both exquisitely danceable and yet never slippery. For my first ball, I had worn satin slippers, and at the end of the night, they had been entirely worn through, my blisters poking out through holes, but still I had not stopped dancing.

We entered another clearing ringed by ancient trees. Several elegant privies waited in a line, and farther on, a vast tent hung from the branches above. Inside, couches and vanities and lanterns were placed for maximum beauty and comfort. I went straight for an empty vanity to check my appearance by the light of a white paper lantern. Of course, I couldn't remove my mask, so I was limited to patting down stray hairs and adjusting the shoulder of my dress over one of Casper's inky smears.

A subtle glance confirmed that even if I was wearing an unusual dress and an overly mysterious mask, no one was paying me any mind. The women chattered and primped and reapplied their bloodred paint as silent servants circulated with trays of bloodwine and pink champagne. I explored the rest of the tent, which floated a few feet off the ground over the stone. In one corner, a small shrine was set up. Red candles and cut roses surrounded a painting of Ravenna with my brother, Alex, sitting at her feet like a dog. But in front of the painting, someone had placed a newspaper clipping with a sketch of Olgha and me. The headline read, "Will the Missing Blud Princesses Ever Be Found?" There was no date, but the newsprint was yellowed with age and curling around the edges.

"Bless them," a woman murmured, and a hand deposited a vial of tears and disappeared before I could determine its owner.

I turned to watch the room. Hundreds of Bludwomen of all ages and types chattered together. All were rich, of course. A few had the traditional Freesian look, with milk-white skin and dark hair and light eyes. Even more had Ravenna's gypsy type, and some had my icy hair and blue eyes. There were even a few dark-skinned girls and one redhead, the very image of Aztarte and full of herself over it. Among these women, there were people who believed in me. Who hoped and prayed for me every day. People who would risk their necks by honoring me with roses and candles and scraps of paper they'd carried for years.

I was close enough to feel the brush of their skirts and smell the oil in their hair, and they didn't even recognize me. But they loved me, and for now, that was enough.

A chime sounded, and the group moved out the other side of the tent and continued along the walkway. The talk was still bright but more quiet now, excited but respectful. When our path angled in again, I all but ran to Casper's side and took his arm.

"All well?" I murmured.

He nodded, but his eyes were guarded, his expression anxious. Being around me held its own dangers, but we had found our equilibrium. Being in a large crowd of his sudden peers for the first time, crowded with puffed-up males trying to find their place in Ravenna's court, would have been uncomfortable even for a born Bludman. But his unsullied costume and face paint told me he at least hadn't found himself in any fights, and that was a fine start.

We were in pairs now, a long line traversing the white stone through the high, silent forest. It felt like a cathedral, like something bigger than hands and hearts, something old and ancient that watched from afar. That was the way of the Sugar Snow Ball: you came only in pairs, although you were free to dance with anyone you chose. I had been accompanied by a string of boring, stuffy, inbred lords strategically selected by my parents, but I had infuriated each of them by night's end and had therefore never had a repeat date, much less a steady beau. I could dance gracefully enough to bring the snow, but I couldn't keep my mouth shut or allow some young upstart to think himself superior for even a moment. Casper was my first agreeable partner, and I could only hope we would live to have an encore.

The forest was so thick around us that it was like walking down a dark hallway. Past the lanterns, the shadows between the trees became an impenetrable wall of sinister green gloom, with subtle rustlings and the eerie growl of wood rubbing on wood. The small creatures would all be in hiding, cowering from such a display of predatory power. But larger blud creatures had occasionally been seen lurking beyond the dance floor, their eyes flashing yellow or green from the darkness as they paid homage to our ancient ritual.

The path ended at a simple staircase climbing upward in the same white stone, and the whispering quieted. I loosed Casper's arm to hold up my dress and kept my eyes on the steps and the grand skirt of the lady before me. When I ran out of stairs at the top of the hill, I looked down on a scene both familiar and yet utterly new.

The Sugar Snow Ball was held in an ancient clearing in the bottom of a bowl-shaped impression, almost as if a mountain had been hollowed out just for that purpose. The forest rose infinitely tall around the wide circle of flat white stone, a ballroom nearly as large as the palace itself. The staircase up the hill had been simple, but the one that led to the dancing floor was grand and twisting. I had watched, bored but too well bred to fidget, as the couples paraded down that staircase every year. The ladies put on the brightest smiles. The gentlemen kept their backs straight, their chins high. Casper's gloved hand gave mine a squeeze, and then we were separated again, step after step in time down the curling, twining staircase, twisting in and out like another dance. At the bottom, the staircases came together by an old carved statue of Aztarte that rose from the earth, glistening as if made of moonstone. Casper and I met, taking the last steps in tandem, and I let go of my skirts and took his arm again, anxious for the connection and glad to feel his strength at my side.

He didn't know the way of things, so I guided him subtly to the back of the crowd, ensuring that there was no way Alex could see me. The wealthiest and highest-ranking couples would be at the front, with the next ring of hopefuls jockeying for position behind them. Most of the people in back would be elders, troublemakers, or foreign semiroyals who knew they would have more fun if they avoided local politics. Here, there was no jostling, just bemused smiles and patience and an occasional nip of something strongly alcoholic.

The orchestra hidden under the twining staircases began with the same sudden frenzy as the bludmares pulling our carriage, with the galloping crescendo of "Aztarte Smiles on Bloodshed," our national song. Hands went to hearts, and all eyes focused on a long, straight staircase on the other side of the clearing. A halo of bright lights glittered, and a couple appeared at the top of the staircase, outlined by the jagged silhouette of the Ice Palace. They paused momentarily for effect. My mother had always been the one to set our pace, always knowing exactly how long to stand, head held high, at the top of that staircase.

This time, the lights shone full on Ravenna.

37

She was ageless, the same as that first time I'd encountered her at the Sugar Snow festival. The same bronze skin, eagle's nose, and sweeping black hair. The same savage grace, as if her spine curved back just a little, like a cobra waiting to strike. Even from the farthest point of the clearing, I could see the magnificence of her costume and the gossamer diamond twinkling of her mask.

But what struck me most was that she had worn black. Black was considered a color of the oppressed. In the big cities of Sangland, many Bludmen were forced to wear black so that all would know what they were. As if my people wished to hide! But I had never heard of anyone wearing black to the Sugar Snow Ball. After all, it was the opposite color of snow.

Just behind her, my brother, Alex, stepped forward to take her arm. He was stiff, proud, alert, his costume done in black and white to coordinate perfectly with hers. He was just the slightest bit taller than she, his eyes shining the bold red that was usual for him and highly strange elsewhere. They descended the staircase, slowly to accommodate Ravenna's proud skirts, and goose bumps rippled over my arms. There was something deeply disturbing about the ritual, and if the whispers around us were any indication, the people felt it, too.

It felt like forever until they reached the floor. As Alex's boots clacked on the stone, a fierce wind began to batter the trees. I looked up to find the green boughs swaying mournfully, straining toward the cold white moon in the center, full and round and perfect and still, untouchable and nearly as bright as the daytime sun. The breeze brought a chill and the welcome and exhilarating scent of snow. I breathed in deeply and looked into Casper's eyes. I wanted to know if he could smell it, too. His face shone with amazement, and his arm snaked possessively around my waist, pulling me close.

Across the clearing, Alex trailed Ravenna as she walked along a line of crystalline red stone inlaid in the white. Her hips swayed, the over-wide skirts of her dress seeming to float along gently. The crowd waited, breathless and anxious for a show. The ball always began with a proclamation, and what was said and by whom was always rather telling.

The orchestra ended the song exactly as they stopped before the circular blud altar in the very center of the clearing. It was smooth and beautifully carved of pure white stone, with a trough down the center that funneled into a hole that supposedly led deep into the earth and to Aztarte herself. Ravenna moved to the fore, her dress blocking the altar entirely. Alex stood to one side, making it clear who ruled here.

My enemy smiled, bloodred lips parting over sharp teeth. Her mask hugged her face like lace spun of moonlight, highlighting her dark brows, black kohl, blacker eyes, and eerie smile.

The wind whipped past her, the feathers of her cape stirring with the iridescent inky shimmer of a raven's wing.

"People of Freesia," she called, her dusky-sweet voice carrying and echoing within the curve of the clearing.

A murmur went through the crowd. Historically, the crowd was to bow, yet . . . no one did. She ignored them.

"I welcome you to the Sugar Snow Ball. May your feet be light, your hearts be open, and the blood of your enemies be ever warm."

The words were mostly correct, but a tremor of unease ran through the crowd. The speech should have come from a Feodor, from someone carrying the blud of Freesia. Ravenna wasn't one of our people, much less a creature bonded by blud and birth to the land. She couldn't even make the traditional offering, just after the Sugar Snow, letting her blud flow into the altar and down into the ground to Aztarte's bones. She must have had plans to use Alex in her place.

When Ravenna bowed to the assembly, Alex bowed, too, which gave me an excuse to return the gesture without betraying my country. The crowd waited, holding our collective breath, as Ravenna raised her arms high and then brought them down dramatically. The orchestra began, and with a grand sweep, Ravenna was waltzing with my brother in the traditional first dance. I struggled to see past a sea of people taller than I. Was Alex hungry and feral, or was he drugged, or had the mad gypsy actually succeeded in calming him to something near normal? The air fairly stank of magic, but I had never had the knack and couldn't tell what exactly Ravenna was using it to accomplish.

The first dance lasted forever, but it always did. At least this time, I was anonymous, squashed between dresses in a crowd. It was harder when you were the one standing before the blood altar, being ogled and judged and measured by the assembled crowd. A heavy skirt nudged me, and I stepped sideways, annoyed to be in what was clearly the smallest dress. As if he could feel my annoyance, Casper squeezed my hand. Bolstered, I squeezed back.

Finally, the first dance was over, and the assembled couples quickly spread out to enjoy the next song. I pulled Casper away from the blud altar, where Ravenna and Alex danced, a dark smudge among the bright jewels of the moonlit crowd.

With a firm and steady hand, Casper twirled me out and drew me near, a cocky smile on his face. His other hand caught my waist in a move both formal and tender, and I let him lead me through the dance, guiding me through the steps with a Bludman's born grace. With such a large floor, it was easy to stay far from the altar and never brush by another couple. In my mother's time, everyone had always gravitated toward the Tsarina, hoping for a benevolent word when skirts accidentally brushed or an especially fine gown caught her eye. This time, they hovered around Ravenna, uncertain and fearful but drawn, deep down, to the most dangerous predator in the area. I didn't want to see it, so I concentrated on Casper.

He was nothing short of magnificent. Had I seen this man from across this very clearing, I would have sought him like a magnet to true north, like lightning to the tallest tree. The intensity of his gaze coupled with the humor in his mouth. The firm cut of his jaw and the soft waves of his hair. The wide shoulders that made the ridiculous jacket into artwork, and the fine figure that made the tight breeches a study of planes and curves. All I missed was the feel of his hands, his dark gloves the only thing between us and possible discovery. I hoped no one else had looked closely enough to notice they weren't a Bludman's claws.

"You're more beautiful than your portrait," he murmured in my ear.

"You can't even see my face."

"I don't have to."

He spun me out and back, the heavy skirt swirling around my ankles. When he caught me close, I smelled his scent rising with the promise of snow, a strange mix of sun and darkness, sandalwood and fir trees, old wood and new blud. The dancers around us became as inconsequential as ashes in a storm, fluttery bits of nothing. Our eyes were caught and burning, our feet moving like leaves on the wind. I didn't realize the song was over until he had spun me out and bowed.

Taking my hand, he led me toward a table of treats tended by low-ranking blud servants. I looked down, hoping they wouldn't recognize me but knowing that it was expected for us to partake and that every drop of blood made me stronger.

Casper had no way of knowing all of the clever and indulgent ways to enjoy a Bludman's feast, so I took up a curl of candied tangerine dipped in blood sugar and held it to his lips. His mouth twitched, and his eyes narrowed, but he knew better than to reject it.

"That is so very weird," he said, chewing. "I like it, and I hate it. But it's familiar."

I popped a piece into my mouth and tried to imagine what it would be like, tasting it for the first time. The tart, bright twist of the orange coupled with the waxy blood and the crystalline coating. But I couldn't tease it apart. I had always loved this taste, just as I had always lived this life in my body.

"Are you happy?" I asked him before my brain caught up with my mouth.

"I exist as I am, and that is enough. If no other in the world be aware I sit content."

"Bah. A ball is no place for your philosophies, Master . . ." I trailed off. Sterling was a Pinky name, the sort of overtly pleasant thing they had adopted when they had begun to take over the parts of the world where Bludmen were considered monsters. His name had to be powerful, careless, cruel. "Master Scathing," I said, liking the flavor of it in my mouth.

"That won't . . . I'm not . . ."

"Sniveling? Strafing? Starving? Savage?"

For just a moment there, he was human again, and struggling. Then, as if shaking off water, he suddenly seemed a foot taller and a foot wider, his eyes filled with thunder and staring over my shoulder at some new threat.

"Would the lady care to dance?"

I turned, mouth open in surprise, to find one of the two dandies I had recognized earlier. Dancing with him was the last thing on Sang that I wanted to do, and yet to deny him would have caused even more aggravation. I forced a smile and nodded, and he took my hand carefully, as if it might suddenly turn in his grasp like a snake. I tried to recall his name and failed.

The next dance was, damnably, a slow one. I placed my hand on his shoulder in the correct place, and he looked at it as if I planned on ripping a hole in his perfectly tailored violet jacket. His other hand landed lightly on my hip, as if I were a piece of furniture instead of a person, and he began to move me mechanically around the floor, whisking me ever farther away from my only ally. The last thing I saw as we passed behind the blood altar was the second dandy sidling up to Casper in a coat the same orange as the sick sunset after a storm.

"You seem rather familiar, my dear. Have we chanced to meet?"

His voice was cultured, affected, and soft. I peered into his face as if trying to place him, and the waxed and curled tips of his mustache twitched. "I don't believe so," I said in the clipped accent of Sangland.

"You've been to the Sugar Snow Ball, surely."

"This is my first time."

"But that dress! Your seamstress is a treat. You must give me her address. In Muscovy, I suppose?" His eyes were quite large behind the slip of the mask, the black around them exaggerated. He was staring at me strangely, not as if I were a woman he found attractive, because that was impossible. And yet there was an odd, anxious hunger that I couldn't place.

"You have been fooled, sir. It is secondhand, I am ashamed to say."

"Is there a tag? A tailor's mark? I simply must know. The beading is exquisite. It's the very image of the debutante gown worn by dear, sweet Princess Ahnastasia, may Aztarte have mercy on her soul. Although the color is just a bit different."

"Mmm," I murmured, nearly tripping over his exaggeratedly long shoes.

"Where do you hail from, darling? Your accent is rather exotic."

"Sangland. London."

"Divine town. I dote upon it severely. Tell me, have you ever been to the opera there?"

"Never."

His hand clenched ever so slightly on my waist, and he looked over my shoulder too quickly. I tried to follow his gaze, but he spun me into a crowd, and I couldn't see back to where Casper had been, beside the table.

"And is your mask from there as well?"

"A gift from my aunt, for the ball."

"Hiding so much." The hand on my waist rose between us, the talon on his thumb raking my chin right under the mask. "Tell me, snowbird. Is your face as beautiful as your dress?"

Thank heavens the Sugar Snow hadn't started yet. My reaction would have plunged the country into anarchy. I jerked back from his claws and stumbled out of his arms, one hand holding the mask to my face before he could pry it off. His mouth curled up slowly, mimicking his mustache, and I spun away to shoulder through the other dancers and return to Casper. The space around the table was empty, with no sign of Casper or the other dandy. The Sugar Snow was close, and the air was tense and expectant, humming with magic. It was almost time.

With a silent hiss, I accepted a flute of champagne-infused blood from a waiting servant and held it up to my mask. I couldn't get it down without making a mess of one sort or another, so I set it on the table and selected a chilled vial of blood slush from a waiting cauldron. Shaking with silent fury and fear, I tossed it back through the mouth hole of my mask as I sought Casper in the crowd.

When I finally found him, the iced blood went heavy in my stomach.

He was dancing with Ravenna.

38

Perhaps Casper led the dance, but it was clear who was in power. They danced slowly, Ravenna's mouth close enough to rip out his jugular as she whispered into his ear. They spun enough for me to see his face, and he was ashen, pale with barely restrained fury. The song ended, but she didn't let go of the hand she had held while dancing. Instead, she dragged him toward the blud altar, and they stood before it together.

"People of Freesia!" she shouted, and everyone crowded around. The scent of the coming Sugar Snow was heavy in the air, the moon obscured by misty clouds that swirled against the indigo like milk in blood.

"My friends, I have great news. Our Sugar Snow is doubly blessed this year. We have with us the greatest musician in all of Sang. The Maestro himself, Casper Sterling!" Polite applause and whispering broke out, and Casper let out a great, shuddering breath. "He has been recently bludded, although he won't reveal the circumstances. For once, an abomination is a welcome member of our ranks. My people, do we wish to hear the Snowsong played by the world's most talented harpsichordist?"

The applause after that was deafening. It had been

a lean few years, and any advantage was welcome. One famous and talented man commanding the instrument he knew best was a better gamble than an entire orchestra when it came to flawless playing and timing.

Then again, no one had ever heard the Snowsong, aside from the Bludmen who came to this ball every year. It wasn't written, it wasn't public, and it was considered a great secret. How he was going to oblige Ravenna and her court without inciting tragedy was beyond me. At least, he had managed to avoid telling her about me; if she had known, I would have been in a fight for my life already. I focused on uncurling my claws and trying to appear as normal and innocent as possible.

As I watched Ravenna lead Casper to the grand white harpsichord under the stairs, a cold hand grasped my wrist.

"May I—"

"I'll sit this one out," I hissed, trying to snatch my wrist back and failing.

"You won't."

It was the dandy. Or dandies. One on either side of me. Their twin smiles, smug and sure, told me they knew more than I wanted them to. They each grasped one of my arms, and when I struggled, the one in violet produced a metal instrument like the one filled with seawater that had been carried by the assassin on the train.

"It's considered a patriotic duty to dance the Snowsong," one said, and the other nodded and added, "Not dancing is often repaid with a good beheading."

I bared my teeth and felt the rush of the hunt flood my veins. I'd rip out their hearts and stomp on their fancy jackets if they didn't loose my wrists.

"Oh, I don't think we want to behead this one, boys."

They spun me around, and I was face-to-face with my enemy at last. Ravenna grinned, a mad look in her dark eyes. My brother, Alex, was nowhere to be seen.

I took a deep breath and held her stare, my wrists caught by the dandies.

"Nothing to say to your queen? Bow to me, then, little peacock."

The anger built inside me, but I was as still as a statue, as still as the blud altar, as still as the high white moon.

Her smile curled up, the bloodred lips mocking me. "Remove her mask."

One of the dandies untied the strings, and the proud peacock's face shattered on the stone. The night air was cool and welcome on my heated skin, but Ravenna's furious cackle of triumph stole the moment of relief. Her jugular pulsed as she threw back her head, and a rush of hunger and anger made me shiver. Nothing smelled so sweet as the enemy's blud. With my wrists pinned, I was helpless to exact my revenge. But I was so close.

I sought Casper across the clearing and found him sitting at the harpsichord. For a fraction of a heartbeat, I smiled to know he was in the place he best belonged, but then reality crushed me again. One of the musicians was scribbling on a piece of paper, and Casper was miming notes on the harpsichord. Should he miss a note or time it wrong, it would mess up the dance, and the company would tear him limb from limb as a sacrifice to Aztarte. It was a clever gamble on Ravenna's part, as if she had known that worry for Casper was the only thing that could leave me unbalanced.

"Ahnastasia," Ravenna said, one claw tracing my cheek

and leaving a hot line behind. "You've run me a pretty chase, princess."

I shrugged. She silently snarled and stepped closer, close enough for me to smell an unnatural scent rising from her skin, something I couldn't quite place.

Across the clearing, a trill rang out from the harpsichord. Four notes. The calling of the dancers.

"May I have this dance?" Ravenna asked with a mocking bow.

And I had to accept, because as much as I needed to kill her, my country needed a well-danced ritual and a perfectly fallen Sugar Snow. And she knew it, damn her. I inclined my head just the tiniest bit, and she held out her arm, as a man would. The dandies loosed me, and I let her lead me to my place at the head of the line. She stood across from me as we waited among hundreds of others, tense and excited, for the first notes to ring out.

It was always beautiful, that song. I could so easily picture Casper's nimble fingers on the keyboard, stroking the ivory keys with an intimacy and strength I knew all too well. As the first notes leaped into the air, I turned to bow to the gentleman on my other side, finding the dandy in the purple coat waiting with a mocking smile. I was trapped among the three of them, but I held my head high and danced with the grace and beauty expected of the crown princess. Whenever it came time to promenade with Ravenna, I had to stop myself from hissing at her damning and flippant power, her grasp stronger than that of any man who had ever led me while dancing. She was all but daring me to ruin my country, her feet stretching to trip me at every opportunity. Keeping up gracefully was a pretty little revenge. Casper played the song perfectly, as if he had written it himself. I was half shocked, half gratified at his success.

"Where have you been, princess?" Ravenna asked, gazing over my shoulder.

"Almanica. Hunting buffalo."

"Liar."

I snorted.

"Does Olgha live?"

"She'll be here soon with an army of daimons to overthrow you."

"I tire of your lies, little tsarling."

"I tire of your meddling, witch."

"I didn't want to do this." She sighed and took my arm. When we began the next figure, she blew some sort of powder into my face, making me blink and nearly trip. I was still shaking my head when she whispered some strange musical words. I went dizzy but didn't misstep.

"Tell me, Ahnastasia. Does Olgha live?"

"No." The word was out of my mouth before I could think it.

"Where have you been?"

I clenched my teeth, but the words leaked out the side of my mouth. "Drained in a valise."

She smiled, almost friendly. "There. That's better. Why are you here?"

"To kill you and take back Freesia."

"Oh, I don't think that's going to happen. You're not doing well so far."

I tried to stick my tongue to the roof of my mouth as I looked over her shoulder. Casper was curled over the harpsichord, his face suffused with rapture. It was truly the most beautiful song I had ever known, and hearing him play it was a once-in-a-lifetime experience, especially since Ravenna seemed to have the upper hand. When I looked up at the moon, I could see the clouds starting to swirl in a circle and sparkle as if tiny fairies flew within. The smell was sweet and heavy, like a bush about to blossom at midnight, except that the blooms were snowflakes. If he was playing well enough and we were dancing well enough, the next chorus would bring the first snow.

"What have you done to Alex?" I asked.

"He's ensorcelled, of course. That began long before I had your parents executed. Alex is on a steady diet of my blud, which calms him and binds him further to me. I'll announce our engagement at the end of the dance. The wedding will happen in summer, I think, at the Basilica of Aztarte."

It had been said to enrage me, and it worked. My talons bit into her shoulder, drawing blood, and the hand I held made a slight crunching noise. She didn't flinch, and neither of us missed a step. If she managed to marry Alex and kill me, she would be Tsarina of Freesia until she died, ending my family's matriarchal reign forever.

"What of the Svedish king?"

A wicked smile. "That's the second act."

"The people will never stand for it," I hissed.

"The people are cattle. But tell me, did you turn Casper?"

"Yes."

"Then I have grounds to drain you, should you live through the dance. Excellent. Ah, the chorus."

Casper shifted into the trickiest part of the song. The dancers had formed two circles, the men a smaller ring inside the larger one formed by the women and their grand dresses. I couldn't see where Ravenna's claws ended and mine began as we spun, around and around, faster and faster.

Her black skirt swung out like a huge bell, a monstrous flower, and mine flared just a little, the iridescent feathers shimmering in the air. The woman on my other side was nothing, just a shadow holding me in place. Across from us, the men's circle whirled in the opposite direction, a blur of dark coats and bright cravats. Casper's song built in speed and strength, and the world seemed to hold its breath, and finally, with a heavy sigh, the first fat flakes of snow began to fall in the center of the circles, right above the blud altar.

The first ones never made it to the ground; you could only see them if you looked up, just right. But then they began to pour, heavy and white and pure, with the scent of hidden flowers and raw wind and wildness. I breathed in deep as we spun, focusing ever upward and sending silent prayers to Aztarte.

Let me kill Ravenna.

Let me save my brother, my country.

Let Casper survive.

I bit my lip hard enough to draw blud and spat into the wind, hoping to hit some snow and help my prayers find the goddess whom I suddenly, desperately needed to be real and listening.

As the song built to the last verse, the circles stopped spinning exactly where they'd started, and the dancers moved to the last set. Ravenna pulled me close, jerking my body into position, as the leading dancer was supposed to do. We were both panting and exhilarated with the touch of the first snow, and a heavy one at that.

"You see? Aztarte smiles on my future rule," she all but purred, and I smiled through closed teeth before spitting a big glob of blud in her face. It spattered over her dainty mask, turning the unicorn hair a strange pink.

Slow and low, she hissed at me. "We finish this dance, and then you and your pet abomination die."

"We shall see."

The dance ended, and we performed the traditional bow, our eyes never unlocking. The entire company clapped and whistled with an unusual enthusiasm. The snow still fell, already gathering in our hair and on the boughs around us, although it never marred the stone of the dancing floor. As I straightened and moved to pounce on Ravenna, the dandies caught my wrists and jerked me painfully back from my leap.

"An auspicious omen!" Ravenna shouted, and the people cheered again with real enthusiasm. She raised her arms and led us to the blud altar, and the dancers formed a ring around us. "Bring the Maestro and the sacrifice," she called, disappearing among the guests and leaving me with the dandies.

As the crowd gathered, the whispering began. They could see my face. Did they recognize me, or were they simply curious about my lack of a mask and the fact that I was being restrained like a criminal?

"Ahna?" My brother appeared, his voice deeper than I remembered but his face still youthful and anxious.

"Greetings, Alex." I kept my tone even, proud, my chin held high.

"Did you know I'm better? Where have you been? We've been looking forever."

I chuckled. "That's my baby brother, always worrying about himself first."

"Do you know where Mother and Father have been?"

"Yes." I cocked my head, confused at his lack of sorrow. "Do you?"

"A diplomatic mission. Ravenna says they'll be back soon."

"I'm sure they will," I said gently.

The crowd parted, and Ravenna marched through with Casper on her arm. His lips were curled back, his teeth bared. But I smelled fear on him, too, which was a surprise. In that moment, anger should have consumed him, as it consumed me.

A murmur rippled through the party, and I smelled something strange, my hackles rising. An interloper, a non-Blud, at the Sugar Snow Ball? When I breathed in deeper, fear clutched my heart, too, and I understood Casper's strange reaction. It was no surprise when the crowd parted to reveal a servant carrying a bound Pinky.

Keen.

The servant set her on the ground, and she growled around a gag and thrashed in the ropes. Ravenna put one hand on her head. "You'll never guess what we found in the city, trying to pawn a royal diamond the size of her thumbnail."

I groaned and glared at Keen, but her eyes were too wide and terrified for it to have any sort of effect, not even the flippant and dangerous eye rolling I had hoped to see. She knew, with the prey animal's deep-down fear, that she was doomed.

"We have Aztarte's blessing, my people! And now we will honor her with the blood of retribution!"

The crowd seemed unsure how to respond, outside of scattered applause and whispering. The clearing went dark for a moment, a cloud passing over the moon. I shivered, and not because of the snow falling like kisses on my hair and shoulders. The very worst had come to pass: she had all three of us in her power and Aztarte's blessing to rule. I had wished to see Keen again, but never like this.

Ravenna picked up Keen as if the girl weighed nothing and tossed her roughly onto the blood altar. Keen's face was as white as the stone, and she fought against the bonds, her eyes pinned on Casper and pleading.

"This insignificant creature has told me all your secrets." Ravenna spoke to me, but her voice was purposefully loud. "First, you will give me the ring of succession, and I will wear it as I drain her in the name of Aztarte. When the sacrifice has been made, I will destroy this abomination and punish you for putting the royal blud of Freesia into a commoner. Three is a sacred number, and your blud will seal our victory. Aztarte will bless us above all others as we join with Sveden and march on Sangland to topple the Coppers and rule forever."

The crowd was silent. I was silent. Ravenna held out her hand. I reached into my corset and withdrew the ring of succession, the sapphire glinting, cold and blue in the moonlight. With a heavy sigh, I placed it in her outstretched palm, her black fingers curling around it and a smile of pure joy spreading over her face. She slipped it over the proper finger and held her hand aloft, and the crowd clapped sadly, as if they had no choice. The empire's death hung heavy over the clearing, which should have sparkled with music and dancers. And yet no one could protest. I watched my ring twinkle on my enemy's finger as the dandies yet again captured my wrists.

"Are you not patriots?" I whispered, and one of them whispered back, "The winner writes the history, sweetness."

Ravenna approached Keen and stroked her tear-stained face, turning her cheek away. In a savage strike, she swiped the girl's throat open with one talon. Blood poured down Keen's tender neck and into the trough, funneling it straight down into the soil, to Aztarte herself. Casper roared and jumped for Ravenna's throat, but the strangest thing I could possibly imagine happened. An arrow from nowhere landed to quiver in his shoulder, and he fell to the ground.

The crowd went mad, as weapons were strictly forbidden at the Sugar Snow Ball. Some people hissed and got into fighting stances, others ran for cover, and several just stared up at the sky, amazed. I looked up to see the dark hull of an airship hovering just beyond the trees. Ropes unfurled, and bodies slid down, shadows against the moon and light flickering off crossbows.

I was torn. Go to Casper and remove the arrow, try to help Keen, or kill Ravenna? Instinct took over, and I howled and slammed into the gypsy witch. We rolled over and over on the dancing floor, teeth and claws slashing for exposed skin. All around us, heavy boots struck the hard stone. The scent of unwashed flesh merged with the magic of the Sugar Snow and the hot reek of spilled blud. I glanced away from Ravenna for just a second and saw a familiar smile behind a curving sword.

It was Mikhail, the pirate.

All around me, Bludmen in ball gowns and tailcoats grappled and fought with the pirates. Underneath me, Ravenna growled and scratched and bit, slippery in her silk dress, the wide hoops of her skirt making it impossible to hold her down. She tossed me onto my back, and over her shoulder, I saw Keen's shape on the altar, no longer thrashing. Casper was gone.

"Give up, little brat," Ravenna said.

"Never!" My shout rang out as sharp as metal on ice.

"Do you want to know what I saw as your fortune, all those years ago?"

"You told me. Rebellion."

"I lied. I saw your blud dripping off the altar. I saw this." She caught my wrist in her hand, clenching hard enough

to make the bones rub together. With a heavy grunt, I reared
back and drove my forehead into her nose with a wet crunch
that reminded me all too well of the pirate we'd sent overboard. She shrieked and pulled back, burbling blud, and
I saw my moment. I reached for the ring on her hand and
twisted the center stone.

She shuddered, her grip loosening. I flung myself back,
dragging my body out from under her skirt and away from
her. Touching her skin just then would have been suicide.

It was almost beautiful, the way her body danced amid
all that fighting. She was on her back, the great bell of her
skirt billowing as she writhed. Blud pooled in her eyes and
dribbled out her nose and mouth and ears to stain the
cracks between the white stones. The fighting slowed, and
the people of Freesia moved near, making a wide circle
around Ravenna, watching her die in silence.

A hand found my shoulder, and I stiffened and growled
before I realized it was Mikhail.

"Cyanote?" he asked.

I nodded. "A hidden compartment. As if the ring had
been made for this day."

"I told you we would be here, my queen. Your word,
my life."

Alex floundered out of the crowd and across the stone
to kneel by Ravenna's side.

As he reached for her hand, I barked, "No! Don't touch
her unless you wish to die."

His hand stopped in midair, considering. It fell to his
side, and the blud tears began to roll down his pale cheeks.
When she gave a final twitch and went still, Alex threw his
head back and screamed, a sound that was all too familiar
from him.

"Your kill, my queen," Mikhail murmured, pushing me forward just a little.

One foot in front of the other, I walked to the corpse of my greatest enemy. I knelt on her other side and used the sleeve of my dress to pull the ring from her stiff, already curling finger.

"A glass of blood," I called, and with a welcome quickness, one appeared. I set the glass on the stone and dropped in the ring, pulling my skirts back. The blood bubbled and fumed, a little green cloud roiling down the glass and drifting along the stone. When it stilled, the blood had gone thick and chunky. I dumped out the ring and slipped it onto my finger.

I stood and held up my bloody hand.

"My people, Aztarte has spoken. I, Tsarina Ahnastasia Feodor, assume the throne of Freesia, as is my right by blud and by birthright. I shout my challenge over the blud of the enemy and the rime of the Sugar Snow. If you wish to face me, do it now, and I will destroy you!"

I stood defiant, my eyes meeting face after face. Every single person there cast his or her eyes to the ground, even Alex. No one was willing to challenge me. And that was right, too.

Mikhail stepped forward. "Three cheers for Tsarina Ahnastasia!"

After a deafening moment of silence, the crowd erupted, their call loud enough to shake the snow from the boughs of the trees.

"Hurrah! Hurrah! Hurrah!"

One fist to the sky, I answered in a primal scream that sealed my monarchy.

As my howl reverberated through the forest, I heard a quiet cough and a gasp.

Casper.

39

I found him clinging to the altar, a trail of blud marking his path.

"You have to help her," he said.

I snorted and muttered, "I have to help you first, fool."

"No. Her."

"Mikhail! Get the arrow out of him!" I shouted.

"Not him." Casper drew back and coughed a spray of blud. "Don't pull out the arrow. I need a doctor."

Mikhail appeared beside us, a bemused smile on his face. "Don't know what a doctor is, comrade, but a little arrow is hardly an impediment. Once the point is out, you'll heal quickly enough. Lucky you joined the right side, eh?"

With a grim nod, I turned back to Keen. Her eyelids fluttered, her pulse weak. She was so broken that she barely registered as food. A great chill crept over me, seeing her nearly dead, and I looked up to the cold moon. Would Aztarte forgive me for what I was about to do? And did I really need anyone's forgiveness anymore?

"My people, I hereby adopt this child as a Feodor. The traitor Ravenna made an unpure sacrifice to Aztarte, and I will redeem this creature with the blud of our people.

She will replace my sister, Princess Olgha Feodor, murdered by Ravenna's hand. Blood for blud."

A murmur went through the crowd, but no one objected or moved forward. With a silent plea to the moon and her mistress, I pulled back the gem-crusted sleeve of my gown to bite my wrist and let the blud pour into Keen's open mouth. At first, nothing happened, and the blud slipped from her lips to dribble down the white face of the altar. For just a second, as I watched the bright spatter fall, I was a child in a gypsy tent, staring at a woman with a crocodile's smile, and then I was back with Keen, willing her to live. My heart stuttered to watch the bright red paint her dry tongue. Then, miracle of miracles, her broken throat moved. After a few moments, she licked her lips, and her eyes popped open.

"More," she said with a gurgle, and I laughed.

"So you're back to yourself, then, urchin?"

She grabbed my wrist and pulled it close, sucking hard. It wasn't like it had been with Casper—not at all. It hurt, as if she were trying to draw the very soul out of my body with her teeth. But I was determined to show my people that I was untouchable, and I was desperate to keep Keen alive. For me and for Casper. So I held my head high, letting her drink and daring anyone to challenge me. Inside, I was screaming.

"She's going to live?" Casper said quietly.

I turned to give him a wobbling smile. "I know nothing else but miracles," I said with a half-sobbing chuckle at how everything had turned out.

"I'm getting there myself."

"Welcome to the Blud Court, Maestro."

40

It wasn't easy after that. Bludding Keen took time and caused us both excruciating pain. By the end, we were curled together on the hard ground under a mound of capes and jackets, shivering with the cold and the ache of draining and covered in frozen blud. Casper had stayed with us the entire time, guarding us as if I was a bitch with a new pup.

Keen finally dragged herself out from beneath my arm and stood, as wobbly as a new fawn.

"I think we're finally even," she muttered. She shook herself and grinned with new energy before following her nose to the banquet table.

Casper pulled me onto his lap, and I tucked my head into his neck and watched Mikhail and his crew clean up the chaos they'd wrought. They had seemed like a multitude, sliding down from the sky in a rain of arrows, but in truth, it was a skeleton crew of fewer than a dozen Bludmen, sons of Freesia who had mutinied under Mikhail's lead and stolen the pirate airship while Captain Corvus drank himself insensible between Miss May's thighs.

My first act as Tsarina was to pardon Mikhail and the rest of the Blud Barons driven out by Ravenna. My second act was to send everyone home to spread the word that the traitor was dead and the true queen returned, along with the heaviest Sugar Snow that had been seen in a century. Alex was still distraught at Ravenna's death, and I ordered the servants to take him back to his room at the palace and lock him up, if need be, until his ensorcelled attachment could be broken.

There was so much more work to be done fixing Ravenna's mess. The weeks to come would take hard days and longs nights of restoring the diplomacy, the pacts, the affairs of state. The rioting Pinkies needed to be dealt with, but not in the cruel way that my people expected. Ravenna had let them run wild to distract the Bludmen from her other sins, but I wanted them to have rights of their own now, which was going to take some tricky footwork in the Blud Council. I would simply have to persuade my people that happy food tasted better. The vials the servants brought me to replenish myself after the bludding hardly seemed to make a dent in my own hunger, but with Casper by my side, I doubted I'd be drinking from live Pinkies again, no matter how much I craved it. The Tsarina would live by example.

When the last of the crowd had dispersed, I turned to wrap my arms around Casper's neck. My limbs were heavy with exhaustion, my dress splattered with blud and torn by Keen's frantic fingernails, but he didn't flinch from the gore. The airship bobbed high above us, brushing the highest boughs of the trees and dusting our heads with snow. I could hear the pirates celebrating up there, drinking their grog mixed with blood and singing "Aztarte Smiles on Bloodshed." We were as alone as we had been since the carriage.

"How did you do it?" I asked him as his fingers stroked my fallen hair.

"Do what?"

"Play a song you'd never heard before, a secret song, as if you had written it? How did you play it so well that the snow is still falling?"

He chuckled into my neck, his entire body shaking with laughter. "I was scared at first. But when I saw the first notes, I knew. It's the 'Dance of the Sugar Plum Fairy' from Tchaikovsky's *Nutcracker*. It's one of the most well-known songs ever written in my world. I learned it before I was ten." He couldn't stop giggling, but I didn't have enough breath to join in. "Of all the music Sang has never seen, I can't believe that song's the Bludmen's great secret."

I smiled weakly and sighed, glad that Aztarte, or fortune, was on our side. Casper pulled me closer, and over his shoulder, I watched Keen pillaging the dessert table, delighting in her first taste of bloodsweets as she tried to fill the emptiness from repeated draining, a feeling I knew all too well.

"She's a tenacious creature, that one," I said.

"You're one to talk."

"Bah. All in a day's work for the Tsarina. I'm nearly invulnerable."

"I never felt that way until you came along. Walt Whitman once said that those who love each other shall become invincible. I understand it now."

"Did he say anything about sleep?"

He thought for a moment, one arm idly stroking my back. "He said that making the best person involves open air and good food and sleeping with the earth."

I grinned and stood on shaky feet, holding out a hand to pull him up beside me. "Forget the earth. I've got an enormous bed, over there in that palace. Let me introduce you."

41

Some days later, I woke to the sound of the harpsichord. With my ermine robe dragging on the carpet behind me, I padded down the stairs to the parlor. The scene before me was like a dream. All of the people I had fought for at the Sugar Snow Ball were there, together, breakfasting in the golden-warm morning of the Ice Palace.

Casper sat curled over the keyboard in breeches and open shirt, playing some strange song from his world, a mirror of the first time I met him. Keen lounged on the floor before the fire, taunting a brood of wolfhound puppies with her clockwork tortoise as my brother excitedly tried to explain the dogs' lineage. Ravenna's magic was hard to break, which meant that Alex's ailment was all but cured, yet he still mourned the woman he had believed to be his fiancée. Casper had already written to Criminy Stain, requesting his aid in separating the spells so that Alex could live a normal life but give up Ravenna's ghost.

As for Keen, she had taken to the bludding better than expected. I had called her tenacious, but it was more than that. She had a fierce will to live and survive against all odds, and even she seemed to recognize that she had little right to complain. Her life in the other world had been a hard one, and her life in London had been harder, and now she was nearly invulnerable and living in the biggest castle on the continent, with all the food, free time, and bludponies she'd ever wanted. She hadn't shown me any gratitude for saving her life, but I didn't expect her to. I'd said often enough myself that princesses didn't say thank you, and she was officially Olgha II of Freesia, as much as she hated the name. She would have several years of freedom before her responsibilities actually became an impediment, but I dreaded the day of her majority, when I would have to force her into a dress and a crown to sit for her portrait. For now, it was enough that she was alive and smiling.

I curled up in my favorite chaise by the window, and a servant placed a steaming cup of blud tea in my hand, the porcelain painted with tiny violets.

"Not playing about Jude today?" I called to Casper, and he grinned and ended the song with a little trill. I watched him walk to my chaise, the very picture of a Bludman, confident and beautiful and sure. He moved my feet aside and sat.

"That one's called 'And I Love Her,'" he said. "By the same band but a little less mournful."

"You've come to terms with your miserable little life, then?"

He glanced around the grandest parlor in the northern hemisphere. "The world is before me. Although I'll always regret not taking one more swim in the sea."

"The sea. How revolting." I sipped my blood-tinged tea.

He took my bare feet into his lap, tracing my ankles in a way that made shivers run up my legs. "Is there anything you regret, Ahna?"

"Mmm," I murmured. "I regret not getting to rip out Ravenna's throat. She died horribly, but I had so looked forward to that part."

"You used to want my head on a pike," he offered.

"Mine, too!" Keen called.

I chuckled. "That was before you proved yourselves useful."

"I'm still not useful," Keen hollered, and I smiled indulgently. I wasn't about to tell her how useful a princess could be.

"So what now?" Casper asked.

I raised my hands. "For you? This. Just this."

"Sitting around, sipping blood? Doing nothing? That doesn't sound like the Ahna I know."

I sighed. "Let's see. We need to hammer out a new peace accord with the king of Sveden, and we'll start by sending him some decapitated dandy heads. We need to send thanks to Reve and an assassin to Mr. Sweeting. My sister's head needs a proper burial on Freesian soil. We must find a way to shift the balance between Bludmen and Pinkies so that Pinkies are servants instead of slaves. I need to call Verusha back to the palace, since no one can do my hair quite like she can. I need to send a bag of silvers to Miss May to pay for the parachutes and the glass tank I broke on the *Maybuck*. I need to rewrite the laws regarding tsarinas marrying musicians." I looked to the wolfhounds by the fire. "And I think we need to start importing cats."

"And what shall I do?" He held out his hand, which had darkened properly, and I took it in mine.

"Your first act as court composer is to write a song for me. About our adventures. A ballad."

He chuckled and looked down. "A song of ourselves?"

"Exactly that."

"And then I'm going to write a book. It's going to be called *Blades of Grass*."

I leaned over to kiss him. "What will it be about?"

"Loss. Redemption. Rebirth. Living many lives. Love. Death. Art. Beasts. About how fortunes come true in the strangest ways and not knowing what you need until it finds you. I finally realized why it doesn't exist here."

"Because you haven't written it yet?"

"That's exactly what I was thinking, my Tsarina. Do you approve?"

I gave him a benign, queenly smile. "Do anything you wish, Maestro, but let it produce joy."

With a hasty glance at Keen and Alex, he yanked me onto his lap and stood, carrying me like a child. Pulling me close and ignoring their mortified stares, his breath hot on my ear, he whispered, "I'll tell you what I wish to do, and I assure you it will produce more than joy." I struggled to squirm out of his grasp, but he held me tight and set his teeth gently in the curve of my ear.

I shrieked as he carried me upstairs, glad to know I couldn't escape him, gladder still to know I didn't wish to do so. It was good being the one who made the rules.

Turn the page
for an exclusive sneak peek
at the next sexy romance in the BLUD series

WICKED AFTER MIDNIGHT

by Delilah S. Dawson

Available from Pocket Books
Spring 2014

"Criminy's going to kill us."

I rolled my eyes at Cherie and leaned my head against the worn cushion of the jouncing carriage, which was moving across Franchia at a fast clip, spiriting us from Ruin to Paris. My best friend sounded way too much like my conscience. I was fairly certain she would nag me to death long before our ex-boss discovered that we had escaped from our chaperone and taken off on our own. My idea, of course.

"He's got to find us before he can kill us. Paris is a big city, *mon petit chouchou*." I elbowed her in the ribs.

"What's that supposed to mean, Demi?" She elbowed me right back.

"It means I called you a cabbage. It's a French—I mean, Franchian—term of endearment. And did you know you have seriously pointy elbows?"

"I just don't think it's right, running out on Mademoiselle Caprice and taking all her coppers. Criminy's going to kill her, too, for being a bad chaperone. What was so horrible about going to the University of Ruin, anyway?"

We hit a pothole, and my head was knocked against the wood, loosening a long dark brown curl to dangle in my eyes. I sat up straighter and sighed. "I wanted an adventure. I didn't want to be a boring contortionist in the boring caravan anymore, and I didn't want to go back to college, either."

"*Back* to college?"

I put my head on her shoulder, my mouth to her ear behind a curled glove. The other passengers didn't know we were Bludmen or that I was a Stranger from another world called Earth. We would be in serious trouble if they found out we were bloodsuckers—not the nice, normal, Pinky girls we appeared to be. "I guess I never told you. I was at university when I . . . when I ended up in Sang. When Criminy found me and saved me. Bludded me. I was a student, in my world. I hated it."

"Why?"

I scowled behind my hand, but her confusion was genuine.

It was easy to forget that Cherie had grown up poor and freezing in the forests of Freesia. To her, the caravan was a life of warmth and wealth and security. And I had taken that from her when I decided to leave. Breathing in the scent of pine and vanilla, her favorite shampoo, I felt a rush of love for the first person who'd reached out to me when I arrived in Criminy's caravan, naked and confused and newly blood-hungry. She'd hugged me and taken me in like a lost duckling, teaching me how to drink blood from vials without staining my clothes and showing me how to line my eyes with kohl like the other girls.

When I looked at her, I saw only my dear friend, the closest thing I'd ever had to a sister. Golden curls, eyes too innocent for a Bludwoman, pink cheeks, and an upturned nose. She looked like a little shepherdess doll. But to her, the University of Ruin represented untold wealth and opportunity. Most likely, no one in her entire family had ever been to university, much less a woman. I would have to remember, before we hit the city, that women in Sang didn't have the sort of freedom I had known back home in Greenville, South Carolina.

"I guess I thought that once I left home and got to a new city, everything would be different. That I would make friends and get a boyfriend and do well in my classes without really trying. I thought life would be as pretty as it looked in the brochures. I thought that just getting away from my parents would suddenly make everything better."

"It didn't?"

"Nope. Kind of the opposite."

The Pinky gentleman across the carriage watched our whispered closeness with an unhealthy fascination, a creepy gleam growing behind his monocle. My instinct was to flash my fangs at him and hiss, but that would get us thrown off the carriage, if not killed. Instead, I pulled my head away from Cherie and locked eyes with the older man. After a few moments of my intense glaring, he cleared his throat juicily and looked away. The prim nursemaid beside him sniffed in disdain and sidled closer to her charge, a girl of about seventeen. The girl gave us an innocent, hopeful smile, which I was sure Cherie would return. We might have looked her age, but I was twenty-six, and Cherie was twenty-seven. There were benefits to being bludded, after all.

"Well, I think it's important that we—"

I never found out what was important. Two sharp thuds set the bludmares screaming as the scent of fire reached my sensitive nose. Cherie's head whipped around, her eyes wide and alert. The coach shuddered with sudden violence, throwing us against each other and the walls. Flames caught at the curtains, black smoke rolling into the stuffy, airless space. The gentleman who'd ogled us earlier threw open the door and froze, before tumbling out onto the ground, a flaming arrow lodged in his jabot. I leaped out, tugging Cherie behind me, trying to make sense of the chaos, while the young girl behind us clutched at her nurse with one hand and the carriage seat with the other and screamed bloody murder. I forgot myself and turned to hiss at her, which really only made her more annoyingly hysterical.

A loud screech outside caught my attention. It was a metal conveyance, shaking and belching smoke. Dark, eyeless figures appeared in the haze, and I tried to run in the opposite direction. Cherie was motionless, stiff with fear.

"Run, you idiot!" I hissed.

"I—I can't."

The figures hovered closer, dark arms up as if to calm us, as if creepy ghost figures with torches could ever calm anyone. Gritting my teeth, I slapped Cherie's white face.

"You're a goddamn predator, Cherie. Act like it. Run."

"You start. I'll follow."

"Promise?"

"Promise."

I took a deep breath and coughed out black smoke. Springing into action, I vaulted over the thrashing, burning, screaming bodies of the once-white bludmares and charged into the waist-high grass of the moors. Arrows *thwack*ed over my head, and I dived and rolled, clawing through the grass and into a thick pricker bush that would have torn apart anyone not wearing so many layers of city clothes.

"Come on. Come on come on come on," I chanted, waiting for Cherie to follow me.

With the screaming of the girl in the coach and the bludmares dying on the ground, the conveyance's rattling, the sound of fire, and the thrashing of the grass as the cloaked figures hunted me, I couldn't hear anything. I didn't dare peek up or call out for Cherie. I would have to hope that her inner strength had overcome her fear, that she was waiting somewhere, crouched, as I was, hiding under the heavy gray sky. I was one of the few people who understood Cherie's quiet tenacity and power, and I prayed it wouldn't fail her now.

The screaming stopped all at once, leaving only the rumbling of the conveyance and the eerie whispering of the wind in the grass. I took a deep breath, trying to scent Cherie, but only smoke and charred meat reached me. When the conveyance's rattling quieted, I rubbed my ears. It took me an extra moment to realize the sound was fading as the vehicle moved rapidly away. I stood in a crouch and found only a trail of exhaust lingering over the road. The machine was far off now, low-slung, dark, and mean, like a charred raven's skull. And faster than anything I'd seen since coming to Sang.

"Cherie?"

The only sound that reached me was the crackling of the burning coach. And the burning bodies around it. I was about to rush over and hunt for Cherie when I heard the loud, nasal sound of a horn.

I dropped to the ground, the adrenaline finally running out and leaving me cold and wobbly. A bludbunny darted past me with a bleeding human finger in its mouth. The next one stopped by my boot to hiss, nearly dropping an ear.

"Keep it," I muttered. "I'm not that desperate." I started to sit up and fell back, dizzy.

What the hell had just happened? We had been attacked. But why? And where was Cherie?

The horn sounded again, and I put my hands over my ears. My head was pounding—at least, I thought it was. Then the pounding turned into the slamming of hoof-beats against the packed road. A large group of horsemen was coming, and there was no way to know whether they were friends or foes. All I cared about was finding Cherie, and whoever they were, I didn't want their help. Or their hindrance. I burrowed deeper into the bushes and flopped onto my back, pretending to be unconscious.

"Damn. Just missed them!" an older man's gruff voice shouted.

"Nicely done, Vale." That voice was younger, smug and nasty.

"Oh, sure. Blame the guy who had to take a piss." A third voice, sarcastic and dry.

The horses skidded to a stop somewhere to my left. The way they screamed and pawed at the earth told me that they were bludmares, and lots of them, far more than necessary for the three voices I'd heard. I struggled to hold very, very still. Bludman or not, with a crowd of any males, the likelihood of a lone young woman being raped on the roads of Sang was just as high as at a frat party back home.

"Ten of you—swords out and after the slavers. Three

more in each direction, hunting for survivors. Don't return until you hear the horn. Lorn and Vale, with me." The old man sighed, and I could imagine him. Paunchy, starting to stoop, a barbarian in decline, wiping his balding head under the Franchian gloom. "I'm getting too old for this *merde*."

Even with my eyes closed and my body hidden, I could sense a strange tension in the drawn-out pause.

"I'm going to look over there, Father."

"There's nothing over there, Vale."

"Exactly."

Soft footsteps spelled anger in the dirt. The sarcastic one was moving toward me, and if he got too close, the pricker bush and grasses wouldn't conceal my overly bright teal dress. Damn it. Why couldn't I have just stayed unconscious for this part or dressed in the boring green of the moors? And where was Cherie? I couldn't smell her. Couldn't smell any of the bodies I knew so well from our time jostling together in the carriage.

"Only the coachman and a gentleman, Father. No women." The smug voice was far away and muffled, and I could easily picture a swarthy pirate with the arm of his floofy blouse over his mouth and nose to keep out the scent of burning flesh.

"Vale? Anything?"

Nearer me, Vale struck the bushes with a stick. I could smell him, a strange mélange of good and bad and spices. He reminded me a little of Veruca the Abyssinian, the caravan's sword swallower, and I guessed he was a half-breed of some sort. The overall effect was like a succulent piece of meat under a dusting of herbs that wasn't exactly to your taste.

"I found a bush!" The shout was falsely bright, and I struggled not to grin. My teeth clacked together seconds later as his stick poked my thigh through several layers of skirt.

"What the devil?"

I could hear twigs breaking under his hands, and in a moment of panic, I sat straight up and grabbed him by the collar, yanking him dangerously close without time to look at his face. To his credit, he didn't topple over or shout. Into a golden tan ear with three gleaming rings in the lobe, I whispered, "Silence. I am not in the mood to be identified. Or raped."

With a soft laugh, he whispered, "Excellent. I'm not in the mood to rape."

When he didn't shout or otherwise broadcast my existence, I let go of his shirt, noting that up close, he smelled like a chai latte mixed with hearth smoke and starlight, a gypsy in ways that Criminy Stain was not. He pulled away gently, no sudden moves, and studied me. I scooted back and wrapped my arms around my trembling knees, realizing how close my lips had been to a seriously hot guy.

Chardonnay-colored eyes lined in black and set in molten tan skin regarded me with a cat's mixed disdain and curiosity. He had a two-day beard that framed full lips and matched his recently shorn hair, which wasn't normally my style but totally worked in his favor. He was dressed all in black, like the Dread Pirate Roberts, sitting back on his haunches with a loose-limbed confidence that made my limbs a little looser, too. His eyes blended in with the moors perfectly, an endless, shifting amber green like a glass of chilled wine that made me feel thirsty all over.

"Anything behind that bush, Vale?"

I jerked and flailed at his father's shouted words, and Vale's lips curled up, revealing white teeth.

His eyes raked from my mussed hat down to the tall leather boots peeking out from beneath foamy black layers of petticoats, as if he were pondering which end of a Chinese buffet to start at. I'd felt like a stone-cold predator since waking in Sang under Criminy's bloody wrist, but now my middle went hot and soft.

"Just the prettiest girl I've ever seen." My mouth dropped open.

"Lazy, lying bugger!"

Something *plink*ed against Vale's back, and he laughed and held up a river-smooth stone for me to see.

"Get to work, you worthless ass!"

He shrugged, unaffected. Barely loud enough to be heard, he said, "Sometimes I tell the truth. It keeps them guessing." Another stone *thwack*ed him in the head, and he rubbed it with a black-gloved hand. "Stay here. I'll be back." Before I could respond, he had disappeared, leaving shivering leaves and skin in his wake.

I flopped onto my back, just in case one of the other men should doubt his lie this time. Eyes open, staring at the lavender-gray clouds, I listened for more footsteps. Partly because I wanted to avoid notice and partly because I wanted Vale to come back and look at me as if I were a candy apple waiting to be licked all over. But most of all, I wanted them all to leave so I could find Cherie.

I didn't smell her anywhere near, couldn't smell anything over the smoke and, now, the gypsies. But from the men's shouts, at least I knew they hadn't found a body. She was small and agile and clever, and I could only hope she was hiding in another copse or backed into an empty bludbadger den, waiting for the pesky band of gypsies to finish its plundering and go the hell home. Maybe Cherie was a predator, but she was also a beautiful young woman, and all we knew of Franchia was ancient history from our daimon dancing mistress. Who knew what dangers actually lurked here?

The hooves of a single horse pounded close, the bludmare's scream protesting her rider's harsh treatment.

"You were right, boss. The same slavers riding hellbent for Paris in that damnable fast conveyance. Farther along than we thought. But the others might still catch 'em before they're into the underground."

"Great humping Hades!" I could hear echoes of the old man's greatness in the bellow of his baritone. Bludmare squeals and the squeaks of butts in saddles meant I would soon be alone again. "Lorn, you're with me. Vale, you keep poking around your precious bushes. Dig through the rubble. Bring in at least a silver's worth of plunder, or don't bother to come home." He spit in the dirt, and despite my ambivalence, I flinched. That was some cold shit.

I barely heard Vale's muttered "Have fun in the catacombs, arsehole."

The horn sounded, and the horses took off amid the men's whoops and hollers. I sat up before Vale could pry his way through the bushes, smoothing my bangs and licking my lips and hoping I looked less like a twitterpated girl and more like a sophisticated, exotic, and possibly dangerous lady on a mission gone awry.

"We keep meeting like this." He grinned and held out a hand, and I took it, well aware that the two gloves between us lessened the heat no more than grabbing a hot cast-iron skillet with a paper towel. I stood, but he didn't let me loose. "I'm Vale Hildebrand, first son of Curse Hildebrand." He paused as if waiting for a response. "Lord of the Infamous Brigands of Ruin . . . ? Nothing? Really?" Dark eyebrows swept up, and he rubbed the stubble on his chin. "Damn, you're hard to impress."

"I'm not from around here. Name's Demi Ward." Then, before he could derail me, "Have you seen another girl, about my age and size but blond?"

"Unfortunately, you're the only one today. Maybe I should start setting snares."

He released my hand, and I stood tall, but not quite tall enough to look him in the eye. "My best friend is gone. We were on the coach together—it was just us and another girl and her chaperone and a gentleman. Headed to Paris."

He put a hand on the small crossbow on his belt but refused to look away. "Who wore the pumpkin-colored dress?"

"The chaperone. An old nursemaid."

Vale exhaled and jerked his head toward the smoking coach. "There's a bloodstained scrap of orange ribbon. Old bat must've fought hard. No sign of your friend or the other girl." His hand landed on the puffed shoulder of my gown, and I took a deep breath to meet it. "I'm sorry. We try to catch the slavers before they swoop in, but they're fast."

"Slavers?"

"We call them slavers, although we honestly don't know what happens to them once they get into the catacombs under Paris. They mostly take young girls, although they'll sometimes take an older woman or a young man. Probably sell 'em as servants or concubines, once they're into the city."

I couldn't breathe, and my back felt more boneless than usual. "Do you never find them?"

"Not once they're underground." His eyes went skittery, and I knew he was lying. "Sometimes we can catch the slavers at the scene, scare them off before they take down the coach. They wear dark cloaks and masks, favor flaming arrows over a personal attack. They shoot the bludmares, set the carriage aflame, then everyone runs out flapping like chickens. Easy pickings."

"I know. I saw. What about my friend?"

He squeezed my shoulder and gave me the warm but useless smile someone might give a child at a funeral. "I know I'm a complete failure, but the rest of 'em are sharp as hell and twice as fast. There's still time."

I nodded once and walked to his giant black-and-white-spotted bludmare where she stomped around a picket driven deep into the earth. She tossed her muzzle at me, and I shoved the metal cap away, sending bloody froth flying.

Vale blanched. "You're going to want to——"

"Hang on to your waist really tightly? Yeah, I know. Let's go."

He allowed himself a smirk. "Look, *bébé*. Just wait until the rest of the band gets back. We'll take you to our camp, and the women will feed you and help you wash up. We're brigands, but we're honorable, and we can get you home safely in a wagon with a lot less bouncing and biting." He winked. "Not that I would mind you bumping against me for an hour."

"You're wasting time."

"And you're wasting your breath. Nice girls don't ride into Paris bareback on a brigand's hellbitch."

With a snort, I stepped out of the mare's reach, took a deep breath, and bent over backward into a C. From the backbend, I walked my hands between my feet, curling under until my forearms were on the ground beneath my skirt. Putting my boots on my own shoulders, I felt the frothy layers of the dress fall down around me, giving him a fine look at the slim-fitting trousers I favored for just such an occasion.

"I'm not that nice. And I'm not a girl." I grinned, showing fangs.

To his credit, he didn't freak out. Just put his head to the side like a crow watching a jewel glint in the sun. For the first time, his tone went serious, quiet. "Now, that I did not expect. Tell me, Demi. What is it that you want?"

"Right now?" I did a front walkover and turned to face him with a swirl of skirts. "I want you to take me to Paris and help me find my best friend."

"Say we find her. Say we don't. What's your endgame, *bébé*? Why Paris?"

I windmilled my arms, loosening up. I was a little sore after the crash, not to mention the previous hours I'd spent crammed between Cherie's shoulder and the wooden wall of the carriage. Just to see what he would do and to stretch out further, I slowly lifted one leg until it was right beside my ear, perfectly pointed straight up.

"I want to go to Mortmartre and be the star of the cabaret, of course."

"There are no Bludmen in the cabarets—"

"Not yet. There will be. After I find Cherie, there will be two. We're an act." I dropped my leg—and my smile. "So are we going or what?"

He crossed his arms over his chest and looked off into

the hazy distance where a single dark spear pierced the clouds. The Tower, they called it—some daimon scientist's clever way to attract and channel lightning into electricity for the City of Light. Paris wasn't tall and humpbacked like Sanglish cities but sprawled, orderly and leisurely, in neat squares. The daimons weren't known for leading lives of fear, nor were the humans who had taken up residence alongside them. There was a wall, of course, but they'd given the artists free rein to make it beautiful, from what I'd heard. Daimons made things much nicer than Pinkies, as I was learning since touching down in Franchia.

"It'll be a hard ride. If you fall off, I'm going to laugh at you. Odalisque is a bitch of a mare, and there's no room for you on the saddle. And when we get to Paris, sneaking in is going to be messy. But if you're determined, I'll do it."

"If you don't take me now, I'll start walking." I realized what I'd said a heartbeat after he did and almost dived back into the bush to die of embarrassment in peace.

"How can a gentleman turn down a threat like that?"

With practiced movements, he snatched out the mare's tether and slid the picket spike through a slot in the metal muzzle cap to make reins. He threw them over Odalisque's head as she danced, then leaped onto the saddle and held down an arm for me. I took it, surprised at his strength as he swung me up behind him, his wide, crystal-green eyes showing in turn his own surprise at my strength. The mare screamed and crow-hopped, trying to shake me loose, and he jerked the reins and kicked her.

I held on for dear life as Odalisque reared and bucked before collecting herself for a pounding gallop. I fastened my arms around Vale's lean waist and settled my cheek against his muscled back, inhaling deeply and willing the horse beast to run faster toward Cherie, toward a city where I could at least focus on something besides the strange man under the worn black shirt. Back in the caravan, I had ached for a goal, a quest, something to care about. My wish had definitely been answered, but not in the way I had hoped. The adventure wasn't important, not until I got my best friend back.

"Aren't you afraid I'm going to rip you to shreds?" I asked, trying to cover the fact that I'd all but nuzzled the hard muscles of his back.

"I'm half Abyssinian. My blood would drive you mad!" he shouted into the wind. "But please, *bébé*. Keep trying."